Elocution Lessons

By

J. William Patrick

Printed in the United States of America

Version 4

ISBN 9781734011807

Cover illustration by Melisa Labra
Cover design by Alvineer Cortum

Dedication

This book is dedicated to my mother, who taught me how to read

and appreciate the beauty of knowledge.

Acknowledgments

The author would like to thank Sonia, Meg, Linda, and my editor

Chelsea Carter - for their keen observations and insights.

"Lovers don't finally meet somewhere. They're in each other all along."

~ Rumi

Contents

Part I

"A smile is the chosen vehicle of all ambiguities."

~ Herman Melville

Chapter 1

Bryce's Estate, Charlotte, North Carolina
Friday March 2, 2018

Bryce knew exactly why he was in North Carolina - the new banking capital of America - but it felt better, lying to himself. *I know my inaction was unspoken approval of the duplicitous dealings at the bank. It doesn't matter that I'm not directly involved. I want no part of their unethical behavior. Hell, it's fucking criminal what they do.*

Almost exactly four years ago, he accepted the promotion to Vice President of International Growth and Market Finance. This was the part of his life that he took seriously. There was no fooling around when it came to making money. But he was ready for a change. He was ready to have more fun in his life, more adventure, and more freedom from the constraints of corporate life - and the lies and deception that came with it. Everything he owned was already packed in boxes.

He considered the possibility that he might be going through a midlife crisis. Though it wasn't clear how that would even apply to him. He wasn't even close to 50 and didn't feel the need to go out and buy a new shiny red convertible. He already had one parked in the long circuitous driveway that led to his southern estate.

It was the beginning of spring, his favorite time of year. The days were getting longer. He rose to the sun every morning, never too early - banker's hours. And he was able to make it home by a decent hour to enjoy a quiet part of the day before it got dark. Recently, he wasn't really enjoying the daylight hours. From anyone else's perspective, he had it made. He was a wealthy, good-looking guy with a large estate and a red convertible.

While Bryce had plenty of fun and dated many fine Southern women, and had satisfying sex with most of them, he never felt entirely comfortable around women from the south. He didn't feel a deep connection with them. After sex, the conversations were awkward and sometimes forced. The sex was good though, so he couldn't complain.

He tried to look back on his life and evaluate his accomplishments. He had accomplished more than he expected of himself when he was 23 and only recently graduated from St. Thomas Aquinas College, in Santa Paula, California. At that age, he felt the freedom just to have his own car. And allowed himself the excitement of dating those hot Southern California ladies.

Compared to what he had become; he felt like he had been such a pauper. But even though he had to work through college, he felt his life was much more satisfying when he had practically nothing of material wealth compared to now. So, he was looking for a change.

As an economist in high finance, Bryce estimated he could conservatively liquidate all of his stocks, bonds, and real estate and easily pocket seven-figures. More, if he decided to live in the Cayman Islands and avoid paying half of that to the bloodsucking IRS. He thought about how money could buy someone to love you, but only for your money. But money could never buy that undefined satisfaction that he desired.

His house was white, with large columns that supported the roof of an expansive veranda. The deck boards were stained a pale white, coated with five layers of marine varnish. The house was set back over one hundred and fifty yards from the front gate. At that distance, it looked like no one lived there - even when the house was filled with wine and guests. The sense of vacancy came from the architectural proportions.

A fine southern architect designed the house to Bryce's precise specifications: "I want to be left alone and not bothered, and I don't want the house to be visible from the street." These were the only instructions he had given the architect. During the design of the house, the architect insisted that the owner approve the conceptual plans but had been rebuffed at every turn. Bryce felt he gave the necessary instructions, and it was now the architect's job to fulfill his wishes, which he had.

The paint hadn't even dried before the owner received numerous offers of twice what he had paid for it. He received countless unsolicited offered throughout his 4-year residency at that home. At one point, he actually called the architect to complain (in a friendly sort of way) that his wishes had not been satisfied because people wouldn't leave him in peace because they kept making offers to buy his *private abode.*

So, Bryce St. James stood in the living room, having just accepted a ridiculous offer for the home. This offer provided a handsome profit of eight times the money he had invested. When it came to investments, he was a whiz. It was for this reason that the Swedish Bank of Uppsala offered him the position in the first place; the one that he just resigned from. The bank executives couldn't understand why anyone would want to quit. So, they offered him more money, which Bryce turned down. They thought he may need more time off, so they arranged an unprecedented deal of two months paid vacation a year. He was briefly tempted by the offer, but ultimately declined.

The Senior Vice President of the bank flew in from Stockholm, just to try and persuade Bryce to stay. Bryce was flattered but didn't change his mind. The Senior V.P. told Bryce that he had a special gift for determining how to make a vast profit from extremely complicated financial deals. However, Bryce was modest and didn't think it was that big of a deal. He said all he did was digest mountains of arbitrage data in his head, condense it down to something he could literally put down on an 8.5 X 11 sheet of white paper with a crayon. The Senior V.P. secretly thought Bryce was an eccentric genius, but Bryce just wanted to be the surfer dude of his youth.

Even after all the flattery and insane offers to make him stay, in the end, management thought Bryce would steal all their clients and financial data. Truth be told, he never intended to do so. Nevertheless, the bank kicked him to the curb, shut off his computer, and escorted him from the building with armed guards. For a moment, Bryce thought that maybe now he would steal their clients, just to spite them. But the thought of doing more financial analysis just bored him, and he let the indignity drop. No, he was looking for something else, something different, something not like what he had become, or those he had previously associated with, and that's where she came in. He smiled and thought; *God, her elocution lessons make me laugh. I'm so glad she is my best friend forever.*

Bryce was an audiophile. A high-fidelity sound system conveyed music throughout the entire house. As he was about to go inside the song "Canto, Desde el Fondo de las Ruinas" by the Buenos Aires' progressive rock band Aquelarre started to play. Bryce had no idea what they were saying and thought, *Tina would know.* He made a mental note to call her as he rocked out to the music, playing air-guitar on his large white veranda, forgetting about the Bank and international finance.

Erin's Apartment, Charlotte, North Carolina

The sun was already high in the sky by the time Erin stirred in bed. She was always a sound sleeper, but last night, she almost reached a comatose level. She didn't get to bed until after 2 am, having been out for most of the day. When she pushed the covers off - trying to regain consciousness - she thought to herself, *those Indians have quite the racket going on there.* She had entered the billiards tournament at the Cherokee Indian reservation just outside of Charlotte. A $100 entry fee, but the winner took all. It was the first time she played there, so the locals didn't quite know what to make of her.

She was a forty-something blonde woman from California with a spider web tattoo on her forearm. Soaking wet, she weighed a hundred and twenty pounds and a lot of that was bust. She never wore stockings, and her dresses were something that northern California hippies would wear.

She loved pool so much; almost to the point of addiction, so she limited her playing time to tournaments where she could hustle the locals with her innocent hippy act. The twenty-something guys were the most pissed off when she won;

to be beaten by a girl (a hippie girl, no less) got them really angry.

Erin kept winning and stayed until the end of the tournament. She went all out on the game until 1 AM. She won the break and the older gentleman she played against didn't get a shot. She never missed. As part of her act, she even brought a *lady's aid*, which she used on the last shot. It was a difficult shot - she had to bank the cue ball around the eight ball. And she made it look way more difficult than it was.

When she collected her winnings at the pay window, the old guy asked her angrily, "Where did you learn how to play like that? I think you're nothing but a hustler."

She looked at him with a slight smile.

There's a reason it's called being snookered, she thought but instead answered slyly, "My older brother taught me." Erin was going to challenge him to best two out of three but was tired and thought better of it. She still had to make it to her car alive with the $2,800 in cash she had just won. She didn't want any sore losers confronting her in the parking lot and demanding their money back from the hippy hustler.

Bryce's Estate, Charlotte

"… Ninety-eight, ninety-nine, one hundred," he grunted as he did arm curls with the barbell. For some reason, probably dating back to the modern Olympics, men have always lifted weights shirtless. And since the invention of the mirror, they lifted weights topless, in front of it. Bryce was no exception. He admired himself in the mirror, infatuated with how his sweat enhanced the outline of his biceps as he set the barbell down and posed, flexing his arms. Ever since he decided to quit his job, he had been working out more. He danced around in his private gymnasium to the thumping sounds of Sly Stone's *Thank You Falettinme Be Mice Elf Agin*. He felt invigorated and ready to take on the world.

Erin's Apartment, Charlotte, North Carolina

As Erin Clarisse Wallace lay in bed trying to find the motivation to raise herself from the horizontal position, she hoped she could just rest for another ten minutes. Thirty minutes later, a slender tattooed arm pushed the covers away from her naked body. Ever since she was a child, growing up in Tarzana, she wore only a T-shirt to bed. Last night, she was too hot and took the T-shirt off. She doesn't remember doing so, but now it lay on the floor with the rest of her clothes, and shoes that covered the floor since the last time she did the laundry; almost two weeks before.

The Charlotte Arts and Crafts Fair is happening today, she remembered. With her recent winnings, she wasn't so hard up for cash. If she could sell some of the jewelry she made, then she could perhaps make a dent in her credit card bills.

Maybe I'll meet some cute guy trying to get something to impress a girl, she thought. That was the motivation she needed to get out of bed and make some coffee.

Chapter 2

Bards College Rink, St. Andrews, Minnesota
Friday March 2, 2018

It all happened so innocently. Jeff was the hockey coach. In his youth, he was quite athletic. He even made it into the NHL. He played one season for the New York Rangers but was cut the next year before training camp began.

Well, Tina stopped by the Bards College rink one morning to surprise Jeff. She even brought him his favorite coffee from Starbucks. Unfortunately, the timing couldn't have been worse. Tina never really followed the college hockey team that Jeff coached. So, she was unaware that they just lost the last four games. When practice started - way before Tina arrived - the guys weren't serious about doing the fundamental drills.

The team was really only Lollygagging, so Jeff flipped out. He started cursing at the guys, calling them "pussies" and threatening to bench them. To teach the team a lesson they wouldn't forget, he started to drill them, hard. Skating drills. Shooting drills. Wind sprints. He never let them stop. The guys were really dragging, but Jeff was relentless. He was so frustrated at them.

Brad Robinson was a psychology major and had no delusions that playing hockey would take him anywhere. He was primarily a student of the game. He played as a kid in Ohio and tried out for the team as a walk-on his first year at Bards. The coach didn't particularly like Brad. He was going to cut him but offered him the backup goalie position. Brad had never played the position before but was willing to give it a try.

Jeff's only instructions were to, "Look big and don't flinch when the puck is shot at you." He didn't add that the puck was traveling at almost 100 miles an hour. Jeff didn't need a backup goalie, but it was league rules to have one, so Brad was as good as anyone.

The Bards College Tigers were a Division III school, according to the Amateur Athletic Union, or AAU. The season hadn't been going very well for the Tigers. They were in last place, and Jeff was pissed.

In a lot of ways, Brad and Jeff had opposite personalities. Jeff was one of the only ones in the rink that day that thought the Tigers were a steppingstone to something bigger. He thought that if he could turn the hapless Tigers into a winning team, any big college or NHL farm team would hire him. Brad, however, didn't even make plans further than dinnertime. He was the kind of guy to take life as it comes.

Since the goalies had so much gear on, and they wore those clumsy goalie skates, they didn't practice the line drills that Jeff was having the rest of the team do. Jeff was so annoyed and was swearing every second word. Brad quietly left the ice and sat in the stands, kicking back and taking a nap, or trying to. Jeff's yelling, swearing and incessantly blowing his whistle interrupted his slumber.

"What's going on?" Tina asked as she walked up to a napping Brad.

Without opening his eyes Brad replied, "Coach is on one of his tears and I'm keeping a wide berth."

From the stands, adjacent to the front entrance, you could hear Jeff going off. "Pick it up! You girls don't even deserve to be here!"

Tina had been dating Jeff on and off for the better part of the last semester. She was an Associate Professor of French and Latin, which was a fancy way of saying her salary allowed her to pay her rent and occasionally buy coffee at Starbucks. This was something she did do on occasion, wanting to surprise Jeff at the rink. Listening to his swearing, she agreed with Brad to keep a wide berth. So, she sat down in the seat next to him.

"Here," Tina offered, extending the second cup of coffee - Jeff's coffee - over to Brad. Brad opened his eyes and sat up. Sitting up, he was easily a foot taller than Tina and spilled out of the seat with his bulky goalie pads. His big hand moved over Tina's to accept the coffee.

"Gee thanks, just what I needed."

"It has chocolate sprinkles, just the way uh… Jeff likes it."

"Oh, I don't want to drink coach's coffee," Brad protested.

"No problem, go ahead," Tina replied as she heard Jeff's cussing echoing off the ice.

Not waiting, Brad took a deep sip. "Yum, chocolate sprinkles."

"So, how is school going?" Tina asked.

"Fine. I have just one more exam, but it's a take-home and I'm almost done. How about you? Are you finished teaching?"

"Yes," Tina said, "I just collected the last papers this morning. Class finished early, so I thought I'd come over here and…"

She faded out, just as Jeff's booming voice took over. "No! That's all wrong, you're a bunch of idiots!" The team obviously wasn't doing the hockey drill in a manner that would satisfy this now raving lunatic.

"How's your sister?" Tina asked, trying to change the subject.

"She moved to Arizona to take a job as an account manager for a woman's clothing chain," Brad replied.

Tina's grandparents and Brad were from Columbus, Ohio. She was twelve years his senior. Brad's oldest sister, Patsy, played volleyball on the high school team. When Tina visited Columbus, she would play intermural volleyball on a team with Patsy. Tina was a senior, and Patsy a freshman. They became fast friends but fell out of contact when Tina moved to Minnesota to teach. She met Brad when he was much younger, and due to their age difference, never thought of him again until he came to Bards College. They hit it off as friends, much like Tina had done with Patsy. There was the familiarity of knowing someone from your hometown, and Brad needed that when he first arrived in St. Andrews. He got homesick from time-to-time and he and Tina talked for hours on the phone, over coffee at

Starbucks, in the park, and at the Blind Barber Pub. Everything was strictly platonic. They each had other romantic interests.

Brad sat straight up in the seat and stretched his arms up over his head. It was the first time Tina looked at Brad as anything more than her friend's little brother. She looked at him intently and he didn't notice she was watching him.

He had certainly grown up and filled out, she thought to herself, *a young psychologist listening to the problems of wealthy spoiled women in his wood paneled office charging three hundred and fifty dollars an hour. Brad was certainly going to have a nice life.*

"Robinson! Robinson! Where the fuck are you?" Jeff shouted from the far side of the rink.

"Uh oh, gotta go. Coach is beckoning me," Brad said to Tina in a hurried but unflustered fashion. Brad stood up. On his hockey skates, he towered over Tina and gave her a big bear hug. "Call me later," he said as he jumped over the boards onto the ice, and then skated toward the cluster of the team on the far side of the rink.

"Jeff can be a real asshole," Tina whispered to herself. She picked up the empty coffee cups and walked out of the rink. *That didn't go as I had planned*, she thought. But she didn't care. School was out for spring break and she had loads of free time, which she looked forward to wasting. After the long, dark, cold Minnesota winter, Tina desperately needed the sunshine, leaves on the trees, the grass turning green and beginning to grow again.

As she walked across the concrete floor of the rink's foyer, her high heels clicked with each step. She thought about how nice it would be to not have to wear those things for a while. *I'm going to splurge and get a new pair of loafers.*

As Tina opened the door of her four-wheel-drive Ram pickup, she surveyed the landscape. She turned completely around 360° to take it all in as if she was looking for something that she hadn't quite found in the one and a half years she had lived in St. Andrews. Assuming she had captured it all, she got in and started the engine. "California Dreamin" by the Mamas and the Papas came blaring out of the speakers. Tina loved her music loud while she thought, *Ah. California! Now that's more like it. Way better than this dump.*

Tina left southern Ohio for St. Andrews in the summer. Minnesota is beautiful in the summer. She had accepted the Associate Professor's position and graduated the year before with a Ph.D. in linguistics from Columbia.

She also really liked New York City. Actually, she loved New York. Unfortunately, it was no place to live as a starving student.

Chapter 3

Columbia University, Manhattan, New York
Tuesday February 7, 2012

Tina's dissertation was on the linguistic similarities of the languages spoken in the Middle East. On a cold rainy day in New York, the Dean of the School of Linguistics, Kim Reed, came to her small, cramped office to request that she join him for a meeting. She had been working long nights on her thesis and was a little frazzled. She said she needed to finish this one thought and would join him in five minutes. Twenty minutes later, she realized she had forgotten the Dean because she was so immersed in thought. She raced down the hall with her leather-soled shoes echoing loudly off the terrazzo floor. She burst into the Dean's office.

The Dean's administrative assistant, Holly Hayworth, stopped her, "Dear, you look dreadful."

"All the long nights," Tina replied as she tucked her white wrinkled blouse into her navy pencil skirt.

"Pull your hair back, my dear," Holly said.

Tina removed the hair tie and moved her hand to the front of her head to gather her light brown hair and pulled it back into tight alignment. Then she twisted the hair band over her neatly gathered hair.

"Much better," Holly said approvingly. Holly announced on the intercom, "Dean, Tina is here to see you."

The door opened slowly, and the Dean peered through the threshold, while still holding the doorknob. "Tina! Please, come in."

Tina moved forward as the Dean moved aside slightly to let her pass and then closed the door quickly behind him. Two men in black polyester suits stood up in unison and put out their hands to greet Tina.

Immediately behind her, the Dean said, "Tina, these men are from the government. They're here to help you."

Tina broke out into robust laughter and shook the hand of each of the men. The Dean was a bit of a wise-ass, and that's one of the reasons he and Tina got along well.

"Agent Steve Foley of the New York FBI," said the tall man, who was slightly overweight, balding, and had a cheesy polyester tie that was tied too short and didn't match his jacket. Tina sized him up as a cross between the good looks of Sidney Poitier, with the no nonsense attitude of Samuel L. Jackson.

"Tina Wood," she replied politely.

"تشرق الشمس في الجبال," the second man said in Arabic. Which loosely translates to *the sun rises beyond in the mountains…*

Tina replied, "ويطل على البحر," in perfect Arabic, completing the sentence … *and sets over the sea.*

"So, you know the poet Marrash?" the man asked.

"A little," Tina replied self-effacingly.

"Come, come Dr. Wood, we know your work well."

"And who are you?" Tina asked rather bluntly.

"Tina, this is Allan Romandi, Agent Allan Romandi," Agent Foley said.

Tina sized *him* up for a moment. He was about five feet - nine inches, maybe ten - with dark thick hair. Although it was eleven in the morning, his facial hair was starting to grow back, even though he had cleanly shaven that morning. A slightly dark complexion that could be mistaken for a tan, but Tina knew better. Upon closer examination, she could tell that his suit was designer, and form fitted by a tailor. Not like the cheap off the rack job of Agent Foley. He was slightly handsome. Not like other men, though. He was rougher, with blocky features. She took him to be in his mid-50's – married, but from his demeanor, not in love.

The Dean began, "Tina these gentlemen are interested in your work with Arabic. Particularly your understanding of ancient Middle Eastern poetry."

"Thank you, Dean," Agent Foley interrupted. "Tina, Dean, perhaps there is a place where we could talk in more comfort. The academic setting is so formal."

"Well, yes there is," said the Dean. "We can meet at the President's Club."

"Splendid," Agent Foley replied. "Let's have lunch there. Of course, if that's alright with you, Dr. Wood?"

Tina sized up the two G-men again, thinking, *what was she getting herself into? What could these two clowns want? Christ, she was immersed in her research; could she spare the time?*

"Fine with me," Tina said in her straightforward way. "It's 11:40 AM. I'll meet you gentlemen there at noon. I have some things here that I have to wrap up." Tina turned and exited the Dean's office without waiting for a reply, indicating to all three men that she was not easily intimidated. Although none of them verbalized it, they all thought the same thing.

Chapter 4

Bard's College Rink
Friday March 2, 2018

When Brad got back on the ice, Coach Jeff was still in his sour mood - perhaps worse than before. He split the squad into two halves of the rink. The starting line, forwards and centers were on the north half; the defensemen and the third line were on the south side. Typically, the starting goalie defended the net against the starting line. This was obvious because they were the best shooters and it would test the skill of the shooter and the goalie. But Jeff was finally changing it up.

Brad was set to guard the north net. The forwards loved this drill because they could take blistering slap shots straight at the goal, as if on a breakaway - something that rarely happened during a game.

The drill started with the first line at center ice. The center passed the puck to the right-winger. The right-winger carried the puck over the blue line along the boards and then cut sharply to the center as he attacked the goal. He raised his stick and let fly a powerful slap shot. The stick blade hit the frozen puck like a rifle shot.

Brad's eyes traced the trajectory of the puck as it soared toward him. He slid into position and was able to block the puck with his shin pad with the lighting reflexes of a kicking motion. The puck rebounded off his pad directly out to the center, who was closing in. The center nimbly controlled the rebounded puck and made a sweeping move to the right, knowing that Brad's momentum was carrying him left.

This opened up the net for a perfect scoring opportunity. The center flicked his wrists and shoveled a backhand shot toward the open net. Brad dug his skates into the ice to slow his forward momentum and arched his body to block the backhand shot. He snow-coned the puck in his catcher and fell to the ice, sprawled out in the crease.

The left-winger, who was trailing the others, sped up toward Brad, turning his skates perpendicular to his direction of motion to carve a spray of frozen wet ice right into Brad's face. This was the ultimate insult in hockey - when a player is lying prone on the ice, like Brad was. So, Brad jumped up onto his skates and rushed the left-winger, ready to clean his clock.

Jeff saw the fight developing and rushed toward the players. He was able to grab the winger's jersey before they were pulled apart by the center, who had circled around and saw the whole thing.

"Well, it looks like Robinson has some fight in him. Must be that he's trying to impress the French teacher," the left-winger spat at Brad.

Brad thought that no one noticed him and Tina talking on the far side of the rink. He pushed off the hold of the center and raced the left-winger again.

"You fucking prick," Brad cursed, "I'll fucking kill you." Brad was trying to get a swing off, but by this time the whole team had a chance to react and gather round.

"That's enough, you assholes," Jeff commanded as he shoved Brad and the winger apart. "Save it for St. Mary's on Saturday."

After practice, Brad showered with the rest of the team. It was one large shower room with thirty naked men, grab-assing and snapping towels at each other. Brad wasn't in a happy mood after what had happened on the ice and didn't partake in the horseplay, like he normally did.

The guys ribbed him about being the French teacher's pet and tried to insult him by talking with a fake French accent. Brad had cooled off enough and wasn't taking the bait to get into an argument. He arched his head back and let the water wash over the top of his head. The force of the steaming hot water washed away his anxiety and restored in him a sense of calm. He tilted his head up and observed the other naked men in the room playing like juveniles, but with much larger pectorals, biceps, and cocks covered in pubic hair.

Being a student of psychology, Brad reflected on why he got so angry when the winger made fun of him and Tina. He couldn't quite pinpoint the reason, but jealousy and protecting of the womenfolk are two sides of the same coin. He filed away his feelings to be revisited later, when he wasn't in a room with thirty naked men who were waving their junk at each other, while they wrestled and tried to put each other in headlocks.

After his long hot shower Brad quickly dressed and left the rink. His piece of shit car refused to turn over.

"Fuck!" He cursed, slamming his fist on the dashboard. A tapping on the window made him jump in his seat. It was Peter Trammell, the captain of the hockey team.

"Hey dude, looks like you need a jump."

Downtown St. Andrews

Not only did Tina like loud music, she also liked fast cars. The wheels of her Hemi charged Ram pickup screeched as she pulled out of the parking lot. She was happy that the days were getting longer and especially warmer. She lowered the window and you could hear the music blare from her truck a block away. She didn't think any more of Jeff and how he was behaving toward the team. She had played her fair share of competitive sports and the common denominator with all coaches was the desire to win. Most were obnoxious about it, but there was the rare exception. It just so happened that Jeff fell into the obnoxious category of coaching.

Tina spent the rest of the day shopping. Something she hadn't done in quite some time, given that Associate Professors of French don't get paid a whole heck of a lot. Since she had a break, she felt like indulging. Although she wasn't much of a girly girl, she still liked feminine things. The first stop was the shoe store on Spring Street - and what remained of downtown St. Andrews. Since the big box stores had arrived, business downtown had dwindled significantly, but certain stores held on.

Tina was able to find a parking spot almost in front of Tom's Shoes. When she walked up to the window display, she could tell that there certainly wasn't equal representation in the shoe business. Men's shoe styles hadn't really changed over the years, yet women's styles changed almost monthly. So, she felt a tinge of regret for being out of fashion, and something she was aiming to change.

Tina spent almost an hour trying on shoes. The clerk, a young man, was very pleasant and patient. Tina was enjoying herself as she shopped, oblivious to the world around her. When she finally snapped out of it, she had selected three pairs of shoes: summer espadrilles, low heel loafers, and of course another pair of black high heels. Surprisingly, Tina was not shocked at how she had splurged in the store. She hadn't shopped like that in some time, and it felt good.

It felt so good that she wanted to keep doing it. The next stop was the Lady Chic Boutique for some lingerie to spice it up. She bought some practical, and also some naughty items that made her feel sexy. It certainly helped that the young men outside, waiting for their girlfriends, were checking her out when she emerged from the store. Although she only gazed at those men, she could tell that they were undressing her with their eyes, imagining what naughty items she bought.

When Tina returned to her truck, she was exhausted. *Shopping really zaps the energy out*, she thought. It was spring, and the days were getting longer, so she decided to drive over to Starbucks for a latte pick-up. She had lost track of time. Plus, she usually wasn't outside most of the day. Her iPhone died earlier in the day and she hadn't bothered to charge it. After she turned the ignition, she plugged in her phone. The phone came to life in a short while indicating numerous texts and missed calls.

"Christ, it's almost 7 pm," she said aloud. She put the phone on the dashboard and thought she would catch up on the missed messages after she had her coffee. Getting a lot of messages was nothing new - she had many friends. She also transferred her work emails and business calls to her personal cell phone.

When Tina finally sat down with her latte, she saw that Jeff had called a few times but hadn't left a message. As she went through her text messages, she saw that he had texted, "Where are you?!!!"

She didn't think anything of it and replied with, "Shopping." She didn't get an immediate reply, so she sipped her coffee and read the new e-book she had downloaded on her tablet.

Starbucks, Downtown, St. Andrews

Tina's phone beeped, signifying a new text. She immediately thought it was Jeff. She picked up her phone and read "LL ..." It was Dean Reed. She recognized his phone number, but was curious why he was texting, and so late.

He had requested a call once before on an LL (landline) and when Tina called him, he joked, "This is a test of the emergency broadcast system," and then proceeded to make small talk about nothing particularly important, mostly about what was going on at the Columbia Linguistics Department - conversation that certainly didn't need the security of a landline.

At the time, it seemed a bit odd that he wanted her to call on a landline and she didn't think any more of it until now. She needed to gather her things and her coffee and find a payphone. There weren't many of those left, and there certainly weren't any at Starbucks.

Tina remembered seeing one at the AM/PM when she got gas there a while ago. So, she headed out. When she went outside, daylight was dimming. Not because she could see it, but because she felt it. People used to joke that she was psychic. She was beginning to believe it, herself. So, she took a deep sip of coffee, put the rest of her things in her purse, and left to find a pay phone.

Chapter 5

Erin's Apartment, Charlotte, North Carolina
Friday February 2, 2018

Erin had lived in North Carolina for about ten years. She moved from Tarzana California with her then boyfriend, on her birthday. As a Scorpio, she was a free spirit and lived for the present, not worrying about the future. She broke up with her boyfriend after three years in Charlotte. He wanted to move back to Southern California, but she wasn't interested. They both knew a long-distance relationship wouldn't work out, so they parted as friends. He moved to Venice California when house prices were still somewhat reasonable.

Since that time, she dated many different men but had come to enjoy her own space and time. She was growing tired of the demands guys made of her. Some thought that just because they took her to dinner and a movie that she was going to go back to their place and give them a blowjob.

At times - especially just before Valentine's Day - Erin would get a little lonely and want the company of a man, even if it did involve a blowjob - except she definitely wasn't going to swallow. After dating a string of real losers – even one that wanted to tie her up and give her a golden shower – she decided that she needed to up her game in the dating scene. So, she deleted her profile on Tinder.

"What fucking losers," she uttered out loud as she pressed the delete button with self-righteous indignation. No, she figured if she was going to do this, that she needed to do it in the right way. She investigated several dating sites, and quickly narrowed her top choices to OkCupid and Match. After an unscientific poll of the other single women she knew, she decided on Match. The consensus amongst the women was that OkCupid was primarily for sex. The monthly membership to Match was a little steeper, but Erin figured she wouldn't be on it that long before it would pay for itself, with her finally finding the right guy that would make her happy.

Erin had professional photos taken of herself and spent an entire weekend working on her profile; something witty, playful, saucy, and a little spice thrown in for good measure. She didn't want to come across as desperate, or worse - a pushover.

Erin didn't have a close tell-all girlfriend, but she knew she needed a second opinion on what she was going to post. So, she asked some of the single women she knew over to her place for a wine and cheese party, and once they had a little to drink then she would get them to critique her profile. After consuming several bottles of the Napa Valley Chardonnay, they were all pleased with the end product and Erin's profile went live. Then they waited for the Mr. Right competition to begin.

The results were a disaster. Initially worse than Tinder, none of the guys that messaged her even bothered to read her profile, the profile she had poured her heart and soul into. Erin thought most guys lie like crazy on dating sites (as do some women). However, she found that men would promise the moon and stars, and some are only looking for is an easy hookup. Her girlfriends agreed that most guys just figure it's just a numbers game, and all they need to be is a little patient. To them, guy math is like this: be on their best behavior for three or four dates (five dates tops), because most women won't have sex with a guy on the first date. Much to her chagrin, Erin didn't have such pedestrian restrictions. If she was physically attracted to a guy (he didn't even necessarily have to be cute) she would have sex with them that night. Now truth be told, there were a few times she had sex within a few hours of meeting a guy that she thought they shared the same chemistry. Unfortunately for Erin, guys couldn't be charted on the periodic table.

On her profile, Erin listed the age range of 30 to 50 for men she'd date, she would even date twenty-somethings, but 50 was her upper most range. And by modern standards this age range probably wasn't unusual (especially for women who didn't have children). And she certainly didn't fret about being a cougar if some cute twenty-something asked her out.

Well the messages arrived like all the others that filled her inbox on any dating site. She skimmed through them like she normally did at 1:30 AM, when she was feeling lonely, horny, or both. Sometimes, she would read her messages and watch soft porn - she particularly liked to watch scenes with two guys and a girl. This particular night she was feeling both lonely and horny. With a tinge of self-pity, she read the message. It stood out from all the rest. First, because it was more than *Hey*, or *Yo*, or even worse, *hi gorgeous, do you want to meet up?* However, this message was personal and directed just at her.

This guy took the time to actually read Erin's profile and compose an individual note to her. Erin looked more closely at his picture. Unfortunately, in his profile picture this guy was wearing sunglasses. She usually immediately dismissed these profiles because she thought the guy was trying to hide something. Although, his individual note intrigued her, and she browsed his profile and photos. The second photo was of him with his shirt off - another demerit under normal conditions.

He was posing with a nonchalant grin like he didn't have a care in the world. He wasn't flexing or straining, and a six-pack could be clearly made out. Guys that were buff always had beefcake photos of themselves flexing their biceps and puffing out their chests. This guy's photos were different though. They were the standard fare but different; at least from Erin's discerning taste. Or perhaps it was that she was just horny and had begun playing with her clit.

She tried not to get her hopes up. She knew the drill. Guys on dating sites aren't as selective as the ladies. The guys' basic theory is it's a matter of mass marketing. Plaster out as many, "likes" and "hey :-)" and eventually some woman would bite. Also, ladies (especially the really attractive ones) get way too many would-be suitors, to reasonably sort through. So, women develop a sorting metric and immediately ignore the profiles that don't interest them and don't meet the sorting metric.

On dating sites, women quickly learn not to respond to messages from guys they have no interest in. All guys are delusional, and think they are hot. So, when rejected (especially by a woman they see as less desirable than them) they take great offense and reply with very hurtful and abrasive messages and won't let up until the woman blocks their profile. When a woman politely declines an invitation to meet, they're usually greeted with a response like, *Yeah, you're probably just a stuck-up bitch, anyway*, or something similar following the same theme.

Well, as an attractive blonde woman with big tits, Erin got a lot of messages. Being in the South, the messages were usually polite and chivalrous. But there were still the occasional jerks, and she just ignored them. Although she wondered what kind of woman would even date a guy like that. They'd have to be pretty hard up, or just a slut.

Erin started to watch porn on her tablet. It was 2 AM, and she wasn't tired. She thought that if she just imagined him making love to her, she could make herself come, and then she could fall asleep, imagining being held in his powerful arms.

Jack's Apartment, Charlotte, North Carolina

Jack Beauchamp was a twenty-six-year-old ex-Marine. He served two tours of duty overseas. He also served time in prison, which was conveniently not mentioned in his dating profile. Jack was the real jealous type and he would get very angry when he started drinking. He beat the crap out of a guy that started to talk to his then girlfriend, when they were at a bar in Raleigh. He could have easily killed the guy but luckily the bouncer jumped in to break the fight up.

Since he was a Marine, this was his first civil offense, and the guy lived, the judge gave Jack one year in the state penitentiary for battery. Being away from booze, Jack was a model prisoner. Jack wasn't the intellectual type so there wasn't much he did in prison except lift weights and jack off, which suited him just fine.

While in prison, Jack decided to turn his life around and found Jesus. He went to the group therapy sessions offered during his sentence. He did find some comfort in the sessions but still harbored deep resentment that his girlfriend dumped him, and he rarely got visitors. Nevertheless, Jack was contrite that he made a mistake and had no one to blame other than himself.

His Marine Corps training certainly came in handy at his parole hearing. Lucky for Jack, there were three women on the five-member parole board. The women practically swooned for this good-looking buff guy. However, his ex-girlfriend knew better and had a different judge put a restraining order on him. Having read so many self-help books, she knew that Jack's jealousy was not a sign of love for her, but a manifestation of his insecurities. Something that was not likely to change.

When his ex-girlfriend thought about her relationship with Jack, she could recall his moody behavior and the signs of insecurity and possessiveness. She once caught him with her iPhone, going through her text messages and recent calls, accusing her of being unfaithful. He got so mad that he threw her phone against the wall. He then stormed out yelling that it was her fault that the phone was smashed because she dressed like a slut.

Erin's Apartment, Charlotte, North Carolina

By this time, Erin's clit was totally swollen from the excitement of watching porn and she began playing with herself. She closed out the porn site and opened Match to read Jack's profile. As she rubbed herself, she kept reading the message he sent her. There was no denying that he was really hot. She removed her hand from between her legs and sent a message in reply.

To her delight, he was on the site and replied right away. They texted back and forth, which turned to outright flirting. They agreed to meet the next day, which it already was.

Erin closed her last text to Jack with "nighty night" and an emoji of a kiss on the cheek. She then shut off her tablet and lay back in bed, fantasizing about making love to Jack. By this time, she was rubbing her clit hard, thinking about how Jack responded to one of the websites questions: "He likes sex both gentle and hard." And with that thought seared in her brain, Erin climaxed.

Sunny's Bar & Grill, Charlotte, North Carolina
Saturday February 3, 2018

They agreed to meet at 6 PM at a bar close to Erin's place called Sunny's. Erin was very punctual and arrived early, at about ten to six. It was a popular bar, but Erin lucked out and got a table near the back. It was half past six and Erin was getting annoyed thinking that she'd been stood up. Just as she was about to leave Jack walked in.

Her mood immediately changed, and she greeted him with a smile and a friendly hug. Jack didn't apologize for being late. The snaps on his Lee denim shirt were half undone, revealing his ripped chest. Erin mentally confirmed that Jack looked just like his profile pictures - a rare occurrence in the online dating world. He was taller than she had imagined and when he squeezed her in his strong arms, she creamed her panties.

They had a few drinks and chit chatted. "So, your profile said you were a Marine," Erin said, trying to get the conversation going.

"Yeah," Jack said with a one-word response.

"Was it dangerous?"

"Yeah, I guess so. I was mostly involved with electronic communication systems."

This was the first military guy Erin dated. Heck, Jack was the first military guy Erin ever met. She figured he was just the strong silent type. And she needed to carry the conversation, because she felt so flattered that a twenty-six-year-old hot veteran stud would want to go out with a much older woman.

She wanted the date to work out. To make up for Jack's reticence, Erin started yammering away about her theories of the military industrial complex and how all Americans are manipulated by the government into seeing others (that don't agree with our way of life) as the evil enemy.

Jack didn't say much, only occasionally nodded, which led her to believe that he agreed with her. By this time, they'd had a few drinks and Erin was feeling very tipsy.

"Listen, do you want to get out of this place?" Jack asked.

"Yeah, sure."

"Okay, I'll be right back. I have to go pee."

Erin was left alone at the table. The waiter came back and asked, "Do you want anything else?"

Erin said, "No thanks."

Just then, a guy walked up to her table and said, "Hi, can I buy you a drink? I cannot believe such a lovely lady is sitting alone."

Then suddenly, the guy is pushed from behind into Erin and spilled his drink on her.

"What the fuck do you think you are doing?" Jack said in a raised voice. "Look what you've done, asshole. You spilled your drink on my lady."

"I'm so sorry," the guy apologized as he backed away from Jack, not wanting to get into a fight.

Erin didn't make a big deal of Jack getting jealous. In fact, she thought it a little charming the way southern men try to protect the honor of their lady folk. Plus, this wasn't the first time two guys fought over her.

Erin got up from the table and came right up to Jack and put her hands on his chest.

"Hey, you know what? Let's get out of here and go back to my place. It isn't far from here." She reached up on her tippy toes and gave Jack a kiss on the mouth. She had now broken one of her cardinal dating rules: not to let the guy she just met know where she lives, until she gets to know him better and confirm that he's not a stalker or serial killer.

Jack seemed pissed off and wasn't making any moves to pay the bar tab. Erin motioned to the bartender to get the check. She reached into her purse and pulled out her wallet. Her bag was filled with a bunch of stuff she figured she needed at some time in the next millennium, and several items she probably could do without. Unfortunately, the two things she didn't have in her bag were a credit card that wasn't maxed out, and condoms.

*   *   *

The parking lot for the bar was on the side of the building. It was dark, and the lot was dimly lit from the streetlight. There were a few guys huddled near the back. They saw Jack walking out with Erin holding his arm.

From the pack of guys, someone shouted, "Yeah, going home with mommy!"

Jack turned and headed straight for the group of guys. Erin chased him and tried to hold his hand, but he pushed her away.

"Which one of you faggots said that?" Jack demanded, standing right next to the gang in a fighting stance. "Not so brave now, are you? You bunch of pussies."

Erin caught up to Jack and moved between him and the gang. "Listen," she started, "it's not worth it. Let's get out of here."

"If I hear another peep from you pussies, you'll all get a piece of me!" Jack shouted over Erin into the gang, waving his clenched fist in the air.

Erin put both of her hands over Jack's fist and pulled it down. "Come on tough guy, let's go." Erin pulled his hand as she turned toward her car. She had to tug Jack's arm to get him to turn away from the gang.

Erin's Apartment, Charlotte, North Carolina

Nothing was said between Erin and Jack as she drove back to her place in her 4X4 Jeep with a stick shift. She said that the stick got better gas mileage. On this night, she was driving faster than normal and missed the driveway entrance by a tiny bit. One of the wheels climbed the curb as Erin and Jack bounced back from the shock.

When the Jeep came to rest in her parking spot behind the two-story Victorian house, she thought *I don't know why I'm driving so fast and missed the driveway*. Perhaps it was because she was upset about the confrontation at the bar, that she had too much to drink, or that she was a bit horny. Maybe a combination of all three.

"We're here," Erin announced as she turned off the Jeep. "I'm in the upstairs apartment."

Jack followed Erin up the stairs not saying a word. She unlocked the door like a jailer because her key ring had about seven keys on it, including a small flashlight that didn't work anymore; the batteries burned out well over a year ago.

"Ta-da!" Erin exclaimed as she swung open the door and turned the light on. Jack waited at the threshold as Erin entered.

She turned to him and said, "Come on in and make yourself at home. Are you hungry? I can make you something to eat."

"No, I'm good, thanks," Jack replied.

"Okay, how about something to drink?"

"Sure, do you have any bourbon?"

"Hmm, not sure. I'll check. Please, go into the living room and have a seat."

Lucky for Jack, Erin's last boyfriend also liked bourbon and there was a near full bottle in the kitchen cabinet.

"How do you like it?" Erin shouted from the kitchen.

"Just straight in a glass. And bring the bottle!"

In a moment, Erin appeared at the living room door with two glasses and the open bottle of bourbon.

"You lucked out. I found this bottle left here... Uh." Erin stopped talking, thinking the better of telling Jack that this was her old boyfriend's bourbon.

Jack rose from the couch as Erin entered. "Nice place you have here."

"Yeah. Thanks. I lucked out when I moved here. This place was available, and I really like it here." Erin said as she set the bottle on the coffee table, "Please, sit down and relax," Erin said as she took a seat on the couch next to Jack. "You southern men are all so polite," ignoring the fight that Jack almost got into within half an hour of meeting her.

The sink was full of dishes and there weren't any clean glasses, so Erin just washed two. The glasses were different, and Erin gave Jack the larger of the two as she poured two inches of bourbon into each. Erin raised her glass and Jack followed her lead.

"Spit in your eye," Jack said as they clinked glasses. Jack took a huge swig of his and wiped his mouth with the back of his hand as he finished.

"Wow! Just like the wild west," Erin joked, thinking that Jack's drinking reminded her of a western movie. Erin took a sip of her drink. She'd already had too much to drink. She didn't mind the taste of bourbon, as much as she did when her old boyfriend still lived with her.

Jack took Erin's glass out of her hand and set it beside his on the coffee table. He moved closer to her on the couch and wrapped his arms around her. He held the back of her head as he gave her a deep kiss. She opened her mouth and accepted his probing tongue.

Erin was trying to move away from her past and made a cardinal dating rule: not to have sex with a guy on the first date. She broke that rule at least half a dozen times that night, as Jack fucked her in different positions on the couch and in her bedroom. Erin didn't get much sleep that night as Jack kept waking her up to do it again, and again. The last time was early in the morning about twenty-four hours after the first text Erin sent to Jack on the dating website.

She lay on her side because her legs, and especially her hip joints, were sore from being spread apart by Jack as he mounted her and thrust into her hard and deep and finally fell asleep, full of Jack's semen.

Seeing Erin was asleep, Jack quietly got up, got dressed, and left.

*   *   *

Erin woke close to noon and wondered where Jack went. She rubbed her eyes and then reached for her iPhone on the bedside table. She clicked her text messages expecting a sweet love note from Jack, but nothing. She was too tired to immediately get out of bed. So, she laid back and closed her eyes, resting; thinking out what happened that night.

She started to get aroused. Her clit was swollen, so she masturbated again, thinking of how Jack spread her apart and fucked her hard, with their bodies slamming together, and then turned her over and did it to her from behind. After about half hour of this, Erin was finally sexually spent. She got out of bed and did a quick survey of the kitchen, thinking that Jack may have left a note. There was nothing.

She took a shower and washed out her cum covered pussy. She then regretted breaking her rule about having the guy wear a condom before she could confirm he wasn't HIV positive. *Too late*, she shrugged, as she knew she was just impulsive and hoped for the best. Making a mental note to talk to Jack about using condoms next time.

Erin was disappointed that she didn't hear from Jack all day. She wondered if last night was just a one-night stand. She remained pragmatic in these things, knowing that she had fucked other guys the night she met them, and never saw them again, although she didn't do it very often - especially with someone almost twenty years her junior.

30

A week passed, and Erin tried to forget the sex filled escapade with Jack. She was on her sun porch making jewelry. The sun porch was at the back of her large apartment. A very inviting space where Erin spent a great deal of her time doing her creative projects. She would never move back to L.A. because she could never afford a place like that one, on the little money she made. And she enjoyed her free time and had no desire to work harder.

The apartment had its own entry and the older couple that owned the place pretty much left her alone, seeing that Erin always made the rent payment on the first of the month and didn't make much noise. She heard a rather loud car pull up, but from where she was sitting, she couldn't see who it was. Besides, she was concentrating on her work.

She wanted to make some nice stuff for the upcoming Charlotte Arts Fair. She looked up as the screen door cracked open. Jack was standing in the doorway. The sun was behind him, illuminating his half open Lee jean shirt with snaps. His jeans were more faded than his shirt and Erin could make out the bulge of his manhood. Of course, Jack wore the obligatory cowboy boots that made his 5'-9" frame seem even bigger and more imposing.

Erin tried to play it cool, but inside she was excited to see him. She'd dated a ton of guys (thanks to Tinder) and experienced all types. She even dated a guy that wanted to wear her bra and panties. At first, she thought he was joking but when she realized he was serious, she dumped him. Although with Jack this was something all new to her. She never dated a guy with such a large age difference. *Oh, the guilty pleasures of a cougar*, she thought.

In the week since she first met him, Erin was careful not to text him, although there were times when she was close to doing so. She had actually spent a few late evenings writing and rewriting the text she wanted to send. However, she couldn't find the right words to convey what she wanted to say. In the end, she decided not to send Jack a text for fear of appearing somewhat desperate.

Jack was standing, waiting, in the doorway. Waiting for Erin to invite him in. But she doesn't. She makes him wait. Jack is tough and cool and has an easy way with the ladies but now he's going to be schooled by the master. Erin doesn't take shit from anyone.

"Listen dude," using the California colloquialism not common in these parts, "you can't just show up here. I just met you, and what if I had another gentleman caller," switching to the sarcastic southern term to both poke fun at Jack, make him a little jealous, and show that she's not as big of a pushover as six coital orgasms would leave you to believe.

"Uh… Sorry, I just thought," Jack said, with no thought of ever apologizing about having left her without saying goodbye and not communicating with her for a week.

"Oh, come on in," Erin said, "I'm just messing with you. But from now on you must call ahead. I've been very busy with my work." She was trying to get the upper hand but couldn't hide her excitement about the hot young guy coming around to see her.

Jack just nodded slightly to indicate acknowledgment, although he'd never before listened to any other request a woman asked of him, and he figured he wasn't going to change his ways anytime soon.

In Jack's absence, Erin did buy her own bottle of bourbon. Thinking, hoping, that she would see him again. "Can I get you a drink?" Erin asked, turning away from Jack and going into the kitchen.

"Sure."

"The usual?" Erin said, laughing.

"Yeah, sure."

While she was in the kitchen fixing the drinks, she thought to herself, *you have to play it cool. You're not just some cheap slut. Get it together girl.* This time, she poured much more moderate drinks. Two fingers, max. And she had clean matching glasses. They sat out on the sun porch, in separate chairs. After Jack took a sip of his drink, he made an advance on Erin.

Erin didn't want to appear like a whore and brushed off Jack's advancement. "Listen," she said, "let's go get something to eat. I know the best burger place, not far from here."

"Yeah, sure," Jack said with slight disappointment knowing that he wasn't going to get into Erin's pants right away.

"You just stay here and let me go freshen up, and I'll be right back."

"Yeah, sure."

Erin knew that most guys didn't like waiting for women to get ready. So, she hurried the preparation to go out. She put on eyeliner, eye shadow and mascara. She looked in the mirror at herself and decided to brush her hair and pull it back in a bun. Lipstick was the final touch.

One final look in the bathroom mirror, and Erin said to herself, "Show time," making a motion to shoot herself with her finger and then blowing out the imaginary gun smoke with a puff of breath.

"You look great," Jack said, making a rare complement.

"Why, thank you, kind sir," Erin replied in her fake southern accent, grateful that Jack had something to say other than *yeah sure*.

*   *   *

They descend the wooden stairs to Jack's waiting Camaro. Erin waved to the nice couple she rented from, sitting on their sun porch, which was just below hers.

"Goodnight," the couple said in unison, returning the salutation.

Erin felt their eyes burning into the back of her head. She figured they disapproved and thought it shameful that she was dating a much younger guy. Erin came to expect this kind of uptight puritan behavior, having now lived in the Bible Belt all these years.

Jack turned over the ignition of his hot rod and the four-barrel carburetor screamed to life, pushing the ignited gas out of the dual exhaust. Erin could feel the vibration of all four hundred and forty-two cubic inches of cylinder displacement. The muscle car's engine roared as Jack put the car in gear and squealed out of the driveway; leaving eye rolls from the nice older couple on their sun porch sipping their tea and gossiping about Erin's rather loose lifestyle.

Chapter 6

AM/PM Convenience Store, Downtown, St. Andrews
Friday March 2, 2018

As Tina turned on Elm Street it was getting noticeably darker and so she turned on her headlights. Ambient music from the Swedish band Carbon Based Lifeforms played from her iPod. She hadn't been to the AM/PM in some time and thought it was closer. As she turned into the driveway, she saw the payphone had been removed.

"Damn," she said under her breath. It figured. Who uses payphones anymore? Not wanting to wait any longer, Tina called the Dean on her cell phone.

He answered, "Hello -" in a weak, uncertain voice.

Tina said, "Hi Dean, sorry I couldn't call from a landline, what's up?"

"Tina, my dear. Everything's fine here. I'm so glad you called." Then he switched to speaking Latin, "Volumus aliquid futurum mali esset, salvum te fac volui."

Tina mentally translated to, *I had a premonition that something bad is going to happen, and I wanted to make sure you were safe.*

"Yes, Dean the weather is fine. I love spring," Tina reassured the Dean; speaking in the code they had established when she started to do translation assignments for the FBI.

"Wonderful, my dear. Have a good night," and the Dean hung up.

The Dean was not one to hang on the phone for any length of time, and he rarely, if ever said goodbye. Tina was used to this by now.

That was strange. A premonition, huh, Tina thought. *It was just the Dean being a fuddy-duddy*. And with that Tina finally headed for home.

Tina's Apartment, St. Andrews

Tina pulled her truck into her parking spot at the Oak Meadow apartment complex at the outer edge of the town limits. It was a new development, too far out as far as Tina was concerned. You had to drive for miles to be near all the conveniences of the city. However, Tina did enjoy the quiet peacefulness of country living. Before she got out of the truck, she reached into the back seat to grab the shopping bags from her numerous purchases.

When she closed the truck door, she could see that Jeff's car was not parked perpendicular to the stall. Jeff drove fast. Too fast really and was constantly getting speeding tickets. He probably peeled in and skidded to a stop, not bothering to turn the wheels to straighten his car. *Most likely in a hurry and still pissed off*, Tina imagined. She fumbled with her keys at the apartment door and couldn't immediately find the front door key because the porch light had burned out.

Tina managed to open the door and enter the front hallway where she dropped her packages on the floor. Then gently closed the door behind her. As she entered the living room there was one dim light on by the lazy boy chair. Jeff was passed out in the chair, reclined all the way back. Tina thought she could walk past him and into the bedroom without waking him.

As she gently passed by Jeff, he said without opening his eyes, "Where the fuck have you been?"

Not wanting to get into a fight Tina kept walking, now quicker and said, "Out shopping."

Jeff lunged forward and grabbed Tina's arm just above the wrist and held her from advancing. Jeff easily had 100 pounds on Tina, so there wasn't much she could do when he was holding on.

"What's the big deal showing me up at practice today?" Jeff angrily accused Tina.

"I thought I would surprise you," Tina replied innocently.

"Yeah right," Jeff said as he got up and pulled Tina toward him.

Tina could smell the liquor on his breath. Jeff let go of Tina's arm. She didn't see it coming, but certainly felt it. There is a special name for this pain. All who have been on the receiving end would call it a "sucker punch." His fist hit the left side of her face with such intensity that her jaw snapped shut. The sting was something she never felt before. It was like breathing ammonia; she wanted to run from the pain.

The shock of being hit by someone who was supposed to care for her, more than the actual punch, hurt Tina the most. From her training, her self-defense reflexes took over.

Tina recoiled and struck back with a vicious left jab to Jeff's throat that hit him square in the Adam's apple. Jeff staggered back and leaned forward, bent over, trying to catch his breath. He dropped to his knees and put his hands out in front of him.

Spitting blood on the floor, he yelled, "You fucking whore," as he struggled to breathe. Tina's brain had a moment to operate at a cognitive level. If she had continued to act only on reflexes, as her training had taught her, she would have kicked Jeff in the soft part of his exposed belly. But she held back for a moment and put her hand up to her cheek, trying to subdue the sting. She turned and walked toward the door. While she felt like slamming it, she didn't. She didn't want to give Jeff the satisfaction of knowing he had hurt her.

Fuck! What brought this on? She tried to figure it out as she sat in her pickup truck, holding her cheek and trying not to cry. She had dated many guys in the past and thought she could identify the manipulative jealous jerks that wanted to control every aspect of her life, but somehow, she missed this.

When they first met, Jeff was such a gentleman. He never pressed her to have sex. He behaved almost exactly the opposite.

He told her, "I want it to be right between us. I don't want to rush into a relationship, and have it just based on sex." So, to her, he said and did all the right things. But looking back, it seemed like he was setting a trap; a big fucking bear trap, to lure her in and eventually control her.

As soon as she brought her clothes and toothbrush over to his apartment, he was on her about whom she spoke to or saw during the day.

Beginning almost innocently with, "How was your day? Did you meet anyone interesting?" Then it progressed to, "But you had coffee with Brad last week as well."

"Well, so what?" Tina would defiantly reply. She was not one to be pushed around.

After they first moved in together, just before Christmas, his behavior changed. He started taking her phone - asking her prying questions about who she talked or texted with. Tina was an attractive thirty-four-year-old woman. She made friends easily and had no problem holding her own. When he confronted her about who she talked to, she told Jeff the truth. Looking back, she figured he didn't believe her and suspected that she was cheating on him. She brushed this all off as the sorting out phase all couples go through when they first start living together. She was wrong.

Tina went straight to her truck. She fought back the tears from being hurt physically as well as emotionally. It was over between her and Jeff. She could never live with someone who even dared to hit a woman.

"What a fucking asshole! What fucking warped view of the world was he raised in thinking he could do this? Yeah, the hockey goons fight with each other, but it stops there," Tina angrily shouted to herself with clenched teeth. She was ready to slam her fist onto the dashboard but channeled her energy into what her next moves would be. She was not going to be bullied out of her home. She took out the Leatherman from the glove box and marched defiantly back to the apartment.

She swiftly opened the front door. "If you come near me, I'll fucking kill you," she said in a raised but controlled voice as she closed the front door. Jeff was now lying on the couch. Tina walked right by him.

"I'm so sorry," he whimpered through his wheezing.

"Shut up, asshole!" Tina commanded.

He reached out to try and touch her, but she pushed his arm away and went into the bedroom to pack her things. She packed enough clothes, shoes and toiletries to last for a few days. She went back to the living room with her suitcase in tow. I'll be back for the rest of my things in a few days. I'll call you to tell you when I'll be getting my stuff. Do not be here when I come back. Are we clear?"

"Yes," Jeff mumbled.

"I didn't hear you!" Tina barked.

"Yes," Jeff said slightly louder like a schoolboy being called out by the teacher.

Tina calmly went to the front door, picked up the parcels from her shopping spree and left with her suitcase. She loaded them into the jump seat of her truck, where they were not 30 minutes earlier. She got into the driver's seat, put her face in her hands and started to cry. Since she was alone, she let all of the pent-up emotions overwhelm her every synapse and started to shake, she was crying so hard. The sobs were powerful.

Tina didn't try to stop crying. She let it all come out. After two solid minutes of tears, sobs and shaking she started to calm slightly. Her breathing was shallow, and she had to take deep breaths in order to get enough air into her lungs because her diaphragm kept contracting making it hard for her to catch her breath.

I'm not gonna let this ruin me, Tina thought to herself. She blamed herself for not spotting Jeff's hang-ups earlier.

"Now where should I go? I should have made Jeff leave, but I need to get the fuck out of this one-horse town" she said out loud as she was regaining her composure, drying her tears, and getting her bearings straight. She thought about it for over a minute. *I don't know, so I'll go to the Blind Barber and try and figure out my next move. And get some ice for my jaw. I'm too embarrassed to call my mother.*

The Blind Barber, St. Andrews

The Blind Barber was a small bar, like other small bars in other small college towns. Slightly better than a dive bar, which made it hip with the hipster, middle American college kids that attended Bards College to study liberal arts and spend their parent's money. Tina had to go back into town, but it didn't matter because she had to get away from Jeff, their apartment, and the bad vibe both were sending out, stinking up her atmosphere. Tina pulled into the parking lot of the Barber – as everyone called it. There were only a few cars.

Good, she thought, *I hope there's nobody in there that I recognize.*

Tina selected a booth off to the side, which was dimly lit. She sat so the left side of her face was away from the room. There was a small noisy group in the back room, but otherwise the place was empty. Usually you order at the bar, except when you're a woman who sits by herself in a dimly lit booth on the side. The barkeep dried his hands on the bar towel and came out from around the bar to serve Tina. As he approached her table, he recognized her.

"Dr. Wood welcome to The Blind Barber. What's your poison?"

Tina had been sitting quietly not really looking around trying to keep her head still and nurse the left side of her jaw. She turned slightly to look at the bar keep.

"Oh, hi," she said vaguely remembering him from one of her first-year classes. "Rum and coke, a glass of ice, and a small towel."

"You got it Dr. Wood. Coming right up."

When the barkeep returned with her order, Tina was looking at an anonymous text she just received, "You were right to leave the bum." She turned to accept the drink and ice and forgot the text.

"Jesus, what happened?" The barkeep said as he now saw the redness and swelling on Tina's lower jaw.

"I got hit by the car door," Tina lied as she placed the ice cubes in the towel and moved it up to her jaw.

"Better be more careful Dr. Wood. Bottoms up."

Tina smiled faintly as the keep turned to go back to the bar. The ice was cold, and it made her wound hurt more. But she knew that the ice would keep the swelling down.

Tina's Apartment, St. Andrews

A black late-model Mercedes with New York license plates turned on Elm Street. The car passed just across the street from Tina's apartment and turned off its headlights. Rather than turn into the parking lot, it coasted to the far end of the dead-end street and parked beyond the illumination of the streetlight.

Two heavy set men got out, quietly closed the car door and walked toward the back side of the apartment complex, beyond the range of the security cameras. They obviously had been there before because they opened the basement door to the laundry by entering the correct number on the security keypad. This wasn't terribly difficult to do because the numbers were posted inside on the bulletin board, "Remember the passkey number has been changed to 1324." The note was signed "management." Having gained access, the two strangers were immediately below Tina's apartment.

The Blind Barber, St. Andrews

Tina was minding her own business and feeling sorry for herself when she put the towel with ice down and lifted her glass to take another swig of rum and coke. This was her second and it was going down smoothly and holding down her feelings of rage.

"Jesus, what happened?" She heard as a figure approached out of the dimness. When he was almost at the table, she recognized that it was Brad.

A few of the guys from the hockey team were the ones in the back making all the noise. Brad was returning from the john when he noticed Tina. Tina didn't answer right away, and Brad slipped into the booth bench right up next to her. Tina turned her face away to block Brad from seeing the extent of her injury.

"Wow!" he said. Her cheek looked worse than it felt. The ice helped the swelling go down, but the left side of her face was a bright red.

"Jeff and I got into a fight," Tina said softly.

"I'll kill that fucking prick," Brad shot back angrily.

"No need, he already got his."

"I don't care. I can't let him do this to you."

"Just let it go, okay?"

Brad didn't reply, he was already thinking of how he was going to really mess Jeff up. *That fucking asshole really has it coming now*, Brad thought to himself as he slammed his fist on the table.

Tina lifted her glass and downed the last bit of rum and coke. "Now I have to get myself straight," Tina said aloud, not immediately addressing Brad.

"What do you mean?" Brad said to her.

"Well, I left my apartment and I'll have to hole up in a hotel for a couple of days till I get a new place."

"Nonsense, you can stay at my place."

"No, it's okay, I can make do. You're sweet to offer, though."

"You're staying at my place, till you get back on your feet and I won't hear another word on the subject." Brad said with a commanding voice. "I'm ready to leave, you can follow me home."

Tina shrugged and didn't protest. She left a sizable tip on the table and followed Brad up to the door.

"Thanks," she waved to the barkeep.

"Take care of yourself Dr. Wood" came the happy reply from the barkeep mixing another round of drinks for the hockey team that could be heard yelling in the back, most likely because of someone's prowess at a videogame.

Parking Lot of the Blind Barber

Brad's car wouldn't start.

"Fuck!" he yelled, getting pissed off at the piece of shit. It was too late to call the garage. He didn't feel like going back into the bar to ask one of the guys for a jump, so he walked over to Tina's truck and asked for a jump. After trying several times, the BMW Z4 wouldn't turn over.

Brad said, "It's the nicest looking steaming pile of shit around." He unhooked the jumper cables and got into Tina's truck. He looked over at her and thought she looked a little tipsy, and he offered to drive. She didn't protest and so they switched seats. Brad adjusted the driver seat way back to accommodate his 6'4" frame and they drove off to his apartment peeling out of the parking lot and almost running over a stray cat.

Tina put her head back in the passenger's seat and closed her eyes. *Christ, what a day*, she thought. It was nice not having to drive again and to be in the presence of such a nice man who didn't demand anything from her.

Brad's Apartment, St. Andrews

Brad didn't live too far from the bar, so of course he was a regular there and it didn't take any time to get home; especially the way he drove. Brad's apartment complex was open. More like a motel than a traditional closed apartment building. The owner tried to make a go of it as a motel, but the venture failed financially. There weren't enough steady visitors to make it profitable, so he converted the building into apartments instead. Brad had lived there since he arrived in St. Andrews. The dorm was full by the time he decided to go to Bards College, rather than Ohio State (like everyone else from his hometown). The owners, an elderly couple, of German heritage took an immediate liking to Brad - the strapping clean-cut, well-mannered, well-spoken kid. Brad parked Tina's truck in front of his apartment.

When he turned off the ignition, Tina reached over and gently put her hand on Brad's forearm saying, "Thanks for helping me out."

They climbed the stairs to Brad's small apartment. Two motel rooms were combined into a cozy living area. Brad placed Tina's truck keys on the kitchen counter. "Can I get you something to drink or eat?"

"Yeah, I'll have a rum and coke if you have it." Tina said as she sat down on the couch, after removing the large textbooks that had kept the seat warm.

"Coming right up. I hope you don't mind if it's diet coke."

"No problem."

Brad returned from the kitchenette with two rum and cokes and handed one to Tina as he sat on the couch next to her.

"Skoal," Brad said

"Skoal," Tina replied, as they clicked glasses filled with the magic elixir of caffeine and alcohol.

Brad's weight pushed the couch cushion down, like the force of gravity, which caused Tina to be pulled in closer to him. As she was pulled in, she didn't resist and let her hip and leg meet Brad's. They each took a deep drink, as Brad put his arm around her shoulder and gave her a hug with his strong arm. Tina hadn't turned on a light in the living room, so they sat in the glow of the light from the kitchen as they sipped their rum and cokes.

Tina started to unwind - now that her face was starting to feel better - and she pulled off her shoes. She put her feet up on the coffee table in front of them and rubbed her foot on Brad's leg. She put her drink down and turned to look at him, with her face moving closer to his. She reached her hand around the back of his head and pulled their faces together. Their mouths touched with a warm wet kiss that lasted a while. Tina moved her face back slightly and said, "I don't want to sleep alone tonight."

Brad nodded slightly and put his other arm under Tina's legs and lifted her up at the same time he rose from the couch.

Tina exclaimed, "Oh my!" being impressed by Brad's strength, power, and balance. He carried her to the bedroom like a bride on her wedding night and set her down gently on the bed. Her head reclined into the pillow. Brad put a knee on the outside edge of the bed and gracefully flipped himself to the other side of Tina. He came to rest on the bed beside her with his leg over hers.

The ambient light in the room was very dim, illuminated only from the light in the hallway. Brad moved his head over Tina, and they kissed again. This time they didn't stop until they had both tasted the rum on the tongue of the other. Tina felt both the sweet gentleness and the brute power of Brad.

He moved his hand over her and caressed her breast as they kissed. His hand moved down and undid each button of her blouse. He gently tugged the blouse out from Tina's blue jeans and moved on top of her. Tina put her hands under Brad's T-shirt and pulled it up. Without missing a beat, Brad reached behind and pulled the rest of his T-shirt off. Straddling her on his knees, she could see his big biceps and pecs. He bent over her again and placed each hand beside her head and kissed her again. While she was being kissed Tina reached up and undid the belt buckle from Brad's pants, twisted the button to his jeans and pulled down the zipper. He rolled off Tina and stood at the side of the bed.

Tina watched intently as Brad pulled his pants and socks off. Standing next to the bed Tina gazed longingly at Brad in his under-armor briefs. His erection was evident, and Brad posed for Tina, back lit, in the dim light. Tina sat up in the bed and took off her blouse and bra. Brad straddled Tina again and caressed her breasts as he bent down to suck the nipple of each one. Tina felt Brad's warm mouth and tongue and wanted all of him.

Brad moved down, toward Tina's feet. He undid her belt and the button to her jeans and pulled down her zipper. Tina lifted herself slightly, so Brad could pull her jeans and panties down. She lifted each leg as he pulled them all the way off. Then kneeling beside her, he took off his briefs.

Brad spread Tina's legs and pushed them up as he knelt between them, so he could put his face deep in her lips. Brad tasted Tina's wetness as he gently licked her pussy, which he spread open, so he could kiss her clit. Tina arched her back and groaned as Brad focused his mouth on her clit, gently licking and sucking it. Tina put her hands-on Brad's head and pushed his face into her as she began to gyrate on his mouth.

She pushed her fingers into his hair as he focused his tongue on her clit. Tina's body was now moving in a rhythmic motion toward and away from Brad's face. All her senses were focused on what was happening between her legs, and the excitement of someone new doing something so intimate to her. She liked the way Brad was going down on her, he did it differently than all the other guys she had had sex with; and she loved what he was doing. Panting with labored breath, she pushed up and pulled Brad's head inward as she began to climax. Brad could feel Tina's clit move in his mouth repeatedly as she kept coming.

Tina loosened the grip on Brad's head and gently rubbed his hair in a kneading motion. Brad kissed her labia lips and moved on top of Tina. He reached into the nightstand for a condom and rolled it down his hard-on.

She was so open and wet that he slipped inside her with ease. He moved in and out slowly at first. Tina moved her hips to meet him with the same rhythmic cycle. She could feel his weight on her body as they moved in unison. Tina stroked Brad's head and put her hands on his butt as she met him on each stroke. Brad was kissing Tina's face, neck and breasts.

His movement became harder and deeper as his breathing intensified. Tina could feel the sweat on his back and moved her legs wider apart to allow Brad full access to her as he moved in and out. They were both panting as Brad made his final thrust and held on tightly to her. Tina could feel his warmth fill her as she dug her fingers into his back and climaxed with him.

Brad put all his weight on Tina as they became one and sunk into the bed as he pulled up the covers. The sex was so intense that they were both exhausted and it took a while to catch their breath. Brad rolled off Tina onto the bed beside her. They spooned.

Tina felt secure in Brad's arms. She never thought that she would be in bed with her friend's kid brother but here she was; and she loved it. In Brad's caress Tina was able to erase the bad things of that day. His warm breath on the back of her head, his legs tucked up into hers, and his crotch pushed up to meet the curve of her butt. Brad's warmth enveloped her, and she felt complete satisfaction as she fell deeply into sleep.

Chapter 7

**Charlotte Art Fair, Charlotte
Friday March 2, 2018**

Erin had been working her tail off, making jewelry for the upcoming Charlotte Art Fair. She figured she could get a better price at the fair than online, so she wanted to have some really nice stuff to show off and capture top dollar.

Her friend Rex called again. She had dated him on and off over the past year or so. She wasn't that crazy about him, but he did have some redeeming qualities. Plus, he was a gentleman and he paid for everything. He was a lot older than Erin and she was beginning to think of him as a sugar daddy. She politely declined his dinner invitation and told him that she would take a rain check. He said that he understood that she was busy getting ready for the fair, and they could go out the following week. She thought, *what happened to Jack? God he was gorgeous. I guess our fling was just a one-nightstand. C'est la vie.*

The vendor's admission price for the Charlotte Arts and Crafts Fair had just been raised. This pissed Erin off and she was considering whether it was worth it. At the last fair she had sold just over a couple hundred dollars' worth of jewelry. After she paid the entry fee, she figured that she was working for less than wages paid to fishermen in Southeast Asia.

She rationalized that at least she had her freedom and didn't have to answer to *the man* - trying to console herself as she laid out the cash to pay the entry fee.

*   *   *

She arrived late and all the prime setup spots were already taken. Erin shrugged it off figuring the people that would buy her stuff would not be looking for cheaply made folk art from the vendors in the front rows. So, she pulled her cart to the far side of the park and set up under a shade tree. From experience she set her prices based on where she was selling and who was interested in buying. She didn't mind haggling if the person that was buying valued the time and creativity that she had put into making her unique pieces of jewelry.

It was late morning and there were a few lookie-loos but no serious buyers. Erin thought, *shit, I better make enough money to at least cover the entry fee, or I'll never do this art fair again.* As she waited for a serious buyer, she got out her smartphone. She started to be enthralled by a YouTube video of an international banking conspiracy - something about the Rothschilds - and was not paying attention to the shoppers she had.

"How much is this?" came a deep voice.

Erin hadn't noticed him walk up to her booth. She was ready to give a wiseass response before she looked up. She started her response but stopped as she caught a glimpse of this hunk of a guy holding the most expensive piece in her collection.

"How much will you offer me?" Erin replied.

"Eight hundred," the man answered without hesitation.

Erin, being a hustler, didn't even move an eyelash but inside she was jumping up and down thinking, *holy shit that's like a seven-hundred-dollar profit.*

"Okay, a thousand," the man said, not waiting for Erin's reply.

"Twelve hundred, and you've got yourself a deal mister," Erin cunningly said.

"Deal," the man said as he pulled out a huge wad of bills and peeled off two William McKinley's and two Ben Franklin's. "Can you model it for me?"

"Sure can," Erin said moving her hand out to take the necklace out of the man's large hand. She felt his soft skin and said, "You must be a banker."

"How did you know that?"

"I'm psychic," Erin said sarcastically but not jokingly. They both smiled. "No, silly. You have the soft hands and manicured fingernails of someone who works in an upscale office, and you don't have to shake a stick too hard in Charlotte to hit a banker."

"The necklace looks really good on you."

"Thanks, it's an original, one-of-a-kind," Erin said proudly beaming from the compliment.

"Beautiful, you must have lunch with me."

"Sure, that's the best offer I've had all day. When do you want to go?" Erin asked without hesitation. Not feeling so hard up for money now that she had the winnings from the pool tournament stashed safely away.

"Now, it's almost noon. Bankers hours, you know," The man said returning the sarcasm with the smile of a GQ model.

"But of course," Erin said making a hand gesture on her forehead. "Let me lock up, and I'll meet you at the entrance gate in ten minutes."

"Sounds good."

"My name is Erin, by the way."

"Nice to meet you, Erin. I'm Bryce."

"Nice to meet you," Erin said as she put out her delicate hand to Bryce. Bryce extended his hand to meet hers, and that is when Erin really took in his physique. His forearm had bulging veins, and his hands were massive, even though soft. His tailored shirt hugged his huge biceps. They shook hands.

"I hope I did not offend you with the soft hands remark. I'm prone to say whatever's on my mind," Erin said in her straightforward way of cutting through any bullshit.

"No offense taken," Bryce said with a wry smile, immediately taking a liking to her.

"Good, see you in ten."

They held hands for longer than was customary to shake hands for the first time. Erin certainly liked Bryce's hot looks. And from everything she'd seen in their brief encounter, he was a perfect gentleman and a GQ model to boot.

Erin hurriedly put away her jewelry in a large case and padlocked it to a large tree. Still wearing the necklace that Bryce bought she sashayed up to the front gate. She tucked her arm under Bryce's and said, "Shall we go?"

"Sure, my car is this way."

They walked along the side of the street in the grass parkway with Erin holding on to Bryce's arm and leaning her head closer to him. On the opposite side of the street Jack drove by in his late model Camaro.

His arrival at the fair was once again unannounced to Erin. This behavior was typical of the dark moody type, which he represented well. As he drove by, he saw Erin walk off with Bryce, with her arm locked with his and get into his fancy red sports car.

Bryce pulled his keys from his pocket and pressed the keyless entry button to unlock the doors to his flashy red Bentley Continental GT convertible.

"Cool car!" Erin said admiringly. She wasn't aware that Jack just drove by and saw her.

"Thanks," Bryce said, opening the door for her.

Erin got in Bryce's flashy car and sunk into the deep leather seat. Bryce walked around and got in the driver's seat. He turned the car over, and the engine purred to life. She thought, *I'm in for a ride* - she thought he would peel out into the street to impress her. Instead, Bryce checked in his side mirror and then just eased out into the travel lane.

"You're not from here, are you?" Bryce asked.

"No. I'm from California."

"Oh, really!" Bryce exclaimed with self-satisfaction when he confirmed that his hunch was right about Erin. Which also confirmed why he had an immediate affinity for her.

"Yeah, Southern California. I'm actually a Valley girl."

"No way, really?"

"Yeah. I've lost most of my accent."

Bryce turned on his tunes - a random playlist of straight-ahead jazz with a little funk. "My Funny Valentine" by Chet Baker started to play in the background, which was appropriate under the conditions of their chance meeting.

"So where are you from?" Erin asked.

"Ojai."

"No way!" Erin shrieked. "I've lived in North Carolina for almost ten years now and haven't met anyone from California; or at least they wouldn't admit it."

"I'm going back you know."

"Really. Oh, too bad. I just met you."

Charlotte Country Club and Golf Course, Charlotte

They had been chatting away and Erin hadn't really been paying attention to where they were going; and she hadn't bothered to ask. Bryce turned his car into the long southern estate driveway of the Charlotte Country Club and Golf Course.

"Do you golf?" Erin asked in a highly sarcastic tone.

"What I do on a course couldn't be considered golfing," Bryce chuckled.

Erin didn't get the joke because she never played the game. She thought the whole idea was rather silly. Bryce pulled the car up to the valet in front of the main entrance to the club.

"Good afternoon Mr. St. James, good to see you sir," the valet said.

"Good afternoon, Jimmy. It's a nice day." Bryce replied

"Yes sir. It is a nice day. Good to be alive."

As they were walking up the white steps into the massive veranda of the country club, Erin again put her arm in Bryce's and leaned her head onto his shoulder. "You didn't tell me we were going to such a swanky place," she whispered in his ear.

"Oh, I hope you like it. It's a bit much at times. We're in the South you know, and they are proper."

"Yes, I guess they are," Erin said as she squeezed Bryce's arm.

*   *   *

A black Mercedes with dark tinted windows and New York license plates crept along the backcountry road. The same backcountry road Bryce's place was on. A car like that stuck out in these parts of North Carolina, but it seemed like no one was paying attention. The car pulled over as the driver checked his GPS.

A farmer in a late model Ford pickup stopped on the road and rolled down his window to shout out, "Looks like you're lost, do you need directions?"

This startled the driver of the Mercedes who turned to look at the farmer. He did not even acknowledge the farmer or lower his black tinted window as he sped away with his tires making a squealing sound when they hit the pavement.

That was strange, the farmer thought to himself, but he had noticed the New York plates and didn't think anything of it because he assumed all Yankees were rude assholes.

*   *   *

Erin and Bryce had a very long lazy lunch at the country club. They talked about everything from politics to the sexual revolution, and from religion to conspiracy theories. After her second mint julep Erin excused herself to go to the lady's room. As she was sitting on the toilet, she did a Google search of "Bryce St. James." Since he was such a big shot here in Charlotte, she expected to get many hits on his name. But surprisingly nothing came up, except for one mention in an obscure article on international banking in the New Yorker magazine. And that's what made Erin suspicious that something was up.

Bryce was mentioned in passing in the New Yorker, "The international banker Bryce St. James has assumed a new role as vice president of overseas business development for the Swedish Bank of Uppsala." And that was it.

Erin thought, *yeah right, the 'New Yorker', that liberal claptrap with articles that no one read and jokes that no one got.*

53

When Erin got back to the table, Bryce was typing like crazy on his smartphone.

"So, tell me your story, Mr. St. James," Erin said sitting back down in a slightly tipsy voice and exaggerating the "Mr. St. James."

"What do you mean?" Bryce replied, somewhat taken back by the question.

"Well, when I was powdering my nose, I did a Google search on you. And being the big shot that you are I expected lots of hits. And I only got one stupid article in the 'New Yorker'."

Bryce smiled wryly and didn't say anything at first - secretly thinking that his best friend Billy had done a good job keeping his name off the Internet.

He just looked at her and said, "Perhaps I'm not the big shot that you made me out to be."

Bryce's Estate, Charlotte

Erin and Bryce finished their leisurely lunch and after lunch drinks. The waiter returned to notify Bryce that his car was waiting outside. "So, what would you like to do now?" Erin asked not particularly interested in returning to the Art Fair.

"We can go back to my place and I can fix you some real southern comfort."

"Oh, my sir, I am much obliged," Erin said, faking the accent of a southern belle. As they started to get up Erin said, "Oh shoot, I have to go back to the fair and get my stuff."

"No need to worry it's already been taking care of," Bryce said with the voice of a man that knew how to take charge.

"My that's pretty presumptuous of you," Erin said, slightly peeved but more impressed with a man that took charge.

"Trust me, I never presume anything," Bryce said faking a James Bond accent.

"You sly devil, you. I can see we're going to get along just fine," Erin said giving Bryce a hug and kissing him on the cheek.

Bryce's car had been washed, polished, and detailed while they were enjoying their fine lunch. Not that it was dirty to begin with, this was just one of the many perks that came with membership to the upper crust of southern society.

"Your case has been brought round to my place. Perhaps you can model other pieces for me?" Bryce asked as he got into his shiny red sports car.

Erin was already seated comfortably and said, "Oh yeah, sure." As she reached behind her head and started to take off the necklace Bryce had bought.

"Please keep it on. I couldn't dare accept it. It looks so nice on you."

Erin smiled and leaned over and kissed Bryce again, but this time squarely on the lips. Bryce put the car in gear and pulled out into the driveway. "Would you like the top down? It's such a nice day and the sunshine will feel really good."

"Sounds good! It would be just like home, cruzin' down Ventura Boulevard," Erin said giddily.

They pulled out onto the two-lane highway, with Bill Evan's "When I Fall in Love" playing in the background, and a slight buzz, as they cautiously drove toward his place. They had gone only a couple of miles when they passed the black Mercedes from New York going in the opposite direction. Erin wasn't paying attention because she was singing and humming to the song on the car stereo. Bryce saw the car and looked hard at it, without appearing conspicuous. He followed the car in his rearview mirror as it went by. Bryce always paid attention to detail and the New York plates stuck out to him.

"Everything okay?" Erin asked, noticing Bryce's cautious appearance as he studied the rear-view mirror.

"Couldn't be better. The sun is shining in and outside of my car."

Erin blushed slightly and said, "You are such a tease," as she gave him a playful push on his arm.

Bryce pressed the button on the driver side of the mid-console and a screen opened up on the dashboard. An image snapped to life. It made a few soft beeps as Bryce touched the screen and scrolled through a few computer pages. He tapped the screen and it went dark.

"What's that?" Erin asked inquisitively.

"The security system console to my place."

"Anything wrong?"

"Everything's shipshape," Bryce lied, not wanting to divulge that someone had tried to breach the security system during the short time he was away. He doubted it was a false alarm, or a malfunction. He made a mental note to check it out later.

Bryce slowed down to turn into his estate. The green canopy of trees that lined his driveway created a cooling cover in the warm sunshine. With the top down Erin and Bryce could hear birds singing in the cover of the trees. In the few short trips Erin had taken that day Bryce had never sped up.

She thought to herself, *this is certainly a man in control. Every action was purposeful.*

From the highway you could not see the house. The architect had purposely sited the house for maximum privacy. And Bryce liked his privacy. The security screen flashed again on the dashboard. Bryce could tell that there had been a breach. So as not to alarm Erin he quickly turned the security monitoring screen off and drove on.

Erin could see the magnificent house up on a slight rise in the topography of the lush grass that covered the expanse. The house was white with large glass areas; it certainly was not like any other house in the surrounding countryside. As they approached, Erin could see that her jewelry case had indeed been placed on the front veranda and locked to one of the columns that held up the expansive roof. It didn't dawn on her to ask how they had undone the lock she used to lock the case to the tree in the park. Bryce thought that possibly his guy Friday could have set off the alarm by entering the wrong code when he brought Erin's case over. He pulled the car alongside the front steps.

Erin jumped out of the car and swirled herself around, making herself a little dizzy but taking it all in. Bryce stayed in the car a moment longer to check the security system again. He could see that his guy Friday had indeed used the right code to access the place. So that ruled that out as he checked the day log. *Hmm*, he thought to himself, *must be a glitch in the system.*

"Stop playing with that gizmo and show me around!" Erin said laughing.

Bryce realized he wasn't being the best host and turned the car off and got out. "Welcome to my humble abode," he said self-effacingly.

Erin laughed again, "You're such a kidder."

Bryce smiled, "I can see they brought your case. I'll have it delivered to your place later on."

"No rush," Erin said as she bounded up the stairs to the large white veranda.

Bryce thought it was refreshing talking to one of his own from Southern California, where you didn't have to be so proper; so formal. Bryce welcomed that and invited Erin in, ironically for the southern comfort he had promised her.

Erin was a little startled by all the moving boxes. There were a few things left to pack; the things Bryce needed as he stayed there the final few days before the movers came. Erin poked around while Bryce went into the kitchen. She could hear the clinking of glasses and the blender turn on. She sat at the grand piano in the living room and started to play Satie's Gymnopedie No. 1. A soft rhythmic piece she enjoyed playing as a kid. She didn't notice that Bryce had returned with their drinks. He stood behind her, quietly listening to her playing and enjoying the new unique use of tones.

When she finished, she heard, "Bravo, bravo that was amazing! I'd clap but my hands are full."

"I'm so glad you liked it. It was something I learned as a kid in Tarzana."

"Well here's looking at you, kid." Bryce said as he handed Erin the glass of a frozen concoction of ice and booze.

"Spit in your eye!" Erin replied as she raised her glass and clinked it with Bryce's. "Oh, my that is good" Erin said after the first sip, I think I'm going to get brain freeze. "What do you call this thing again?"

"Not sure. It's something I made up, and never thought to name it."

"Why don't you call it a Mason-Dixon? You know something Californians always heard about the south."

"I'll drink to that," and they clinked their glasses again and downed a large gulp.

Bryce walked over to the couch. Erin got up from the piano bench and followed. Bryce sat on one end and kicked off his shoes and put his feet up on the coffee table. Erin took off her shoes and sat on the opposite end of the couch and swung her legs up onto the seat between them. Bryce lifted her feet and put them on his lap and started to massage her feet with his strong gentle hands. Erin was in heaven.

It was getting late in the afternoon. Bryce preferred ambient lighting. Erin didn't mind either way but, in this instance, she didn't think it necessary to turn any lights on. They were now next to each other on Bryce's large couch. He had his arm around Erin's shoulder, and he rotated his body to face hers and lay his other hand on top of hers. Erin placed both hands on either side of Bryce's face, next to his ears, and gently pulled his face to hers. Their lips met in a passionate kiss. Erin opened her mouth and accepted Bryce's tongue. He probed deeply in her mouth. Then she returned the favor. She was getting incredibly aroused and could feel herself getting wet. Bryce was moving his hips. They were entwined in a zipless fuck.

"Do you want to go upstairs?" Bryce managed to ask in love-labored breath.

"No, I don't want to interrupt the moment," Erin replied.

He took no for an answer and unbuttoned her blouse. He moved his hands to caress her breasts with her bra still on. He reached behind his back and pulled his shirt off over his head. She watched him in the dusk light flex his upper body as he pulled off his shirt with his upper arms. The shirt was loose fitting and she couldn't tell the full extent of his physique until now, when his shirt was off, and he carelessly tossed it onto the coffee table. His six-pack rippled in the soft light.

Oh my, Erin thought, *she had never made love to a man with one of those* (temporarily forgetting about Jack).

Bryce put his hand under Erin's skirt and moved his hand up to the top of her legs. Her panties were already wet from the excitement.

"Take your pants off," she said to him in a soft panting voice.

Bryce stood by the couch and pulled his pants and bikini briefs off. His member was hard and when released from the confines of his briefs flopped out in front, stiff and at attention. Erin sat on the couch as Bryce moved toward her and she took it into her mouth. Bryce never thought the day would turn out this way. He was planning a lazy day off, just hanging out doing nothing in particular. Now here he was, naked in his own living room, with an incredibly beautiful California woman going down on him. He took it all in. Stroking her head and gently pulling her blonde hair back so he could get a better look at his member in such a beautiful mouth.

Erin reached up and moved her hands over Bryce's six-pack. Keeping her mouth open so Bryce could move in and out freely but with enough pressure to make it feel great. She moved her hand down to caress his balls and Bryce almost came.

As much as he didn't want to, Bryce pulled out of Erin's mouth and said, "God that was so good."

He gently pushed her back on the couch and reached behind her to undo her skirt. She lifted her hips, so he could pull her skirt and panties off. She spread her legs wide so Bryce could get between them.

Bryce excused himself and went into the hallway. He opened one of the packed boxes and found his condoms. Erin smiled as she watched him put it on in front of her, knowing that Bryce was a classy guy. She held his hard on and gently guided it into her wet inviting pussy. Bryce gently eased it in, taking short strokes to work it in all the way. Erin spread her legs further apart, lifting them so Bryce could get deeper, all the way into her. She was so wet, and he was so hard that with ease they met each other's stroke: Bryce inward, and Erin's upward.

"How do you like it?" Bryce asked with a wry smile.

"Just like this," Erin replied, her face and chest flushed with excitement.

Bryce reached down with his hand and found Erin's clit. He stroked it in a circular motion as he pumped her. He increased the intensity of both actions. Erin moved her legs up over her head, so Bryce had full access to her clit. She moved her hands and rubbed his back while he pumped her hard and fast. Her breathing was becoming so rapid that Bryce could sense that she was about to climax. He thrust in deep this time and held it.

Erin came at the same time with such intensity that she let out a soft yell, "Oh yes!" As Bryce filled her with his come. As they were climaxing together Bryce put his mouth on Erin's open mouth and kissed her as he shot his load deep into her. Her hot breath made his face wet as he collapsed on her. Erin felt his weight on top of her and his shaft deep inside. She moved her legs down and squeezed them around Bryce.

Bryce pulled out and got off Erin. She turned to her side as Bryce held her. He kissed her hair and squeezed her in his arms. It was a warm evening and they lay on the couch, entwined, for about twenty minutes before they stirred. Erin thought, at one time, that Bryce had fallen asleep; which he had.

Bryce got up and went to the bathroom to get a towel for Erin. The house was now dark, as the sun had set, and the moon had yet to rise. Bryce turned the light on in the bathroom and went inside. Standing in front of the toilet, taking a piss, a shot rang out. The bullet smashed through the bathroom window, whizzed by Bryce's head, and smashed the glass medicine cabinet on the far wall. Bryce hit the floor. Trying to avoid the broken glass as he crawled to the door and turned off the bathroom light.

Erin came running toward the bathroom, "Jesus! What was that?"

Bryce grabbed her and pulled her down to the floor. "I don't know. Stay down and don't move." He opened the linen closet and got a large towel out for Erin to wrap herself with. "Stay here and don't move until I get back," Bryce said with a firm voice.

Erin nodded in obedience. "Be careful," she whispered.

Bryce went back to the living room and found his clothes strewn on the floor. While sitting on the floor he started to put on his underwear. He could hear a car's engine start and the tires squeal as it pulled out of the driveway. He rushed to his study and opened the security panel, fumbling in the dark to check the status of the security system infrared sensors. The light from the panel illuminated the room. Bryce could see the murky image of a large car pulling out of the driveway. It was too fuzzy to determine the make of the car or the license plate number. *Somebody has been fucking with the security system*, he thought, *otherwise it should have picked up the intruder as soon as they entered his property*, Bryce concluded.

Erin heard the car pull away and came back into the living room. She saw the glow from Bryce's study and walked over to that room. She gently pushed the door open and saw Bryce at his desk looking at the computer screens with graphs of data. Nothing she could make out or understand. She stood in the doorway with a large white terry cloth towel wrapped around her body like a short mini dress.

"Christ what was that? Why would anyone want to kill you? We have to call the police!"

Bryce went over to Erin and put his arms around her in a gesture of protection. They stood there, he and his briefs and her in a towel, illuminated by his computer screen and a security panel displaying the infrared image of the driveway. "Why would anyone want to kill you?" She asked again.

"I don't know," Bryce replied, "but I'm going to find out."

Chapter 8

Tina's Apartment, St. Andrews
Friday March 2, 2018

The two men who had entered Tina's apartment building through the laundry room were now at the door to her apartment. One was on a bended knee with a locksmith's pick trying to open the door to her apartment. The other had his back turned to the door, standing guard. This was the Midwest. With the low crime rate, the security cameras were spaced too far apart to be effective. And none were aimed at the door to Tina's apartment. The lock presented only a minor annoyance to the pick and was easily opened in less than thirty seconds.

The man rose from the floor and gently opened the door and the two men in black quickly went inside and closed the door behind them. Snoring could be heard in the front hall from a passed-out Jeff on the couch. The two men split up and like cats quickly and effectively cased the entire apartment. They both met up in the bedroom to conclude that Tina was not at home. And from the looks of things (the opened closet door, clothes on the floor, and an empty bureau) it appeared that she had hurriedly packed for a sustained trip.

The two men returned to the living room. One stood at the head of the couch and the other at the foot. The man at the foot of the couch kicked Jeff's feet and said, "Get up," in a firm, and not too loud voice spoken by someone with a Middle Eastern accent.

Jeff did not respond so the man kicked him again. This time, he kicked harder. Jeff groggily awoke and said in a rather annoyed voice, "What?" as he sat up and rubbed his face.

"Alright, tell us where she is," The man at the foot of the couch said.

"How did you get in here?" Jeff replied angrily trying to get up.

The man behind Jeff smacked him in the face with the back of his hand, "We're the ones asking the questions. Now, where is she?"

Jeff wasn't ready to back down from someone who hit him. And so, he started to get up again and the man behind him pulled on his hair, pulling Jeff back onto the couch.

"She left you, dumb shit."

"Where did she go?"

"How would I know?"

The man in front hit Jeff again, but harder this time. Jeff started to lunge at him but was restrained from behind. Jeff tried to fight him off, but the man was too strong, in a superior position, and Jeff was still feeling the effects of the alcohol, which slowed him down and impaired his judgment, strength, and agility.

"Okay, I'm going to ask this one last time; where is she?"

"I told you I don't know. And even if I did, I wouldn't tell you fucks."

The man from behind put Jeff in a chokehold. The other man went to the kitchen and returned with a paring knife. The man in back pulled Jeff over the top of the couch exposing his abdomen. The man in front thrust the knife with a forward motion and plunged it to Jeff's lower belly, deep into his liver.

Jeff struggled wildly but was restrained by the chokehold. Blood came oozing from the wound and filled Jeff's shirt and spilled over onto the couch. The man from behind choked him until Jeff stopped flailing. And then he stopped. Then the man let go. Jeff slumped back onto the couch and the cushion became soggy with his blood.

The men canvassed the apartment one last time, taking pictures with their smartphones. They left quickly, leaving the lights on and Jeff to die on his own couch, drunk, alone, and not knowing what just happened.

Tina woke with a start. She tried to focus her eyes and figure out where she was. Then it all came back to her. She was alone in Brad's apartment. She got up quickly and went to the bathroom to freshen up.

She felt like shit and slightly hung-over from the night before. Her hair was a mess and her skin was dirty and sticky. She thought she would get her suitcase from the truck. But first she needed to find Brad. She didn't want it to appear like she was moving in with him, if she went to get her suitcase. She went back to the bedroom and put on her clothes. It was a small apartment, so it didn't take long for her to find the note Brad left. "Gone to hockey practice. We can talk when I get back. Brad."

She drew a happy face on the note. This was not a standard practice of hers, but she needed to do something to let the kid down easy.

Tina thought about it. *Did she really want to tell her problems to her friend's kid brother, many years her junior?* She thought the better of it and decided she needed to get out of this fucked up town.

But where to go? Okay girl, first things first, she thought to herself, slowing the pace of her breathing and trying not to get panicked. *Get cleaned up and then figure out your next move, once you've had a chance to analyze your options.*

Tina quickly went to her truck and got her suitcase from the backseat. When she brought her Ram pickup, she was only looking for a two door. Now she was happy that the salesman talked her into getting the extended cab with the back doors. That backspace certainly came in handy.

The hot water from the steaming shower felt good on the back of her neck. She massaged her scalp as she washed her hair. "What to do next?" She kept repeating out loud. "You know what? Fuck it. I'm going to drive to California."

When she was dressed, and with her hair still wet, she went on Google Maps and did a map search of St. Andrews,

Minnesota to Los Angeles, California. The answer came back: 1,926 miles. She figured she could do it in as little as three or four days. She'd take I-35 to Des Moines, then I-80 to Omaha. She had never been to Iowa or Nebraska, so visiting a new state was a small consolation prize. From there, she would head to Julesburg, Colorado. And then take I-76 from Denver to Utah. The thought of being in Utah gave her some small comfort. She had fond memories of her family vacations there, both in the summer and winter.

Maybe I should call my mother, Tina thought to herself. *No, I just need some time to think. I don't want my mother to start solving my problems.* "Okay, Tina concentrate." She said aloud, being temporarily distracted by the task. She scrolled the map down to read, "Denver to Sulfurdale, Utah on I-70. Then take I-15 to Las Vegas and on to L.A. on I-15."

Tina sat back in the chair and steeled herself for the adventure that lay ahead. This trip would close a chapter in her life and open another.

Tina was never afraid of change. Her only desire was that change happen when she had some control over it. It was a little unsettling for her to realize that she didn't have complete control. And maybe that was okay. Regardless, it was out of her hands now and she had no choice but to go with it.

What would Dad do? Tina thought. A smile came to her face when she thought of him and the way he would talk. At times when she was younger, he would give her advice - just like she was a member of the SEAL team. She could visualize him saying "SNAFU, Seaman Wood: situation normal all fucked up. What are you gonna do?"

"Use my wits and my training to take charge, sir!" Tina would bark out to the Major's interrogative, and then they would both laugh and high-five.

Part II

"We are all in the gutter, but some of us are looking at the stars"

~ Oscar Wilde

Chapter 9

American Naval Base, Yokosuka, Japan
Saturday August 24, 1996

"Very good. Now do you think you can do the same thing blindfolded?" Tina's father asked.

"Yes," Tina replied confidently.

"Okay, let's see. Disassemble the weapon and place the pieces neatly on the table."

Tina did as instructed and placed the pieces to her father's .45 MM MEU (SOC) pistol neatly in front of her. Her father got a small towel from his work bench and tied it around Tina's head, over her eyes, and under her long light brown ponytail.

"Can you see anything?" Her father asked.

"No," she replied, getting excited.

"Okay good, I'm going to time you to see how long it takes. And we'll keep track each time you do it, to judge your improvement. Ready?"

"Yes," Tina said, sitting in front of the table with a stern look on her face. This was her game face.

"Okay. Ready? Begin."

The small hands of a twelve-year-old girl deftly assembled each piece of the weapon. Working in quick succession, almost robotically she snapped the pieces together with precision. Just as she was pushing in the clip her mother came out to the garage to see what was going on.

"Oh, Hank," Tina's mother sighed. "We have a daughter, not a Navy SEAL."

"It's okay mom, I like learning all this neat stuff from Dad," Tina said as she pulled off the blindfold, proud of her accomplishment.

"Forty-two seconds," replied Tina's father while he ignored the previous comment from his wife.

"We have to leave soon for your haiku class, dear," Tina's mother said. "Please go inside, clean up, and put on something nice. That new dress we just bought would serve perfectly."

"Yes mother," Tina said, placing the weapon on the table. She got up from the chair and gave her father a kiss and a bear hug (at least what a twelve-year-old girl could manage).

"Thanks, pops, for showing me about gun safety," Tina said. She didn't know that other twelve-year-old girls weren't also learning how to assemble and shoot a pistol.

"Certainly, my dear. Now run off and get ready for poetry."

Tina skipped into the house like any twelve-year-old would, without a care in the world.

Tina's mother turned to her husband slightly pissed off, "Hank, now we talked about this."

"Yes, dear we talked, but you may remember we didn't necessarily agree."

"Oh, Hank, you're such a JAG."

"Now, Susan, you don't have to call me names."

They both burst into laughter. Hank reached up and put his arms around Susan. She bent down to accept his embrace and he kissed her on the top of her head.

"The good Lord blessed us with the most wonderful child," Hank said, proud as can be of his daughter.

"Indeed, He did, dear."

They walked arm in arm back into the house, with Tina's father sliding the gun into the back of his trousers.

Tina ran down the hall from the bathroom into her bedroom. "Almost ready!" she yelled to her mother.

Hank went to the fridge and got himself a Sapporo beer. Then he went to the living room to read the paper. Before he sat down on the couch, he locked the gun in the cabinet. It was a rare day off for him and he enjoyed his downtime teaching new things to Tina. *If he drove Susan crazy in the process, then that was just gravy;* he chuckled to himself.

"Hey Sailor, looking for a good time?" Tina said to her father with a slight Japanese accent as she made her entrance into the living room. Her father looked up from his newspaper and let out a whistle like a sailor on leave.

"My, don't you look nice, my dear." Tina certainly did. She cleaned up well with her new navy-blue pencil skirt, white blouse, and espadrilles. Her hair was pulled back and braided. "You're a real heartbreaker, my dear."

Susan came into the living room to join them. "My, now that's better. Let's get going so we can stop at the library before you have to go to your lesson."

"あなたが望むように、母" Tina replied in Japanese and added somewhat patronizingly, "あなたはとても賢い."

Susan rolled her eyes not knowing what to make of her precocious daughter of twelve, and unable to understand that Tina just said "As you wish, mother. You are so wise." Susan gave Hank a kiss before she left the room. He squeezed her hand as she turned away.

"See you later, sailor boy," Tina said to her father as she gave him a hug, continuing her act as a Japanese escort girl.

"Have fun, my dear."

*   *   *

Major Hank Wood was the ranking member of the Navy SEAL team assigned to the American naval base at Yokosuka. The SEALs ran top-secret missions in the Asian theater from this base. Hank was able to station with his family across the globe. The Wood family spent the last nine months in Japan, and Tina loved it. Hank's SEAL team adored Tina and treated her like she was one of the guys. It wasn't just because she was the boss's daughter. Tina was special, and they all knew it. They were amazed at the knowledge that came out of her.

Tina's mother was a flight surgeon at the Naval Hospital. Due to military regulations, Hank and Susan couldn't always be stationed together, especially with Hank being on-call with his SEAL team and the irregular schedule of his assignments. The Woods cherished the time they were all together, and the Japan assignment had been an especially pleasant one. One that Tina didn't want to end, but she knew that it would. Her parents were career military personnel and had traveled the globe many times.

Hank first met Susan when he was brought into the Naval Hospital in Bahrain. Hank's mission didn't go as planned and his Seahawk helicopter was hit by a surface to air missile. The helicopter made a hard-emergency landing behind enemy lines in Yemen. No one was killed. The team spent an erratic night in a firefight but were rescued in less than eight hours by another SEAL team.

Hank took a piece of shrapnel in the neck that required surgery to remove it. It wasn't life threatening, but it was painful; although no one could tell by the way Hank handled his pain.

Susan operated on him. When she did her rounds the next day and stopped in to see how Hank was recovering, they hit it off. Hank immediately developed a school-boy crush on Susan. Susan rebuffed his advances because of the military rules, and especially because a doctor shouldn't date a patient. To pursue Susan, Hank requested that his commander require the hospital to assign him to another doctor. This caught a lot of attention at the small hospital and rumors spread like wildfire.

The great lengths Hank would go just to be able to have a date with Susan flattered her. A week after his release from the hospital, Hank called in for a favor and got a week's R & R in Hawaii. Of course, he invited Susan and she finally said yes. They had a glorious week together of relaxing fun in the sun. Susan was smitten. During that week on the island, they made love every morning, every evening, and sometimes the middle of the afternoon.

After a long, disjointed courtship, Hank and Susan decided to get married. Their wedding ceremony was observed by over two hundred people and held at the naval base in Honolulu. Susan's parents flew in from southern Ohio and her

Dad gave her away in a beautiful traditional wedding ceremony with a measure of her Japanese heritage added to honor her grandmother who had passed away recently in Tokyo. Hank's parents had a much shorter flight from Kauai, where they lived after Hank senior retired from the Navy.

Technically, Tina was a Navy brat, but she was anything but bratty. She made lasting friendships with the other kids she met all over the world. These friendships became invaluable.

Nippon Prep School for Girls, Yokosuka, Japan

"Dr. Wood … Dr. Wood," announced a small, diminutive voice - almost in a whisper.

Susan didn't immediately respond because she was immersed in her new library book.

"Excuse me, Dr. Wood," said the voice a third time.

Susan looked up from her book. "Yes," she said, almost face-to-face with a petite Japanese woman. Susan was sitting down, but the woman stood at eye-level.

"I want to tell you how impressed I am with Tina, and how thankful the school is for having her attend the haiku class," the school's principal told Susan in impeccable English, without a hint of an accent.

"Oh, thank you for saying so," Susan replied, proud that her daughter had made a positive impression on the principal.

"Dr. Wood, I would like you to consider enrolling Tina full-time here at the Nippon Preparatory School for Girls."

"Well, I don't know Principal Woo, Tina doesn't speak Japanese."

"Dr. Wood, please don't be so hasty with your conclusions. Tina has an enormous gift for language. In the ten classes she's had so far, she hasn't struggled at all. Tell me, have you gotten her a private tutor to teach her Japanese?"

"No. What makes you ask that?"

"Come with me, Dr. Wood. I would like you to see your daughter in action, as you say in America."

The principal carried herself as the dignified woman she was and escorted Susan down the hall to a door that led them to a mezzanine above the lecture hall. They stood in a shadow at the back of the room without making a sound. From that vantage point, Susan could see most of the students, but not Tina.

The haiku teacher instructed, "あなた自身の言葉で、詩人が何を言おうとしていたかを説明してください." The principal whispered the translation in Susan's ear, "In your own words, please describe what the poet was trying to say."

The room was silent, as the teacher waited for a student to respond. Then, there was a voice of a young girl - loud enough to be heard by Susan and the principal.

"詩人は愛のあいまいさを表現していた," said the young girl.

Which the principal translated as, "The poet was expressing the ambivalence of love."

"それは非常に洞察力があります," the teacher replied, "しかし、なぜ彼は直接それを言わなかったのでしょう。."

Again, the principal translated, "That's extremely insightful but why didn't he just say it directly?"

"詩はそれが読者の感情にどのように影響するかによって楽しまれる芸術形式です," said another little girl, in clear but slightly hesitant Japanese.

The principal smiled widely and looked at Susan, "That was Tina," she whispered pointing in the direction of the voice. She just said, "Poetry is an art form that is enjoyed by how it affects the reader's emotion."

"No?" Susan asked in disbelief as she moved out of the mezzanine shadows, so she could see all the girls in the classroom.

"俳句には従うべき厳格な規則があります," pressed the teacher.

"Haiku has rigid rules that must be followed," parroted the principal.

"はい、でもすべての芸術に構造があります,"
Tina countered.

"Yes, but there is structure to all art," the principal continued translating Tina.

"時々、楽しみは詩人が流れるようで美しくそして厳格な規則にもかかわらず何かを創造することができた方法から来る," Tina concluded confidently.

"At times, the enjoyment comes from how the poet was able to create something flowing and beautiful in spite of the rigid rules," the principal concluded her translation while boasting a wide smile, proud of Tina.

"Well done, Tina!" the teacher beamed in English, as all the other girls in the class gave a slight bow to Tina to show their respect for her wisdom.

Susan was dumbfounded as she put her hand over her open mouth. They had been in Japan for only nine months. *How could this kid learn to speak Japanese in such a short period? And where did she develop such an insight into poetry? She had only been taking haiku lessons for a few weeks*, Susan asked herself, still somewhat bewildered at her own protégé. Still dazed she shuffled back into the shadow where the principal had stayed. Hesitating for a moment before she spoke, she replied, "Well, I'll have to talk to my husband about this. Ah, arrangements will have to be made. You understand."

"Of course," the principal replied. "You have a few weeks. The next quarter is the best time for Tina to enroll full time."

"Yes, yes. That sounds right," Susan said, still stunned from what she had just witnessed. It was almost like Tina had become a child that she didn't know. She thought to herself, *oh my Lord, what else about this kid don't I know*?

Chapter 10

Columbia University, Manhattan
Monday October 7, 2002

It was announced that Kim Reed would become the new Dean of Linguistics at Columbia University in New York City. It seemed like everyone in the humanities faculty knew Kim and that day well-wishers stopped by to congratulate him and offer their support.

"If you ever need anything, just ask," was the common refrain he heard, to greatly emphasize the cliché.

Along with the promotion came the corner office and a department secretary. The Dean's belongings were moved from his previous constricted office to his new accommodations overlooking the neatly groomed quad four floors below. Kim spent the better part of the day putting his books in the sturdy oak bookcases that lined his office and going through his old papers. Every now and then, he would take a moment to read an old research paper he had written, which brought back many fond memories.

One photo, touched him like he hadn't expected. It fell from a textbook he had carried with him since high school. Kim felt a rush of emotions he hadn't experienced since high school. He was surprised at the sexual arousal he felt when he saw the photo of his best friend. He hadn't seen that friend since their high school graduation ceremony. They lost contact when Kim went away to college and they never tried to keep the friendship going. For Kim, it was a time to break free of the constraints and harsh judgments of that small town in Utah. From his introspection over the years Kim knew there was a psychological incentive to keep troubling times from his conscious mind. He concluded that the self-deception of his sexual identity was the result of growing up in such a repressive place. Unfortunately, he didn't know quite how to apply this new-found knowledge. But that was about to change.

In high school, Kim kept it to himself. He thought he was gay because he never daydreamed about girls. Instead, he had crushes on other boys, especially the inaccessible ones - the guys on the swim team. Southern Utah was Mormon country. The Orthodox Mormons in St. George thought that even Salt Lake was becoming morally loose, just like the Gomorrah of Los Angeles. To *keep the faith*, they had to double-down and keep those immoral hedonists at bay. A prime example was homosexuals.

Kim grew up God-fearing. So how could he possibly go against the church? These were the people he looked up to, admired, and loved. When he was in middle school, he did research on Reparative Therapy offered in Salt Lake. However, the stigma of psychotherapy was too much for such a tender heart. And he had his doubts that they could convert someone into liking girls.

Kim never followed through with the therapy. It would have absolutely devastated his parents if he told them he was gay. And regardless, the cost of the therapy was out of the question. For all those years, Kim hid his sexuality and he always had a deep and lingering dread that it was his fault that he wasn't *normal*.

He dated girls to try to appear normal and fit in with the rest of the guys in St. George, and Mormon society expectations. However, he was not sexually active, and he repressed his feelings deep into his subconscious. Up until he left Utah, Kim truly believed that if he prayed hard enough and lived a solid Mormon life, his prayers would be answered and that his attraction to boys would end.

Since high school, he had become depressed. He overcompensated by throwing himself into his studies. He elected to go to the University of Utah rather than Brigham Young, much to the chagrin of his parents. Kim believed that the University of Utah wouldn't be as conservative and would provide freedom from St. George, which he desperately sought.

*　　*　　*

It was in this reminiscent context, that Kim heard a light knocking on his office door. Kim was sitting on the floor in front of his bookshelf holding the photo of his best friend from high school. He realized that he had become sexually aroused from looking at the photo and had a raging hard-on. Kim turned to check the door but didn't get up for fear that his hard-on would show through his pants.

"Excuse me Dr. Reed. I am sorry for interrupting, but I was wondering if you could please help me," said the sweetest voice from this beautiful boy of nineteen that had so gently knocked on the Dean's office.

"Hmm," Kim said, clearing his throat and trying to hide his boner and flushed complexion.

"If this is a bad time, I can come back. I'm sorry. I can see you are busy."

"Nonsense, my dear boy. I was just tidying up," Kim replied, getting up as he turned away to adjust his dick, so it wouldn't show as much. He remained facing away from the boy as he walked over to sit down behind his large mahogany desk and hide the bulge in his pants. "Please, sit down," Kim said as he motioned to the two chairs in front of his stately desk.

"Uh, thank you, Dr. Reed," replied the young fellow as he crossed the room and moved the chair to take a seat. This was the first time Kim was able to get a good look at the student. He did a double take because he looked so much like his high school friend, in the photo he was still holding.

"Uh, Dr. Reed," the boy began, "I need your advice."

"Ah, I'm being so rude. You know my name, but I don't know yours," Kim said.

"Grayson, sir. Grayson Nash."

"Well, Grayson what brings you here to my office so late on a Friday afternoon. Most of the other students are out having fun and most likely not thinking about their studies."

78

"Well, it's like this. I'm an anthropology major, and I don't like it so much. I want to try something else, and I was thinking that linguistics may be interesting."

"May be interesting? Are you kidding? Linguistics is the sun and the moon, the earth and the stars. Linguistics is the study of who we are. Language separates us from the beasts of the jungle."

"Wow, I had no idea," the young boy said, fidgeting in his seat, clearly not expecting such a passionate response.

"What makes *you* think linguistics would be interesting?" Kim asked.

"Well, I can speak three languages and I thought why not play to a strength I already have."

Kim looked closer at Grayson. The perfectly coiffed sandy blonde hair, pale white skin, blue eyes, and the chiseled body that indicated Grayson worked out and cared for his body. As Kim sat behind his desk, he felt like he was looking at his high school friend, and a twinge came to his already hard penis. He became slightly flushed and had to clear his throat before he began again.

"My, three languages, while you're a perfect candidate to sit for the prerequisite exam. I'm sure in your case this would be a mere formality."

"But I don't know the first thing about linguistics."

"Ah, and that's where you are wrong my young friend," Kim said, getting less formal. "Knowing more than one language gives you the ability to intuitively know the building blocks of communication. And that is what linguistics is all about."

"I don't know, professor," Grayson said, unsure of himself.

"Well, it's late in the day and I was thinking of stopping by the local watering hole to have myself a libation to celebrate my promotion. Why don't you join me, and I can tell you more about linguistics and you can tell me more about yourself," Kim said nearly flirting.

Kim was about to break one of the cardinal rules he established for himself when he first moved to Columbia - *not to get chummy with the students.* Perhaps the reason for this one exception was that he was feeling a little bit lonely. It was, after all, the day he officially started as Dean at one of the most prestigious universities in the United States, hell, the world. He didn't have anybody special to share this occasion with. Although, the real reason was the uncanny resemblance of Grayson to Kim's high school friend, and the fact that Kim was developing a crush on Grayson, indicated by his now fully erect dick that he was trying to hide behind his large mahogany desk.

Misty Moon Bar, Manhattan

  Kim didn't go drinking much, but he had enjoyed a bar near the campus a couple of times. Walking to the Misty Moon Kim learned that Grayson spoke German, French, Italian, and English - all languages that Kim knew fluently. As they went down the stairs to the Misty Moon the door opened and in the dim light Kim could see a few of the University students hanging out with each other. They all had the self-conscious walk of someone who just had too much to drink. Without thinking, Kim put his hand on Grayson's elbow as they walked into the den of rich college students drinking away trust fund money.

  A table opened just as they approached. Kim slid into the chair and motioned Grayson to join him in the adjacent chair. Kim hadn't felt this happy since he had arrived at Columbia. His new crush would be hyper-charged with alcohol that would take complete control of him. When the third round arrived, Kim raised his glass and proposed a toast.

  "To new-found friends. The best kind." They clinked glasses and took a deep sip of the rye whiskey and club soda. They placed their glasses on the table. Grayson put his hand on Kim's, leaned in, and gave him a passionate kiss on the mouth.

  He moved his mouth over to Kim's ear and whispered, "Is there somewhere we can go to be alone?"

  Nothing like this had ever happened to Kim, but he was in the Big Apple and not Southern Utah anymore. There was no turning back. Kim wanted this moment to unfold and go places he had never been, which it did.

Kim turned his face to Grayson's and said, "Yes, my apartment is a short drive away."

Dean Reed's Apartment, Manhattan

In the excitement, they didn't finish their drinks. Back on Lexington Ave., Kim hailed a cab that whisked them the four blocks to Kim's pad. To attract the best and most prestigious professors, Columbia offered very generous living accommodations.

The doorman opened the cab door and said, "Good evening, Dr. Reed"

"Oh, good evening to you, Charles," Kim said getting out of the cab. "It is truly splendid."

"Indeed sir," the doorman replied. Grayson quickly followed Kim into the foyer. In New York City, nobody cared if Kim brought a young man home.

On the elevator ride up to the eleventh floor, they were alone, and Grayson began kissing Kim. Two doors down the hall from the elevator was Kim's apartment. Had it been further away, they would have torn off their clothes in the hallway and had sex in front of the elevator. Kim's hands were shaking when he tried to put the key in the door lock. Grayson gently reached over and steadied his hand as the key slid into the lock and turned.

They burst into activity once they were both safely inside. It was as if Grayson knew the layout of Kim's apartment. He took his hand and led him to the bedroom.

Grayson skillfully undid Kim's belt and unzipped his trousers. He reached behind and pulled his pants down to his knees. Kim had nowhere to hide his full erection as Grayson took it eagerly into his mouth, putting his hands up to gently stroke Kim's butt and balls.

Grayson pulled his mouth off and pushed Kim back onto the waiting bed. Grayson started to take off his clothes as Kim watched, stroking his dick in anticipation of what was going to happen next. Kim was right about one thing that evening, Grayson did work out as evidenced by his toned and tanned body.

"Take off your clothes," Grayson commanded. Kim readily complied, quickly taking off his shoes, socks and pants, but he left his shirt on. Then Grayson kneeled on the bed, turning on the nightstand light.

"The shirt, too," Grayson said in a firm but playful voice.

Kim obliged and then lay back down. Grayson straddled him and put his massive cock into Kim's virgin mouth. Kim thought he must have gotten a male enhancement procedure because it was enormous. Grayson pumped his mass in and out of Kim's mouth, but Kim began to cough. He choked on Grayson's cock going all the way into the back of his throat. Kim sat up and coughed for several seconds.

"I'm so sorry. I've never done this with a guy before," Kim admitted, feeling ashamed.

Grayson sat next to Kim and put his hand around his shoulder. "Hey, there's nothing to be ashamed of," he said this as if he could read his mind. "Let's try that again, shall we?"

Grayson lay back on the bed and motioned Kim to start sucking him off. Kim moved his hands over Grayson's body studying his shape and feeling its stiff form. He put his hand on the base of Grayson's shaft as he lowered his opened mouth onto it.

Grayson put his hands-on Kim's head and moved it up and down on his throbbing member. Kim had never been that excited in his life. His face and chest were flushed red, and his breaths were shallow and rapid. Up until that point, he was always confused about his sexuality. However, when Grayson's steaming white semen hit the back of his throat, there was no denying it anymore. Kim knew he was as gay as any fag in the New York Gay Pride Parade. They spent the rest of the night having sex. The next day, Kim's whole body was sore from the contortions Grayson put him through.

Dean's Office Columbia University, Manhattan
Friday November 15, 2002

There was a very good reason Kim made a rule about not getting too friendly with the students. Those relationships always ended badly. Grayson certainly took advantage of the crush Kim had on him. Grayson did not reciprocate Kim's feelings, which hurt him deeply. Kim felt that he had been a mark, and Grayson set him up and played him.

When Grayson started to pressure Kim into paying him off for not filing a complaint with the university provost, that's when Kim needed help. He turned to Holly Hayworth, the department's secretary, because he was lost, had never been in a situation like this before, and desperately needed to confide in someone. Holly Hayworth was a tall, articulate, black woman from Queens.

Kim sat on the chair next to Holly's desk and started the conversation with, "I feel so ashamed for what I've done and that I have to involve you in my personal matter. You can tell me honestly that you don't want to get involved, and I will not think any the less of you," Kim said to Holly, looking past her gaze because his shame did not allow him to look her in the eye.

"Dr. Reed, please consider me your friend. What's up?" Holly said, trying to be supportive.

Kim then calmly explained the situation; having practiced this moment beforehand to make sure he said what needed to be said. When he heard the words he was speaking, he could hardly believe what he was saying about himself. The only one Kim was fooling about his sexuality was himself. Holly knew from the minute she first met him that he was *a little light in the loafers*.

"My, oh my. You've certainly gotten yourself into a pickle. No pun intended," Holly said with a chuckle slightly waving her arms. "Oh, I don't mean any offense, Dr. Reed. But it does seem like you just fell off the turnip truck from Southern Utah."

"No offense taken, Mrs. Hayworth," Kim said a little wounded, knowing that he had indeed just fallen off the turnip truck from Southern Utah.

"Oh, come now, please call me Holly."

"And me Kim," he said still slightly glum but managing to take in a quick glance of her.

"Okay, now that we got all those pleasantries out of the way we need to do some serious talking," Holly said, taking command of the situation, knowing Kim was out of his league.

Kim motioned toward his office. "Let's be discreet about this."

"Yeah, good idea," Holly said, following Kim into his corner office. She closed the door behind her and walked over to the chair in front of his desk. She sat in the same chair Grayson had, when this completely sordid mess began, a little over a month ago.

"If I'm going to help you, you have to tell me the whole story," Holly began. She had experience dealing with student-professor relationships. In fact, it was quite common, but almost always involved some young good-looking woman charming her way with some willing, overweight, balding professor, who was full of himself - thinking that he deserved such delicacies - and more than willing to inflate her grade each time she inflated the blood vessels in his meat. However, Kim was unaware of such offences by the faculty, being the naïve turnip cart rider that he was.

"Agreed, but you have to swear that you will never tell another living soul," Kim said in a hushed tone, looking around the room, as if someone could be eavesdropping.

"Agreed," Holly said, placing her large hand on Kim's desk.

Kim fidgeted in his large black leather chair. He looked away from Holly and gazed out into the courtyard. This wasn't called Ivy League for nothing. The vines grew on the stately buildings and the leaves were beginning to show a hue of color due to the November chill.

"It was like a summer romance, as best I can describe it, though I never really had one before. But this is what I imagined it would be like," Kim said without further prodding from Holly. Being a scholar, Kim didn't leave out any details except the parts about blowjobs and anal sex. Kim talked nonstop for over forty minutes and Holly didn't once interrupt. She paid careful attention to every word he articulated. This wasn't just a deposition about being blackmailed, this was a full on mea culpa of a grown man describing the pain he had been through his entire life, by hiding his sexuality for so long and finally realizing it, discovering his true self, and yet have it all come crashing down on him harder than the sanctimonious judgments he endured in Southern Utah.

The entire time he was talking, Kim looked out the window and didn't once look at Holly. He knew he had to get this out in the open for his own psychological well-being, but he was too ashamed to look straight at her while he laid bare his soul.

Holly knew this and respected him for it. When Kim finished, he turned and faced Holly once again. She was wiping a tear from her eye with the sleeve of her blouse. She got up from the chair without a word and came around to the other side of the desk. She then reached down and hugged Kim.

She kissed him on the top of his head and said, "You poor man. Of course, I'll help you." Then she turned and walked out of his office, closing the door softly as she exited and walked back to her desk.

Kim was stunned. He sat there for the rest of the evening. The dusk came, and he didn't turn the lights on. Sometimes, he just felt good sitting in the dark, feeling sorry for himself; his own little pity party. To really feel it deeply, to allow himself to feel all the hurt and all the pain, the regrets, the anger, and hatred that welled up from within. Kim allowed himself this luxury - something he rarely allowed himself to do. From that point forward, he was a changed man.

Holly treated this as a purely administrative procedure. The University was very progressive and recognized that strange things will happen when humans interact. Professor-student relationships were common in universities across the globe. It was the first and purest form of grade grubbing. Some women were extremely skilled in the art form and practiced it with sorcerer like acumen. Men were less skilled at the vocation because female professors were much better at not thinking with their dicks.

The Dean's case was rare, and Holly felt that it needed to be treated as special. Besides, she really liked the Dean. She felt that he wasn't an asshole, like many of the other professors she interacted with.

Holly went to the University's Human Resource department and filed a hostile work environment complaint. She hadn't consulted with Kim before doing so. She had special training in this area and part of her job description was dealing with just such events. Holly also assumed that the University would treat the situation cautiously, since she was a black lady from Queens, and Kim was gay.

Monday November 18, 2002

Monday morning arrived with wet weather. The rain dampened everyone spirit just a little bit. Holly gently knocked on Kim's open door, "Dean may I have a word with you?"

"Well certainly. Please come in. Have a seat," Kim gestured.

"I won't be long," Holly said folding her skirt neatly under her as she took a seat and crossed her long black legs.

"What's up?" Kim asked in a rather cheery tone.

"My we're happy today, aren't we?" Holly said noticing the chipper mood Kim was in.

"Yes, we are indeed. I'm a changed man I say. A changed man indeed." Kim beamed in his Southern Utah sort of way.

"Well that's just fantastic," Holly replied somewhat guardedly knowing that the topic of conversation was about to change to something rather unpleasant. "Kim, I filed a complaint with human resources."

"Oh, I see," Kim said with his mood changing to become much more serious.

"Don't worry, it is standard procedure for these sorts of things," Holly stated matter-of-factly not going into details. "You will be interviewed by the human resources department to tell your side of the story. I know you will, but I just want to emphasize that it is best that you tell them the whole story, just as you described it to me. They will also interview the student to get his side as well. There is nothing preventing him from lying or fabricating events. It is best that you come clean and trust that the system will be fair as they adjudicate this most unpleasant event."

"I completely understand. Thank you for your support and kindness. I figured something like this would happen. I was checking up on the human resource rules for this sort of thing. In anticipation of this interview, I spent the weekend typing my side of the story. I know they don't need it in writing but doing so cleared my brain of all the emotions. That is the reason I'm in such a good mood. Ironically, going through this unpleasant experience has allowed me to shed all the emotional baggage weighing me down that I've been carrying all these years. This is the beginning of the new Kim Reed."

"Wow! You have been doing your homework. Good for you!" And with that, Holly rose and walked out of Kim's office.

Kim was interviewed by human resources, as were Holly and Grayson. This time, Kim told every aspect of the sordid story including the blowjobs and anal penetrations. At the end of the interview he slid his typed report across the table to the human resource representative and stated, "Everything I just told you is in my report. You can take this copy, but you will have to sign the non-disclosure agreement that is on top." Kim had found a generic agreement online and modified it slightly to suit his needs.

The human resource rep. said, "Oh my, no one ever provided a written report for such a minor event. I don't know if I can even sign a nondisclosure agreement. I'll tell you what Dr. Reed, just keep this here with you at I'll check with the boss, but I don't think we'll need it."

When the HR rep left Kim's office, he was so relieved. The words *minor event* kept playing repeatedly in his head. He thought to himself, *yeah, I guess I really did just fall off the turnip truck, but I won't be fooled again.*

No formal sanctions were handed out to either Kim, or Grayson. Grayson did eventually drop out of Columbia. The provost visited Kim one evening - to check up on him. The provost was very kind, understanding, and assured Kim that the University valued him very highly. With his pride intact and his newfound identity, Kim set out into the world a gay man with an insatiable appetite for sex with young men.

Chapter 11

Anderson School, Incirlik Airbase, Turkey
Tuesday May 6, 2003

"Okay class please settle down," Miss Dodson, the elocution instructor said in English but with a British accent. Miss Dodson would however take issue with you saying that she had an accent. She spoke, according to her, the proper King's English, and it was indeed everyone else that had an accent. Young ladies from across the globe had been selected for admission to the prestigious Anderson School located at the joint task force base of the North Atlantic Treaty Organization (NATO) located in Incirlik, Turkey, on the Mediterranean Sea. Each year, thousands of women applied for thirty coveted spots for the high school freshman class.

Tina researched numerous schools before selecting this one. Her parents supported her decision to attend an international school, seeing that she had traveled the globe her entire life. It would be good for her to close out her high school education in one location and not to be disrupted by the many moves of the military and her parent's global assignments. Tina completed an enormous amount of research and visited several schools that made her short list. In the end, she only applied to the Anderson All-Girls School. Her mother tried to convince her to apply to at least one other school, to increase her chances of being accepted at one of the schools she had spent so much time researching.

Tina could not be dissuaded and said, "If I don't get accepted, Nana and Pops said I could live with them and go to the school in Columbus."

"All right, my dear. I just don't want you to be disappointed."

"Don't worry, mother. I won't be," Tina said with her usual self-confidence.

Tina was accepted to the Anderson school out of the one thousand four hundred and eighty-two that applied. The other twenty-nine that were accepted were mostly from the NATO countries of Belgium, Canada, Denmark, France, Iceland, Italy, Luxembourg, the Netherlands, Norway, Portugal, the U.K., Greece, and of course Turkey. Tina was the only American selected of the one hundred and twenty-eight that applied.

Tina thrived in the international environment. She soaked up the customs and languages of her classmates and the host country. During spring, summer, and Christmas breaks, she returned to the U.S. and spent most of the time with her mother's parents in Ohio. She particularly enjoyed the vacations her parents attended. Tina understood the demands of the military life on her devoted parents. She didn't place additional demands on them when all of the travel arrangements didn't work out perfectly during her vacations.

The curriculum at the Anderson School was very rigid. This provided a solid basis in the very building blocks of knowledge. One of the requirements was a one-unit class in religion. Tina's parents were not religious, although her grandparents were Catholic on her mother's side and Lutheran on her father's. Tina decided that she would study Islam to learn more about their culture, customs, and what all the fuss was about. This time it wasn't her mother that tried to dissuade her from studying Islam. Her parents were neutral on the subject. This time her maternal grandparents, who Tina was very close to, tried to get Tina to change her mind. In the end, Tina stuck with her initial decision. She didn't think it was such a big deal.

With the additional effort Tina put into her academic studies, she advanced ahead of her age group. Of course, this being an all-girls school meant only one thing: older jealous girls picked on her and treated her as a frenemy. She was in her senior year and the tables were about to turn.

"Are you going to the Founder's Day Ball?" Anne Taylor asked Tina. "It would be nice if you could go and join our table."

Anne Taylor was the most popular girl in Tina's class. They had certainly not seen eye to eye the first three years at the Anderson school. Anne was royalty or some such thing being from the upper crust society of the effete British Lords and Ladies. Being an American, Tina considered this all so medieval and thought the world should be rid of that nonsense. She was quite proud that American society did not have a class system. However, Tina wasn't in the States, and since this was Europe, and the only American at the school, she was certainly in the minority opinion on royalty.

"I haven't thought about it," Tina replied. However, truth be told, she had. She knew the all-boys school from Ankara was going to attend. Being nineteen the youthful exuberance was raging within Tina just waiting to burst out. Turkey was a closed society, especially compared to the States. Every time Tina visited her grandparents, she was able to catch up on all the latest fads and crazes in Ohio. However, she was dying to go to California to get the real American experience. For the moment, that was out of the question. Tina had to settle for the version available to her.

"You have to be there. Everyone is going. I heard that the all-boys school is going to be there, and they have the cutest guys. I want you to go with us and sit at my table," Anne said trying to imitate a genuine California Valley Girl accent.

"Well, if you insist, then yes I'll go," Tina replied in her imitation of an upper crust British accent.

"Oh good," Anne said waving her hands in the air, pretending to be a Valley Girl.

Tina was surprised, and flattered, to be asked to sit with the popular girls at Anne's table. There was an unspoken rivalry between them. They always vied for the best class projects and reports. Always spoke up when their teachers asked for input from the class. However, that was kid's stuff. To Anne's way of thinking the battle was now going to be for boys, and that's where she felt the stakes were the highest.

Anne had the look that came with wealth, breeding, and elocution lessons. However, Tina had the look of an American model. She was tall, slender, short light brown hair, and most importantly, self-confidence. Not a false self-confidence from the crap they teach kids at "leadership club." She had a genuine self-confidence built from perspective, hard work, not being afraid to try something new and even make mistakes. In addition to her wholesome good looks, Tina was also very friendly and accepting of the difference of others. She was slow to pass judgment on others and always looked for the good in another.

Unfortunately, she didn't come from wealth, and on the international stage that she was on, that counted for a lot. That is why Anne was the most popular girl in class. She thought nothing of inviting a friend to go with her on a weekend skiing trip to Austria. All-expense paid weekend junkets were stiff competition for the daughter of a military family.

Tina never felt resentment about her lot in life. Even when it was amplified by the international setting, she placed herself in. In fact, she thrived on being who she was and having friends, true friends, accept her for who she was. Not because she could take someone on daddy's yacht.

"My table is going to be exclusive to the hip crowd," Anne boasted. "The boys will all fight for our attention. Our dance cards will be full," she said using an old cliché, but meaning every word.

"That sounds great Anne. Sure, I'd like to join your table," Tina said sarcastically. "We'll be the hippest people there. I'll find out what the latest craze is from my hipster friends in L.A."

"Oh yes!" Anne exclaimed with a shriek, "That would be so cool."

They were walking in the quad between the campus buildings. The hot afternoon sun was high in the clear blue sky.

"I'd love to stay and chat, but I have to get to class," Tina said, almost cutting Anne off. "I don't want to be late."

"I have others that can cover for me when I want to ditch a class," Anne said with an air of superiority. "I'm going to the bazaar to smoke hash from a hookah. See you later."

History Class, Anderson School

Tina was a little surprised by what Anne had just confessed and thought, *I guess if she gets caught by the Turkish Authorities, Daddy will just bail her out like he always does.* Forgetting about Anne, Tina hurried down the hall with her steps echoing in the empty corridor. She was already late and hoped that she would be in time before her name was called by the teacher-taking role.

Tina could see through the window of the classroom door that class had already begun. She opened the door gently and eased herself inside. She walked to her seat, trying to be inconspicuous.

"Miss Wood, so nice of you to join us. Perhaps you would like to tell the class how you answered the homework assignment," Mrs. Hassan, the history teacher, said sarcastically.

"Yes, of course Mrs. Hassan. I'll be delighted to," Tina said as the girls already seated giggled in relief that they weren't called on to answer the assignment.

Tina turned and walked to the front of the class. She looked out at the twenty-eight young girls seated in their desks. All had stopped giggling and were intently looking at Tina. She wore the school uniform, but on her, it looked different. The plaid skirt was hemmed up an inch and a half and two of the pleats were removed to give the skirt a form fit and reveal her slender legs. The official cut was deeply drooping and unflattering to anyone.

Tina made hers an individual statement of whom she was and that she was not a conformist. The white blouse had also been altered. The back-seam had been taken in and slot seams added to the front just under her breasts to flatter her natural figure. Around her neck was a stylish leather choker, favored by the surf culture in Southern California. On her left wrist, she wore two hoop bracelets made of silver and turquoise from the Hopi Indians of Arizona.

Tina began, "The assignment was to give the main causes of World War I. I researched this topic extensively. Being from a military family, I found the subject very interesting. Most textbooks cite the assassination of Archduke Ferdinand of Austria in Sarajevo as the cause. Some even think the Serbian government was implicated in the machinations of the secret society; The Black Hand. In my opinion, this was not the primary cause but merely a catalyst. The last pebble, as it were, to be added to the others to make a heap."

Tina paused for a second, trying to decide if she should go on. It was certainly a pregnant pause because the class and Mrs. Hassan were waiting for her to continue. "In my research, I discovered something very interesting. Something I had not thought of before. When we read the tragic history of war, we learn about the sacrifice, loss, and the bloody inhumane savagery humans are reduced to. But the one thing I was not aware of was the people who benefited and profited from the misery of others. I don't want to offend anyone, but Sweden was far from neutral in the conflict. Swedish banks financed the war and reaped huge profits in doing so. Being the daughter of two career naval officers, I find war profiteering particularly appalling."

The class sat stunned at what they were hearing. Mrs. Hassan had to clear her throat before she spoke, cutting Tina off.

"Oh my, Tina, you've done it again. I give a straightforward assignment and you go above the call of duty. Bravo, good show. Please do try and not be late for class again."

"Yes, Mrs. Hassan," Tina said with a slight bow as she turned and went to her seat. The class started whispering again, sounding like the low hum of a beehive.

"Settle down," Mrs. Hassan scolded, as she returned to her lesson.

Tina wasn't paying attention. She was into her own thought about what just transpired with Anne. For the entire school year, so far, Anne hadn't given Tina so much as the time of day. *Why was she now being all nice and overly friendly*? She couldn't figure out Anne's motives. *Oh well, it's probably nothing. I'm over-analyzing again*, Tina thought to herself as she turned her attention to Mrs. Hassan's twelfth grade history class.

Turkish Bazaar, Ankara

"Oh God! She makes me sick, that fucking high and mighty American attitude. I'm gonna puke," Beth Campo said just before she took another drag of the hookah pipe. She coughed and then continued in a slightly raspy voice, "If I hear her say one more time that her Dad is a Navy SEAL I'm going to scream." She handed Anne the hookah hose.

The Turkish bazaar was a busy place with small shops that lined the narrow, winding, cobblestone alleyways that led into a labyrinth of haggling commercial undertaking, foul smells, and hash smoking. It was this last item that Anne and Beth came to the bazaar for. Sitting at a small cheap plastic table on wooden folding chairs in the alleyway outside of the Turkish coffee shop Anne felt self-satisfaction that she had turned Beth against Tina. Anne's modus operandi was that of a master manipulator. She wasn't overt in her approach. She would lead her subjects down a path and let them make their own conclusions from the suggestive statements she would release into a conversation over time.

Like Anne, Beth came from a well-to-do British family, the daughters of old money and proper breeding. Over the centuries, it was through the process of exclusion that these blue bloods held onto their wealth and prevented upstarts from acquiring any. Upstarts were the common enemy to be thwarted at every opportunity. Beth's family had the heritage but not the same money as Anne's. However, modern times were catching up with Britain and both of its citizens getting stoned in the bazaar.

Chapter 12

Tina's Dorm Room, Anderson School
Friday May 9, 2003

Tina sat upright in her chair. She put down a thick book on the tiny table in front of her. *Wow, what a story*, she thought to herself. She had just finished reading a two-thousand-page history of Christopher Columbus. Her term paper was going to be on a significant person who had changed the world. She leaned back, and the chair creaked slightly. Tina's bed occupied a significant portion of the small room. It was neatly made with the sheets folded where the corners met. It certainly would pass inspection at Camp Lejeune. She turned her chair. Her roommate, Chanal Aslumani was sitting with her head cradled in one arm propped up on her tiny desk. The white cords of her earbuds stood out against her black hair and dark brown skin.

The school year, as well as Tina's time at the Anderson School, was ending. Final exams were coming up and teachers were assigning long term papers. It was a month before finals - Founder's Day. That night's gala ball was to take place in the President's Hall on the north side of campus. However, it was 10 am and the two girls had much to do before they could start getting ready.

"Hey, Chanal. What's your history term paper going to be on?" Tina asked as she turned completely around in her chair. There was no response, so Tina tapped her gently on the shoulder.

Chanal took her hand and pulled out an ear bud. You could hear the music blaring out of the tiny speaker. "Sorry, I couldn't hear you. My music was up too loud," Chanal said as she turned the volume down on her iPod.

"Oh no problem," Tina said "I just needed a break from studying. I asked what your history term paper is going to be on."

"The British Raj, the pros and cons," Chanal replied. "There were many benefits derived for the people of India and Pakistan. Some positive effects remain in place to this day. But there were many negatives. I'm going to try and be objective in my analysis, but it will be hard, especially after having suffered through the school year putting up with all those British bitches led by Anne and Beth," Chanal said as she removed the other earbud by the time she finished and had turned to face Tina.

"Whoa, why don't you tell me how you really feel about it?" Tina said sarcastically. Both girls chuckled at Anne and Beth's expense.

"How can you say that about Anne and Beth? You've been in their clique all year long?" Tina inquired.

"That's easy for you to say. You're an American and everyone looks up to you. Plus, you're smart, and pretty, and independent. I'm Pakistani, Muslim, with dark skin, and talk with a funny accent. I was asked to be in their group, but I had to pay my dues to hang out with the 'popular' girls," Chanal retorted.

"Just because I'm an American doesn't mean people automatically look up to me. Hey, I didn't mean this to be an inquisitor conversation. I was just surprised with the vitriol in your voice when you mentioned Anne and Beth," Tina said, almost apologetically.

"I feel so ashamed," Chanal said in a quiet slow voice. "I feel like I sold myself just to be with the popular girls. I've lost my dignity."

"What do you mean?" Tina asked supportively.

"What I'm going to tell you cannot leave this room," Chanal said very seriously.

"You have my word," Tina replied lifting her hand and giving the Girl Scout's salute.

"Well it all started innocently," Chanal said. "They wanted to borrow my notes from the classes they missed. But it soon became much, much more, and much worse."

"Yes, go on."

"Well, hmm. It all started at the beginning of this school year," Chanal whispered. She looked from side to side, ensuring no one could hear them. "Beth invited me to a study group meeting with Anne and two other girls. One was from Turkey and one was from Greece. I don't want to tell you their names."

"Ivanna and Balavkia," Tina interjected.

"Yes, so you remember them?" Chanal said with her voice rising a little.

"Yes, of course I remember them. They taught me Turkish and Greek. Until they left for Christmas break. I was disappointed that they didn't come back. I reached out to them, but they wouldn't tell me what happened, and the reason they weren't returning. I stay in contact with both of them." Tina added smartly but not in a condescending way.

"I'll tell you what happened," Chanal continued in her hushed tone. "Ivanna, Balavkia, me and another girl were writing term papers and doing homework for Anne and Beth. The political science teacher suspected something was up when Ivanna turned in a paper that was very similar to Anne's. He dug deeper and found Balavkia's paper was almost exactly like Beth's. Then all hell broke loose. Anne's parents actually sent their barrister here from England to speak on Anne's behalf. That must have impressed the principal because Anne and Beth were allowed to stay, while Ivanna and Balavkia's scholarships were revoked and they were kicked out."

"Wow. I never heard any of this," Tina said, dumbfounded. "I heard rumors, like everyone else, but nothing like this. Why do you know so much about this?"

"Remember," Chanal began, "I was in their clique and we were forced to choose sides. Who would you believe, two scholarship students from relatively poor families who could not afford tuition on their own? Or, two rich party girls, whose estates contribute money for scholarship students? I hate myself for doing it, but I chose popularity and was rewarded for it. I sold out." Chanal's eyes began to well with tears. "I sold out and lied for those two British bitches. The principal interviewed every girl in the study group. The vote was unanimous. We all sided with Anne and Beth and said that Ivanna and Balavkia had copied their term papers. Oh, I'm so angry! God, I'm pissed off," Chanal said with tears rolling down her cheeks.

Tina looked at Chanal and saw a naive young woman, away from home for the first time, desperately trying to fit in and be accepted by the in-crowd. "Listen," Tina began, "in the States, we have a saying - 'don't get mad, get even'."

"Thanks for listening to me blabber away and burden you with my problems," Chanal said sheepishly. "I really shouldn't burden you with my problems. You're being nice, and I feel I don't deserve it after what I did to Ivanna and Balavkia. I think I should go to the principal, confess, and accept whatever the consequence will be."

"Yes, that would be one way to deal with this. But there's another popular saying in America - 'you make your own breaks.' If you don't plan out ahead of time how things will play out, then you're setting yourself up to be treated just like Ivanna and Balavkia were treated. What makes you think things will work out for you better than it did for them?"

"Well, I'll be sincere and honest."

"Yeah right. And they'll believe you now that you've changed your story?"

"But - but"

"Listen," Tina said, cutting off Chanal, "they'll eat you alive. You'll be made out to be the disgruntled one that is seeking revenge for not going along with the clique."

"Yeah, I guess you're right. But I feel I have to come clean."

"You can. I'm not suggesting that you don't come clean. What I'm saying is plan ahead of time and weigh the different scenarios out, and plan for the consequences of each."

"Wow, sounds like you've done this before."

"I don't want to belabor it, but I am..."

"Yes, yes the daughter of a Navy SEAL" Chanal said finishing Tina's sentence. Both girls laughed and gave each other a high five.

"Okay, enough of this serious talk. We must get ready for the Founder's Day Ball. Let's have some fun!" Tina said trying to break Chanal out of her funk.

"You go. I'm not feeling up to it," Chanal said feeling dejected.

"Nonsense! The first part of the plan is for you to act as if there is nothing wrong. You must remain friends with both Anne and Beth. 'Keep your friends close and your enemies closer,' as the saying goes."

"My, you're full of sayings, aren't you?" Chanal teased.

"You betcha," Tina beamed. "Now, here's what we're gonna do for the ball," Tina began to talk slowly and quietly and looking around the room as if someone was eavesdropping, mimicking Chanal.

"Quit it," Chanal scolded, gently slapping Tina's hand.

"Okay, okay, but seriously…"

Grand Hall, Anderson School

Southern Turkey has a Mediterranean climate. Warm during the day and cooling off nicely in the evening. That night was going to be no exception. It was early May. One month before graduation. The days were gloriously long. The evening was still bright and clear as the crowd began to gather in the courtyard outside the ballroom. The olive trees that lined the courtyard were festooned with small white lights that gave a glow to the leaves and harkened that this was a special evening.

The students from the Anderson School started to arrive. Walking across campus dressed in their evening gowns. Some spent weeks planning their outfits, with matching shoes, and jewelry. These proper young ladies had their hair done in fashions not seen before in Turkey, but common in most of Europe.

In a memo to the girls, the principal had stressed conservative dress and most especially no makeup or perfume. She cautioned, "We want to make a good impression for our male guests visiting for the evening. We most certainly don't want to come across in the wrong way."

At the principal's direction, the young ladies of the school - from freshman to seniors - all followed instructions to the *T*, looking quite attractive in their evening wear without their makeup or perfume.

The girls formed circles and they chatted amongst themselves, waiting for the evening's festivities to officially begin. The principal's memo stated that they were to arrive by 7:45 PM sharp, in order to be present and greet their male guests. It was a traditional party, held each year on Founder's Day.

The girls were excited. To go to an all-female school was one thing, but to not be around boys for six months straight was something else altogether.

Alcohol was out of the question; officially that was. Turkey, although a Muslim country, was still a country full of bazaar traders ready to supply just about any need. All the local merchants knew this day; ready for a quick sale of outrageously high priced liquor to naive young girls spending their daddy's money. Liquor, not the cheap stuff, but the real deal was available for a price. And of course, on such an exalted occasion the consensus amongst the student body was that nothing was too good for these young princesses, with their raging sexual urges, killer good looks, and fancy evening gowns.

Elaborate plans to consume vast amounts of alcohol were laid out weeks before the actual event. The supply chain was an apparatus of enormous intrinsic value, created when the Anderson School, seventy-five years before, consisted of only one building. The school had since grown to a sprawling campus of enormous international prestige. And it was now all aflutter with teenage high school princesses; most with an alcoholic buzz.

Shrieks and screams of excitement flew into the air when the first busload of boys arrived on campus. The girls were all very excited. The Founder's Day Ball was a legend, talked about years later by alumni. The urban legend was born and there were over a dozen teenage girls thinking that there was going to be wanton sex, after the ball. While in fact, nothing could be further from the truth.

The administration was well aware of the legend - the loose talk and rumors. They were well prepared with chaperones to make sure nothing got out of hand. In fact, the parents of some of the girls called the principal during the week to get reassurances that absolutely everything was being done to protect the bloom of their little flower; as it were.

Since that was a tradition, all but the freshman class had been to the ball before. When the boys walked into the courtyard, other screams went up as the girls recognized boys they had met at other functions and had kept in contact with through social media. Formal dating was strictly controlled at the Anderson School, which put a damper on anything real from happening. And that's the way most, if not all, parents wanted it. But these girls were all certainly debutants and a fine catch for any boy from the Ankara International School for Boys. The school had an equally impressive reputation as the Anderson School. And wealthy families sent their boys there for a well-rounded education. In recent years, due to the very expensive tuition and the fact that the school was in a Muslim country, the percentage of well to do Middle Eastern boys had increased and made up about a quarter of the student body.

Friends that remained in contact through social media had made plans, as only teenagers could, to maximize their night of fun before the long month crunch to the school year end and those dreaded final exams. The night had been equated to a weekend furlough for a prisoner. Of course, the kids didn't know what they were talking about, but that didn't matter. They were there to have fun and not think about tomorrow and final exams; just like most teenagers. On the other hand, Tina knew she was not like other teenagers.

It was almost 8:00 PM and the chatter had increased to a loud din. Everyone started to talk louder in order to be heard over the crowd. This was drowning out the music supplied by a Turkish D.J. who played the latest songs coming out that year; at least the ones that made it all the way to Turkey. The hall was set, and the staff, dressed in white dinner jackets; black pants, white shirt, and thin black ties - an outfit right out of colonial Europe - opened the French doors into the courtyard. A smallish man walked through the crowd playing random notes on a handheld xylophone to signal that all present were to make their way inside the hall and take their place at the tables that were set for the grand occasion.

The boys and girls, the teachers and the chaperons all filed through the multiple French doors into the grand hall. The hall was stately and commanded attention, signifying that something special was about to happen within its immense confines. There was no assigned seating. Some of the groups of boys and girls had predetermined who they were going to sit with; and who was not welcome at their table. A small, but sizable number of boys and girls broke with tradition and sat at mixed tables. They immediately struck up conversations with the group from the other school. From the hushed tones at the other tables, the girls were already forming rumors and taking inventory of who was with whom. It was sad how petty some of the girls could be, even when this was supposed to be the party of the year.

When all were seated there was still a racket, rising from the hundreds of conversations taking place. The acoustics in the old hall didn't help. It mostly made it worse. So, everyone again began to talk louder over the noise to make themselves heard, but this just made it altogether chaotic.

At the front of the hall, there was a small stage that was decorated with ribbons and flowers. At the center of the stage, was a lectern with the crest of the Anderson School on it. A microphone stuck out from the top of the lectern. The principal of the Anderson School rose from her seat and walked up on stage to the lectern. She tapped gently on the microphone to confirm it was on. A thud from the loudspeakers indicated so. Thus, the principal began to speak.

"Welcome, everyone, welcome." The hum of the crowd began to subside. The principal waited a few moments until she had everyone's attention, before she began again. As the assembled crowd stopped talking, they directed their attention to center stage.

As a hush took over the crowd, laughing was heard outside the closed French doors. The leaves of each door opened simultaneously, and everyone could hear the laughter. The crowd members swiveled their heads away from the principal to the back of the hall. There were two stunning young ladies giggling in their incredibly sexy outfits, makeup, and perfume that drifted in with the cool Mediterranean air. Tina and Chanal made their entrance wearing the shortest hot pink dresses ever worn in Turkey. They were holding hands to steady each other from the swagger caused by their four-inch-high heels and the two rum and cokes consumed while they got ready for the ball.

Every girl in the hall thought to herself, *how come I have to wear this dumpy long gown when these two come here in a strapless cocktail dress with a hemline that just barely covers their ass?*

Tina and Chanal were also wearing ballerina tutus, which only added to the outrageousness of their outfits. Not to mention the diamond tiaras, ten odd bangles on their left wrists and each with a pill-box purse that was barely big enough to carry a tube of lipstick.

Every guy in the place was craning their neck to get a better look and were thinking to themselves, *I bet those two girls aren't wearing any panties*, as their dicks began to straighten from the blood flowing into their newly forming hard-ons.

Hand-in-hand, Tina and Chanal walked forward, as if on a runway in a Paris fashion show to the front of the hall. They navigated between tables and catcalls from some of the boys. They made their way to the table just in front of the stage.

The principal, clearly annoyed, towering over them in stunned silence and disbelief as she watched Tina and Chanal take the opened seats at the head of the table. When they sat down, all the boys in the crowd whistled and clapped in thunderous applause.

The principal took a moment to regain her composure; having never witnessed anything like that before. "Tina and

Chanal, so nice of you to join us, is it okay if we now begin the festivities?"

"Oh yes, Mrs. Chisolm, please begin. No need to wait for us," Tina replied with hoots and laughter from the entire assembled crowd. The principal couldn't help but crack a smile, despite herself.

For Tina, the rest of the dinner was something of a blur. She had never had so much to drink, and it went straight to her head. That, coupled with the fact that their entrance to the party went exactly as planned.

Chanal had texted her boyfriend, Saeed Balmsa (from the boy's school), ahead of time to make sure he sat at the front table and saved two seats for her and Tina. He was under strict instructions to save the seats and make sure no one sat next to him.

Saeed was handsomely rewarded because he had the two hottest girls in the whole hall sitting with him, giggling and carrying on. Tina and Chanal introduced themselves to all the other boys at the table. The boy next to Tina introduced himself and Tina was pleasantly surprised that there was another American in the place. The only other one. They hit it off immediately.

Dinner was served and Tina and Chanal hardly touched theirs, they were too excited about the whole evening, and being at the table with all those cute guys from the all-boys school. It had completely slipped Tina's mind that Anne had invited her to sit with them. Needless to say; Tina and Chanal had the best table; and Anne and Beth were eating their hearts out.

After dinner, Chanal grabbed Saeed by the arm and almost pulled him out of his chair. "Let's dance!"

Tina, being slightly more reserved, turned to the boy next to her. She didn't have to say anything because he was already up and extending his hand to her. They held hands as they waltzed over to the dance floor. Neither of them were great dancers, but they had a good time.

After a few dances, the boys were ready to sit back down. Tina and Chanal weren't ready to quit, so they stayed, dancing with each other.

"We really did it, didn't we?" Tina yelled to Chanal over the loud music.

"Indeed, we did girlfriend. We'll go down in Anderson School lore!" Chanal yelled back.

They were certainly smitten with what they had just pulled off. They knew that the principal was frosted, but she really wouldn't do anything to punish them because they were two of the best students at Anderson. When they finally tired of dancing in their high heels they returned to their table and rejoined the boys.

The boys had spiked their punch drinks with whisky they had hidden in a small pocket flask. "Let's go outside and get some fresh air," Saeed said to Chanal. To the boys that was a signal that they wanted to smoke hash and drink more booze.

The two couples started to head for the French doors at the back but saw a row of chaperones patrolling the area. Most likely to head off teenagers from going outside to smoke hash and drink booze.

The four of them returned to their table and sat down dejected. Tina was the first to speak.

"I know everyone is sick of hearing about my Dad being a Navy SEAL, but this is what a SEAL would do in this situation. We need to create a diversion to draw the chaperones away from the doors, just long enough for us to escape. This is tactical maneuver 101."

"Roger that," Chanal mocked. And they all laughed. "Okay Admiral, what do we do now?"

"Behind the stage there are stacks of chairs that will fall like dominoes. They'll make a thunderously loud noise when they start to fall over. This will draw the chaperone's attention away from the French doors and allow us just enough time to get outside unnoticed. All of you make your way to the area near the doors. When you hear the chairs fall, move calmly and quickly through the doors and out to the far side of the courtyard, in the shadows. I'll meet you out there.

"Got it, captain," Chanal said. "Should we synchronize our watches like they do in the spy movies?" The two girls held up their arms and pretended to adjust their nonexistent watches. The two boys looked on in disbelief and Saeed rolled his eyes.

"Okay, let's roll!" Tina commanded.

Chanal and the two boys headed for the back of the room and sat in some open chairs. Tina disappeared into the scrum of dancers. Within two minutes, there was a crashing noise from behind the stage. The three of them moved towards the French doors when all the chaperones left their posts, just as Tina described they would. They moved swiftly to the doors and exited the building.

They raced across the courtyard laughing and fell on the grass berm in the shadows, on the far side away from the hall. They continued their laughing until they saw a chaperone, next to the French door. The chaperone opened the door and peered outside, looking for the source of the laughter. The three bit their lips trying not to laugh and get caught. The chaperone didn't see anyone, so she went back into the hall and closed the door.

Anderson School Field

"That was a close one," Saeed said. Then he laid back on the grass and gazed up at the stars. The night sky was clear and cool, perfect for seeing the constellations. Saeed had studied astronomy and now impressed the others with his knowledge when Tina finally showed up.

"What took you so long?" Chanal asked, almost in a scolding voice. "I was beginning to worry that you had been caught!"

"Yeah, that was quite a diversion!" Saeed laughed.

"No need to worry, girlfriend," Tina said to Chanal. "After I set the domino collapsing chairs, I went into the kitchen to see if they had any dessert leftover because I hadn't finished mine," Tina said trying to keep a straight face.

The boys howled in laughter over how nonchalant Tina was about the whole thing.

"You're one cool cucumber," Saeed said admiring her composure.

"Who's got the booze?" Chanal said. "After all that excitement, I could use a stiff drink."

Saeed laughed at what Chanal had just said, "Oh, you're so big and mature now. Next thing you'd say is, shaken not stirred."

They all laughed when Chanal smacked Saeed on the arm with a clumsy punch because she didn't like being teased.

"Oh, I'm sorry, baby. I didn't mean to hurt your feelings, but..."

"Enough, already. Let's have a drink," Chanal said, somewhat exasperated. Saeed reached into the breast pocket of his white dinner jacket and produced a metal flask. He unscrewed the top and let it fall to the side, held there by a small chain. He held it out for Chanal to take the first swig.

She smelled it first. "Wow, that's strong!" She said as she put the flask to her lips and took a sip. She began to cough, and everyone laughed again, not directly at her, but to the contrast between her acting all tough and mature against her spewing and coughing from one little taste of liquor.

The flask was passed around a couple of times. At the same time, Saeed reached into his other pocket and pulled out a hash cigarette and lighter.

"My dear, you're pretty resourceful this evening," Chanal said to him.

Saeed straightened his back, lowered his shoulders and gave Chanal a funny expression to get her to laugh again. He put the cigarette up to his mouth and lit it. He held the smoke and handed the cigarette to Chanal. She took a tiny puff and began to cough. Again, all had another chuckle over Chanal's predicament. Even she tried to laugh at herself between her coughing fit.

The flask and cigarette made a few trips around the four of them before they were all consumed. Each one of them put their head back on the grassy berm and watched as the stars swirled above them. They were all pretty stoned by this time.

Chanal was feeling a little chilly so she snuggled up to Saeed. He put his arm around her and pulled her in closer. He propped his head up on one arm and with the other brushed the hair off Chanal's face. Then he moved his face to hers and kissed her on the mouth. She put her hand up around the backside of Saeed's head and pulled him in closer as their mouths locked.

Tina was beginning to feel a bit awkward, being next to the couple making out. So, she turned to the boy next to her and said, "I feel like going for a walk. Would you like to join me?"

"Sure thing," he replied.

Chapter 13

Public Beach, Ankara
Friday May 9, 2003

"I know you told me your name at dinner time, but it was loud, and I was too tipsy to hear it. Not that I'm not too tipsy now but at least I can hear you clearly," Tina said looking at the boy as they sat on the grass, next to the couple making out.

"Bryce - Bryce St. James."

"Nice to meet you, Bryce. I'm Tina Wood."

"Yes, I know. I heard you clearly inside," he said with a smile on his face, almost making fun of Tina.

Bryce stood up and put his hand out to help Tina up from the grass. He pulled her up and as they stood together, they continued to hold hands.

"Wait," Tina said, "I have to take off these heels. They are killing my feet." She reached down and slipped out of her shoes, as she continued to hold Bryce's hand for stability and because it felt nice to hold the hand of the best-looking guy at the party. Tina was going to say something to Chanal but decided against it when she looked over and saw Chanal in a very passionate love embrace with Saeed. So, she turned around and said to Bryce, "The beach isn't that far to walk to. It will be nice on this moonlit evening."

"Sounds swell," Bryce replied.

Tina laughed, "I haven't heard anyone say 'swell' in a very long time. Everyone from all parts of the world but the States has surrounded me. So, imagine the chances of meeting you here at this party."

"Pretty crazy, huh," Bryce agreed.

Tina laughed again "I do remember that you said you were from California."

"Yes, originally from Ojai. It's just northwest of L.A. in Ventura County. Lots of horses and vineyards."

"Sounds very nice. I've only been to San Diego. My ..." Tina stopped herself. She was going to say her Dad was a Navy SEAL but figured she would keep that to herself from now on. "I lived there briefly when I was much younger. I don't remember it though."

Tina and Bryce had covered a significant distance on their way to the beach. They were well beyond the neighborhood of the Anderson School, even though the school was on the outskirts of town. The neighborhood wasn't bad, but it certainly wasn't great. Turkey is a country with a large percentage of the population living in poverty and the homeless wander the countryside. Tina had been to the beach hundreds of times over the four years she had been at Anderson but only during the day.

In Turkey, young American girls did not go out at night wandering around. However, she currently felt safe because she was with Bryce. Tina loved the beach. She felt a sense of connection to the rest of the world looking out at the ocean knowing that the water she was looking at traversed the whole planet. That connection made her feel comfortable wherever she was on the planet, and she rarely got homesick. She had lived in so many places it was hard to figure out where home was at times. She felt a part of everywhere she had lived, a true global citizen.

There was a slight drop from the grassland down to the sand beach. There were no streetlights in this area but by now Tina and Bryce's night vision was wide open. The sky was lit with thousands of stars and looking south they could clearly see the constellation Scorpio. The Milky Way lit the black sky with immense beauty. You could almost see the reddish hues of color from the wide band of stars. Tina held Bryce's hand as they looked up at the stars taking it all in. The walk had helped take the edge off the alcohol and hash that was coursing through their synapses making them feel a little dizzy looking up.

"Let's walk along the beach," Tina suggested.

"Sounds good," Bryce replied with a gentle squeeze of Tina's hand. They slid down the sandbank to the beach and walked to the water's edge. Gentle waves broke on the sand and washed up on Tina's feet. Bryce let go of her hand and hopped up just before he got his dress shoes wet. The cool water felt refreshing on Tina's aching feet.

Bryce sat down on the dry sand and took off his shoes and socks. Tina joined him and sat right next to him, leaving no space between them. Bryce took his arm and put it around Tina's shoulder and hugged her. Tina responded by leaning her head into Bryce's shoulder. She picked her head up and turned to face Bryce. He turned to look at her. Their gazes met, and they looked deeply at each other.

Bryce slightly tilted his head and moved forward to put his lips on Tina's, and she met him with a slightly opened mouth. They kissed with tremendous passion, fueled by teenage hormones, alcohol, and hash. They laid back and put their heads on the sand. Bryce rolled towards Tina and slightly rose above her to look at her face and into her eyes.

"If you're thinking what I'm thinking, I never did this before," Bryce said trying to be honorable.

"It's all right," Tina replied, "we'll just let it flow and see where it goes."

Bryce didn't need to be told twice. He put his hand on the inside of Tina's thigh and moved it up until he lifted her dress and stopped at her G-string panties. He didn't stop to think about when he first saw Tina that evening, wearing that super short dress, if she was wearing panties or not. It didn't matter that he was the only one in the hall of people that had the answer to that question.

"Huh, before we go any further, we need some protection," Tina said as she kissed Bryce's face.

"You're getting way ahead of me," Bryce replied in a panting voice.

"A girl has to be careful about those things."

"Totally agree. I've carried a rubber in my wallet all this time and the occasion has never presented itself."

"The occasion is now," Tina said, relieved that Bryce was able to come through and knowing that he was an honorable guy. They again locked themselves in a mad kissing session sucking each other's tongues. While they were kissing, Bryce moved his hand from Tina's thigh to the space between her legs. Tina responded by opening her legs slightly to give Bryce access.

He moved his hand up, between her legs. His hand moved up and down under her wet panties and he found her clit. Tina arched her hips up to meet Bryce's advances. Bryce started to kiss Tina's neck and the upper part of her chest. He took his hand out of Tina's crotch and pulled the strap of her dress from her shoulders. This allowed him to kiss her breasts as he freed them from the confines of her bra.

Bryce straddled Tina's legs as he was sucking her tit and began to moan softly as he moved in and out, pumping her leg. Tina reached behind him and pulled his shirt out from the waist of his pants and put her hand on his lower back. She slipped her hand into the back of his pants under his underwear to feel the top part of his butt.

Bryce knew it was time. He knelt up and looked down on Tina lying in the sand with her dress pulled down off her shoulders and pushed up above her pubic bone. Tina could make out Bryce clearly in the moonlight. The small waves breaking on the beach in a rhythmic motion beckoned this young couple.

Bryce reached down and undid his belt buckle and pants zipper and pulled them down with his underwear to expose himself to Tina. His pants were pulled halfway down and then he reached under Tina's dress to pull her panties off. She obliged him by lifting her hips up, so he could pull them down. She lifted her feet as her panties were removed and she spread her legs wide, waiting for Bryce. He took out the condom (that had been patiently waiting in his wallet all this time) and rolled it over his erection.

"I never did this before," he said shyly.

"Neither have I," Tina replied, blushing from embarrassment and from the hyper sex-drive within her.

Bryce leaned over and kissed Tina full on. Their tongues darted in and out exchanging saliva and love. Bryce reached down and directed his hard-on into Tina. She pushed up to meet his downward thrust. Although neither of them had had sex before, they had thought of it often, and the actual act was way better than anything they could ever have imagined. Their pulses raced and their breathing labored as Bryce thrust deeply inside Tina.

She moved her legs further apart, so he could go deeper into her. She moved her hand up to unbutton his shirt and put her hand inside it and reach around to his back. Tina moved her head up and kissed Bryce's chest. She took one hand out to find her clit waiting to be stroked. She rubbed it vigorously as Bryce pumped in and out. He was now thrusting harder and his pumping frequency increased. Tina held her breath as she started to climax and with one final thrust Bryce pushed all the way in, ejaculating deep in her at the same time.

Bryce collapsed; his weight was squarely on top of Tina. His entire being was connected and inside of her body and this filled her with a tranquil calm. Bryce's face was planted into Tina's neck and she could feel his warm breath on her. At that moment, there was no distinction of where she stopped and where Bryce began; they were simply one.

Tina took a deep breath and sighed. Regaining his composure, Bryce kissed Tina's neck and ear. He lifted himself off her and rolled to her side with his arm propping up his head. He gave her a hug and pushed up beside her. Tina lay with her back on the sand and looked at the stars.

After a few moments of hugging, Tina was the first to speak, "That's Aldebaran," she said, pointing up into the magnificent sky.

"What?" Bryce asked.

"Lay back and look at the stars," she told Bryce.

He moved his arm away from her and laid his head on the sand.

"Do you see those three stars in a row?" Tina said as she moved her arm up to point them out to Bryce.

"Yes," he replied.

"Those are the three stars of Orion's belt."

"Okay, I see them."

“Now, look slightly up and over.”

“Ah, okay”

“That’s Aldebaran, and the constellation Taurus. It’s the eye of the bull.”

“Yes, now I see it. I think. It’s reddish.”

“Yes, that’s right. Now move a little further over and you’ll see a cluster of stars.”

“Oh yeah, I see them.”

“That cluster is called the Pleiades, the seven sisters.”

“Cool. How do you know all this stuff?”

“Elocution lessons,” Tina said, deadpanned.

Bryce couldn’t help himself and he started to laugh. “You’re such a kidder. Sometimes I can’t figure out when you’re joking and when you’re serious.”

“Oh, one more thing. Look straight down, almost at the horizon,” Tina said with a very serious, almost commanding tone. “See that bright object in the sky?”

“Yes, I can see it,” Bryce said, not completely sure what he was supposed to be looking at.

“Well, do you know what that planet is?”

“No, I don’t. So, tell me smarty-pants,” Bryce said making fun of Tina.

“Okay, well that’s Uranus,” she said as she pinched Bryce’s bare butt.

And both Tina and Bryce burst out in laughter that lasted a while and echoed down the shoreline in the warm air punctuated by the quiet repetitive sound of the waves. And there they lay, spread out on the sand beach, on this warm Mediterranean early summer night.

Tina thought about all the Founder’s Day party tales of conquest that she had heard over the four years she had been at the Anderson School. All along, she thought most of it was embellishment, but she had her tale. A tale that she would never tell another living soul - how she lost her virginity to a boy she had known for less than four hours, having met during the evening of the Founder’s Day Ball. She thought that her secret was way better than the stories she had heard, and it was fine that she wanted to keep this special moment to herself.

Bryce was certainly not one to kiss and tell. So, their love secret was safe. Not that it mattered really, or that they necessarily cared, but it was just comforting that it was something special, very special, that Tina and Bryce shared with each other and did not need anything external to make the moment better. It was just perfect the way it unfolded, unplanned, and genuine.

After stargazing and relaxing, Tina and Bryce each thought they better get back to the ball before they were missed by the umpteen chaperones that were cluelessly watching the other students dance. So, they assembled their clothing and dusted the sand off.

"The sand gets everywhere," Tina remarked as she kept dusting off her thighs and butt.

Bryce tried not to laugh as he assisted her and help straighten the back of her dainty dress. Then they turned for home with Tina holding her high heels shoes in one hand and Bryce's large fist in the other.

*   *   *

They didn't recall walking so far down the beach when they first arrived. Perhaps it was the alcohol and hash that impaired their judgment. The effects of those drugs were wearing off and now they couldn't find their way up the bluff from the beach. It was dark - a perfect night for stargazing and making out on the beach, but not so helpful for climbing a steep bluff. It was much steeper than they remembered.

"Going down is way easier than going up. That's one of the first rules of climbing," Tina said trying to keep a brave face to mask her frustration at being lost. Tina and Bryce walked along the beach at the foot of the bluff but decided to turn around when the bluff just became higher.

116

"We must've passed the spot where we came down," Bryce said.

"Yeah, we must have," Tina said. "Let's turn around and head back the other way, to see if we can find a good place to climb up." So, they turned around and headed in the opposite direction. Almost immediately after they turned around, both realized that they were not alone on the beach. About 50 yards away three males were heading straight toward them.

Oh my God, Tina thought rather startled, *did they see us making love?*

Bryce tightened his grip on Tina's hand and started walking slightly faster and with purpose. They were walking parallel to the foot of the bluff and the three males deliberately moved up from the beach to cut them off. When Bryce and Tina were about 20 feet from the three males, they could see that they were teenagers, eighteen or so. Bryce pivoted and moved outward towards the ocean and attempted to go around the boys.

The boy in the middle-followed Bryce's movements toward the water and yelled, "Hey, o kadar hızlı değil, küçük fahişenle biraz eğlenmek isteriz. Senin yaptığın gibi." Which meant *Hey, not so fast, we'd like to have some fun with your little whore. Like you did.*

Not proficient in Turkish, Bryce had no idea what the boy just said and kept moving. The boy confirmed to Tina's horror, they had been spied on when they were making out. The boy in the middle, lunged at Bryce and pushed him with both arms straight out. Bryce stumbled back a little because he was not expecting that the boy would jump out and push him. Bryce was at least 6 inches taller than the other boy, but they were about equal in weight.

Still holding Bryce's hand Tina addressed the gang leader, "Bela istemiyoruz. Sadece geçmemize izin verin, yolunuzdan çekileceğiz." Which meant, *we don't want any trouble. Just let us pass and we will be out of your way.*

Not knowing quite what to make of Tina's accent, the gang leader replied as he put his hands on his hips, "Oh, fahişeyi dinle. O yolda olmak istiyor. O kadar hızlı değil tatlım. Üçümüz seninle biraz eğlenmek istiyoruz." *Oh, listen to the whore. She wants to be on her way. Well, not so fast sweetheart. The three of us would like to have a little fun with you.*

While he was talking, the other two boys darted out to get behind Bryce and Tina. They were surrounded. The middle boy was clearly the leader of their little gang. He reached into his pocket and pulled out a shiv that he raised in the air. He snapped his wrist and the switchblade sprung out. The metal edge sparkled in the moonlight, a sobering sight for both Bryce and Tina.

The boy immediately behind Bryce dropped down and tried to tackle Bryce by hitting him right behind his knees. Bryce's legs buckled, and he went down hard. His hands were just barely able to brace his fall. The jolt of hitting the hard sand knocked the wind out of him.

Tina had let go of Bryce's hand and leapt into the air with her right foot out. Her bare foot hit the forearm of the gang leader. He was not expecting that a little whore could do such a thing and he inadvertently let go of the shiv with her impact. Tina's kick hurled the shiv into the air. Her left foot landed just in front of the gang leader. She rotated, and her forward momentum was transferred into her right hand that still carried her dancing shoes with the four-inch stiletto heels. The heel hit the gang leader just above the eye socket and cut a deep gash. Blood immediately filled his eye.

The sting of the gash and the flow of his blood caused his reflexes to lift his hands up to cover his eye as he staggered to Tina's left. She moved again, pivoting like a cat and climbed up on the gang leader's back. Her left arm wrapped around him and closed around his neck. She locked her left arm with her right and immediately leveraged her weight to apply tremendous pressure to his windpipe, which cut off his airway. The gang leader started to flail wildly, trying to knock Tina off his back. She held on like she was riding a bucking bronco.

With his oxygen cut off, the gang leader dropped to his knees. While holding the gang leader in a chokehold Tina

screamed, "Kurtul ondan!" *Get off him* in a commanding voice
to the boy that was on top of Bryce.

The boy looked over and saw Tina choking the leader of
the gang. This brief moment allowed Bryce to push himself up
with his arms. Since he was so pissed off about being attacked
from behind his adrenaline rush gave him the strength to bench
press 500 pounds. The boy on his back lost his balance and
rolled off Bryce onto the sand. He put Bryce in a scissor grip
with his legs. Bryce, with his arms and upper body free, landed
blow after blow on the boy's face. Then he directed his punches
to the boy's legs. The boy covered his face with his arms but
held on tight with his scissor grip.

Throughout the whole ordeal, the third gang member
just stood back and watched in stunned silence. Obviously, he
wasn't the swiftest guy in the gang, and didn't immediately
know what to do because his leader wasn't giving him any
commands. Tina could see him move as she was still holding
tight to the chokehold. She glanced over and saw a shiny object
in the sand. The third boy spotted it as well and was rushing over
to pick it up.

Tina let go of the chokehold, slid off the gang leader,
planted her left foot and let go a fast kick of her right foot like
she was going to kick a field goal in football, except she was
aiming for the gang leader's balls. The brutal kick knocked him
flat out on the sand. Tina felt more than morally justified for
what she did to this creep, seeing that only moments before he
had threatened to gang rape her.

The third boy was bending down to pick up the shiv
when Tina looked back that way. She took three large strides like
she was preparing to clear the high bar at a track and field meet.
She launched herself not to clear the bar but the clean the clock
of the third boy. He was on his way up from picking up the knife
when Tina's feet, propelled by the momentum of her strides, hit
him in the side - directly into his kidneys.

The force of her kick went through the guy like an
electrocution shock and his blood turned to battery acid as it
raced through his entire body like poison. He dropped to his

knees and writhed in pain holding his side. Tina landed on the sand just after she delivered this decisive blow to the third creep.

Now Tina got up, ready to finish off the second guy still holding Bryce in the scissor grip. Bryce and the boy holding him were still exchanging blows. She again timed her steps to launch herself at the second boy. But this time the second guy saw her coming and released his scissor grip on Bryce and pushed back to try and get away. Just before he was able to break free, Bryce coldcocked him with a right cross to the face. The second guy fell back on the sand - knocked out cold. Seeing this, Tina slowed her forward motion and now stood above the second guy.

"Hepiniz şehit olmayan bir kişinin ölümüne katlanabilirsiniz! *May you all suffer the death of a non-martyr* Tina shouted at them as she spit on the sand. Thinking this was the worst Muslim insult she could come up with at the spur of the moment.

She reached her hand down and helped Bryce up. He had been hit in the face a number of times but was otherwise okay. She searched around the kicked-up sand and found her shoes. Then she and Bryce continued down the beach a little way and luckily found the spot where they had come down the bluff. Bryce gave Tina a leg up as she scaled the bottom part of the bluff that was steeper. Bryce scurried up behind her. They left the beach with their virginities gone and three wounded young Turks not knowing what just hit them. Tina and Bryce walked back to the Anderson School in silence. Everything that just happened was so raw in their minds, everything from the extreme act of love making to the fight of their lives.

Tina was the first one to break the silence. "Should we call the police?"

"Oh, I don't think so," Bryce said, "The police in Turkey are not anything like the ones in the States. I don't trust them."

"How do you know that?" Tina asked inquisitively, pressing the issue in her search for some justice. "Although I can't recall ever meeting a Turkish policeman."

"Trust me. I've heard my Dad talk about the corruption here. I'd just rather not get mixed up in that. Who knows how it will turn out?"

"How does your Dad know these things?" Tina asked, still pressing for some justice.

"He's the U.S. Ambassador to Turkey. Turkey is a key ally of the U.S., but they have a very different culture than what we're used to."   Bryce paused a moment and turned to Tina, "What did that guy say?"

"Oh, they were just picking a fight," Tina lied. She felt so violated that they were going to rape her. She didn't know how to deal with something so vulgar, so base.

"Hey, where did you learn to fight like that… and to speak Turkish?" Bryce asked, almost shrieking.

"Oh, elocution lessons," Tina replied, trying to crack a smile, in an attempt at gallows humor.

Bryce smiled and put his arm around Tina, hugging her tightly.

They stopped walking when they were in sight of the school. Tina looked up at Bryce and he moved his head down and kissed her on the mouth. She put her arms around his lower back. They squeezed each other again.

"I don't want to go back to the dance," Tina said, "and they won't let you up to the dorm."

"That's okay. Let's just go sit on the bus together until the dance is over and I have to leave."

Rather than head back to the dance and suffer the gaggle of chaperones interrogating them with prying questions, Tina and Bryce walked to the bus from Bryce's school. Bryce tapped the door, the napping driver awoke, and rubbing his eyes, opened the bus door.

"Had enough fun for the night, guv'nor?" the driver asked in a British accent, still sitting in the driver's seat.

"Yes, you can say that again," Bryce replied not looking at the bus driver, as he was trying to hide the bruises on his face. "We're just going to sit on the bus together until everyone's ready to leave."

"No problem, guv'nor."

Tina and Bryce boarded the bus and selected a seat near the back, out of the light from the driveway. The lights on the bus were out, and they just held each other in the darkness. Tina was lying with her head on Bryce's shoulder, and Bryce had his arm extended over Tina's upper body. He could smell the perfume in her hair. She held his forearm with both hands.

"I know you won't tell anybody about what happened tonight," Tina said turning to look into Bryce's face, knowing that he wouldn't tell anyone but still wanting to be sure.

"Of course not. This is our secret."

And from that point forward, they never spoke of the events of the Founder's Day ball. Even years afterward when alumni would brag about their exploits, Bryce and Tina kept their secret safe, even though they had the best story in the history of the Anderson School Ball.

Chapter 14

Anderson School Graduation
Friday June 20, 2003

June arrived with its sweet warm air and the promise of a new beginning. And a new beginning it certainly was for Tina and Chanal. Bryce returned to the International School a man, ready to take on the world. But for the moment, and the rest of the month, the three had to concentrate on their studies. Bryce and Tina texted each other just as often as Chanal and Saeed. Tina's mind would wander to the night of the party and she had the warmest memories of being with Bryce and making love.

Surprisingly, by the time the school year ended, she had gotten over the shock of the fight and the threat of being raped. In her thoughts, she thanked her Dad and his SEAL buddies for teaching her mixed martial arts she had applied so masterfully on that Turkish gang. She also thanked her mother for guiding her to focus on her studies and find the enjoyment of learning something new and mastering it. And that she did.

At first, the principal looked at her askance when she saw Tina in the hall; but didn't say anything to her. Other than that one prank she and Chanal pulled off at the ball, both were model students. Tina aced her final exams, as did Chanal. Since the party, Tina dared not to venture off campus and the safety its confines provided her. She wondered what became of the three gang members. Their physical injuries would not leave permanent scars, but the fact that a young girl kicked their asses would haunt them for the rest of their lives.

Throughout the graduation ceremony Tina and Chanal kept shooting glances at the other and smiling with smug, self-satisfaction. They had composed a long letter describing the countless transgressions of Anne and Beth. The letter was mailed anonymously to the principal. They knew that nothing would change as far as Anne and Beth were concerned, and especially the entitled way they acted. Tina and Chanal just wanted the principal to have a doubt about what she did in allowing such behavior to continue. As a result of the letter, the principal put new procedures in place to prevent such blatant cheating in the future. In addition, neither the principal, nor any of the teachers, would give a positive recommendation to either Anne or Beth.

Anne Taylor was the valedictorian at the graduation ceremony. Tina's parents flew in from Hawaii to attend. They were so proud that their daughter had applied herself and graduated summa cum laude. She was accepted to the U.S. Naval Academy in Annapolis Maryland. She had applied out of respect for her parents. When the three of them were alone, after the ceremony, Tina told them that she decided that a career in the Navy was not for her. She decided to attend the University of California at San Diego (UCSD). To her surprise, Tina's parents were relieved that she had decided not to go to the Naval Academy. Although they both had challenging and rewarding careers, they wanted their only daughter to pick her own field. And that she did. She was going to study linguistics.

Lahore Pakistan

Chanal returned to Pakistan after graduation. She and Tina promised to stay in contact through social media. But they would be worlds apart in terms of distance and culture. Chanal would be attending a small college in Lahore, with the goal of obtaining a visa to study in the United States. The Muslim world did not treat smart women like Chanal well, and she needed to get out of Pakistan. But for now, she had to make do and patiently wait her turn.

Ojai, CA

Bryce was so ready to leave Turkey. He had lived there for over three years while his father was the American Ambassador. He returned to Ojai, California to figure out his next move. While he was doing that, he enrolled at St. Thomas Aquinas College, which is very close to where their family estate was. St. Thomas was a very small college in the Ojai Valley, set in idyllic surroundings. Bryce knew that he wanted to study business and international finance, and the small college setting gave him one-on-one access to the instructors. He thrived on the attention and was ready to apply himself to his studies and move on to the next chapter of his life. Plus living in Ventura County California afforded him ample opportunity to catch up on his surfing, which he dearly missed while living abroad.

La Jolla, CA

La Jolla California (where Tina was attending UCSD) and Ojai were a little over 100 miles apart. When the semester first started Bryce would travel down to La Jolla, with a few of his buddies, to visit Tina and of course to surf at La Jolla's beautiful sand beaches. The place was perfect for surfing, just down the slope of the Scripp's Bluff, which is mantled by majestic Torrey Pines. However, as the school year ran on, and the demands of class assignments increased, the visits became less frequent. Tina and Bryce agreed that their relationship would not be exclusive and that they could date other people. They remained fast friends and stayed in contact with each other. From their brief intimate relationship, they had shared more emotional capital than a lot of couples' experience in more extended relationships over a longer period of time. They would share their innermost feelings with each other, even though they remained separate. This bond would serve them well in the adventures they were about to have.

St. Thomas Aquinas College, Santa Paula, CA
Tuesday September 2, 2003

"If you remember this advice, you will go a long way in investing. You should be able to sketch every investment strategy - that is obviously not fraudulent - out on an 8.5 x 11-inch sheet of paper. The ones actually worth investing in, are the ones that can be written out this way, with only a crayon. All other investments that don't fit this model are either frauds or Ponzi schemes."

The financial instructor stopped pacing and looked up at the class of bright young minds staring back at him, with a dazed look of *what the fuck did he just say?*

In the whole class of Financial Investment 101 at Thomas Aquinas College, only one student was looking down. He sat in the row closest to the windows, in the front row seat. He sat limply in his seat. His long graceful body was turned toward the window but not as much as his head was.

His eyes gazed out on the wooded campus of sycamore trees with leaves larger than your hand. The sky was blue. In the distance, there were rows upon rows of grapevines. This was wine country, just northwest of Los Angeles in Ventura County California.

"Mr. St. James. Mr. St. James!" the instructor repeated a second time, but emphatically. "Would you like to tell the class how this investment strategy would work for you?"

Bryce St. James sat up and turned his 6' 2" frame towards the classroom and without hesitation began to speak, "If I understood you correctly, professor, I have to sell all my shares of Entron stock."

The class burst out in ruckus laughter. Some mocking Bryce for being such an idiot.

"Would you care to elaborate on that?" The instructor asked, caught off guard because he expected that Bryce was not paying attention. Bryce was visualizing the words the instructor spoke.

"It's funny. It's almost uncanny. The stockbroker said that Entron stock was skyrocketing, but he didn't know why. He had read the prospectus several times but couldn't grasp the complex underpinning of derivative companies, arbitrage, the international currency market, and the age of his mother. I think he was joking about his mother part, but the rest I'm quite certain he was serious about," Bryce began as he recalled the events leading up to his purchase of the stock. Again, there was assorted laughter and catcalls from Bryce's friends.

"You see, my grandparents gave me a savings bond when I was a little kid and said I could cash it in when I was accepted to college. I had forgotten all about it, so it had grown into a tidy sum. And I was eager to invest it. A family friend recommended the stockbroker. So, I bought the hot stock without any investigation on my part. I just relied on the broker's recommendation."

"It's funny, almost uncanny," the instructor said jokingly, "but that was going to be my next word of advice. That is, do your own research. Read the prospectus and ask the dumb questions. You don't know how many people have lost their shirt buying the hottest stock on a tip from a broker."

Bryce was again looking off into the distance of the very pleasant view offered from the classroom window. He was digesting the advice from the instructor. Those words would come to serve as his investment mantra.

"Okay, class," the instructor began, "your assignment for next week is to do research on a company listed on the New York Stock Exchange and determine if their stock price will rise or fall within the next quarter. Remember that all companies are required to file their documents with the Security and Exchange Commission and are available online."

Bryce dropped his gaze and rotated his head on his body back towards the class, "Professor Lewis this has been a eureka moment for me! I need to be excused right away to work on the assignment." And without waiting for a reply, Bryce bounded out of the classroom and straight to his red jeep to tear off on the two-lane highway that led west to Ojai and his broker's office.

Wildlife Sanctuary, Ojai, CA

If Bryce was anything, he was patient. He studied the Entron company prospectus and drew his own graph of their business plan and the complex financial transactions the prospectus discussed in a specious way, full of doubletalk accounting terms. In a three-ring binder Bryce was developing a glossary of financial terms. Every time he ran across a new term, he would write it in the binder along with its definition and usage. Out of all the complex terms Bryce found through his research the most interesting by far was the term "revenue." It wasn't so much the term, per se, but how the concept of revenue was manipulated. That was the most interesting, and primary accounting attribute that Bryce paid attention to.

The old adage goes "follow the money." But in accrual-based accounting there is no money (i.e. there is no cash). Only revenue is tracked. Since revenue was not tangible, like cash, it was subject to being manipulated.

The capitalization of a company is the actual cash it has on hand. Cash is the most liquid of all assets, and it is for this reason there is a corollary adage, "cash is king." There is no adage for "revenue." Perhaps there isn't an adage because accountants don't want the unsuspecting public to focus on revenue. Revenue, unlike cash, can be manipulated to mean lots of different things. Whenever there is a financial crisis there is a "call for cash." No one gives a shit about revenue.

Armed with his new knowledge, and the things he picked up along the way, Bryce dove into Entron's financials. *The hot stock, eh?* Bryce mused to himself. *Making money and no one knows how. Hmm, we'll see about that.*

Perhaps it was that he was so young and not knowing what to look for that he found the accounting equivalent of a smoking gun. Of course, this took days of research and Bryce stuck to the task like a dog on a juicy soup bone. He rose early and turned on his computer. He would sit in front of the screen for hours with a cup of coffee reading financial statements and trying to make sense of the complicated financial charts. He took a break to get more coffee and write down his own interpretation of what he was reading. After twelve hours the first day, nothing was adding up or making any financial sense.

That evening, he went out with his buddies to the local bar called the Wildlife Sanctuary. The name was in reference to the California Condor's Wildlife Sanctuary that called Ventura County home. There were only a couple hundred of these magnificent creatures, with wing spans of up to 10 feet, that lived in the Topatopa Mountains of the Sespe Wilderness. The wilderness occupied a large swath of the county. Indeed, they were special, having survived all this time since the last ice age. Bryce looked to these haunting creatures for strength and perseverance.

"If they could outlast the catastrophic events that killed off many other species then I can find out how Entron is making money," Bryce announced to the small group seated at the table in the back of The Sanctuary.

"Oh no, not that again," the guys all moaned. "Give it a rest St. James, we're here to have a little fun."

"Seriously guys, I'm onto something big. And if you're nice to me, and don't piss me off too much, I might let you in on the action," Bryce said pressing his case. Bryce was hopelessly confused by all of the financial documents he was reading, and the more he read the more confused he became.

"Oh Bryce," said the guy next to him, "you're so full of shit." He casually pushed his shoulder to indicate that he couldn't pull one over on the guys.

"No, really guys. This is big." And with that, all the guys at the table threw balled up napkins at Bryce to indicate that the discussion on this topic was over, and they could now discuss the more important topics that they always talked about baseball, girls, and surfing (and not necessarily in that order).

Bryce's mind drifted and he put his elbow on the table to support his chin as he was thinking. He ignored the conversation, or argument, that was taking place around him, and occasionally took a sip of his craft beer and heard snippets of the multiple conversations going on around him.

"The Dodgers suck again this year. There is no way they're even making the playoffs."

"Did you see the tits on that girl? I'd like to take her out surfing, she could ride my wave anytime."

"I heard they are going to have the winter national surf competition at Point Mugu again this year."

Bryce tuned all of this chatter out, which was a little difficult to do because the guys weren't so much talking or discussing these topics but arguing their point of view in loud beer charged voices. Bryce certainly had his point of view on all these topics but for now he was determined to work out the task at hand - to figure out how Entron was making its money.

He took a long sip of his dark microbrew and thought; *maybe this is the wrong question to ask. Not, how are they making money? But more importantly how are they convincing gullible stockbrokers that they were making all this money?*

And this is where the concept of revenue came into the picture. Bryce put his chin on his hand again and tilted his head in thought. His buddies were not about to let Bryce sulk by himself, so the guy on the opposite side of him pushed Bryce's elbow out from the table and Bryce's head drop down, snapping him into awareness of what was going on around him.

"Bryce, the waitress wants to know if you'd like another."

"No thank you, I'm good," Bryce said wishing he could have another but knowing that he wanted to check out his new hunch before he went to bed.

"Guys, I'm going to take off," Bryce said thinking that he was having an eureka moment.

"No! You wimp. You pussy St. James" came the chorus of objection from the guys at the table.

"Thanks, guys. It's been great as usual. But I need to check out another angle on the problem that's been bugging me." And as he began to get up from the table he was showered again with crumpled napkins, coasters, and empty chip bags. For the guys this was the sign that they wished Bryce would stay and hang out with them, shoot the breeze, partake in downing a few fine microbrews, and talk about surfing, and girls.

"Alright ladies. I'll see you around," Bryce said as he departed after giving the waitress a tip.

When he got into his Jeep he sat there for a moment before he turned on the ignition. He said out loud as if he was having a conversation with someone, "What if Entron was just one big fucking scam? What would they be doing to cover up their illicit activities? And what would they be doing to convince all of the mutual fund managers that they were legit and the second coming of John D. Rockefeller?"

The press on the executive managers at Entron was that they were financial geniuses, whiz kids, doing things no one had done before.

What if what they were doing was just a big con game? Bryce mulled over in his head.

Bryce pressed the button to the ignition and the engine turned over. It roared to life just like Bryce was doing about his research. He thought to himself, *I'm glad I didn't have another beer; I think this is going to be a long night.* And with that Bryce put the car in gear and he lit out of the parking lot of The Sanctuary. And like a California Condor launching itself from the peaks of the Topatopa Mountains, Bryce was off to look for accounting carrion, with "California" by the L.A. rock group Fatt Khat, blasting from his Jeep's speakers.

Professor Lewis' Apartment, Santa Paula, CA
Wednesday September 3, 2003

The text arrived with the sound of a chime, like all text messages did, but this one arrived at 4:30 AM and woke Professor Lewis from his sound sleep.

It read, "Can we meet? This is urgent. Thanks, Bryce."

It took a moment for the professor to understand the message, for a couple of reasons. The first was that he had just been woken up from a very deep satisfying sleep. The second, and more important reason was, he didn't recall who Bryce was. So, he turned off the sound of his smartphone, fluffed up his pillow and went back to sleep.

Chapter 15

University of California San Diego, La Jolla, CA
Friday November 21, 2003

The University of California San Diego was in one of the highest rent districts in the United States. The campus sat above the bluffs of La Jolla graced with lush green lawns. The urban legend was that a fair number of the applicants hoped to get accepted to this prestigious institution, so they could go surfing at Black's Beach (the only nudist beach in Southern California). Everyone that first attended UCSD wanted to go surfing at Black's Beach. However, within a month or so of arriving on campus, the freshman class en masse came to realize that surfing was way harder than it looked. And the first thing they learned at UCSD was the word "wipeout."

Tina, like the rest of her freshman class, tried her hand at surfing. Since she knew how to ice skate and snow ski, she had a leg up on her classmates. Those activities help with balance while surfing, but they didn't necessarily help with the propulsion part. For that, you must become one with the ocean. To do that takes practice, strength, and respect; respect for the power of the wave. Tina, unlike the vast majority of her classmates, caught the surfing bug. Luckily for her, there were more female surfers than ever before. Most of the guys were territorial about their beach and their waves, and they were not willing to share. The women on the other hand were way more accepting of newcomers and were willing to share the waves to maximize the fun for everyone with the hopes of gaining new friends.

It had been a very long week and late Friday afternoon Tina was still in the speech lab, listening to Latin tapes. The sign above her, read "Cum Gaudio Doctrina Long Linguae Claris." Which Tina translated as *The Joy of Learning Long Lost Languages*. She didn't place the sign there. Some wiseass did, and Tina wasn't amused. It finally clicked in Tina's mind what a dangling participle was. The concept made no sense in English, but in Latin it was clear as a bell.

With her small victory, Tina thought she could wrap it up early and hit the beach for a late afternoon surf. The speech lab was in the basement of one of the older buildings on campus. And of course, there were no windows. Tina had lost track of time, which happened often when she was deeply immersed in learning a difficult concept. The sun was getting low in the sky when she headed across campus on the neatly trimmed lawn under the Torrey Pines toward her dorm.

Tina's UCSD Dorm

The freshman dorms were on the front side of the campus, furthest from the beach. Theoretically, Tina shared her apartment with five other women. But by the third week, everybody was living wherever they wanted. And some of her roommates had different boys that they slept with. So, Tina never really could keep track of the comings and goings of the people in her apartment. It was no surprise as Tina entered her apartment (the door was already open) that there were approximately 12 to 15 guys and girls (about half of each kind) sprawled out in the common living room that connected the six separate bedrooms and the kitchen/dining area.

Luckily for Tina, she had her own room, and more importantly, a door that locked. She was not against the hippie lifestyle of her roommates. It just wasn't her thing. When she came into the apartment, the assembled crowd immediately offered her a hit from the hookah pipe they had all been sharing for most of the afternoon.

"Hey, Tina, wanna toke?" a cute guy asked, sitting in the middle of the living room.

Tina politely declined as she unlocked the door to her room, "No thanks, surfs up and I want to catch a few waves before the sun goes down."

"Hey, that sounds like fun, do you mind if I join you?" asked the guy that was holding the hookah hose.

"According to the State Coastal Commission the ocean belongs to all of us," Tina said in a wiseass way.

The cute guy took this to mean, "Get your shit together because the sun is setting, and time is a wasting." So, he handed off the hose to the spaced-out girl sitting next to him and dashed from the apartment to get his "shit."

Tina locked the door to her room behind her because she didn't want some stoner to walk in on her while she was changing into her wetsuit. In the corner of her room sat a crisp white short board (the locals called them "potato chips"). Tina had just bought it and was dying to try it out. Her parents had sent her money for textbooks, but she thought the surfboard was a much better investment. Besides the information contained in the textbooks was available online and in the university's library.

She quickly stripped out of her school clothes and put on a skintight wetsuit that highlighted her shapely figure. Since she left Turkey, and arrived back in the states, she had been working out: Pilates, weightlifting, and of course her favorite; mixed martial arts. There was surfing in her life, and she lived for the thrill of catching a wave.

She pulled off the wrapper from Mr. Zog's sex wax and carefully applied it to her surfboard in quick controlled strokes, each side at a slightly different diagonal to the central axis of the board. Satisfied with the waxing, she wrapped the leash around the back of the board and the triple fins, opened the door and was again hit with a blast of pot smoke from the living room. Not wanting to inhale the air, she held her breath as she exited the apartment.

La Jolla Beach

Southern California architecture uses external corridors and staircases to the fullest extent possible. And San Diego, with the best weather in the United States, mastered the application.

Unfortunately, they hadn't mastered the external elevator and the thing kept breaking down, especially at the freshman dorm.

So even though her apartment was on the sixth floor of the six-floor building, Tina never tried the elevator after she first discovered that it was rarely in operation. She quickly descended the staircase with her board tucked under her arm. When she hit the ground floor, she headed off across the quad in the direction of the Pacific Ocean and the thrill that was to be had on its carefully shaped waves.

"Hey, wait up," came a voice across the quad.

Tina didn't turn around or break her stride, "Hurry up the sun's a setting."

She could hear the puffing of heavy breathing slowly catching up to her by the time she reached the far side of the quad. She started down the incline that was cut into the bluff. This was a well-worn beach access path that led through the rocky outcroppings.

"The oceans not going away," came the voice immediately behind her.

"But the sun is," Tina replied in a hurry-up fashion, as she raced down the access path and bolted across the wide expanse of beautiful Southern California sand and jumped into the ocean on top of her brand-new potato chip surfboard. She didn't wait to see if the guy behind her was still there and was going to join her. She wasn't particularly interested in a pothead anyway.

*   *   *

Tina paddled out to the launch point but there was a lull in the waves, so she stopped paddling and sat up on her board. She put her hand up to her forehead to block the sun as she looked to the horizon to watch the waves begin to form as they approach the shore. The cute guy that had followed her to the beach had just started to paddle out when the next wave set hit. Tina learned to let the first wave go by. That wave was for all the alpha males (some with their self-indulging GoPro cameras strapped to the front of their boards to capture their every hipster move).

Tina rolled her eyes and thought, *just as predicted all these guys took off paddling for the first wave*. This set Tina up perfectly for the second wave in the set. She turned her back to the wave, lowered herself on the board and started to paddle like mad toward shore. She passed the guys that didn't catch the first wave but were way out of position to catch the second. Tina could feel the wave behind her now and she paddled harder, digging her arms deeply into the water to propel herself forward. She could feel the wave take hold of her board like a sprocket in a gear. She pressed her hands against the rails of the board and popped herself up, onto her feet. She carefully stayed low and moved her feet to position her center of gravity toward the downslope side of the wave.

She was rewarded with the acceleration of the board down the face of the wave. Tina was a little scared at first, knowing that if she lost her balance, she would wipe out and be driven into the surf and held under until the wave mass passed over her submerged head and body. But the fear turned into elation when she moved her center of gravity to the backside of the board and turned sharply to make her first carve up the wave face. She exploded above the wave and had to turn quickly again so she would land on the front side of the wave and maintain her forward motion.

"Fucking awesome!" Tina screamed as she transferred her weight again to carve into the wave and launch herself again over the top. She sprang off her board and dove into the backside of the wave. The water was cool and refreshing as it surrounded her and crept into the back of her wetsuit. She could feel the tug of the ankle leash as the moving water was pulling her board forward.

Tina surfaced, pulled the leash to retrieve her board, climbed on and paddled out for the next wave. She was stoked! She had only been at UCSD for little over three months but loved it here. She tried to get to the beach as often as she could, but was taking a heavy load of classes, and there was so much to learn, besides surfing.

The red crescent of the sun was setting on the horizon when Tina finally paddled ashore. She was exhausted from her early evening of surfing but very excited. She noticed that the cute guy that followed her to the beach was waiting for her near the pathway that led back up the bluff.

"Wow. You're an incredible surfer," he said.

"Thanks" Tina replied leaning over to pick up the towel she had left on the beach.

"You must have been doing this since you were a little kid."

"No. Actually I picked it up three months ago when I arrived at UCSD."

"No way! You're a liar," he said only half-jokingly. "Regardless, you are awesome. I'm truly impressed."

"Thanks. Things I enjoy I pick up fast. You know, I don't even know your name. I am Tina Wood."

"Yes, I know. I heard you introduce yourself at Dr. Hutchinson's English Literature Class."

"You're in that class? I've never seen you in the lecture hall," Tina responded thinking she would have at least recognized someone from the same class.

"I sit in the back with all of the other lowlifes hoping we won't be called on by Dr. Hutchinson. You're always in the front row and know all the answers to the professor's questions. Oh, I'm Mark Dunphy, by the way."

"Well, it's nice to meet you, Mark," Tina said, extending her hand that she tried to dry on her wetsuit.

"Nice to meet you, too."

"You know, I heard this was supposed to be a nude beach. But I've been here lots of times and I haven't seen any nudists, just a bunch of surfers. I guess the rumor is just an urban legend that someone made up and others perpetuate," Tina said as she shook out her hair and tried to get the water out of her ear.

"I heard it was a nudist beach back in the day, but the only nudists now are gay men giving each other blow job's and

...” his voice tapering off as he realized that it wasn't polite to talk about such things to a lady.

"Oh, I get it," Tina said wishing that she hadn't mentioned the subject in the first place.

"Hey, do you want to get something to eat?" Mark said hoping to get to know this incredible lady better.

"Sure, I'm starving after all that surfing." So, Tina wrapped her leash around the board and followed Mark up the path leading back to campus.

"I know this nice place just off campus that has the best patty melts and beer this side of the Pecos," Mark said as he puffed his way up the stairs and briefly stopped to catch his breath.

"Sounds delicious," Tina said, almost salivating for the grilled onions and beef.

Tina couldn't hold back; she was indeed starving. She forgot to eat lunch because she was so engaged in the fifth century Middle Eastern poetry she was reading and preparing a paper on. So, when they got to the top of the stairway Tina started to jog across campus back to her dorm. Mark tried his best to keep up but halfway across the quad he developed the stitch in his right side and slowed way down. He watched Tina climb the six flights of stairs up to her dorm room, taking two at a time.

The Apple Pan Burger Joint, La Jolla CA

Tina carefully placed her surfboard back in the padded case and stripped out of her wetsuit. She toweled off, considered showering, but that would have to wait until after she devoured a thick, juicy, patty melt. Just the thought of the juice dripping down her chin made her salivate. She put on a sporty short dress she picked up from REI and headed out again. The crowd in the living room was not as animated as they were earlier, having consumed larger amounts of pot smoke cooled by the hookah pipe. Tina paid no attention to them and left quickly.

Mark was waiting for Tina at the bottom of the stairs.

"Are you going to change?" Tina asked Mark, who still had his swimsuit on and was holding his board.

"Oh, I don't live on campus. I live near the burger joint we're going to. I just brought my surfboard and was hanging around the dorms trying to find someone to surf with. Some guys I know invited me up to your place. Next thing I knew, I was holding a hookah and that's when you walked in. I tried a small puff but started coughing and everyone started laughing at me. I tried pot once before in high school with the same effect. One puff and I started coughing. So, I guess pot isn't for me. Besides, I plan on working for the FBI and you can't be smoking pot when you work for the federal government."

"Wow. I guess I misjudged you. So sorry." Tina said a little taken back by Mark's forthright nature.

"What do you mean?" Mark replied as they started walking.

"I thought you were a pothead like the rest of the people currently occupying my apartment."

"Me? Oh no!" Mark laughed. "Apology accepted."

"Are you really going to work for the FBI?"

"Of course," Mark replied wholeheartedly.

"Oh, you're so full of it" Tina replied, not believing that Mark would actually want to work for the FBI as she pushed him on the shoulder in a friendly gesture of disbelief.

"Well, let's get going I'm starving."

"So am I."

The two of them headed off with Mark leading the way because he knew where the burger joint was. It didn't take very long to get there. And that was a good thing because they were both hungry (especially Tina) and the place was packed. It was Friday night and the local culinary institution - The Apple Pan - was doing a brisk business. Not only was it a favorite with the locals but the UCSD student body quickly learned of its gastronomic delights, very quickly after arriving on campus as young freshman. This was to be Tina's freshman experience and boy was she ready. The line moved quickly and soon they were standing in front of the young man who took food orders.

"Patty melt - well done, with extra onions, large fries, and a chocolate shake," Tina said without hesitation.

"Anything else ma'am?" the young attendant inquired.

"Oh yes, and a slice of apple pie."

"Of course. And for you sir?" The attendant turned to Mark.

"I'll have the same," Mark replied.

"You got it," the attendant said as he turned to bark the order at the fast order cooks feverishly working to fry up everyone's order.

Mark handed the attendant his debit card. Tina tried to pay for her own order, but Mark insisted on covering the tab.

"Okay, next time it's on me," Tina said.

"Thanks."

They got their number and looked around but couldn't find a table.

"We can go back to my place when our order is ready," Mark offered. "I'd say we could go to the park but it's already getting dark."

"How far away is your place?" Tina asked not wanting to seem impatient from her hunger.

"Oh, it's just around the corner."

"Sounds like a plan."

Luckily the Apple Pan was at full staff that evening, and Tina and Mark's order didn't take that long.

Chapter 16

Mark's Condo, La Jolla, CA
Friday November 21, 2003

They took their brown paper sack dinners and headed for Mark's place, which was literally around the corner. There was a glass gate off the sidewalk and Mark entered the security code on the keypad next to the gate.

"After you," he said to Tina.

"Thanks," Tina said as she passed Mark and went down the open paved walkway to the front door.

"Mine's the unit in the back," Mark said as he continued past her on the walkway, gently rubbing Tina's shoulder as he passed.

Tina followed him around the side yard to the rear unit.

Mark opened the front door and said, "Please, come in and make yourself at home."

And Tina did. She went straight to the dining room table. Sat down. Tore open the brown paper bag that held her dinner. She peeled off the wax paper that held her patty melt and took a huge, satisfying bite. The juice dripped off the sides of her mouth, down to her chin and off onto the black glass table. She sat back in the chair and chewed the most satisfying bite she had had in quite a while.

Mark put his surfboard down in the living room and watched all this unfold with a smile on his face and said, "My, you are one hungry woman."

"Oh yeah," Tina replied with her mouth still full of food. She put her hand around her chocolate shake and washed down the last bite she had just consumed. She put the cup back down on the table. There was condensation dripping from the cup of the ice-cold yummy concoction inside. Tina wiped her mouth with a napkin that came supplied in the brown paper bag.

"Boy, I needed that," she said to Mark as she reached for the little plastic tube of ketchup she was going to squeeze on her fries. "Eating a patty melt is better than having sex," she said nonchalantly, feeling more comfortable in Mark's presence.

"Hmm…" Mark murmured, "Yeah, it's good, but better than sex? I don't think so."

"Yeah, you're probably right. I guess it depends on who you're having sex with." Tina smiled sheepishly at Mark, as he started to chuckle.

After his full-belly laugh, Mark finally caught his breath and asked, still panting, "Where do you come up with stuff like that?"

"Oh, I don't know," Tina replied with the wide smile of a Cheshire cat. "Elocution lessons, perhaps." And they both laughed this time, with Tina not being so self-conscious.

Mark sat down next to Tina at the dining room table and started to devour his food. They both chomped in silence until the hunger subsided and then took a long slurp of their thick ice-cold milkshakes.

"My eyelids are coated with salt from the ocean," Tina said blinking, trying to open her eyes wider.

"If you'd like we can soak in the Jacuzzi after we finish eating."

"You have a Jacuzzi?" Tina exclaimed. "Yeah I'd love to have a soak. But I don't have a bathing suit."

"Hell, this is Southern California. Wearing a bathing suit in the Jacuzzi is against the law." Mark said trying to keep a straight face.

"Oh yeah?" Tina said thinking that Mark was actually serious for a second.

"Damn right!" Mark replied thinking he had pulled one over on Tina and was thrilled at the prospect of having this stunningly beautiful lady naked in his Jacuzzi.

"Felony or misdemeanor?" Tina said, still flirting with Mark.

"Felony, of course," Mark said with a chuckle as he reached out and squeezed Tina's hand.

Tina felt Mark's touch and looked up, straight into his eyes. She had known him for less than four hours, and she didn't know if she wanted to have sex with him, and that was okay. Mark was a good-looking guy. Tina could tell that he lifted weights and was certainly well off; given that he had a swanky condo in La Jolla, with a Jacuzzi, no less.

"Hey, I don't know anything about you other than your name, we have the same English lit class, and you like to surf" Tina blurted out.

"Well let's see. I'm from Ojai. I'm majoring in economics. I…"

"You're from Ojai?" Tina said cutting him off in mid-sentence. "Do you know Bryce St. James?"

"Why, yes I do know Bryce. How do you know him?"

Tina was going to be a smartass and say, "Well, I lost my virginity to him." But instead she replied, "I met him in Turkey. We both went to international high schools there."

"Yes, that's right. Now I remember that Bryce did go to high school overseas. He traveled a lot because his Dad was an ambassador, or something."

"Wow, what a small world. So, I cut you off. Please continue," Tina said motioning to Mark.

"Well there's not much more to say. What do you want to know?"

"Why did you decide to come to UCSD? And you can't say to surf."

"No, it must be because of the hmm… oh I know, the elocution lessons."

Tina hauled off and slugged Mark in the shoulder as he tried to move away laughing.

"No, seriously?"

"Okay, okay…" Mark said sitting up straight and deepening his voice, "It must've been the elocution lessons." He moved away as Tina tried to grab him. He got up so quickly that he knocked the chair over and ran into the living room laughing. Tina followed him and was able to tackle him on the couch. The couch was very wide and deep. Mark landed a little awkwardly, and Tina landed on top of him.

"Ow! Ow!" Mark said because of his rough landing and Tina's weight landing on him.

"You're so full of it mister," Tina said trying to appear serious as she laid on top of Mark with her face only inches from his.

"No, seriously."

"You should have been serious when I asked you the first time."

"Yeah, you're right."

Tina started to get off Mark, but he pulled her back down by putting his hands around her back. Now they were face-to-face. Tina waited a moment and then moved to kiss Mark with her eyes closed. Mark met her halfway as their lips met. Mark moved his hands over Tina's back and hugged her as their mouths remained locked. Tina tilted her head slightly, so she could breathe while they kissed. Mark slid his hand over Tina's butt and moved it down between her legs. Tina straightened herself out as she lay directly on top of Mark.

Tina could smell Mark's masculinity and felt the whiskers on his face. The masculinity of the musk scent excited her as she became more aroused. As she lifted her head up Mark strained his neck, so he could catch her lips and give her one more kiss. Tina happily obliged this last peck.

She slid off Mark and moved over to the opposite side of the couch.

"Do you want a drink?" Mark asked, adjusting his body.

"Sure," Tina replied.

"I'm not sure what I have but let me check," Mark said as he got up off the couch.

As he stood up, he had to adjust the crotch of his board shorts because his boner was clearly showing. He went back into the kitchen and turned the light on. It was getting dark and dusk had passed and now it was turning into early evening. Mark peeked his head back in the living room. "All I have is Red Bull and vodka. At UCSD we call it a 'panty downer,'" Mark said with a chuckle.

"Ahh… that's okay, I think I'll pass," Tina said reconsidering, and not being enthralled with the 'panty downer' moniker.

"Oh, I'm just kidding. It's the latest craze on campus. Everyone is having it. It's called the Ying Yang because it combines the best of both worlds."

"Okay, but just a small one," Tina said, not wanting to be a party pooper.

Mark returned to the living room with the ice-cold drinks. Walking carefully so as not to spill them. He had made two very strong drinks. He wanted to make sure that he got some tonight, seeing that he was still hard from the deep kissing that had just happened.

Mark handed Tina her drink and sat down beside her. He flopped back into his seat and motioned his drink forward. Clicking Tina's glass, he said, "Bottoms up."

Tina took a sip of her drink and wasn't prepared for how strong it was. She started to cough. She put her hand over her mouth and managed to say, "sorry," because she was embarrassed that she couldn't handle a strong drink. Through her cough, she managed to ask, "What did you put in this?"

Mark rubbed Tina's back and replied, "Oh, a little something special just for you."

Tina regained her composure. And the two of them sat on the couch holding hands and sipping their drinks. Tina consumed a few sips of her drink when she started to feel really dizzy.

"So, are you ready for the Jacuzzi?" Mark asked in a soft voice as he leaned over and whispered directly into Tina's ear with his lips touching her.

"I don't know. It seems like you've already gotten me pretty drunk," Tina said jokingly as she pried herself off the couch and stood up. She could see that Mark had a raging hard-on that he tried to hide as he got off the couch and embarrassingly adjusted his board shorts and crotch again.

"Ahem," Mark cleared his throat as he tried to gain his composure. He wasn't doing too well though because his face and neck were flushed a brilliant red. "Let me get you a towel," he said as he motioned to Tina to follow him to the bathroom.

"You can change in here," Mark said as he pointed out the bathroom. He opened the door to the linen closet and got Tina a large blue towel with the name "Tahiti" embroidered on it.

Mark's Jacuzzi, La Jolla, CA

Mark was already in the Jacuzzi when Tina came out on the back deck. A tall wooden fence enclosed the area, creating an inviting atmosphere of privacy. Tina didn't feel so self-conscious, having consumed the strong drink that Mark made for her. The light from the house provided a dim backlight. The moon was not out, so the sky was dark, and the first stars could be seen. The Jacuzzi was sunken into the deck. The jets produced a steady stream of bubbles. A soft light shone from inside the tub which made the bubbles glow. A soft mist rose from the breaking bubbles in the air directly above the bubbling water surface. All Tina could see was Mark's head. He laid his head back and stretched out his arms.

Tina took off the towel that she had wrapped around her body and placed it on a deck chair. Mark looked intently at her. Even though Tina's skin-tight wetsuit left very little to the imagination of what lay below the thin layer of neoprene, seeing her in the flesh was a whole other world, and Mark wanted to make sure he didn't miss a thing. Tina walked to the side of the Jacuzzi and dipped her toe into the bubbling cauldron.

"Come on in, waters fine," Mark said as he gazed longingly at Tina.

Neither one of them had any idea that their day would end up like this, but they were both very pleased that it had. Tina stepped into the gurgling water and moved down the steps until her whole body was submerged.

She floated over to Mark and said, "So, where were we?" as she gave him a passionate kiss.

They were both up to their chins in the water. And the glow of the light lit their faces and Tina's tits as they floated up. Mark reached around Tina and pulled her closer to him. All was quiet in the backyard and only the occasional sound of a passing car broke the silence as Tina and Mark continued their face sucking from where they left off on the couch. Tina reached down and started to stroke Mark's large erection. His head tilted slightly back as he enjoyed the feeling of this lovely lady giving him a hand job.

Tina was in charge. She kissed Mark's neck and rubbed his chest with her free hand. "Move over a little," Tina said.

And Mark dutifully complied. Tina placed her legs on the outside of Mark's legs and moved up right next to and on top of him. She moved her hand to direct his erect member between her legs. She moved it back and forth so that it would lubricate her opening. She moved her hand away and let gravity take over, but ironically, the water wasn't wet enough to allow Mark's rod to enter her pussy.

Tina was sitting on Mark's lap, riding him cowgirl style, and she continued to give him a hand job. She put her other hand on the side of his head and gently massaged his ear. Then she leaned in and they locked mouths once again. Tina's hand was moving up and down on Mark's rock-hard member. She moved his hand over, so he could rub her clit. She continued to gently rub his member as she arched back slightly, and Mark put his mouth on her breast and started to suck and lick her nipples. This got Tina really excited.

Tina felt Mark tense up, and lift his whole body, led by his member to shoot his semen into the bubbling water. She felt his warm come on her hand. Mark was rubbing her clit and continued to stroke her clit as she kept coming, over and over again. He started to relax after his climax, and he watched Tina enjoying herself. Her chest and breasts were blushed red and she was groaning softly as she climaxed for the fourth time.

She dropped her shoulders and opened her eyes. "Wow, that was intense," she said through puffs of heavy breathing. Mark just smiled and kissed her breasts again.

Then a rush of blood emptied from her brain and Tina said, "I think I'm going to faint," as she got off Mark.

She had enough strength to get out of the Jacuzzi and wrap the large towel around herself. She staggered back into the living room and collapsed on the couch, with the large blue towel wrapped around her.

Chapter 17

**Mark's Condo, La Jolla
Saturday November 22, 2003**

Tina woke up and the room was dark. She had a splitting headache. Her head throbbed, and her mouth was dry. She tried to lift herself off the cushions, but they sucked her back down. She just lied there on the couch unable to get up. She was feeling cold and noticed that she was naked. She moved her hands trying to feel for the towel. She was not able to reach it. She reached behind her for the table lamp. Even as she strained her reach wasn't long enough. So again, she shrugged back onto the couch.

She lay there still for a minute and mustered enough strength to rotate her body around and put her feet on the floor. Again, she felt for the towel but couldn't find it. She pushed herself up and walked slowly, naked, across the living room to the bathroom. She turned on the light and the bright fluorescent bulb over the sink flickered on. Her head was pounding, and she was lightheaded and nauseous.

She squinted as she looked in the mirror. She noticed dried semen on her breasts and on her stomach, just below her navel. She turned to look for her clothes and remembered putting them neatly in the linen closet. She opened the closet door and found her clothes in a pile, not neatly folded as she had left them. A wave of humiliation passed over her. *What happened after I passed out?* She thought to herself, horrified.

She took a clean washcloth out of the linen closet and returned to the sink. She turned the tap and waited until hot water started to flow. She tried to wash the dried semen from her skin and her pubic hair. She rinsed the washcloth in the sink, under steaming hot water and rubbed it between her legs. Tina tried not to look at herself in the mirror, assuming she looked dreadful and was too embarrassed to imagine what happened to her when she was passed out on the couch. She hurriedly dressed and left Mark's condo.

Tina's Dorm Room, UCSD

The night was quiet, as it usually was in toney La Jolla. Tina felt the chill of the ocean air as she navigated the hilly street back to campus and the safety of her dorm room. She crept into the dorm room. The wall clock read 3:12 AM, like an angry parent waiting up and berating her, *where were you and what the hell were you doing.*

Tina hurried past the accusing clock and unlocked the door to her room. She closed the door quietly behind her and slunk down on the floor with her back pressed against the door as if to keep danger out. She pulled her knees up to her body. She buried her head between her knees fighting hard not to cry. She stayed balled up for at least five minutes before she regained enough composure to make it to her bed. She didn't take her clothes off, only tucked her pillow between her legs as she passed into a fitful sleep.

*   *   *

Tina awoke to the sound of her roommates scampering around outside in the common room. She reached for her cell phone and saw that she had unread text messages and a voicemail. It was 11:21 AM and she put her head back on her pillow. It was Saturday morning and she wanted to enjoy her weekend. Then she remembered last night, and a wave of anxiety passed over her. She checked her text messages.

There were seven messages from Mark.

"Where are you?"

"Worried. Please text me back." And five others just like that. Tina cringed, thinking Mark was a fucking creep.

She took a deep breath and regained her composure to text back, "What the fuck did you put in that drink? Why did you take my towel and jerk off all over me when I was passed out? You're a sick fucking creep. You better stay the fuck away from me or I'll call the cops!!!"

151

Right then, she made a promise to herself thinking, *I'll never let anything like that happen, ever again.* She would always want to be present when a guy she didn't know made a drink for her. She was proud of herself that she had texted Mark back and stood up for herself. When she thought about it further, she started to get angry and violent thoughts crossed her mind, like drop kicking Mark in the balls. But Tina bucked up, like the daughter of a Navy SEAL, and was ready to start her day fresh.

Tina exited her room and walked into the dining room where four of her roommates were sitting eating breakfast.

"Look at you, girlfriend. Did you sleep in those clothes?" Keisha said to laughter from the other three girls at the table.

Tina frowned and replied, "I think I was drugged last night and taken advantage of." The laughter stopped. All the girls got up to give Tina a hug.

"Oh, I'm so sorry," Keisha said.

"You want to talk about it?" Asked Karen the senior from Oklahoma City who came to UCSD to study anthropology.

"There's not much to say. I met this guy surfing. He was here yesterday. We went back to his place and made out in his Jacuzzi. I think he slipped a Mickey into my drink. I passed out on his couch and woke up covered in come."

"Oh, you poor thing," Karen said, giving Tina a hug. "As difficult as all of this is, I think you need to go to the clinic and get checked. And I think you should file a police report."

"Yeah, you're probably right," Tina replied in disbelief that she was even in such a predicament.

"Thank you everyone for being so supportive," Tina said with a renewed feeling of determination.

Health Clinic, UCSD

Tina went to the clinic that day to get checked for venereal disease and see if Mark had sexual intercourse with her when she was naked and passed out on his couch. Luckily, all the tests came back negative. She decided against filing a police report mostly because she knew it would come down to a "he said, she said" argument, that she did make out with Mark in the Jacuzzi, and she felt that she had to put this behind her and get on with her life. As the wave of relief passed over her that the tests were negative, Tina thought, *I must be way more cautious in the future. I just met that guy, and I jumped into the hot tub with him, ready to have sex. Stupid.*

Tina's Dorm, UCSD

Tina's mother called later that day to check up on how college was going. Tina did like all college kids do; lied that everything was okay. That evening the five girls in the dorm room decided they wanted to take Tina out, to take her mind off the happenings of the last day. So, they all went to Wahoo's to have fish tacos and then caught a 9 PM movie at the United Artist theater in downtown La Jolla. Tina was so grateful for her roommate's support. Although they had lived together for months, they didn't really know each other. Especially Tina. She kept to herself and went surfing and to class. And when she wasn't doing that she was studying. Out of something shitty, a little sunshine appeared.

*   *   *

When they got back from the movies it was past midnight. All of Tina's roommates felt compelled to give her a goodnight hug - something that had never happened before. She was touched by the compassion and understanding that her roommates were showing her.

Tina retired to her room and started to watch YouTube on her Samsung Galaxy tablet. She enjoyed watching foreign films from all over the world. Plus, it helped her learn new languages and practice her pronunciation, so she could talk like a

153

native. This skill came in handy one day after the semester began, when she met a freshman from Poland at the Student Union Building.

This young cute guy, with a long brown hair and strong Slavic looks, looked so lost. Tina asked him, "So, can I help you?"

The guy smiled – relieved that someone reached out to help him - and replied in a very heavy Polish accent, "I just arrived. Late for school year. I having trouble with student visa."

Tina replied to him, "Mam przyjaciela, który może ci pomóc z twoją wizą." Meaning, *I have a friend that may be able to help you with your visa.*

Tina's accent was so impeccable that the guy asked her, "z jakiej części Polski była?" W*hat part of Poland are you from?"*

They both had a good laugh when Tina told him that she wasn't from Poland, that she was studying linguistics. Eventually she got Bryce's help with the guy's student visa because Bryce's father had connections in the State Department.

Tina was just settling down to watch another foreign video when Bryce called.

"Hey kiddo, this is your lucky day!" Bryce said in his usual easygoing manner.

With all the shit that had happened, Tina wasn't so sure. "Okay, whatever you say."

"Listen kiddo, I'm planning on driving down tomorrow first thing. Surf is supposed to be great. Can you meet me at 5 AM at the Scripps Pier and we can surf our brains out?"

"Well, I… Don't know. It's sort of last minute."

"Exactly! That's what's great about it. Those who choose in haste get to seize the day."

"What?"

"Never mind, just meet me or be square. Listen kiddo, I gotta go. Need all the shuteye I can get before I drive down."

"Oh, do be careful Bryce," Tina said being more protective than usual.

"You know it. Kisses," Bryce said ready to hang up the phone.

"Kisses." Tina said, and was ready to add, "I've missed you," but Bryce hung up too fast. He wasn't one to linger on the phone; and he rarely, if ever, said goodbye.

And with that, Tina's Sunday was set. She was glad Bryce was coming down to visit but was worried that things between them may be moving too fast; or not at all. She was confused about what their relationship had become, and seeing other people maybe wasn't such a great idea after all.

Chapter 18

**La Jolla Beach
Saturday November 22, 2003**

Bryce was right - the surfing was great. They had breakfast burritos afterward at the local taco place, next to the Pacific Coast Highway, and washed it down with café au lait. Just as they were about finished Bryce reached across the picnic table and held Tina's hand.

"Listen kiddo, we gotta talk."

Tina was a little startled by this, but with Bryce she knew he was always planning. Always thinking ahead.

"I've made up my mind that I'm not going to go to grad school. Even the classes I'm taking now are sort of lame."

"You're not thinking of quitting, are you?" Tina asked, not fully prepared for a deep conversation; being that she was a little raw from what Mark had done to her.

"No. Course not. It would kill my parents, especially my mother. No, I'm going to finish my degree and get a job in New York at a big financial house and make a ton of money," Bryce said laughing, but completely serious.

"Wow, New York, huh?" Tina replied not knowing where the conversation was heading.

"So… I was thinking about us."

"Yes?" Tina said hesitating.

"Well, I think it best that we not get too committed to each other. You know, be friends. Best friends, but not let our relationship get in the way of our careers."

Tina was dumbstruck by this. She knew that her relationship with Bryce wasn't exclusive. And she felt a little guilty having just had sex with Mark - even though it was certainly strange and not entirely consensual. She knew Bryce wasn't seeing anybody else, and probably felt more attached to her than she did to him. For a moment she thought about bringing up Mark but decided against it.

"I'm glad you have your life and career figured out," she said with a slight feeling of hurt. "You jet off to New York and I'm stuck here soaking up the sun, surfing and having a good time." Tina said trying to make light of the serious conversation.

"Oh, don't feel bad kiddo. Everything will work out," Bryce said squeezing her hand.

"I hope so… I hope you know what you're doing."

"Listen, I gotta go. I have a paper due tomorrow that I haven't started yet." Bryce slid out from the picnic table came to the other side and gave Tina a monster hug and kissed her on her lips. And with that, he was gone.

Tina didn't know what to make of the conversation. In one aspect she was relieved because for a moment there she thought Bryce was going to propose marriage to her. She recognized her own thoughts of not wanting to get too serious with anyone. But this happened so fast, and she wasn't the one to bring it up. So, she felt that she had lost control of the relationship; and Tina liked being in control.

The salt from the ocean was drying on Tina's skin and hair. She saw that others were waiting for a table, so she decided to go back to campus.

Student Union Building, UCSD

When she was walking across the quad, she received a text from Mark. She hadn't heard from him since the last angry text she had sent. She opened the text expecting an apology, but instead received the following,

"Why are you seeing that jerk, Bryce? I'm going to kill him if he comes near you again!!"

Tina was shocked. She didn't immediately know what to think or to reply. So, she decided to change out of her wetsuit and confront Mark head-on.

She texted him in reply, "I don't know what you think you are doing, but it better stop. We need to straighten things out. Meet me at noon at the Student Union Building cafeteria."

The one thing she was sure of is that she didn't want to be alone with this guy, and meeting in a public place would provide the needed safety.

*   *   *

Mark was already there when Tina arrived at the Student Union. The cafeteria was large and there were a few scattered diners. Mark waved to Tina - he saw her before she saw him. She didn't acknowledge Mark's wave but started walking toward him. He was smiling and rose from his chair ready to give her a hug.

"Don't you touch me," Tina said gritting her teeth working hard to control her anger, and not drop kick him in the balls.

Mark didn't expect that kind of greeting. "Please sit down. Let's talk. I know what I did was wrong but let me make it up to you. The evening started off so right. But I guess I got a little carried away."

"Jerking off and ejaculating on an unconscious woman is not getting carried away. It's fucking wrong. Probably criminal," Tina said with her voice rising.

"Yes, yes you're right. I am so sorry, so sorry for my despicable behavior. Please, forgive me and let me make it up to you," Mark said trying to calm Tina down and not let her make a scene in this public place.

"And where'd you get off threatening Bryce and telling me who I can see," Tina demanded, not intimidated by Mark.

"Yes, yes you're right that was wrong. I'm so sorry let me make it up to you."

"I'm so angry with you now. I can't bring myself to forgive you."

"Yeah, you're right again. Let's take a little time to sort things out."

158

"You better not have taken pictures of me when I was passed out," Tina demanded, emphatically staring right at Mark waving her finger in his face.

"No! Of course not. No way," Mark lied.

"And what did you put in my drink? Did you slip me a Mickey?"

"No! No way. I'd never do that. I like you too much. I think I'm in love with you."

"Well, you certainly have a strange way of showing it" Tina said trying to keep her cool.

"Listen," Mark said reaching his hand across the table trying to hold Tina's hand. Tina pulled her hand back out of reach of Mark's grasp. "I promise I'll make it up to you. You'll see."

At this point, Tina was too pissed off to even care if she even wanted Mark to make it up to her.

"We'll see," she said as she cut the conversation off.

And with that, Tina rose and left without looking back at Mark, leaving no uncertainty of her feelings.

Tina's Dorm, UCSD

When she got back to her dorm room, she told her roommates what had just happened with Bryce and Mark. Again, they were supportive, seeing what Tina was going through. However, a couple of her roommates harbored jealous feelings. Tina had two cute guys that wanted her badly, and they hadn't had a decent date since they arrived on campus. For them, a lot of the guys at UCSD were too immature, wouldn't commit, flaked on dates, played video games all day long, and some fantasized about being laid by cougars their mother's age.

Tina was proud of the way she stood up to Mark for taking advantage of her. What she neglected to do was to find out how Mark knew she had met with Bryce. She resolved to herself to get over Mark. Bryce. *Oh Bryce, why did he have to be so fucking organized and practical?* Tina thought to herself. *It must be because he's a Capricorn she laughed to herself,* mistakenly because he was actually a Sagittarius.

Cafeteria, Student Union Building, UCSD

Mark saw the whole interaction quite different than Tina. To him, Tina was his girl, and no one else had better touch her. Mark wished Tina would have stayed at the cafeteria with him. *Oh well,* he thought, *I'll just have a malted milk before I go back to my place and catalog all the pictures I took of Tina when she was passed out. God is she gorgeous,* Mark said to himself - getting a hard-on just thinking of the compromising positions he had placed Tina in, when he took the photos. He decided to skip the malted milk and go straight back to his condo and jerk off, looking at the photos of Tina naked, with her legs spread apart, passed out on his couch.

After the meeting in the cafeteria, Tina avoided Mark. She tried to shrug it off as just bad judgment and a poor choice of who to date. Mark became obsessed with Tina. He understood that she wanted her space, so he tried not to call or text her too much. But there were times when he just couldn't help himself. This happened when he was insecure and afraid he was going to lose her. Even though he was delusional to think that Tina was his to lose.

Chapter 19

Surfer's Point Beach, Ventura, CA
Thursday January 1, 2004

"Outside!" yelled one of the surfers in the lineup.

Bryce knew exactly what it meant. It was New Year's Day and the swell graced the beaches of Ventura County with incredible surf waves. From high school science, everyone remembered the class on wave theory - how waves can cancel each other out or be added together.

"Outside" meant that Mother Nature had combined two waves together to create that rogue unsurfable wave that would most certainly swallow you, or worse, if you stayed on the beach side of the break. Bryce turned without thinking and paddled like mad toward the wave and duck-dove right under it, letting it pass over him.

For those not used to surfing, the whole experience would be terrifying. But for Bryce - who had surfed since grade school - the whole ordeal was a small inconvenience in the overall pursuit of surfing thrills. However, even with all his experience, the sensation of a massive body of water passing over him could be daunting, to say the least.

Bryce recalled from high school science that momentum was mass times velocity. A wave isn't traveling that fast, but it has a lot of mass. And he felt that powerful momentum as it passed over him. He was lying on his board, prostrate, on the altar of Mother Nature, praying to the goddess of the ocean, *please don't kick my ass.*

Bryce emerged on the outside - the ocean side - of the wave. The cold water had seeped into the back of his wetsuit and sent a shiver down his spine as the cold Pacific displaced the warmer water formerly occupying the tight, insulating space between his wetsuit and his skin. This was stimulating and refreshing to Bryce as he wiped the water from his face to survey the ocean landscape and get ready for the next surfable wave that was sure to follow.

Bryce and his buddies had been surfing this beach since they were little kids, and although they were very competitive at getting waves, they had each other's back. Bryce sat up and straddled his board. He put his hand on his forehead to block the sun as he looked up and down the row of surfers to make sure everyone made it outside in time. The sun was bright even though it was still low in the eastern sky.

At first, Bryce thought he saw a large clump of seaweed floating on the surface of the water. He squinted to get a better look though. The saltwater that dripped from his hair stung his eyes. No, it wasn't seaweed. It was someone floating face down with the back of their wetsuit bobbing at the surface of the water.

Bryce laid on his board and started paddling furiously towards the bobbing object that was a little over 25 yards away. Bryce knew the drill on rescuing someone in the surf. He flipped his board over, so the fin was up as he dove into the water and swam to the person floating face down. He came up from behind and put his arms around the front of the person and gently flipped their head out of the water. Just then a wave hit, and Bryce was pushed down into the water, along with the person he was holding on to. He frantically did a rotating whip kick to keep both of them afloat as he started to swim for his board. But his board had been pushed by the wave further from where he had left it, straining on his ankle leash as he kicked.

His head was right at the water surface, so his field-of-view was very limited. He started to kick and move his free arm toward shore, while holding onto the person he was trying to rescue. He couldn't tell who it was because from the back the person's hair kept getting in his face. The person was unresponsive. Bryce had to make a choice; continue to swim for his board in the direction he thought it traveled or try to start mouth-to-mouth resuscitation in the surf. He quickly chose the latter and moved around to the front side.

It was the first time Bryce could see the guys face. It was his friend Billy del Toro. Bryce tilted Billy's head back and held his nose as he gave him a deep breath. Bryce was kicking hard to keep both of them afloat in the surf. When giving mouth-to-mouth resuscitation you don't go fast. However, you have to give steady forceful breaths, which Bryce did. He kept Billy's head above the water as he kicked to move closer to shore. After about forty-five seconds (which seemed much longer) Billy started to cough, breathing on his own.

Bryce got behind Billy again and kept an arm around him as he kicked toward his board. After he finally reached his board, he put Billy up against the back of it as he maneuvered himself to the opposite side. He reached across the board with both hands and lifted Billy's arms up across the board. Billy was facing away from Bryce.

Bryce put his feet up on the rail of the board and held tightly onto the far side to keep Billy balanced. In one quick motion, he lifted himself onto his side of the board. The equal and opposite reaction forced the board to rotate and lift Billy's body up onto the front side of the board, all in a swift skilled motion. It worked! Bryce was so happy and exhausted. He checked that Billy was still breathing as they headed for shore.

Bryce's swift action wasn't unnoticed. The lifeguard on the first shift had arrived early to try and get a little surfing in before his shift began. As Bryce and Billy were heading in, he was heading out into the surf to assist in the rescue. The lifeguard came up on the far side of the surfboard, held on, and added propulsion to get Billy safely back to shore. Some of the local surfers, that had just arrived, also entered the water to help.

When they were in water shallow enough to stand up Bryce said, "Let's lift him up." There were four guys around the board and they each held their side and lifted the board when Bryce said, "Okay, one two three lift!"

They walked out of the surf and onto the sand beach. Before he went into the water the lifeguard had called 911 and a Ventura County fire paramedic was already speeding its way to the beach.

Billy coughed again, rolled on his side and threw up. It was then that they all knew he was breathing on his own.

"Dude you just saved this guy's life," the lifeguard said to Bryce.

"Yeah, that was fast thinking," one of the local guys said, "any longer without breathing would have caused permanent brain damage."

Bryce understood the gravity of the situation but was not ready to be crowned a hero. He said, "Yeah I know, but any of you guys would've done the same thing."

The quiet peaceful environs of the beach were punctuated with the sound of the paramedic's siren. A calm came over Bryce because he knew his friend Billy was going to be okay.

Bank of Uppsala, Stockholm, Sweden

Money laundering is a puzzling concept. Strictly speaking laws against money laundering have mostly to do with the source of the dirty funds; which can be a whole host of crimes: extortion, insider trading, drug trafficking, illegal arms sales (you name it). The list of illicit activities is only limited by a criminal's devious imagination.

The easiest way to be caught is to use the dirty money directly. The FBI is constantly monitoring large money transactions in the United States. Thus, in order not to draw attention to your illegal dealings the dirty money you 'earned' needs to be cleansed i.e. laundered, such that the bank transaction gives the appearance that the source of the funds was derived from legal activities.

Banks and financial institutions are required to report large monetary transactions to the government. And thus, the process of laundering requires deceit and obfuscation. However, the actual mechanics of laundering can become far less complex if you are dealing with a financial institution that is somewhat accommodating, provided it's worth their while to do so. The one main ingredient of an 'accommodating' financial institution is one with a corrupt corporate culture. Such as an unspoken

motto of "Don't ask and don't tell, if the profit is large enough."
And that's where Bryce comes in. Correction. That's where the
bank that Bryce works for comes in.

A corporate culture is the undercurrent that defines the
work ethic of the institution. The Bank of Uppsala was the
financier of Sweden's heavy industry before the start of the
Second World War. At that time the bank cooperated fully with
the German war effort in providing steel and heavy industry for
the German war machine. It is now a matter of public shame that
the Swedes allowed the Germans to use their railroads to attack
Norway during the war. Although officially Sweden was neutral
during the war, that was far from true in practice. The attitude
held at the time was one of submission; "We are in no position to
openly contest Germany and so we may as well make
concessions." This naturally evolved into the culture of the bank,
i.e. "Don't ask too many questions as long as we make a profit.
And, it's not my problem to question what's going on."

The practicality of this position served them very well,
because Sweden was not involved in any hostilities during the
war, they came through unscathed. With a stable populace,
ample natural resources, and an intact industrial base Sweden
was one of the richest European countries at the end of the
Second World War. This only reinforced the corporate culture of
don't ask too many questions, and who could argue against it.
Profits flowed, and everyone was very happy.

The bank remained in private hands, far from the prying
eyes and the pesky rules of a publicly traded company. To fill
the 'less than on the up and up' banking void the Bank of
Uppsala went international and set up base in many unsavory
places. But if there was a profit to be made, don't ask too many
questions. The Bank operated on a simple formula: the riskier
the deal, the more unsavory the place, the larger the profit
margin demanded. The Bank of Uppsala (or B of U, as the
employees affectionately called it) was performing probability
risk analysis before it was even taught in business school. After
all of this unsavory financial history, they didn't have any
particular hang-ups financing Muslim extremists in the Middle

East or anyone else for that matter. To the B of U, it was business as usual - just another day at the office.

So how did clean-cut Bryce Christian St. James, surfer dude and financial whiz come to work at such a place as the B of U?

St. Thomas Aquinas College, Santa Paula, CA
Wednesday April 28, 2004

"Okay, class settle down. As you know this is the final exam of International Finance 560. You will have three hours to complete the exam. And from the looks of the assignments some of you just turned in, you'll need every minute of it," Professor Wright said as he quickly paced the class passing out the exam booklets face down, on the desk of each student. A look of terror was on the face of many. When he came to the back of the last row, he stopped. The student hadn't been paying attention to the instructions Professor Wright had just given.

"Mr. St. James," he addressed Bryce.

Bryce slowly broke his gaze out of the window and turned to face the front of the class.

"Yes, Professor?"

"Do you understand the exam instructions?"

"Perfectly Sir. International Finance 560. Three hours. Some will need every minute," Bryce said, parroting what the professor had just said, which brought on hoots of gallows laughter from the other students.

"Good, Mr. St. James," the professor said, ignoring the laughter, as he continued down the last aisle handing out the last of the exam booklets.

"Okay, class settle down. I now have 8:10 AM on my watch. You will have three hours to complete the exam. There'll be no talking or communication of any kind during the exam. If you have a question, just raise your hand and I'll come over and talk to you. Turn your exam booklets over and begin."

Bryce turned over his booklet and read the exam questions rather quickly. Then a smile came to his face. He stretched his hands out in front, clasping them together as he twisted them towards his face. He knew he was going to need to relax his arm and hand because he was about to write a ton of shit on international finance and he didn't want them to cramp up.

*   *   *

As was customary at most colleges, including St. Thomas Aquinas College in bucolic Santa Paula, California, grades were posted on the window of the door to the professor's office exactly one week after the day of the exam. International Finance 560 was Bryce's last exam of his senior year. He wasn't exactly sure what he was going to do after college but continuing with graduate school was out of the question.

Bryce applied himself rigorously to the last four years of study, taking the hard classes and really pushing himself. And of course, keeping the partying to a minimum, although he did make a special exception for surfing, and an occasional visit to Tina at UCSD. He felt a great sense of relief and accomplishment, after final exams were over, he spent the week surfing, and waiting for his final grades to be posted. The surf splashing his face cleared his mind, and he knew he was ready for his next challenge and adventure. He did so much surfing that his arms felt weak like spaghetti from all the paddling.

It was with a clear head that Bryce entered the Wainwright Building on campus. The stately brick building housed the offices of the professors and the college administration. Bryce bounded up the stairs and glided through the hall visiting each professor's office to see what his final grades were for each class that he took during the last semester at St. Thomas. He was anxious to graduate and get on in life. He had taken five classes and received an A+ in the first four, as indicated on the lists posted on each professor's office window.

He headed up the stairway to visit Professor Wright's office. It was early – 7 AM in the morning. Way before anyone occupied the building, so Bryce's footsteps echoed on the tile floor of the historic structure. Only the hall night-lights were on, which provided minimal illumination. Bryce stood in front of the door to Professor Wright's office. There were four sheets of white paper taped to the inside of the window. Each sheet represented the grades of the four classes the professor taught.

Bryce found his class, International Finance 560 and scanned down the list of student numbers. To ensure confidentiality, no one's actual name was listed on any of the sheets, only their student number. Bryce found his student number and scanned across to see the word *Incomplete* where a letter grade should have been. Bryce's head jerked back slightly, "Hmm," he said to himself, "there must be some mistake."

Bryce flipped his phone and shined it on the piece of paper taped to the window. He confirmed the class name, and his student number lined up with the *Incomplete* grade. Everyone else in the class had received a grade. The highest grade was a B. The vast majority received a C and there were a few Ds and Fs. But Bryce's grade was the only Incomplete.

"Shit," Bryce swore, thinking *what the hell could this mean?* His mind raced as he thought back on the entire semester. The class was a yearlong, starting in September of the previous year. His mid-semester grade was an A that he received just after Christmas break and the grueling winter exam. This led him to think that something was amiss, during the second half of the yearlong class. *What could it be*? He thought to himself but could not come up with an answer. He took out his phone and called the number for the Economics Department.

"Hello, you've reached the office of the Economics Department at St. Thomas Aquinas College in Santa Paula California. Our office is currently closed. If you'd like to leave a message, please do so after the tone," The voice recording said, then Bryce heard a beep.

"Hello. This is Bryce St. James. I would like to meet with Professor Wright. Please call or text me back when he will be available. Thanks. Oh, and my number is …" as Bryce carefully recited his phone number and then hung up. "Fuck," he said as he turned away and headed down the hall. It was no consolation that he had received an A in all his other classes. International finance was the subject he was most interested in, so how could it be messed up so much after all of his hard work?

Chapter 20

Rincon Beach, Carpinteria, CA
Wednesday May 5, 2004

Bryce turned over the ignition to his Jeep Wrangler. His surfboard protruded from the back. Sparklehorse's "Don't Take my Sunshine Away" shot out from the Blaupunkt speakers. In usual form, Bryce peeled out of the parking lot. *It was going to take some serious surfing to pull out of this funk*, Bryce thought to himself as he weaved on State Route 150 back toward Carpinteria and the famous right break at Rincon Beach.

*   *   *

The world of international finance is indeed byzantine. The word *arbitrage* comes from the French word, *arbitre*. It was used to describe exchange rates and profit taking to settle a bill of exchange. The practice by international financial institutions involves complicated financial transactions that capitalize on an imbalance in the marketplace between two currencies. Successful arbitrageurs have the skill of a reptile. Like an alligator they are extremely patient and will wait for the right opportunity. With their lightning fast reflexes, they can snap up their prey when the right deal comes along. Bryce was just such a person.

Bryce's arms had the strength of limp noodles when he finally got out of the surf after four hours. His face was a little sunburned, but he felt refreshed and alive when he wiped his head with his towel. When he got back to his Jeep, he noticed the voicemail indicator on his smartphone, and he hit the voicemail button.

"Hello Bryce, this is Professor Wright. I am returning your message. Please be at my office at 2 PM today, and we can discuss your grade."

"Shit," Bryce said. He had been surfing all morning and had lost track of time. It was already 12:40 PM and he hadn't eaten anything. He quickly loaded his surfboard in the back of his Jeep and sprinted out of the dirt parking lot onto the highway that led back to the college. Led Zeppelin's "Achilles Last Stand" was playing as he wound his way through Ojai and the stately horse ranches lined with white palisade fences.

There has to be some misunderstanding that can be easily cleared up, Bryce thought to himself. He pulled off the road and stopped at a taco stand; more of a glorified roach coach really but they had the best fish tacos in Ventura County. Bryce wolfed down three to satisfy his ravenous appetite and then gulped down an extra-large Cactus Cooler. The ice-cold liquid quenched his thirst and gave him a little brain freeze.

Professor Wright's Office, St. Thomas Aquinas College

Bryce's brain was anything but frozen when he climbed the stairs of the Wainwright Administration Building, up to Professor Wright's office. He didn't have a chance to change from his knee long board shorts, and he still had on his skintight rash guard that revealed every ripple of his physique. The seawater dripped off his shorts and he left a slight water stain on the tile floor where his flip-flops echoed in the hallway announcing his arrival. The door to Professor Wright's office was open, and Bryce gently knocked on the door. It was almost 2 PM, so Bryce had made it just in time.

"Come in," the professor said. "Bryce. Thanks for coming. Please have a seat and I'll be right with you."

Bryce hesitated for a moment, thinking that his wet shorts would stain the upholstery of the chair, but he thought, *what the hell*, and sat in the first of two chairs facing the professor's desk.

"I've asked the provost to join us," Professor Wright said and just then Dr. Evans, provost of St. Thomas Aquinas College came into the room, also on time for the 2 PM meeting.

"Right on time," Professor Wright said. "I'm not sure if you know Bryce St. James."

"No, I have not met this fine young man, but I've heard so many good things about him. It's a shame to finally meet him under such circumstances," Dr. Evans replied extending a hand to Bryce.

"Nice to meet you, sir," Bryce said politely, although a little perplexed from not knowing what he meant by the 'such circumstances' remark.

The provost sat in the chair next to Bryce as Professor Wright began, "Bryce you are by far my best student. Well hell, you're probably the best student I ever had. So, I don't quite know how to put this, and so I'll just come right out and say it. Where did you get the questions that were on the final exam?"

Bryce looked at Professor Wright like he was speaking a foreign language, not knowing how to reply. "I… don't know what you mean," Bryce stuttered.

"Come now Bryce. I purposely made the final exam extremely hard and put some questions on it that would be nearly impossible to answer completely. Yet you answered the questions like you were taking dictation."

"Let me get this straight," Bryce said sitting up straight, getting a little indignant and glad his shorts were staining the upholstery of the chair. "Are you accusing me of cheating?"

"I know the pressure students place on themselves, and there is the desire to maintain an A average."

"You didn't answer my question. Are you accusing me of cheating?"

"Well, yes," Professor Wright said, looking away from Bryce.

Bryce gripped the armrests of the chair - trying to restrain his temper. He took a deep breath and began, "I do not cheat. No one gave me the questions that would be on the exam. There is much about me that you do not know. On the other hand, there's plenty I know about you. Your reputation of having the most difficult classes and being a hard grader are well known on campus," Bryce stated, restraining his voice and moving forward in his chair.

The professor gave a quick shit-eating grin to the provost as Bryce continued, "When I started to study for final exams, I did a risk and probability analysis of what I thought you would ask on the final exam, knowing that the exam was going to cover the entire year's work. I isolated those topics that I wasn't as familiar with. Seeing that I had an A at the Christmas break and an A in the last midterm, I figured I needed to concentrate my studies on the topics you covered in the last half of the semester. I looked at the course syllabus and noticed that there were topics that you had only briefly covered, and knowing your reputation of being a real prick, I made a calculated determination of what you would put on the final exam and I prepared for those topics. And sure enough, I was right."

"We only briefly covered arbitrage. That is a graduate level topic. No undergraduate would have the knowledge of this subject and write what you wrote on the exam," Professor Wright shot back.

"So, I take it that I aced the final exam," Bryce said, with his voice slightly rising.

"Where did you get the questions from?" Professor Wright asked again.

"What was my grade on the final exam?" Bryce asked again, this time measuring his words and catching himself before he lost his temper.

"Yes, just what was his grade on the final exam?" The provost asked, rather calmly putting his hand on Bryce's forearm, trying to diffuse the situation.

"He had to have been given the questions that were on the exam," Professor Wright said looking straight at the provost.

"Please answer my question," the provost said again, very calmly leaning back in his chair.

"He got an A+," Professor Wright said after a long pause.

"Good. Thank you," the provost replied. "Bryce, please tell me how you know so much about the esoteric topic of international arbitrage."

Bryce took a deep breath and moved back in his chair. A small puddle had formed on the floor beside his flip-flops from the water coming off his board shorts. The chair's upholstery would now most definitely be stained.

"My father has served as an ambassador, or on the staff at the consulate, of many foreign countries."

Professor Wright rolled his eyes. Thinking that he was hearing the bullshit from a skilled cheat. Bryce ignored the professor's gesture and continued.

"I have traveled the globe since I was a little kid and have become immersed in foreign culture, politics, and finance. I intend to go into international banking when I graduate from this fine institution. When I started college, I cashed in the savings bond my grandfather had given me many years ago, and I started investing in the stock market. I made a little money, but I was looking for a way to get a greater return because I was willing to take more risk based on my own research. I opened an arbitrage account at the Credit Suisse Bank in Bern Switzerland. Most small investors that go into arbitrage lose their ass. Not because there is so much risk, which there is, but because they are impatient, and they are not willing to do the painstaking research necessary to know when to make the trade. They either act too quickly or wait too long. I've made a tiny sum over the last four years. So much so that I do not intend on going to graduate school. Unfortunately, this current escapade has taught me that some college professors are more interested in academic exercises than what happens in the real world. So, I didn't steal the questions to your exam. I studied and prepared for this test for the past four years, by putting in the time to know the intricate details of international finance and arbitrage trading. So, yes I do deserve the A+ because I did it the old-fashioned way; I earned it."

Bryce paused for affect. Then he leaned forward again staring straight at Professor Wright and said, "Another thing I learned in life is that I won't be bullied. So, either you agree to give me the grade I deserve, or I will have my lawyer contact this fine institution," Bryce said as he turned to face the provost, making sure that he knew that he was not bluffing.

"That won't be necessary," Dr. Evans said, putting his hand again on Bryce's forearm to calm him down. "Based on your stellar performance to date, and the evidence you just presented, you will have the grade you deserve and graduate from this fine institution."

"But, but -" Professor Wright started to talk.

"I'll deal with you later, Professor Wright," the provost said giving him a stern look and placing his other hand firmly on the desk signifying that the meeting was over. "Bryce, please excuse us and go wait in my office and I'll join you shortly."

Bryce was obviously all riled up and wanted satisfaction from Professor Wright. He wanted to carve his pound of flesh from that academic weasel by wiping that shit eating grin off Professor Wright's face. He looked at Dr. Evans and was ready to speak.

"Bryce, trust me. I'll straighten this all out." And with that reassurance, Bryce got up from the chair and left the room and a very large wet stain on Professor Wright's upholstered chair.

Provost's Office, St. Thomas Aquinas College

Bryce was sitting on the bench in front of the provost's office when Dr. Evans came down the hall about ten minutes later. Dr. Evans opened the door to his office and said, "Please come in and have a seat."

Bryce put away his Xiaomi smartphone, that he had been using to check his investments and followed the provost into his office.

"I've cleared up this misunderstanding with Professor Wright," Dr. Evans said as Bryce sat down.

In the four years he had been at Thomas Aquinas, Bryce had never been in this office. There was no need to. Bryce was a model student: Straight A's, always did the work, and never raised a fuss.

"I completely understand your frustration back there. You will receive an A+ for that class and graduate with honors. I'm very proud of you son."

"Thank you, Dr. Evans. Sorry I got a little hot, but I put in the work and I was annoyed at being falsely accused of cheating."

"No need to apologize, my boy. Listen, I'm very impressed with your academic achievements and see that you have a bright future ahead of you. I have a friend in New York who works at an international bank. He graduated from Thomas Aquinas about five years ago and has done very well for himself. I'll contact him and give you a great reference and tell him that you're going to give him a call. One piece of advice though; when you go and see him, make sure you wear a suit and tie." Both Bryce and the provost smiled, seeing that Bryce's board shorts were dripping on the provost floor as well. The provost gave Bryce the contact information for his future boss at the Bank of Uppsala.

Bank of Uppsala, New York, N.Y.
Tuesday June 1, 2004

Bryce St. James - California surfer dude, and now international financier - went to New York for an interview that the provost had made possible. The management staff at the B of U that interviewed Bryce was so impressed with his knowledge of arbitrage and international finance, that they offered him a job on the spot, not wanting Bryce to go to the competition.

Things happened so fast. Bryce hadn't socialized much during college and saw Tina less frequently as the years went by. They stayed in touch but mutually agreed that they wanted their careers to come first. Bryce thought that after college let out that he would take a month or more and just surf, hang with his buddies, and visit Tina in San Diego. But here he was heading to the Big Apple and a new career far from the laid-back backwater of Ojai. Bryce didn't believe in goodbyes, especially when it came to Tina. They had a special connection a 'je ne sais quoi' that they both understood implicitly. Although at times Tina wished that Bryce was more explicit.

Bryce had his friend Billy del Toro do research into the place of his future employment. Billy's methods were very unorthodox. The dark side of the Internet is a phantom place that exists only in hyperspace. Billy would tunnel into restricted networks. Dark web information cannot be found in a Google search. It is essentially unsearchable because the data is stored in formats that are not easy to read or are encrypted. Additionally, the dark web is intentionally hidden and accessible only to those who know exactly what to look for and have all the correct passcodes. The dark web is everywhere, yet nowhere. Not just anyone can connect to this decentralized system.

Well, it just so happened that Bryce's best friend Billy wasn't just anybody. Billy dropped out of Caltech, in Pasadena, California, because he didn't think they had anything useful to teach him, which was mostly due to technology moving so quickly and that Billy didn't want to be left behind. And so, Billy did the research on the Bank of Uppsala and gave his report to Bryce.

Bryce read widely and witnessed many unsavory things in his travels and living abroad. He expected Billy would pull up some dirt, which he did.

The bank was no better or worse than any other bank that dealt in international finance, as far as Billy could tell. Although he prefaced his statements with, "now that's just the ramblings of a jaded Libertarian."

Bryce accepted the job and within a month of graduating from St. Thomas Aquinas's College in St. Paula California, he was living in New York City. The contrast could not have been more extreme, and Bryce embraced the challenge, although he did miss surfing every day.

*   *   *

    The Bank of Uppsala International Division had a culture of 'don't ask too many questions of the people they dealt with, so long as they made a substantial profit.' Unfortunately, that attitude doesn't fly when you do business in the United States, and the bank was always on the FBI radar in New York City. Fortunately for the bank, there was so much corruption happening in New York and New Jersey that the Bureau was easily overworked. A dedicated G-man can only take so much corruption and paperwork in a single day. And that was a big part of the problem. There was so much paperwork that a financial institution had to fill out and so much red tape to wade through to properly address the mountain of regulations that cover international banking. At times it was nearly impossible to separate the scofflaws from the real corruption that was going on.

    Bryce had just settled into his new office on Wall Street when his boss - the guy from St. Thomas Aquinas College that Bryce was thinking would mentor him - up and quits without any notice. The guy gave Bryce some lame excuse as to why he was leaving. Bryce didn't know what to believe. When he arrived at the bank Bryce felt this guy had his back. He didn't know who he could turn to. Bryce shook it off and made the best of the situation.

    Bryce quickly found out that his boss was forced out because he wasn't keeping up with the paperwork required to file with the Federal Banking Authorities. There was a backlog of work that needed to be done. The final straw came in the form of a letter from the FBI stating clearly that unless the paperwork was cleared up immediately; they would launch a thorough investigation, a detailed audit, and possibly levy some very stiff fines.

    Within a month of quitting the B of U, the guy that hired Bryce was dead. He died in a mysterious car accident in Ventura County. Bryce never heard a satisfactory answer as to what caused the accident. Apparently, the guy just drove off the steep, curvy part of Highway 150, just past Dennison Park. There were no skid marks on the pavement to indicate that the guy tried to brake before he left the pavement. He was burned beyond recognition when his car burst into flames upon hitting a rock outcropping, 200 feet below the highway. The California Highway Patrol thought there could have been foul play but could never prove anything.

Silicon Beach, Venice, CA
Tuesday June 1, 2004

Almost imperceptibly the brainpower of the cyber world had shifted from the Valley to the Beach. Yes, certainly all the established firms, with household names, still dominated the Silicon Valley and commanded the capital to be made in this industry. However, the cyber world moves very quickly, brought on in most part by its own success. So now most of the new generation of coders wanted to be part of the L. A. hipster culture of Silicon Beach rather than the perceived stodginess of Silicone Valley.

Whether the stodgy characterization was fair or not was not the point. The point was that the best and the brightest believed it, and so in the brave new cyber world that was all the truth anyone required. And thus, it is with this perception that one of the brightest stars arrived at the hipster confines of L.A. Billy del Toro was far from being either a hippie or a hipster. He was a savant when it came to computer code. He also quickly learned the ways of the dark web. The part of the web not found by any Google search.

Chapter 21

Pakistani Airline Flight, London to Islamabad Pakistan
Sunday June 6, 2004

After a long, unexplained delay, the Pakistani Airlines flight took off from London's Heathrow Airport. Dean Reed tried to relax when they passed 10,000 feet and the announcement came on that the passengers were cleared to use their approved electronic devices. Perhaps it was that he was clearly overtired from the red eye flight from New York's JFK to London earlier that day. Perhaps it was the problem of changing airlines in London, which turned into a colossal hassle of customs, security assholes, baggage claim, and lugging your stuff to a different airline terminal (Pakistani Airlines no less). No matter, the Dean kept fidgeting in his seat.

"Dude, you don't look okay. Is something wrong?" said the guy in the window seat.

The Dean stopped and turned to look at the guy. It was hard to make out his face immediately because the sun's glare came through the window, as the plane cleared the London gloom on its way to 30,000 feet.

"Yes, I am okay. Thanks for asking," the Dean replied as he caught a quick glimpse of the guy's face.

"No problem. Hey, you're the first American I've met since I arrived in England."

"Well it's certainly nice to meet you as well," replied the Dean holding out his hand, "Dean, oh I mean, Kim Reed."

"Billy del Toro. So, you are a Dean, eh?" Billy said in his easy way that put people at ease.

"Yes. Dean of Linguistics at Columbia" the Dean replied; always impressed with himself every time he said those words.

"I'm very impressed to meet a scholar. I'm just a beach bum from Ojai, California." Billy said self-effacingly. As he chuckled to himself knowing that in the business of exploiting the vulnerabilities of the Internet through the dark web, he always had to be cautious about who he spoke to and what he said about himself.

The Dean smiled and said, "What takes you to Pakistan?"

"I'm going to climb in the Himalayas" Billy said, proud of himself.

"Oh wow! Mount Everest?"

"No. That mountain is way too commercial and covered with spent bottles of oxygen, frozen corpses, and human excrement."

"Oh my!" Exclaimed Dean Reed.

"Sorry. Perhaps it's not that bad but it certainly isn't the place for serious climbing."

"Really? Hmm. So, what is the place for serious climbing?"

"Nanga Parbat" Billy replied in a somewhat cocky way, which was not his usual style, but he felt obligated to impress the scholar he was now addressing.

"Hmm…" Dean Reed said, "Do you know what that means in Urdu?"

"Ahh...no," Billy replied hoping the Dean would not go into a long explanation.

"It literally means naked mountain."

"Cool. I have to tell the others on the climbing team."

"Be careful up there. Nanga Parbat is known as the killer mountain. Not just because so many climbers have died trying to summit. Now militant Muslim extremists are threatening foreigners in the Gilgit-Baltistan region of Kashmir."

"Kashmir eh... Yeah I like that Led Zeppelin song," Billy said, shaking off the warning. "Trust me, we are not looking for any trouble."

"You may not, but it may come looking for you."

"Understood." Billy paused trying to figure out if he should now be more cautious than his normally over-cautious self. To change the subject Billy inquired, "So, what brings you to Pakistan? Especially given all of the strife you are aware of?"

"I am on sabbatical and I want to continue my research on the languages spoken in Pakistan. Did you know that almost 98% had its origin in Iran? But there are smaller ethnic groups found mainly in the northern part of the country. Our task as scholars is to study these languages, catalog them, and make sure they are preserved for posterity. It would be a tragic shame on humanity if we let these languages die. It would be the equivalent of letting a species of wildlife go extinct."

"Wow. Sounds like some serious stuff," Billy said, not knowing what else to say but wanting to appear interested and polite.

The Dean saw this as his opening to start in on one of his lectures about the great service linguistics must provide to society and the tragedy of having lost languages in the past and his commitment to make sure that it never happened again.

Billy sat there not knowing how to get out of the conversation and regretting that he had initiated the contact in the first place. But the Dean recognized that he was boring Billy and said "Oh I'm sorry. I can drone on and on about my passion."

"Hey, no problem bro," Billy replied. "It seems like all the talk about languages has put your mind at ease."

"Yes, yes I guess it has. Thanks for listening." And with that, the Dean sat back and reclined in the seat and chilled, as the two chatted amicably on and off during the remainder of the flight.

Islamabad, Pakistan

Billy thought it smelled bad inside the plane. That was until the door opened and a full draft of the City's air wafted inside, as he was about to exit. A rickety aluminum ramp had been wheeled up on the tarmac to the side of the plane. He squinted his eyes to block the glare of the sun. Ahead of him he saw the ragtag group of mountaineers with their scruffy beards and backpacks amble across the hot tarmac to the terminal building. This was the jumping off point for those western tourists with enough money and a lot less sense, to head off into the Himalayas and find something they couldn't back in Britain, New Zealand, or some other British colonial country. Billy was the odd man out, as the only American in the group.

Dean Reed was a different type of tourist altogether. The Dean had struck up a conversation with a handsome young man from Ojai, California of all places. He had learned a great deal from this fellow on the bumpy flight across Europe to the Pakistani countryside.

Billy del Toro was mostly a surf bum from a wealthy family that owned large tracts of land in Southern California. This allowed Billy to join the leisure class and to afford to jet clear across the face of the earth and try his hand at climbing the freaking tall mountains of the Himalayas; more than twice the height of the Sierra Nevada range back home in California.

Billy followed the Dean down the jetway stairs to the hot asphalt tarmac.

"Best of luck to you on your climbing expedition, Billy," The Dean said.

"Thanks Dean. I also wish you well on saving the languages you are seeking out," Billy replied graciously.

"Whenever you are in New York City look me up" the Dean said as he extended his hand in friendship.

"I will indeed," Billy said shaking the Dean's hand and not knowing if he'd ever see the Dean again.

Kim Reed had made several trips to Pakistan, so he knew his way around. As he had done on past trips, he arranged for local handlers to pick him up at the airport.

Saeed's and Chanal's Apartment in Islamabad
Two Days Earlier

"Oh no! I don't feel good about this," Chanal exclaimed pacing back and forth across the dimly lit dining room floor. Her belly expanded by her womb carrying their first child; a boy.

"Don't worry. Everything will be okay. I've got it totally under control," Saeed stated with his false bravado. "Besides, we need the extra money to feed and clothe our little bundle of joy, he said, bending over and talking to Chanal's belly and finishing the sentence in a baby talk voice. Saeed was more upbeat about the prospect of having a child once he learned that it would be a boy. The baby talk was a recent addition to his usual antics. She granted him this minor indulgence. Although, she had no choice. Saeed always got his way with her.

"What if you get caught? Then what are we going to do?" Chanal pressed further, worried that Saeed didn't have it all figured out.

"I'm not going to get caught," Saeed said in frustration at being second-guessed by a woman.

"I don't know…Do you know the penalty for messing with these Islamic extremists? They only have one penalty, it seems: death."

"Those extremists are a bunch of assholes. They don't know what they are doing," Saeed said continuing with his mightier than thou attitude.

"Yeah, but they have guns and they are very trigger-happy."

"Listen, I said I have it under control," he said, reaching out to give Chanal a reassuring hug. The hugs had become less frequent since Chanal gained weight during her pregnancy.

*   *   *

It had just rained, which was common for this time of year. The asphalt pavement on the jam-packed road in front of the Islamabad International Airport, gave off a humidity that soaked your clothing. Kim had gotten used to the feeling. He looked forward to touching the wet skin of the young men he was about to meet. As he began to daydream of the waiting wanton pleasures, the honk of a car horn brought him back.

"Professor! Professor!" Saeed yelled above the din of the scrum of cars that packed the frontage road and made driving nearly impossible.

Kim turned and saw Saeed waving as he stood beside the open door of his beat up faded pale green Toyota Corolla sedan. The Dean grabbed the handle of his roller bag and moved in the direction of the waiting car. Saeed left the car running and ignored the angry honking of the other cars he was blocking as he came running to the aid of the most esteemed Dean.

"Oh, Professor I am so happy to see you again," Saeed exclaimed grabbing Kim's hand and shaking it with both of his as he gently bowed, bobbing like a bobble head.

"Good to see you as well, Saeed."

"Let me take your bag. The car is ready."

"Yes, I can see that, Kim grimaced a little embarrassed that his ride had created a traffic jam, making vehicular movement impossible. They both jogged back to the car. Saeed opened the trunk and lifted Kim's bag. He tossed it in the trunk and slammed the hood closed.

"Wow, that's a heavy bag!"

"Yes," Kim explained, "I plan to be here for a couple of weeks."

The sedan was decorated in traditional Pakistani style with red dingle balls festooned from all the windows. With this being his fifth trip to Pakistan, Kim was well accustomed to the idiosyncrasies of the Pakistani ways and customs. On his first few trips it all seemed quite odd to a guy from Southern Utah. Now he was a seasoned pro and these things just faded into the landscape.

Kim slid into the backseat. The front seat was piled high with miscellaneous junk. Saeed got into the car but before doing so flipped off all the people he had been blocking with the common Pakistani insult by raising his right hand with his fingers spread apart. The insult is loosely translated as, "You may know who your mother is but anyone of the five could be your father."

The roadway was packed, and the Dean was exhausted from his long trip from New York. Since they weren't moving too fast, he put his head back on the seat rest. Pakistani drivers think it is important to honk their horn, as it is to use the brake pedal. A nearly continuous blaring of horns and five-finger gestures accompanied them to the Dean's hotel. Saeed was certainly not immune to this practice and employed it frequently.

Downtown Islamabad was a noisy, dirty place - the complete opposite of Southern Utah. Kim enjoyed the contrast and freedom that came with being away from the confines and mores of the United States. He was still very naïve, however. Even though he fully embraced his newfound sexuality, in Pakistan he didn't recognize the sinister forces that would conspire against him. In his mind, he mistakenly replaced his denial of sexuality with a sense of himself as being worldly, with the ability to assimilate into this new bizarre culture.

International Hotel, Islamabad

"Professor! Professor! We are here," Saeed said reaching behind the front seat and gently nudging Kim as they pulled into the driveway of the five-star hotel. A five-star rating in Pakistan pretty much equated to having indoor plumbing and very gaudy architecture. There was certainly no comparison to the rating of American hotels. What it lacked in grandeur and ambience it made up for in helpers. Servants were everywhere. It took a little getting used to, but the professor quickly got the knack of it and enjoyed having someone do pretty much everything for him. Unfortunately, an American could get spoiled with this kind of treatment and it was certainly an adjustment Kim had to make when he got back to the States.

Kim had fallen asleep in the back of the car despite the constant blasting of car horns and five-finger gestures. He awoke a little groggy and replied back to Saeed, "Thanks for taking care of the arrangements, you are a good friend."

Saeed nodded at the complement but felt a slight pain of guilt inside at being called a "good friend."

The professor was well known as a big tipper. He unwittingly fell into this on his first trip to Pakistan. Not fully understanding the value of the currency, and the average take-home pay of a helper, he kept handing out coins the size of an American quarter; thinking that this was a reasonable tip for someone that just opened the door for you, and not much else. He didn't realize at the time that the coin he so freely handed out, represented almost a full day's pay for the very poor helpers that hung around the hotel looking to be of assistance to wealthy guests. The professor obtained the best service of any westerner that had visited Islamabad in some time.

It was not until he was ready to leave that one of the helpers he tipped pointed out the folly of the professor's largesse. Kim was so touched by the honesty of this helper, that he sought him out on his next trip. Kim felt that if this young man would bring to his attention a practice that would cut into his own earning potential, he was a person with honesty and integrity. These traits were in general shortage in the Third World, as far as Kim was concerned. This young man was Saeed. Over time the Dean relied more and more on Saeed's assistance. And Saeed was certainly accommodating. This trip would be no exception.

The bellhop, who immediately opened the trunk and carried the professor's bags inside, opened the car door. Saeed was Kim's handler and took care of all of the mundane tasks, such as administering the tips. Much to the chagrin of the helpers, Saeed was not as generous as the professor had once been. The doorman opened the large front door for Kim and his small entourage of helpers. The smell of curry greeted them as they entered the main foyer. Kim had become accustomed to the smell, as it lingered everywhere, even in his clothes. Luckily, the olfactory nerves take pity on you by diminishing the unpleasant smell over a short period of time.

"Oh Dr. Reed. So wonderful that you can join us again," came the greeting of the front desk clerk. "We're hoping you have a wonderful stay with us."

Saeed approached the desk and filled in the guest registration book. Kim learned that he had to allow the help to do as many of these tasks as possible. It took Kim a little getting used to, but he now considered himself a seasoned pro. If he did the small things himself, the help would think that he was cutting into their rice bowl, so to speak. Thus, Kim allowed Saeed free reign in those areas.

"بہت بہت شکریہ", *Thank you very much,* Kim replied to the desk clerk in flawless Urdu. He had even learned the speech inflection of the local accent and applied it masterfully. Kim, Saeed, and one of the helpers - that managed to cut off the others clamoring for the professor's attention - all crammed into the small elevator that took them to the penthouse suite. Even though the smell was very stale in the elevator, Kim hesitated when the elevator door opened.

"This is not my usual floor," he said, remembering the explicit instructions he had given to Saeed, when he was planning his trip.

"Yes, Professor. I booked you into the master suite. Only the best for you, you know," Saeed replied slyly, as he exited the elevator and motioned the professor to follow. "You can put the bags there," Saeed directed the bellhop. He handed the bellhop his tip and said, "That will be all for now."

Kim and Saeed were left alone. "Saeed you have been most helpful as usual," Kim said reaching out to shake Saeed's hand. "I'm going to freshen up and I'll call on you later."

"But of course, Professor. You know you can call me anytime, day or night. I'll leave the key on the table beside the front door."

"Yes, that will be fine."

Kim was alone in the master suite. It was much bigger than he needed, and he thought back to when he was making the arrangements with Saeed, hoping that the suite did not cost him more than the regular room he stayed in the last time. He thought it a little odd. *What the hell, celebrate a little,* he thought to himself, relieved that he had finally made it.

The long trip from New York made Kim's skin grimy, and he decided to take a shower. There wasn't much water pressure from the showerhead, but it felt good to wash away the oil and sweat from the long day's travel. He started to stroke himself, fantasizing of the fun he was planning on having. He lathered up and was stroking faster but decided not to come because he wanted to save every drop of semen for the real encounters he was going to have with the young Pakistani boys he craved. This was the main reason for his trip. The linguistics study was really just a sideshow, a guise, to cover for his wanton cravings.

Kim stepped out of the shower, reaching for a white terry cloth towel that hung on the towel rack, as he dried his body and his still rigid member. He then remembered the cologne he brought with him. He wanted to wear it for this special occasion, and to be fully rested for the night ahead. So, he went into the bedroom and laid down on the huge king bed. Kim's exhaustion put him fast to sleep within moments of his head touching the pillow.

Kim woke in the dark to the strange sounds of the city below. It was rare that the air conditioning worked and so the large windows were left open to allow a breeze to cascade through his room carrying the sounds and smells Kim had grown accustomed to. The venetian blinds partially obscured the city's light and it took him a little while to orient himself and to realize that he was in Pakistan. He rolled onto his back and put his hands behind his head. Kim thought back to the months that had just passed. To the preparation and anticipation that went into this trip. And here he was. Kim reached for the bedside lamp and turned it on. He sat up and turned his feet to the floor as he dialed the phone. Kim was ready for the fun to begin.

"Hello professor, I was expecting your call," Saeed said as he answered the phone.

"I'm ready to go out for dinner," Kim said as he cleared his throat.

"But of course. I'll be right over," Saeed said hanging up the phone and not waiting for a reply.

Kim had just finished getting dressed when he heard a light knock on the door.

"My, that didn't take much time at all," he said as he opened the door to his patiently waiting servant.

"Indeed. I moved my apartment. I now live closer to the hotel. I can now take the back way to get here. I planned a wonderful dinner for you, that I know you will really enjoy," Saeed beamed knowing that the professor would be happy with his services and preparations.

"Sounds great. Let's go," Kim said excitedly knowing that Saeed had planned for some real entertainment, the kind of entertainment that he liked. Kim didn't keep his sexuality hidden from Saeed, who realized the income he could make catering to Kim's sex trade.

It didn't take long to get to the restaurant. Saeed valeted his car. As Kim exited the backseat, he could hear sitar music playing from the live band inside. Kim didn't particularly care for the local indigenous music. Being from the west he preferred country music; the old stuff, like Hank Williams, Loretta Lynn, and Johnny Cash. Although, he didn't think that contemporary 'country music' was 'country music' at all. He joked that it was 'bad rock music with a fiddle." He let the sitar music fade out of his mind as he entered the restaurant. He was there to have a good time, and he wasn't going to let some annoying music spoil his evening, as the powerful smell of curry hit him full on.

The host had been expecting them, and immediately showed them to their table, up front, and close to the band.

As the dark-skinned Pakistani host handed out the menus, Kim asked in flawless Urdu, "آپ کے اچھے ساتھی کی کیا رائے ہے", meaning: what do you recommend, my good fellow?"

"Oh, professor. We are so honored that you are able to join us this evening. You simply must try the lamb curry. It is the best in the whole city of Islamabad," the host said, in broken English.

Kim was used to the hyperbole from Pakistanis and replied with a wry smile, "Yeah, somehow I thought it was going to come down to that," as he began to chuckle at his inside joke.

Saeed smiled back at the professor but didn't get the joke. As it turned out, he didn't get a lot of the things that pleased the professor. But he paid well, and Saeed was proud that the professor allowed and trusted him to make the arrangements.

Kim did in fact enjoy the lamb he was served. The spices were diminished by the copious amounts of coconut yogurt that he consumed to wash the curry down.

While they were having their after-dinner coffee Saeed said, "I've made arrangements at a new club, that I know you will enjoy. It is new and one of the best in town." Having served the professor for a number of years, Saeed had grown out of the Pakistani habit of gross exaggeration. He knew that the professor was an easy sell and would go along with pretty much anything he planned as long as it led to the ultimate prize.

"Oh, splendid," Kim replied, trying to contain his excitement as his skin became flushed thinking of the fun that lay ahead.

"It is right next door, so we can walk there," Saeed said knowing that he had 'done good,' as they say in Southern Utah.

*   *   *

Middle eastern rock music came from speakers that had a broken tweeter. If the sitar music got on the professor's nerves the music distorted in the high frequencies was really going to test his patience. Kim and Saeed had to talk loudly, right next to each other's ear, in order to be heard over the blaring music and the chatter from the packed house. Two young men immediately came up to Kim and simultaneously said, "Can we get you something to drink?"

"Sure. Saeed, what do you want?"

191

"I'll have Perrier water, thank you," Saeed said having acquired a taste for the finer things in life since meeting the professor.

"Same for me," Kim motioned to the two servers in front of him.

Chapter 22

The one thing a government worker doesn't want to do is work a lot of overtime. So, the call went out to hire new staff to the New York branch of the FBI. Seasoned veterans from other offices with seniority could pass on these undesirable assignments. Rookies were the first to be called, and unlike his colleagues Mark jumped at the chance to be in New York: The Big Apple. His attitude was *a bloody war was the way to a quick promotion.* Being a recent graduate of the FBI Academy, and graduating with honors near the top of his class, Mark was welcomed to the New York office. They initially treated him like a superstar that was drafted out of the minors to win 20 games for the Yankees.

At first, Mark was a little taken back at the depravity that took place in the underworld. There were strict laws that governed the work of an FBI Agent. However, with a slight tilt in his moral compass, Mark soon discovered ways around all the rules. He actually felt it was his duty to get results, regardless of the rules and procedures.

There are countless hidden services available on the dark web, for a price. This notorious online marketplace served as a modern-day Silk Road, and Mark was going to be Marco Polo and find all the illegal trade; everything from drugs to weapons, to porn.

To find this illicit trade, Mark had to discover the trade methods that were being used. Of course, none of this stuff was in the FBI Field Manual. Mark enjoyed the challenge and he thought it ironic that the basic architecture of the dark web had been created by the U.S. government to store and share classified information amongst those who had the proper security clearance. Back in the day, encrypted data was routed through countless servers making it virtually impossible to trace the online activity back to a specific person or location. One needed both the decoding software and the correct access codes to retrieve the data.

Now the private marketplace operated the really cool stuff. The dark web, as put in place by people in the private sector, was a way to make a buck and keep out of the sight from guys like Mark. However, on the modern-day Silk Road there needed to be some honor among the thieves. Out of necessity, escrow services had been created to keep paying customers from being ripped off. The Internet is full of scam artists. But the dark web had the worst ones, including plenty of pasty skinned juveniles in their mother's basements trying to hack into the system just for pure sport. Their motives were to create as much mayhem as possible.

On the other hand, computer savvy hipsters were highly entrepreneurial. They ran the online escrow services because they could remain anonymous and could keep the transactions untraceable. To do this, 'onion routers' were set up in a series to anonymously forward traffic. The routers had been designed to only have knowledge of the router immediately upstream and downstream, and no further, making it extremely difficult and time consuming (for a G-man like Mark) to trace a transaction. The path to the destination server was completely random, and it disguised the Internet provided address. If all this didn't make it hard enough to trace, all the data was encrypted and was in a format that prevented it from being saved on a hard drive.

In spite of the obstacles, Mark certainly dove into his work. He had dated a few times using various Internet dating sites, but he found that the women he dated were all interested in getting married and settling down. The only thing Mark was married to was his career and to getting ahead. As a person of malleable scruples Mark quickly learned the ways of the corrupt world. He twisted the FBI's rules in the name of getting results. And boy did he thrive. Mark started small and the brass turned a blind eye to the very questionable techniques he used. This tacit approval only emboldened Mark to stretch, bend, and break the rules even more.

It wasn't long before Mark was investigating the B of U, not knowing that this was the bank that Bryce worked for. A few routine loans to a Dubai Sheikh came to the Bureau's attention and Mark was assigned to investigate irregularities in the paperwork that was required to be submitted to the New York Department of Commerce. Most Agents at the Bureau hated this type of work. It was dull and monotonous and just added more misery to their already monotonous and dull lives. Mark didn't look at it in this way at all. He was taught at the FBI Academy, in one of the numerous classes that covered the illegal activities of unscrupulous people, to trace the complete circle. What at first may appear to be incomplete paperwork would inevitably lead to something larger in an ever-expanding array of corruption. Mark was so infatuated with the case that he took his laptop home to his apartment in the lower Bronx, to continue his work.

Mark's Apartment, Lower Bronx, N.Y.

Mark lived in a crummy neighborhood, which was about all a rookie Agent at the Manhattan Bureau could afford. There were areas of the Bronx that were being populated by hipsters but somehow Mark's part of the city was left out of the gentrification craze. This was okay with him at the time, because he didn't socialize much and it kept his rent low, even if the garbage was piled high on the street.

The bell rang on the microwave oven signaling, once again, that Mark's dinner of canned Campbell's cream of corn soup was ready. Mark used oven mitts to carry the hot bowl to the little Ikea kitchen table. He blew over the top of the bowl in an effort to cool the soup. His laptop was already opened, and he had just finished logging into the Bureau's website. He composed a well-written and concise email to the Turkish Investigation Agency's Bureau Chief in Ankara Turkey asking what he knew about the Islamic Sheikh he was investigating. Satisfied with his email, he sent it off and picked up the spoon to ladle some soup into his hungrily awaiting mouth.

High atop a golden skyscraper in midtown Manhattan, Bryce had worked at the Bank of Uppsala for over ten years since graduating from college. Life at the office was hectic, which made the days go by quickly. This was fine with Bryce. He felt he knew a lot when he first came to the bank. They liked his swagger and his slightly cocky attitude, which fit in well with the brash New Yorkers that worked there. Bryce tried hard to hide the surfer boy in him, which at times wasn't hard to do. It was December - the end of the year, and Bryce knew that the bank took a tally of how well they did that year.

A Senior Vice President from Sweden flew in to oversee the final audit of the New York office. The whole office was in a twitter over his presence. Bryce didn't seem to notice and continued as usual. He went to work early. He was an early riser - part of the surfer culture he was trying to hide. Most days, he was the first in and had to unlock the main office door.

It was early on a Friday morning and Bryce unlocked the front door and closed and locked it behind him. His office was down the hall, away from the reception area. Floor to ceiling glass lined his office, he had a clear view to the east. The sun was rising, and the sky was glowing a brilliant red in the distance. Bryce turned on his computer and began to scan the spreadsheet he was looking at the night before. Something just didn't make sense, so he wanted to go over it first thing.

"Hello Bryce," came a voice with a foreign accent.

Bryce looked up from his computer screen a little startled because he didn't think anyone else was in the office that early. At the doorway was the Senior Vice President from Sweden.

"Oh hello, beautiful day," Bryce said in his friendly California way.

"Yes, it is indeed. Mind if I interrupt?" the Senior V.P. said trying to appear like he was just one of the guys in the office.

"No - not at all. I was just checking this spreadsheet that wasn't quite adding up."

"I'm Ulf Samuellson from headquarters."

"Yes, I know. I'm Bryce. Bryce St. James from Ojai," Bryce replied rising from his seat and extending his hand. "Please, have a seat."

"Oh, I won't stay long," Ulf said taking a seat. "You're in early."

"Yes, it's just a habit of getting up early. The best waves are early in the morning before the onshore winds pick up."

"Hmm. I'm not sure what that means."

"I'm from California. And I surfed a lot. Or I used to before I moved to New York."

"Oh, yes I see. You're the up and coming talent I've heard so much about," Ulf said, knowing full well who Bryce was, but pretending otherwise.

"I hope some of it was positive," Bryce said jokingly.

"Oh yes. Yes indeed. In fact, all of it was positive. Very impressive stuff."

"Well that's good to hear," Bryce said smiling, knowing it was always a positive career move to make the boss happy.

"Do you like it here?" Ulf asked in an open-ended way.

Bryce measured the man in front of him before he replied. Here was a Senior Vice President wearing jeans, loafers, and an opened collar white pressed dress shirt sitting down to chit chat with a young staff member.

"Yes, I do. I do indeed. I am learning something new every day and trying my best to make a contribution."

"Well, Bryce we certainly appreciate all of your efforts. If there is anything you need, or want to talk, please feel free to call me. The Bank of Uppsala is a privately held company and thus immune to the quarterly fluctuations that seem to grip the publicly traded banks. We are in it for the long haul and avoid the up and down cycles of the crazy marketplace that we work in."

"Thanks for your offer Mr. Samuellson."

"Please, call me Ulf."

"Will do."

And with that, Ulf rose up and extended his hand. "So good to chat with you Bryce. I see a bright future here for you at the B of U."

"Thank you, sir." Bryce said giving Ulf a firm handshake. And with that Ulf turned and exited the office, but not Bryce's thoughts.

Main Conference Room, Bank of Uppsala, Manhattan

Later that afternoon, the New York Branch Manager called for a general staff meeting. There was already a large crowd assembled when Bryce arrived in the large conference room, which was enormous. Even so, the room wasn't large enough to hold everyone in the office, so many of the staff had to stand in the hall. Bryce was fortunate enough to be inside the conference room but was too late to get a seat. So, he stood against the wall on the far end of the room.

"Thanks for coming," the Branch Manager began. "As most of you know, we had our yearly audit and Mr. Ulf Samuellson from the head office in Sweden was here for a few days to oversee it. I am pleased to announce that the audit is complete, and the New York office has once again made a record profit."

A gasp of enthusiasm and chatter rose upon hearing the good news.

"Mr. Samuellson had to catch a flight back to Sweden, so he couldn't join us this afternoon. He told me to tell you that he is extremely pleased with our performance and wishes everyone a happy holiday and joyous Christmas. With that out of the way, I want to make sure everyone will be able to attend our office Christmas party tonight. As most of you know it will be at the Waldorf Astoria just down the street. And in anticipation of the expected exuberant celebrating we are covering the cost of everyone's cab fare. We want to make sure you make it home safely and report to work on Monday, to make even more money for the company." The boss said jokingly.

The assembled crowd laughed, because it was always a good career move to laugh at the boss' jokes and the din rose again, drowning out the office manager, so he had to shout, "Thanks for coming. The meeting is over. See you all tonight." And with that invitation, the branch manager got up and made his way through the crowd out of the conference room.

To further raise Christmas spirits, and as was traditional in the company since its founding, Christmas bonus checks were given to each employee after the branch audit was completed. The company founders thought that was one of the most important and concrete ways to show your employees, who worked all year for the benefit of the company, that their contribution mattered.

And so, when Bryce returned to his office, he noticed that a new email had arrived from the company's payroll department. Attached to the email was a 'thank you' note from the company Senior Vice President, in charge of New York affairs, Mr. Ulf Samuellson. Also, attached was the deposit slip of a fat bonus check that amounted to about five eighths of Bryce's annual salary. Bryce was blown away. He leaned back in his chair and just let the feeling of Christmas joy wash over him. He thought about calling Tina to share the good news but decided against it. He had made his choice and boy, was he going to party that night to celebrate his wise career move.

Chapter 23

Waldorf Astoria, Manhattan
Friday December 12, 2014

Bryce hailed a cab on Lexington Avenue just in front of the office. A Checker Marathon cut across four lanes to come to a screeching stop just in front of him.

"Where to?" asked the cabbie as Bryce climbed into the back.

"The Waldorf, please."

"You're not from here?" the cabbie asked, looking back and not paying attention to traffic as he raced forward into the eight-lane maze of cars.

"No, no I'm not. How can you tell?"

"New Yorkers never say please," the cabbie laughed as he honked the horn to help in the flow of traffic, in typical New York style.

Bryce sat back and thought of the day he had just had. He was gazing off looking at the streetscape as his mind tuned in the music coming from the cabbie's boom box.

"What's that you're playing on the radio?" Bryce asked.

"Oh, that's a recording of my recital at Carnegie Hall. I'm playing Eric Satie's Gymnopedie No. 3," the cabbie said, again looking back and not paying attention to traffic.

"Really? Wow! Very beautiful I must say you have real talent. So, if you have this incredible musical talent, why are you driving a cab?"

"Why, thank you! Now I really know you're not from here. New Yorkers never give compliments. Well I'm driving a cab to pay off my student loan. It costs a small fortune to go to The Juilliard, even with a scholarship. Being a musician just doesn't cut it."

Listening to the cabbie, Bryce was glad that he didn't pursue a career in music. He remembered that his teacher thought he had tremendous musical talent in his youth. Bryce continued to daydream about the incredibly terrific day he had. He was in a weird mood when he arrived at the Waldorf. He took the company up on their cab fare offer and gave the cabbie a huge tip; way more than is customary - even during Christmas time.

"Gee, thanks mister! Merry Christmas to you," the cabbie said leaning out the window.

"And you as well," Bryce said as he closed the cab door and turned to walk up the granite stairs to the excitement of the company's Christmas party. Bryce was a free, and very eligible bachelor, although not exactly by choice. His brief tryst with a ballerina from the New York Ballet had just ended.

She dumped him with a non-ceremonial text, which read, "I think this is over. It's just not going to work for me."

Bryce wasn't too upset. He agreed that their brief relationship wasn't going to work either. Although he had to admit, the sex was fantastic. He was amazed at how she could contort herself to get into those crazy positions. Well that was then, and Bryce was ready to move on, but the night was for celebration, and not to dwell on the past.

"Good evening sir," said the concierge as Bryce entered the hotel lobby. The place was festooned with spruce garlands and a very large well decorated Christmas tree. The Christmas tree rose to the height of at least 20 feet, with an angel on top. Bryce could smell the spruce and the hardwood burning in an unbelievably large fireplace, that made the place smell like the Hudson River Lodge.

"Ah yes, good evening. The --"

"The Bank of Uppsala party, I presume?" Came the reply from the concierge finishing Bryce's sentence.

"Yes. How did you know?"

"A number of guests have already arrived looking very happy and festive. You look very happy and festive, so voilà."

"Well, my good man you are very astute," Bryce said handing the concierge a tip for having done pretty much nothing but be astute, and a little rude.

"Straight down the hallway on the far side of the lobby, first door to the right. You'll be in the Empire State Ballroom."

"Okay, thanks," Bryce said as he started walking across the foyer.

Bryce could hear the music and laughter of the early party crowd. It turned out that Bryce was one of the last to arrive, even though he wasn't late. Officially, the party wasn't supposed to start for another twenty minutes. However, the tradition in the New York office was to start the celebration pretty much right after the staff meeting, and of course after the bonus checks arrived.

Bryce hadn't noticed the staff sneak out of the office; he was too focused on the paper trail of this loan to the Sheikh. Something just wasn't adding up, so Bryce knew that he had to do some forensic accounting to get the paperwork in order to be able to submit it to the New York Commerce Commission. He tried to push that aside and get into the holiday spirit. Not that he was in a funk, even though his girlfriend had just dumped him. He was single again and it was time to party and have some fun.

When he entered the ballroom, the music was thunderous. He knew in past years the older guys always hired a New York jazz band to play live, but the times were changing. The company wanted the up-and-coming talent to start making decisions, so the hipsters decided to hire one of New York's hottest DJs. And so, the music of the hip, alcohol charged generation came pumping out of the loudspeakers.

After a long day of looking at numbers that didn't add up, Bryce needed a stiff drink. He made his way over to the bar and as he did all his colleagues either shook his hand, slapped him on the back, or gave him a hug. He certainly liked all the beautiful women giving him a hug. By that point, the women had a little too much to drink so their hugs were a little harder and more personal than professional decorum would otherwise dictate. The company had over two hundred staff in the New York office. Bryce was struck by the fact that he knew so many of them. He met most of the staff by working on different assignments and by taking on more responsibility. He finally made it over to the open bar.

"Three fingers of rye and seven, please," Bryce asked the bartender as he placed a twenty-dollar bill in the tip jar. Bryce thought it was always good karma to spread the wealth.

"Yes sir. Coming right up. Thank you, sir," the bartender nodded, seeing the large tip.

Three fingers to start was a lot, but Bryce felt like celebrating.

"Here you go, sir. Three fingers of the good stuff, black label," said the bartender sliding the drink across the polished countertop.

Bryce lifted the drink and nodded back to the bartender, "Merry Christmas," as he took his first sip of the stiff drink.

"Merry Christmas, sir," said the barkeep.

Bryce turned and faced the stage. The DJ was playing, "Sexy Mother Fucker," by Prince. At these large corporate events you weren't allowed to play any music that could possibly offend anyone. So that meant no Christmas carols - religious freedom protocols. It was alright to play Prince, but not Bing Crosby. Modern times…go figure.

After the first taste of booze Bryce dropped his shoulders and tried to relax. *Christ, what an intense day*, he thought to himself. *It's Christmas time and everyone is enjoying it, so I need to get into the Christmas spirit too.* And with each sip of his drink the stress of the day started to fade.

"Let's get out of this corporate bullshit party and have some real fun," said the man that was pulling on Bryce's arm, directing him to the door.

"But I just got here..." Bryce's voice tapered off as he allowed himself to be pulled by the man to the entrance coat check. All Bryce could see was the back of the guy's head and he was trying to figure out who it was. After a brief stint of weaving through partygoers they arrived at the coat check. The guy stopped pulling Bryce's arm and turned around. Bryce could now see that it was the guy from the North Carolina office that he had met just a week or so before.

"Quick, quick let's get our coats and go to a place with some real excitement. A bunch of us from the New York office are going."

On this command Bryce reached into the breast pocket of his suit coat and produced a coat check ticket and handed it to Lars Anderson, a transplant from Sweden, now stationed in Charlotte. Once the older gentleman fetched their coats, with a slight limp and a hunched back, Lars gave him a tip and he and Bryce were off. They headed out of the main ballroom entrance and Bryce turned to go back into the hotel foyer. Again, Lars grabbed Bryce's arm.

"No, this way. Out the back."

Club 69, Manhattan

Bryce was impressed that Lars seemed to know his way around. Lars swung open the side entrance door to the chill of the New York night and a waiting limo. A very gentle snow was falling, and the alleyway was now dusted in a white powder. Bryce was starting to feel the Christmas spirit as he and Lars climbed into the limo. Bryce's eyes needed to adjust to the darkness of the limo. He couldn't make out the faces, but he could tell that not everyone in the limo was male, and he was glad that it wasn't going to be a 'sausage party'. Nellie's "Hot in Here" was playing too loud and the sub-woofer was thrusting out the bass.

Over the din, Lars shouted to the driver, "Everyone's here, off to the party!"

A cheer rose from the crowd as the limo driver waved receipt of Lars' direction and sped off into the New York night cutting a swath through the snow flurries.

The three fingers of rye whisky had taken hold of Bryce. The limo swerved through traffic as it sped to their destination, wherever that was. At this point in time Bryce was just along for the ride. He tried to strike up a conversation with the attractive young lady next to him - while trying not to be distracted by the intoxicating aroma of her perfume - but the music was so loud that they just ended up shouting at each other; and even then, they didn't really know what the other person was saying.

In what seemed like no time at all, the limo slowed and turned into a dark alley. They crept along slowly making a crunching sound on the fallen snow. Then an automatic garage door opened, and the limo disappeared into the cavern. A soft yellow light gave off an eerie glow. The limo stopped, and the garage door closed behind them. Bryce had absolutely no idea where they were. The group of about twelve alighted the limo. The garage was a little chilly due to the cold coming from the outside air vent. The small group headed for a red painted door directly ahead of the limo.

Lars held Bryce's elbow and whispered in his ear, "The big man himself got the club owner as one of his first clients when the B of U opened its first U.S. branch here in New York. The club owner always throws the best parties, and a select group from the office is invited. You must have impressed the boss." And with that, Lars let go of Bryce's arm and caught up with the hot young lady that sat next to Bryce on the limo ride to the club.

Bryce's gait slowed slightly as his neurons competed with the three fingers of rye to try and assimilate the information he was just told: *the big man? The big man?* Bryce thought to himself. *Does he mean Ulf Samuellson?*

By the time Bryce reached this postulate he was already inside the club, and the entire entourage from the limo had passed him. The door swung open and he saw a glimmer of light and heard a waft of thumping music escape.

The bouncer opened the door for Bryce, "Good evening, sir. Have a wonderful time."

"Thanks," Bryce replied stuffing a twenty-dollar bill into the man's very large hand, with fingers the size of German sausages.

Max Frost's, "White Lies" was playing as the door closed behind Bryce and he again had to adjust his eyes to the inside light. It didn't help much that there was a strobe light blinking, which caused everyone's motions to look robotic. A faint scent of marijuana filled the atmosphere and Bryce thought to himself, *you're not in Ojai anymore. Just relax and have a good time. And don't do anything stupid.*

Mark's Apartment, Bronx, N.Y.

Across town Mark just finished his dinner and turned off his FBI issued laptop. The floor of his fifth-floor walk-up squeaked as he walked across it. He could hear his neighbors above, beside, and below him. The older couple next door were the worst. They would fight at all hours of the day or night. The walls were so thin Mark could hear every bickering conversation like they were all in the same room. At times, the fighting got so bad Mark felt like he should call the cops, and he wondered why the couple even stayed together if they were so incompatible.

Mark went to the bedroom of his one-bedroom apartment. At least it was on the opposite side of the bickering couple's apartment. He turned on the Ikea desk lamp and booted his own Toshiba desktop PC. There were multiple levels of firewalls and passwords necessary to get to the desktop page. It had been a long day and Mark needed to unwind.

When Mark was doing research on the main computer at work, he often transferred case files to his FBI laptop. Mark would claim that he came by the files innocently enough but that was irrelevant, it was against standard protocol; something he had little regard for. The Bureau had been investigating a child pornography ring run out of the warehouse district in Queens with ties to the Russian mafia. Mark did in fact come upon the files by accident when he was doing his own research on bank fraud. In a moment of moral lapse (which happened often), he downloaded the files to a stick-drive, so he could later copy them to his own PC.

The files from the stick drive finished loading on the PC's hard disc. Mark started to go through the thousands of images by clicking on photos of young Russian children. The photos were of teenage boys and girls who looked to be in their teens – 14 to 17 years old. Mark knew that even possession of these photos was a serious offense. A first-time offense for possession of child pornography faced a statutory minimum of five years in prison. Since he was an FBI Agent, sworn to uphold the law, he could easily get twenty years, no question.

Prior to leaving the kitchen, Mark had poured himself a stiff drink of Kentucky bourbon straight over two ice cubes. He took long sips of the bourbon and studied the photos. There were a couple thousand and Mark took his time going through them. He knew it was wrong on so many levels, but he started to get aroused and excited experiencing the absolutely illicit nature of the porn. As he clicked through the photos, he made a mental note of the ones he liked best. It took over an hour for him to click through most of the photos that were in the folder. Some he just flicked through, but others he would spend a little time studying and zooming in for a closer look.

He finished his drink and went back into the kitchen to make himself another. When he returned from the kitchen with the second drink, he stood next to the table. The room was dark, except for the light coming from the computer screen. He decided to close the curtains, being paranoid that someone was watching, and he would be caught.

The computer screen light created a faint glow that lit Mark's face. He studied the photo on the screen and took a gulp of bourbon and then set the drink down on the table. A condensation ring formed on the table from the cool glass, as he undid his belt and the button on his pants. He pushed his pants and underwear down below his knees. His erection moved out, away from his thick black pubic hair, with the tip glistening in the light of the photo. Mark sat down on the chair. He lifted his left hand to his mouth and licked it. Then he moved his wet hand down between his legs and started to stroke his erection and became fixated on the photo of two teenage boys, possibly sixteen, jerking off each other. There was a series of photos of the two boys in various sexual poses. He went through the photo deck making a note that this series of photos aroused him the most.

He clicked through the photos, and as he did his breathing became more pronounced. His pulse increased with the increased pace of his hand stroking his tool. He clicked on a photo of one of the boys giving the other a blowjob. The photo showed the boy's hand cupped around the other boy's balls. Each boy had the first indications of adolescent pubic hair.

Mark stroked himself furiously and arched his back as he shot his load out of his stiff tool, which almost hit the computer screen. His head was spinning with excitement from the porn and the two glasses of bourbon. The wet sticky goo covered his left hand and made a mess on the table and floor. Just as soon as he had relaxed and slunk back into the chair, he felt a slight pang of guilt. He quickly cleaned up ejaculate and permanently deleted all the photos he had downloaded from the FBI evidence folder. He scrubbed the stick drive and his PC's hard drive to remove all evidence that the photos had once been in his possession.

Chapter 24

Club 69, Manhattan
Friday December 12, 2014

A waitress wearing only body paint, a few strategically placed sequins, and a feather boa sashayed up to Bryce with a silver tray of drinks crooked in her left arm. With her right arm, she gently grabbed Bryce's silk scarf and put her face right up to his and said with the deepest sultry voice he had ever heard, "New in town, sailor?" And she gave him a quick kiss on the lips. Not waiting for an answer, she did a pirouette on her spiked high heels and as she turned, she took a glass from the tray and glided it into Bryce's hand without spilling a drop. "See you topside, lover-boy," as she blew him another kiss, and then was off.

Not quite knowing what to make of all of this, Bryce took a sip of the vodka martini cocktail he was just handed. He knew this was a classy place by the way the lemon twist was stabbed with the little cocktail sword. As he lifted the glass to his mouth, he saw that a crowd had gathered in front of him standing around what seemed like a round glass enclosure.

The coolness of the drink was refreshing. As he came closer to the crowd, he was able to confirm that the glass enclosure was about 25 feet in diameter. The crowd was at least two persons deep, spread around the circular extent of the class. All the lights went out for a brief moment and Justin Timberlake's "Sexy Back" started to play. Then a small spotlight lit the far side of the enclosure and a black door opened at the back of the enclosure.

The crowd pressed up to the glass to get a better look. Bryce was caught up in the moment and moved forward as well. By coincidence, the young lady that sat next to him on the limo ride over to the club was on his right, and Lars was just off to the right of her. They didn't notice Bryce as they stared into the enclosure. Bryce started to think that perhaps those two were an item. But the music was so loud that Bryce couldn't think or hear anything else, but he could sense the harmonic movement of the glass wall keeping rhythm to the beat of the music. Then two male and one female dancers emerged from the far opening and the black door immediately closed behind them by an unseen hand.

The dancers twirled and strutted to the beat of the music, "I'm your slave. I'll let you whip me if I misbehave..."

The two guys were buff and wore tight-fitting black suits with straight pant legs and a thin black tie over their tight fitted dress shirts. They pranced around and made suggestive motions with their hips and arms; dry humping in the air. The crowd went wild, whistling and shouting catcalls. Bryce took the last sip of his martini and when he looked through the glass, he recognized the female dancer. She was the waitress who had brought him his drink.

A spotlight followed her around the circular glass enclosure. She dragged her feather boa on the floor and then whipped it against the glass. Wherever it hit the glass she would come up right next to it and make very suggestive moves; either spreading her legs or turning her back and bending over to touch the floor. Wearing only blue body paint left essentially nothing to the imagination of the adoring crowd.

Unbeknownst to the party guests, their host (the manager of the club) was watching the festivities from his lair high above the club floor. A two-way mirror clerestory separated his office from the club. His office was soundproof, but he could still feel the vibration of the music. Ahmed Ali Raheem stood by the mirror and peered out. A smile came to his face as he thought about all that he had accomplished in the last year.

He looked at the Americans below with contempt as they lustfully watched the erotic dancers. As a shrewd businessman he had developed a theory of doing business in the United States. To him, Americans were somewhat childlike in their view of the world. But he could not deny that Americans made the absolute best weapons. That is why he was here in New York to trade in arms and launder the money transactions.

Ahmed spent a number of years in London doing essentially the same thing, but British weapons were second rate (nowhere near the quality of the Americans). Although he did acquire a taste for cucumber sandwiches and tea, which he was now just finishing off as the dancers began. In his opinion, there were too many Muslims in London and it was bringing the place down. Those fucking foreigners were so crass and uncouth that he was embarrassed to be one. So, he was happy to leave and set up business in New York.

Almost immediately, he had found the right connections. From his perspective, everything in America was for sale at the right price. He found the right bank to launder money through and more importantly the right bankers: guys that didn't ask too many questions and went with the flow if the bank made a substantial profit.

Mark's Apartment, The Bronx

Mark had just laid down on his single bed. He could hear the horns honking of the New York traffic below. He was thinking of the image of those two sixteen-year-old boys and felt both guilty and horny at the same time. For a brief moment, he regretted deleting all the pictures.

Mark was a little startled when his fax machine beeped giving notice that a message was incoming. For all the technological advances in communication, Mark learned that if you wanted to send a message and not have someone intercept it; send it by fax. Proven old school technology.

Mark also purchased disposable cell phones; or burner phone as the street vendors call them. A different vendor and model of cell phone each time. He purposely had no pattern to when, what, or where he bought cheap cell phones. He figured if someone really wanted to hack into his phone, they could, given enough time. And time was really the only variable Mark controlled; i.e. how long he actually used the disposable cell phone. For highly sensitive critical communications he would use the phone only once and then throw it away (usually in the East River). All of this was against FBI policy, but of course Mark didn't care.

Mark had set up a hotspot with the burner phone and linked the fax machine to it. Being that this was Friday night he didn't expect any sensitive communications. So, he was a little startled when the fax machine turned on with its signature high pitch sound. He was also startled because he felt like he was caught with his pants down, masturbating to child pornography. But this would be his secret; like so many other things.

As the paper began to unfurl from the fax machine Mark immediately knew it was from the National Intelligence Organization Chief in Ankara, Turkey, in response to his information requested earlier that evening.

The communication read:

"We believe the person of interest (your so-called Dubai Sheikh) is neither a Sheikh nor is he from Dubai. We have been tracking him for years, but our leads turned cold approximately a year ago.

His real name is Aarav Arjun Khurmi and he is originally from Islamabad Pakistan. It was believed that he maintained very close contact with militant Muslim factions in Pakistan. We know that he is not ideological. He is strictly a businessman and would sell his own mother for a price.

He goes by a number of aliases. The last known was Ahmed Ali Raheem. Which is sometimes Americanized as Al Ross. We also have reason to believe that he has been laundering money from Middle Eastern arms dealers. From your communiqué we understand that he has been having dealings with a certain Swedish bank called the Bank of Uppsala. That bank is also a bank of interest. Consider the suspect to be armed and dangerous. Attached is the last photo we have on him. Please send the additional information you have on Khurmi, so we can continue our investigation."

-     Emre Demir, Bureau Chief, National
Intelligence Organization of Turkey

Mark read the fax with intrigue and thought; *this could be my big break. Of course, I'm not going to share this intelligence with my bureau supervisors. They wouldn't suspect a thing because they'll be thinking that I'm investigating bank fraud and tax evasion. And this Emre character... Well, I'll just have to string him along, so I can get the rest of the information he has on this Ahmed guy.*

As Mark was scheming a relatively clear headshot of Ahmed Ali unfurled from the fax machine. Mark ripped the page from the machine, stared intently at the photo and said, "You are mine, you son of a bitch."

Mark pulled out the plastic chair from beneath the IKEA desk and thought, *so they lost the trace on this guy.* He heard that the Pakistanis could be sneaky, but they must've learned of the cyber interception techniques being used overseas and changed their methods. Better encryption most likely.

He pulled out the top drawer of the desk and a pill bottle rolled forward because it was the only thing in the drawer. It was a stolen prescription for anadrol-oxymetholone - a very strong anabolic steroid. Mark popped two pills into the back of his throat and gulped them down with the bourbon and ice that were still in the glass. He was stoked from the porn and now the good news that would surely lead to the big break in his case. So, he decided to lift weights.

The weight bench dominated what could be called the living area of this tiny apartment. Mark carefully wrapped black Velcro straps tightly around each wrist. He had been lifting weights for about a year now because he thought it would help him meet women that were more desirable. He saw women as very shallow creatures that only cared for hot looking men with a lot of money. Since he didn't have a ton of money, he wanted to improve his body, thinking that men with big muscles and large cocks turned women on.

Mark tried the online dating sites but struck out. Yeah there were women that wanted to go out with him, but he wasn't the least bit attracted to them, though there were a few older divorced women that he had dated. He found that older women were not as complicated as women his own age. And most of the older women wanted to have sex just after one or two dates.

Hell, there were some real sluts that wanted to get laid on the first date, he thought. From Mark's experience, slutty divorced women, who were older really enjoyed sex because they knew what they liked and weren't shy to ask for it. Plus, they had big tits, which he liked to play with and suck when they had sex. These cougars always found it charming that Mark got so excited sucking their breasts that they happily indulged him.

However, Mark found that they were just too demanding after the sex was over and kept dropping hints of wanting to be married again or go on vacations to Europe. So, beyond good sex, these relationships didn't amount to anything; and they never could. These women had had so many sexual partners because they used sex just to satisfy their narcissistic appetites. They quickly dumped Mark when they realized that he wouldn't concede to their demands for a committed relationship leading to marriage. So, they quickly were looking past Mark for their next sex partner.

Before he tried the dating sites again, he wanted to improve himself. Figuring that he would attract a more desirable woman (someone younger than the baggy-breasted cougars he had been banging). The other part of the equation was that Mark had also become hooked on anabolic steroids. Two of which he had just popped. This required him to buy them on the black market since there was no reason for an FBI tax fraud investigator, who lived in a shady one-bedroom Bronx apartment - that smelled like fish - to get a legal prescription.

Mark slipped under the barbell resting on the frame of the bench. He puffed short breaths, lifted the 140 pounds from the bracket, and lowered it down to his chest. He grunted, "one," as he pushed the bar back up.

Chapter 25

FBI Headquarters, Manhattan
Tuesday December 16, 2014

The Turkish language dates back to antiquity. Turkey, being at the crossroads of Europe and the Middle East, was highly influenced by other ethnic cultures, particularly Arabic and Persian. After the First World War and the defeat of the Ottoman Turks, the Allied powers created the Turkish alphabet as a way to break up and control the various ethnic factions that comprised the unruly Ottoman Empire. Thus, modern Turkish is a relatively new language with many interpretations for the same sentence.

Mark exchanged a number of meaningless bank investigation documents with Emre, and in return obtained more background information on the Sheikh (as Mark now referred to him).

Late one evening when Mark returned to his apartment there was a very long fax waiting for him. The only problem was that it was in Turkish. It seemed like Special Agent Emre was wise to Mark's scheme of stringing him along and that two could play that game.

Turkish has a bizarre alphabet of twenty-nine letters with multiple letters being the same, only modified with strangely placed accents. There was no way Mark could use the Google translator for this. He knew he needed a professional translator and thus asked around at the Bureau to find someone who did such things. Through his frustrating search he ended up in the basement of the Bureau's building on Wirth and Broadway, in lower Manhattan.

The rickety elevator opened to a corridor dimly lit with incandescent light bulbs that glowed yellow against the puke green government paint of the walls. As the elevator door opened, Mark could see the sign on the wall opposite the elevator which read "Language Services" with a small arrow that pointed to the right.

The place smelled like a government office. A mixture of musky old paper files rotting slowly in filing cabinets and a gym locker full of sweaty clothes. There was a handwritten sign scotch taped to the frosted glass window in the middle of the door, which read, "Closed. Back at 3 PM." He was really annoyed at seeing this, seeing that it was just 1:30 PM. But he had other things to catch up on and decided to come back.

The door was opened when he returned. As he entered the office Mark was surprised at how cramped it was. Boxes were stacked everywhere. It looked like a hoarder was in charge of the filing system. There was no one immediately present so Mark called out, "Hello!"

He heard shuffling coming from the back and a muffled, "Hello."

Mark started to head back to where the voice had come from and then he heard, "Please wait there. I'll be with you shortly."

Mark wasn't the most patient person, but he had nowhere else to turn to, to get the documents translated. He didn't want to ask Emre because he didn't want to have to return the favor. Within a few minutes, but to Mark it seemed much longer, a small frail woman emerged from behind the stack of boxes and filing cabinets.

"Can I help you?" Rae Donaldson asked. She was a short rotund woman with small white Reebok tennis shoes, a yellow blouse, and tight light brown (almost orange) polyester pants.

"Well I hope so. I have a document in Turkish that needs to be translated."

"Oh my, we don't have much call for that here. We'll have to send it out."

"Send it out?"

"Yes, we'll have to get one of our private contractors to do it."

"Well, this is top secret!"

"Yes of course. All of our contractors have top-secret security clearance, some with level five clearances. It'll take about two weeks, maybe more depending on the availability of our contractor fluent in Turkish, and the length of your document."

"Oh no. I don't have two weeks. I need it back right away. How do I get ahold of the translator?"

"You can't. Everything has to go through me. That's the protocol. And you have to fill out this form, supply a cost code for the work, and have it signed by your supervisor. Please return everything in a business-sized envelope. If I'm not in, you can slip it in the mail slot."

Mark thought for a moment. Obviously, this woman didn't want to be cut out of the food chain, so she was deliberately creating needless bureaucratic red tape, which was ironic coming from an employee of the Federal Government.

"Okay fine, I'll bring the signed form back shortly."

Midtown Manhattan
Wednesday December 17, 2014

The sun was shining as Tina exited the subway station at Columbus Circle. But the morning air was chilly. She decided that she had been cooped up too long and decided to walk through Central Park on her way up to W. 63rd St. Tina tolerated New York at times and loved it at others. Perhaps it was that she just needed a change of pace; so, she welcomed these translation assignments. Some would think that it would be tedious to translate a document, especially one in Turkish. But she jumped at the chance when the sweet lady from the FBI local Bureau called. The lady mentioned that it was a rush job, but she understood if Tina would need more time. Tina didn't regret saying that she would get on it right away, despite this would be taking her away from her postdoctoral work at Columbia. Besides, she needed a break from that as well.

It was early, and the majestic oak trees stood naked against the Manhattan skyline. The hipsters were out of course: jogging, doing Tai Chi, and other such things they thought would impress the opposite sex, or the same sex. Tina was immune to this behavior, having now been in New York for over 10 years, and chose to get her exercise at the ultimate fighting club on campus. The guys were pretty cool and allowed Tina to participate in their matches. Although there were still some guys who didn't want a girl to participate. Not that they were chauvinistic (which they were) they were just afraid to get their ass kicked by a girl because they saw how good she was; and she had indeed kicked more than one guys ass.

Tina bounded up the steps of the stately brick building. She pulled her hood over her head. This was not abnormal for someone going to work out at the YWCA. Although that is not why Tina was there. To protect her identity Miss Donaldson used the YWCA as an anonymous assignment drop-off and pickup location. She passed the receptionist that didn't even look up. She wound her way down the narrow stairway to the women's locker room. She could smell the chlorine from the swimming pool as she placed her FBI issued key into the padlock of her locker.

A brown business envelope was sitting on the top shelf. Tina took the envelope and looked around to see if anyone could see her. Satisfied that she was alone she carefully lifted her sweatshirt and placed the envelope in the back of her pants, half sticking out - also where she would typically keep her pistol. Then she lowered her sweatshirt back down. She put the hood over her head again and quickly exited the building.

She didn't notice the black Chevy Suburban parked on the opposite side of the street. The windows were tinted so Tina didn't notice that she was being videotaped.

Bryce's Condo, Upper West Side Manhattan

Christmas vacation for Bryce had just started. Actually, Bryce didn't take a vacation. He didn't go into the office. He had too much work to do and too many things on his mind. He woke up at 2 AM thinking he had made a big mistake moving to New York City. He thought he shouldn't have told Tina that it was best that they just be friends and not get too serious. Shit it was even his idea to not have an exclusive relationship since they were so young, and let their respective careers take priority. He got out of bed dressed only in his bikini underwear and went into the living room.

The curtains on the full wall window were pulled all the way back. Bryce went to the window, which was floor-to-ceiling tempered glass. The snow had stopped, and the moon was shining on the Hudson River, which lay eighty-three stories below him to the west. Bryce pressed his face and body against the glass and felt the coldness. He didn't pull back. He felt that if he pressed himself even harder, he would be that much closer to California, way off in the distant West. He stayed there for a few minutes and thought about all that happened during his years in New York City. He had advanced rapidly at the bank. Hell, he deserved it, having made a shit load of money for the bank and its clients. Now he was beginning to feel some resentment and jealousy from the more senior guys in the office. And while this bothered him slightly, he was never going to back down.

"Too fucking bad those guys didn't do the research and have the balls to make the investment decisions I made," Bryce said aloud as he turned from the window and made his way to the kitchen.

He opened the Sub-Zero fridge and pulled out a chilled Perrier sparkling mineral water. He downed the whole bottle in two gulps.

"Yes. Yes, God dammit!" Bryce said slamming the bottle down on the granite countertop. Yes, meaning that taking the assignment in Charlotte was the right move. It was a big promotion and had the backing of all the brass in Sweden.

Over the years he worked at the B of U, Bryce developed some very sophisticated computer algorithms that solved complex arbitrage strategies using a Monte Carlo risk probability scheme that learned as each investment was made. From the profit percentage the algorithm learned what to do next time and what to avoid. It was a form of artificial intelligence. The program he implemented was so successful that he was written up in the New York Times and the Wall Street Journal. Heck, the New Yorker magazine did a piece on him saying he was the new blonde-haired whiz kid from California and likened his business acumen to none other than John D. Rockefeller himself.

However, for the most part Bryce avoided the spotlight and was quoted in the New Yorker as saying, "There are some days that I think I'll give all this up in exchange for the great right break at Rincon Beach," south of Santa Barbara in California.

But the surf would have to wait because Bryce had just taken on a Herculean task and everyone was watching him, and more importantly the investors were counting on him. Most (over 90%) didn't even take a dividend that year to plow all of their profits back into the Bank of Uppsala and Bryce's international investment fund.

The California surf would have to wait and so would Tina. Bryce didn't even know if Tina was still available. He thought some whiz-bang Navy SEAL he-man would swoop in and steal her heart. Unfortunately, there was no fancy Monte Carlo probability risk analysis when it came to matters of the heart. So, Bryce was just going to have to take his chances. Something he was a master at.

To get prepared for his new assignment the Charlotte office sent five bankers' boxes full of financial data and analysis to Bryce's New York condominium. The boxes arrived on Christmas Eve like a present from some greedy Scrooge one-percenter that was going all in on Bryce's acumen of the financial markets. Bryce had taken a week off and hadn't opened the boxes. He felt like he should at least peek before he went back to the office. He went to the foyer of his condominium where the boxes were stacked just as FedEx had left them. The FedEx delivery guy was happy to be on the receiving end of one of Bryce's Christmas tips.

The Charlotte branch president was so excited to have Bryce transferred to North Carolina that he had commissioned an architect to design a house for Bryce. The branch president subdivided a large parcel he had in the countryside and had sent Bryce pictures. It all looked nice and the architect put Bryce at ease. At one point in the meeting, Bryce confided that he didn't know the first thing about architectural design. The only two requests he had were that the house be set back and hidden from the road and that it had a large wraparound veranda. The architect assured him that both requests could be easily and satisfactorily met.

Bryce had almost forgotten that the architect had sent the roll of drawings over for his review. He turned the light on in the foyer, and there sat the role of drawings on top of the stack of banker's boxes. He rethought his original intent of looking at the financial data, instead took the drawings and went to the dining room table to lay them out.

Bryce turned up the dimmer switch and the crystal chandelier cascaded light on the colored renderings of his new house that was to be built on the outskirts of Charlotte. It was a bone chilling 32° outside and a light but stiff breeze pressed against the window as Bryce sat in his underwear, looking at his new house and the next phase of his life. A smirk came over his face as he thought of life in the California sunshine. That too would have to wait as Bryce texted the architect, "Looks good, let's get started right away! I want the house constructed as soon as possible." He closed out the text with a happy face emoji. Bryce left the drawings on the table and went back to bed, again ignoring the stuff in the banker's boxes. He was going to need all his rest for the tasks that lay ahead.

Columbia University, Manhattan

Tina jogged back through Central Park to the subway station at Columbus Circle. The station was dingy and stank from urine the homeless left as their calling card. She raced down the tiled stairway to the waiting train and was able to jump aboard just before the doors closed. The train wheels squealed as it barreled through the tunnel north on the west side of Manhattan on the way to Morningside Heights. The lights would flicker on and off periodically, which was disconcerting for New York City newbies.

Tina had been in the Big Apple for so long she considered herself almost a native although she wasn't rude, pushy, obnoxious, or speak with a funny accent. She pushed her way off the train and raced up the stairs at the Columbia University station stop, glad to be able to see the sky again. Although she wasn't claustrophobic, she tried to limit her time in the New York subway for some very good reasons.

Tina kept up her quick pace across campus to her office building. Postdoctoral researchers were treated only slightly better than the french fry makers at McDonald's and made about the same pay. So, Tina welcomed these extracurricular activities from Miss Donaldson, the sweet woman at the FBI language service. She was grateful that all the work was done with the utmost secrecy because she undoubtedly made many enemies doing this top-secret work. The work was to remain anonymous to protect Tina yes, but for the FBI they wanted to protect their Agents more importantly. Special Agents put their life on the line every day and thus needed the protection anonymity gave them. It was the least the bureau could do.

Tina's code name was Miss Amber. She selected it because Amber was the name of the main character in a favorite childhood book about intrigue and mystery. Tina never knew what to expect from these translation assignments, and she enjoyed the challenge. She was still breathing hard from her jaunt across midtown Manhattan when she closed the door to her office. As an extra precaution, she locked the door and did not turn on the ceiling light. She was a little paranoid that someone was watching. She didn't have any proof; it was just a hunch. Her father had a saying about being in combat, "When there's a doubt, there is no doubt."

Tina placed the manila colored envelope on the desk. It was slightly creased because it had been stuffed into the back of her pants. For a difficult translation assignment such as this, Tina was paid by the hour. She looked up at the clock on the wall. It was 3:30 PM. Tina broke the seal of the envelope and removed its contents. She quickly flipped through the pages and noted that there were thirty-nine.

"Thirty-nine pages of Turkish is going to take some time to translate," she said aloud. "Better get cracking," She smiled to herself, remembering her Dad used to say this corny expression.

Tina turned on her computer and logged on to the hard disk, but not the server. This was another precaution. She didn't want someone to hack into her computer through the Internet. The text of the document was not crisp and clear. It looked like it was printed on heat sensitive fax paper.

Tina exclaimed, "Sheesh, I wonder what Luddite is still using a fax machine? This is going to be a bitch to decipher."

Tina ran her hand over the stack of papers to flatten them out. She pushed her chair back and rose from the desk. The chair made a squeaking sound as it slid across the floor. She walked to the scanner that was on top of the filing cabinet. She set the scanner resolution to 1200 dots per inch. This was the highest resolution it would go. Tina was glad she paid the extra money for the Hewlett-Packard scanner. For this project, she was going to need it. She placed a thumb drive in the scanner to save the image file. At this resolution, the file was going to be huge, but it was necessary. It was going to take a while to scan all these documents, so Tina decided to make herself a cup of coffee - it was going to be a long night.

Chapter 26

Club 69, Manhattan
Saturday February 14, 2015

The lights went out. The place was pitch black. So dark you couldn't even see your own hand placed directly in front of your face. Jay-Z's "Friend or Foe" came exploding out of the loudspeakers. A small spotlight hit the glass enclosure. The assembled Valentine's Day crowd went nuts stamping their feet to the beat, whistling, and hollering. Some started to pound the glass enclosure but were immediately stopped by a bar bouncer weighing at least 275 pounds with a very grumpy disposition. Ahmed assumed he was most likely neglected as a child and never hugged enough.

Just then, a leg stuck through the black door and the place went wild with shouting, jeers, and whistling. High above the dance floor Ahmed sat motionless initially watching what was going on below. He had worked all day laundering the Saudi funds through countless transactions, mostly brokered by the local branch of the Bank of Uppsala.

This financial obfuscation would make it nearly impossible to trace how funds from a Saudi Arabian Sheikh were used to purchase a dozen FIM-92 stinger missiles from Turkey and have them delivered to the Muslim extremist front-line fighters.

This was international finance at the most sophisticated level. There was no one better at it than Ahmed, and he knew it. It was one of the reasons his fees were so high. He was a Muslim alright, but not a fanatic. There were limits with his religious beliefs, though there were absolutely no limits when it came to business. He was an expert when it came to the dark net marketplace. His codename was Onion, because he created so many layers that anyone who tried to trace his steps and peel back each layer of the onion, would start to cry. Ahmed knew that the FBI had been tracking him for years. He thought the best place to hide was in broad daylight where they wouldn't think to look.

Ahmed had such contempt for authority. His New York club was the most exclusive. He maintained twenty-four hours security, three hundred and sixty-five days a year. He paid double time to the guards, so they didn't mind working on holidays such as Thanksgiving or Christmas. Since Ahmed wasn't from the U.S., these holidays meant nothing to him. His observance of Ramadan had begun to wane as well. With each passing day in America, he was becoming increasingly secular. He thought to himself, *at least I'm not a sanctimonious prick, like other guys. I just think religion is outdated and mostly full of shit. If I had to say honestly, the only reason I'm in this movement is for the money.*

Ahmed knew how to make money. He was one of the first to recognize the true potential of online virtual currency. The FBI called it crypto currency, but Ahmed called it *untraceable.*

Ahmed loved New York. He just didn't like New Yorkers (at least the native ones). The young hipsters that were members of his club never met Ahmed. He was an extremely private person, but a world traveler. His international travels allowed him to feel completely comfortable setting up a global transaction ledger of his huge virtual digital wallet. His personality, void of all scruples, allowed him to exercise the computational power of the dark net to deal in drugs, weapons, and launder the proceeds. The thing that made the most profit (as a percentage of investment) was catering to pedophiles that shared their kiddy porn. When it came to making money, nothing was off-limits to Ahmed.

In all his worldly travels, Ahmed came across some extreme sexually deviant behavior. But the U.S. was the undisputed champion when it came to raunchy porn, as far as he was concerned. So, his club catered to these bizarre behaviors. The acts were different each night so his very wealthy clientele - with various sexual proclivities - never became bored and kept coming back to satisfy their deviant fantasies.

*   *   *

Rachel had made her way through the black door and was prancing around the glass enclosure like the slut she was. Well technically, she was still a he. Being a pre-operative transsexual. Rachel (formally known as Wayne) still had an enormous prick, which bulged from the crotch of her red G-string banana hanger.

Rachel wore 5-inch-high heels, danced, and twirled to the sound of Jay-Z's rap. Without knowing any better, and with a second gin and tonic, Rachel looked like a big buxom bleach blonde-haired woman. She was taking estrogen hormones, and a fistful of other meds on the transition process from male to female. It was sort of like a second puberty.

Unfortunately, the hormone therapy wasn't enough to completely stop the facial hair from growing. So, Rachel shaved and dyed at least twice a day and applied gobs of foundation makeup to hide her 5 o'clock shadow. She dyed her hair blonde, because she was naturally a brunette. The dark hair showed through more prominently, and she was obsessively covering her roots. But tonight, she looked stunning. The high heels accentuated her thighs. The one thing she was particularly proud of was the silicone breast implants that she flaunted through a very skimpy bikini top - colored red, white, and blue. Her whole body was shaved, and she shook her butt with just the hint of her G-string showing through. The crowd loved it.

*   *   *

Ahmed moved his chair closer to the two-way mirror, so he could get a better view of the dance show unfolding. He had the space designed so that the audience would never block his view; no matter how rowdy they got; jumping up and down. He positioned his chair under a hook protruding from the ceiling. He stepped on the chair, carefully balancing himself so as not to tip over, and threaded a small diameter cord through the hook. He looped the rope and tied a knot on one end. He gently tugged to confirm that the knot was secure. Holding the rope, he jumped off the chair onto the floor.

He went to the door and locked it. The slip block fit tightly into a small recess in the threshold. He turned the overhead light off and turned up the dimmer switch for the mood lighting sconces. He turned up the volume of the music that was being played full blast on the dance floor below his elevated office. "Imaginary Lover" by the Atlanta Rhythm Section began to play.

Ahmed quickly looked around and being satisfied with the room set up, he returned to his chair. As he started to walk across the room, he undid his belt and the button to his pants. He kicked off his shoes and lowered his pants and cotton underwear, as he maneuvered his butt into the chair. The wooden chair rocked back slightly from the force of his weight and he sat looking forward toward the stage.

*   *   *

By this time Rachel had been joined on stage by the two beefcake guys wearing black G-strings, bulging muscles, and an *I'm going to fuck you* look. They strutted to the music and flirted with Rachel pretending to dry hump her. She of course returned the favor pantomiming giving them a blowjob.

*   *   *

Ahmed fitted a padded collar around his neck and fastened the drawstring to the cord hung from the ceiling. He pulled the cord to remove all the slack. He tried to reach for his pants, but the cord restrained him. So, he had to remove the collar to reach into his pants pocket to pull out a stolen bottle of Percodan.

227

He popped four tablets in his mouth and swallowed. The narcotic went to work almost immediately, bringing a feeling of intense relaxation, and euphoria. Ahmed cupped his hand and stroked himself. As he sat back down, he placed the collar back around his neck. When he leaned back in the chair the collar tightened and choked him. Ahmed gasped for air and tried to clear his throat. He had a raging hard-on, which he kept stroking as he watched Rachel and her two companions dance like they were only dancing for his enjoyment. There was a heightened sense of excitement as Ahmed imagined all the people below watching him jerk off.

The brain is fed oxygen by two arteries on either side of the neck - the carotid arteries. As the collar became tighter restricting these arteries Ahmed's brain was being deprived of oxygen. Carbon dioxide started to build up in his brain cells causing a semi-hallucinogenic state of hypoxia.

*   *   *

Rachel and her two friends had completely stripped down, not that they were wearing much to begin with. Rachel was on her hands and knees pretending to 69 the first guy, who was lying on the floor, enjoying the view. The second guy was dancing behind Rachel, dry humping her raised ass as if readying himself to fuck her from behind.

*   *   *

Ahmed's pace quickened as he stroked his purple-headed dick. He gasped for air as the masturbatory neurotransmitter sensation passed between the synapses of his brain cells. The abnormalities in his cerebral neurochemistry, caused by the hypoxia, gave him the most euphoric orgasm. Ejaculate shot from his dick 3 feet to spray the two-way mirror separating Ahmed from his imaginary lover on stage. Ahmed

228

collapsed with his head drooping forward as he slipped into an unconscious state with his hand still holding his rock-hard dick now covered in come and his neck being choked by the padded collar.

Roketsen Headquarters, Anatolian Province, Turkey

The principles of war have evolved from antiquity. The book of Deuteronomy describes how the Army was to fight. Forbidding them to harm fruit bearing trees, but plunder and enslavement of the enemies' women was okay.

The U.S. Army's Field Manual lists nine main principles of warfare. It stresses clearly defined and decisive objectives. War is messy. In addition, it is difficult to prepare clear and uncomplicated plans. Regardless, the main tenant of the manual is the use of overwhelming combat power when engaging the enemy.

*   *   *

The FIM-92 is a man portable air defense system (or MAN PADS in Army jargon), commonly called a Stinger. It operates using an infrared homing device and can destroy an airplane or helicopter with a single shot. The U.S. government allowed TRX - a chartered member of the American military industrial complex- to extend its production license to a Turkish company called Roketsen. Roketsen was based in the central Anatolian province of Ankara and had quickly risen to become one of Turkey's top one hundred industrial establishments. There was no surprise there, given Turkey's connections to the Middle East where the clear majority of the Earth's guerrilla wars are fought and the demands for armaments (such as the FIM-92, Stinger missile launchers) are so high. The FIM-92 fulfills the field manual tenant of overwhelming combat power when engaging the enemy.

As NATO members, the National Intelligence Organization of Turkey (or NIOT) and FBI were supposed to share information. This wasn't always the case. But on this particular instance something of interest came to the attention of the NIOT field operative monitoring Roketsen. With battles raging all over the Middle East, in a geographic area similar to the Ottoman Empire of old, the great neutralizer was the MAN PADS. Yeah, yeah it seemed like everyone had the rocket launcher, but they were always running out of the Stinger missiles to launch. The launcher isn't much good without something to fire.

Business was booming at Roketsen. Unfortunately for all the combatants in the market, for a new Stinger (there wasn't much call for used ones) the U.S. Army put a quota on the number of stingers Roketsen could make in a month. Given the law of supply and demand, when supply is being limited this meant the price was skyrocketing on the black market. Roketsen pressured TRX and the U.S. Army to allow them to produce more, with no dice.

The current administration in Washington was already worried about these things getting into the wrong hands. Well, the administration needn't worry anymore because MAN PADS were already in the wrong hands. Helped in large part by Arab oil money, Swedish bankers who would finance anything for a price, and a man known only as The Professor who had a proclivity for teenage boys.

The NIOT paid very good money for good information, like the money laundering that was taking place to get MAN PADS into the wrong hands.

NIOT Headquarters, Ankara, Turkey

The geographic area of the former Ottoman Empire was like the Wild West. There was certainly better money to be made doing something illegal than what meager existence could be had from any legitimate business. And in this dog eat dog world the best money of all to be gotten was that of a NIOT informant. Obviously, there were a few hazards to this occupation. Well you were a snitch, and no one liked a traitor. Hell, the NIOT didn't even like these guys but tolerated them because who else was going to do this dirty work. No one trusts a snitch. It is for this obvious reason that all information from these sources had to be independently corroborated.

The best informant in these parts was a man with the nom de guerre of 'The Executioner'. This guy was so secretive, even the NIOT didn't know his true identity, and The Executioner wanted it kept that way. His theory was the fewer people who knew what you did the greater your chances for survival in the wild west of the Middle East. The information The Executioner provided was golden - always accurate and timely. He certainly knew his business. The only problem was that he couldn't write anything in English; although he could speak it. So, all of his information - sold to the NIOT - had to be translated from Turkish, a tedious task indeed.

*   *   *

This fine morning, the NIOT Bureau Chief in Ankara arrived at the embassy to find a thick brown folder placed squarely in the middle of his desk. He immediately recognized it as the work of The Executioner. The Bureau Chief tore the package open and began to read.

In the world of money laundering and illegal arms sales, timing was everything. So, when he read about a possible connection between a Swedish international bank in New York and a possible American professor, he faxed the document through a secured line to his only daily operative in the U.S. The only guy he thought was interested in receiving such information.

He thought about sending it to the CIA headquarters in Virginia but decided he would not go through proper channels to get it transmitted. The document would most likely languish as it

231

cleared the appropriate protocols to allow it to be released to another bureau. And by the time all that happened the usefulness of the information would be too dated and stale to be of any real value. So, the Bureau Chief broke protocol and faxed the document to FBI Special Agent Mark Dunphy in New York City. The Chief rolled his eyes and thought, *these faxes to Dunphy are becoming routine. I hope that bastard has some useful information to give me in return.*

Chapter 27

**Bank of Uppsala, Charlotte, North Carolina
Tuesday February 24, 2015**

Bryce leased an apartment on Market Street, so he could walk to the office. It was February and although North Carolina is in the south it sure could get cold. This was something the Charlotte newspaper - The Confederate - attributed to the solar minimum. There were still plenty of people, even newspaper people, who thought that global warming was a hoax, perpetuated by the Yankee liberal elite. Bryce didn't go into any of those details.

All he knew was that you better watch out for a phenomenon called "black ice." If you weren't careful you could slip and fall and break your neck. Bryce learned that the hard way the evening he arrived when his feet slipped out from under him on what he thought was a perfectly smooth and dry sidewalk. Little did he know at the time, that this was the sign of things to come.

Bryce studied the files that were sent to him when he was in New York. He thought he understood complicated financial transactions, but those files and accounts made absolutely no sense. He tried to come at the problem a couple of different ways. So, when all else failed he turned to his secret weapon: Billy.

For a genius, Billy was pretty patient with Bryce, and he didn't extend his patience to very many people. Bryce did save his life after all, but neither of them dwelled on it. And Bryce never brought up the subject. It was on a Tuesday afternoon; Bryce's first full work week in Charlotte that Bryce decided to call Billy.

"NorthStar Communications," answered the receptionist. "How may I direct your call?"

Bryce was always a little surprised that the most cutting-edge software company on the earth still had a receptionist and that you couldn't directly dial an employee. Billy explained one time to Bryce that it had to do with cyber security; something he called the gate and the drawbridge. But Bryce's eyes glazed over, and Billy didn't elaborate further.

"Can I please speak with Mr. William del Toro," Bryce asked politely, as he rolled his eyes thinking of the silly formality for calling his surfer buddy.

"One moment please as I patch you through. Who can I say is calling?"

"Bryce St. James."

"Thank you, sir. One moment," and the phone went dead. For a second, Bryce thought he had lost the connection.

"Bryce! You old skin dog. How you doin'?" Billy said in the buoyant voice of a surfer dude.

"I'm doing great. I miss the SoCal weather though."

"Yeah, I thought you were going to take some time off and come surfing with the guys. There's a northwest swell and the break at Sunset is killer."

"Yeah, that was my original plan, but things got in the way."

"Gratitude is the sickness suffered by dogs."

"What?"

"A great quote from Joseph Stalin."

"Oh, that's great. A real role model" Bryce said sarcastically.

"What can I do you for?" Billy asked, knowing from Bryce's tone that he had been in deep thought and needed a second opinion from a rational human being, i.e. someone who was not involved in international finance.

"I've been reviewing the details of this overseas account and it just doesn't add up. It's impossible to follow because the identity of the participants keep changing. And it appears that they've been converting hard dollar currency into crypto currency."

"Hmm," Billy said. Thinking about what Bryce had just told him. "So, you think they're laundering money?"

"Duh, yeah!" Bryce shot back with his frustration showing.

"Dude, it was a rhetorical question. Every time you call it has to do with some illegal activity at your bank. You know what the fundamental problem is?"

"No, what?"

"You think too much like a prissy Boy Scout. You have to start thinking about these types of transactions more like a guy from the Middle East or a corrupt Scandinavian. You have to put yourself into their mind and culture."

"Yeah, I get that. You said that the last time we talked."

"Ah dude, you haven't changed."

"Okay, so how is some Middle Eastern guy going to get into international currency trading dealing in crypto currency and using random number generators?" Bryce asked in a huffy tone.

"Don't underestimate them. Illegal arms traders make for very strange bedfellows. Some international banks are always looking to maximize profits however they can. Did you know that World War I ended over a hundred years ago, but the debt has only recently been paid off, and a few people got very rich off the suffering of millions? And this is just one example."

"Yes, yes, okay already" Bryce said a little exasperated at being lectured.

"Sorry for the lecture Bryce, but you're dealing with people who are rotten to the core. They will not stop at just eating your lunch. They will eat your breakfast, dinner and bedtime snack as well!"

"Got it! They are rotten to the core. I need your help on understanding crypto currency usage."

Billy began from memory, as if he was reading a script, "On the darknet, there are sites that deal only with creating fake IDs. The guys running the sites are cutting edge tech savvy. Contrary to public perception they have no interest in creating mayhem; you know computer viruses and shit like that. The primary reason is they see it as bad for business. These guys are entrepreneurial hipsters. The reason they're not nerds is that they make a ton of money, drive red sports cars, and get all of the foxy ladies."

"Are you speaking from experience?" Bryce chuckled at Billy's expense.

"Very funny. Do you want my help or not?" Billy shot back.

"Sorry dude, please continue."

"The trick to being successful, and not getting caught by the FBI or legitimate bankers, such as yourself, is to constantly change your identity. That's why you're having such a hard time following the transactions. They are purposely obfuscating their dealings. You've heard of a 'nonce'?"

"Yes. Yes of course. It's a computer-generated random number," Bryce said happy to contribute to the conversation.

"Yes, that's correct, but what we're talking about is that and way more. Nonces are used in an online authentication protocol to constantly change access usernames or passwords, making it virtually impossible to trace. The funny thing about money laundering in the virtual world is that it is done pretty much in the open, meaning that there are both a public as well as a private key to a communal virtual wallet. The trick, and what these traders have figured out, is the authentication of a user while maintaining anonymity."

"Huh?" Bryce said, trying to follow these seemingly contradictory statements.

"Just stay with me and it will become clear," Billy continued. "These money laundering clearance houses create communal pools of crypto currency. Tumbling involves figuring out who put in how much while remaining anonymous. Peers in the network log each transaction, by the many parties that contribute, into a virtual ledger. It's like three-card monte done by honorable thieves."

"Honorable thieves?" Bryce said incredulously, "I don't see how that's going to work. It's hard enough to get honest banks to do the right thing."

"Well, maybe honesty is the wrong description. It's more like there are sufficient checks and balances that give the appearance of integrity. The exchange service prevents tracing a transaction by obfuscation. And there are a couple of ways this is done."

"Wait, don't tell me," Bryce interrupted. "Let me guess. The others in the network log each transaction simultaneously. Amounts are distributed to virtual wallets by the tumbler, but it makes sure that the amounts deposited don't match the amount withdrawn, making it virtually impossible to trace. And of course, all of this is done for a small fee by the online bank."

"But of course. Those greedy bankers always have to get their cut," Billy interjected, getting a dig in on Bryce. "Wow, it seems like you been doing your homework."

"Yeah, you have to get up pretty early to get ahead of me. Listen, I need a favor. I've been working at the Bank of Uppsala for about eleven years now, but there is something weird going on and I need you to do some investigative work for me. Very hush-hush."

"Okay, good who do you need the poop on?" Billy said, expecting all along that this was what Bryce was after.

"I can't tell you on the phone. I just expect that everything I say is being recorded. So, I'll send you an envelope by FedEx, with the name and the information I have. But your research has to be top-secret, and nothing linked to me."

"Yes. Yes, of course. That's what we do best here at NorthStar."

"Very good. Expect the package in a day or so."

"I'll get right on it as soon as it arrives, assuming that the surf is not up at that time."

Both Bryce and Billy got a good chuckle. Bryce did because he thought Billy was just kidding. Billy did because he was not. And with that, they closed their conversation without saying goodbye.

Just as expected, a FedEx package arrived at the office of NorthStar Communications. The office building was a nondescript concrete tilt up - one of several dozen in Playa Del Vista California. The FedEx guy in his polyester uniform liked to ogle at the receptionists for these Silicone Beach high-tech companies. In the back offices were these nerdy pale white geeks (the average IQ being a hundred and fifty-five) and on the cutting edge of technology – some with Asperger's, or borderline personalities. Yet inevitably, out front (in each one of these tilt up offices) sat a gorgeous buxom blonde-haired woman.

Carol, the receptionist for NorthStar Communications (who fit the receptionist stereotype perfectly) accepted the package and thanked the FedEx guy. She got up from behind her desk and walked down the corridor to Billy's office. The FedEx guy watched her ass move in her tight pencil skirt as she walked away from him.

*   *   *

The package was thicker than what Billy expected. Though it had been less than a year since Billy last saw Bryce he thought he knew him really well. But now he wasn't so sure. Bryce had changed. Or it was more like Bryce had aged. Some would call it maturity, but Billy knew Bryce better than that.

Billy opened the package and removed its contents. On the front page was a post-it-note handwritten by Bryce, which read…

"Hey dude, thanks again for all your help. As usual, keep all the stuff very hush-hush. I want you to pull up everything you can on Ulf Samuellson. He's a Senior VP at the Bank of Uppsala. A very powerful man, but I think he's up to no good and I don't want to be around when the shit hits the fan. I would guess that your usual rate still applies. I'll pay you in crypto currency (LOL!) Take care, Bryce."

And with that, Billy opened a file folder on his Dell laptop for Ulf Samuellson.

Chapter 28

Club 69, Manhattan
Tuesday March 5, 2015

If Ahmed had been conscious, he may have seen the door handle move. Mark had been tracking Ahmed for some time now. He knew of Ahmed's existence and illegal arms dealings long before he got the faxes of information from Turkey. Mark couldn't wait for the translation to be done, and just figured that the fax would confirm what he already knew. After he received the fax, Mark pretty much ignored the NIOT. Thinking they would just get in his way with bullshit like investigation protocol and search warrants.

The door was way easier to pick than Mark had anticipated. He heard the click of the last tumbler in the lock and he was in. He quickly opened the door, stepped inside, and swiftly closed the door behind them.

"What the fuck?" Mark said to himself when he saw Ahmed unconscious, leaning back in the chair with a noose around his neck and his pants pulled down around his ankles. Mark checked the gun in his holster and looked around to see if there were any CCTV security cameras. He didn't see any cameras, and figured if there were, Ahmed would've turned them off before he started to jerk off. With his Blackberry smartphone Mark took multiple pictures of the man he had been chasing for some time, in this most compromising of positions.

With the knife on his keychain Mark began to cut the top cord secured around the hook in the ceiling. Mark rolled his eyes thinking; *this is not the first time this fuck has done this. Who else would put an eye bolt hook in the ceiling*? (And he was right. The neurochemistry of the hypoxia caused by self-strangulation was addictive. Nothing compared to the euphoric orgasm. Anything short of this high was not worth the bother, even if it was a blowjob from a Baywatch Lifeguard). As the last fiber of the cord was cut, Ahmed crashed to the floor, falling backwards in the chair. Ahmed's head smacked the floor, but remarkably he didn't respond. Mark checked his carotid artery and detected a very weak pulse.

In a strange way, Ahmed should consider himself fortunate that Mark found him just in time to cut him down. The noose had cut off most of the oxygen to Ahmed's brain. And over time he would have suffocated and died or suffered severe brain damage. So, in reality Mark saved the life of someone he despised. But Mark wasn't shortsighted. He didn't expect to find Ahmed literally with his pants down. Mark's brain was working, scheming, and in the brief time that he was in the room he had devised a plan. He started to do what he went there to do. And that was to go through Ahmed's desk and computer to track the movements of this guy and his connections in international crime.

Breaking into Ahmed's computer was child's play for Mark. Soon he had copied the contents of the hard disk to the solid-state drive that he brought with him just for this purpose. He didn't spend a lot of time reading the files. He wanted to move swiftly before Ahmed regained consciousness.

But for a moment, Mark debated if he should wait for Ahmed to wake up so he could interrogate him about the arms dealing and money laundering. Mark decided against this, because he saw the long game play out in his devious mind. He had sunk the hook into the big fish and wanted to let out some line before he started to pull him in. Mark installed a cyber cryptic forwarding program onto Ahmed's computer. The device would be undetectable and would forward all traffic into and out of Ahmed's computer directly to his FBI computer account downtown. Satisfied with himself that his actions would lead to a big payoff, Mark took one more look around and then quickly left.

A soft beep from the microwave signaled that the cup of water was heated to Tina's specifications. She measured out an even spoonful of Taster's Choice instant coffee and placed it in the hot water. The cup handle was warm to the touch. Tina preferred her coffee piping hot and black. This was an acquired taste by choice. Truth be told, she loved the frothy mocha coffee from Starbucks, but on the scant wages of a postdoctoral researcher, that luxury wasn't in her meager budget. She lifted the cup and held it in both hands as she took a sip. Its warmth gave her a small degree of comfort as she turned to face the arduous task ahead.

The natural light through the large window in Tina's office was beginning to fade. She turned on the desk lamp to illuminate the area immediately around it. She let her suspicions about being followed fade as she put the thumb drive into the USB port of her HP desktop computer. She created a subfolder on the external hard disk to save the images she just scanned. Each page of the document snapped into place on her computer monitor.

She had had tremendous success using the optical character recognition (or OCR, as it was usually referred to) in a slick computer program called Bluebeam that could manipulate a file seven-ways to Sunday. She was hoping like hell that it wouldn't fail her on her current assignment; otherwise typing all that text would be a real bitch.

Tina did get paid by the hour, but even still, typing all that would not be the least bit enjoyable. Simply put, OCR converts a scanned page into electronic text. It works quite well for documents in English; one of the reasons is that English has no accents. Turkish on the other hand has lots of accents and similar letters, so Tina was hoping for the best. To Tina that meant that the OCR would get close enough, and then she could sort out the rest.

The files were large because of the high resolution and the OCR process took way longer than Tina first estimated it would take. She was feeling a little frustrated when she took her last sip of coffee, which was now lukewarm. Tina had lost track of time because she was concentrating on the technical aspects of manipulating the files into a format she could use. Even though it was laborious, she knew that careful file preparation now, would pay off later on when she was translating the text into English.

The sun had set, and Tina rose from her chair and went to the large window that framed her office. She stretched to get the kinks out from having sat for so long.

The desk lamp only illuminated the area immediately around it, so she could see clearly out the window and down to the parking lot below. Her office was on the third floor of the language arts building. Tina took a moment to scan the extent of the campus visible to her.

Her paranoia returned when she saw a black Chevy Suburban parked adjacent to the building. Nothing said *Federal Government* more than a black Suburban. Tina thought she was just being paranoid about being followed and tried not to think about it. However, as a matter of precaution she closed the Venetian blinds and returned to her work.

Tina saved the OCR files as Microsoft Word documents and used the Turkish language modules she had downloaded (that included all the unique characters and accents she would need). She was right; her initial investment paid off. Word recognized the text and did a spell check to correct the missing accents.

"So far so good," Tina mumbled, not believing her good fortune.

Tina hadn't conversed in Turkish since she left the international school in Turkey, when she graduated from high school, but it all came back to her after recently translating a number of Turkish documents for the FBI. The first page of the document flashed up on the computer screen. She translated the first line in her head and then began to read the Turkish aloud, softly to herself, "The Black Hand has risen again, and we fear that it is stronger and more insidious than ever before. They have adopted the motto from the original group widely known as being responsible for the start of World War I. They are a pan-Muslim group who see Osman Gozi as their spiritual leader. In 1299, A.D. Osman founded the Ottoman Empire. The inspiration comes from Osman's fighting strength and strong leadership. The Empire started as a small principality but grew to a world empire. The Black Hand sees the western imperialist governments as their sworn enemy and blames them for destroying their empire in 1922 with the abolition of the Ottoman Sultanate. They see the 1923 Treaty of Lausanne as the ultimate embarrassment and vowed to restore the greatness of the Muslim empire and will suffer death as a martyr before they surrender."

Tina's hands began to shake from fear. She realized with great clarity that she was reading about the Vortex of Evil. Tina's heart rate became rapid from her rising anxiety. She held her breath and tried to swallow but her mouth was too dry. She couldn't turn away. She was being pulled into the gravity of the unfathomable vile immorality. She kept reading until she thought she heard a rattling chain. And then a gentle knock came to her door and she froze in fear for her life, not able to move. Her ears were ringing as her pulse rate had shot up.

The knock came again; this time accompanied by a faint voice, "Tina my dear, are you in there?"

Tina slowly let out the breath she was holding. She pushed her chair back away from the desk and stood up. Not seeing the bottom drawer she had left open, her shin hit it hard as she was walking around the desk.

"Fuck," she said emphatically, letting off a little tension as well as her leg really hurt. She limped to the door and in a commanding voice said, "Who is it?"

"It's Dean Reed, my dear," the Dean replied in a voice that was sorry to have bothered her in the first place. Especially after hearing Tina curse (which she rarely did).

"Oh, Dean!" Tina said as she hurriedly undid the deadbolt and flung open her office door.

"Are you okay my dear? I'm sorry to bother you but I was taking Elton John for a walk on the Quad and saw your light on, so I thought I'd pop in to say hi and introduce my new dog."

Tina realized the source of the rattling chain, for on the floor sat the cutest little puppy with his new collar and a metal dog tag that clanged every time his paw scratched at his neck.

"Oh, what a cutie! When did you get him?"

A Dark Site in the Syrian Desert
Wednesday July 8, 2015

The two incandescent light bulbs that hung from the ceiling briefly dimmed as the dial was turned. Saeed was too exhausted to scream so his body just convulsed as the electric current passed through the metal chair he was strapped to. His head jerked to the left as his teeth clenched and a white froth of saliva formed on his lips and dripped from his chin.

Two other men occupied the concrete bunker made with cinder block walls. One sat behind Saeed out of the cone of the light from the ceiling fixture. The only thing visible was the red glow from his Turkish cigarette each time he took a drag. The other man sat directly in front of Saeed at a small wooden table that wobbled because one of the legs was too short and the concrete floor was not perfectly flat. On the table was a small black box with a dial to regulate the flow of electric current. Two black wires crossed the table, crossed the floor, and were connected to the metal chair where Saeed's limp body sat.

The man at the wood table leaned back in his chair and a sadistic smirk framed his Pakistani face, as beads of sweat formed on his balding head. The small room was stifling hot and a stench of excrement and urine filled the humid air. The man in the dark waved his hand and the Pakistani turned the dial to stop the free flow of electric current that was passing through Saeed's body. When the current was cut Saeed slumped in the chair with his head bowed down.

"Okay, let's go through this again because I think you're leaving something out," said the man in the dark, in a thick Turkish accent.

There was a moment of silence as Saeed tried to catch his breath. A high-pitched cry came from him, "Stop, stop, I beg you to stop… I'll, I'll tell you whatever you want to know."

"I'm going to say this slowly because this is the last time I am going to ask. You've admitted that you've been stealing weapons from the shipments."

"Yes. I'm so sorry it will never happen again."

"Who was helping you sell the weapons?"

Saeed paused again. He swallowed hard. He figured he was a dead man however this sad ordeal turned out. All he could do now was to try and protect Chanal and their little boy. He had to give them a name, but he didn't know anyone. He was just a pawn. And then through the fog of his drug infused brain he had an idea.

"Please, you must leave my family out of this. There was a man that comes from America. New York City, I think" Saeed said, pausing to catch his breath. "He likes boys. He goes to Pakistan to fuck young boys."

There was a long pause. "Yes, go on," said the man in the dark leaning forward on his chair with his face just barely lit from the yellow glow of the ceiling lamp. "What was the man's name? I need a name."

"I don't know his name. I'm telling you I called him The Professor. That's all I know."

And with that, the man behind Saeed moved back out of the light. He rose from his chair, dropped his cigarette onto the floor, and with his shoe stepped on the butt and gently twisted it to extinguish the flame. The man turned and walked to the far end of the bunker and exited the back door. As the door closed, the light from the two incandescent light bulbs dimmed again as electric current passed through Saeed's body, stopping his heart.

Chapter 29

Charlotte, North Carolina
Saturday March 3, 2018

Jack wrote a long text, apologizing for being a jerk and asked forgiveness and a second chance to make it up to Erin. He invited her on an outing (a hike in the rolling hills far from town) to someplace special with a great view.

Erin was so touched by Jack's text that she got a little wet just thinking about him and what great sex they had. And seeing that Bryce already moved back to California, she figured what the hell. She would give the guy a second chance to make it up to her.

Jack showed up at Erin's place at 11AM on Sunday morning. Exactly when he said he would be there. The older couple (Erin's landlords) that lived just below her on the main floor were away at a Southern Baptist Church service. So, they were not there to frown on Erin's choice of men - a man much younger than her.

Lake Houser, North Carolina

Jack's car didn't have air conditioning, so the windows were opened to let in a breeze. Erin and Jack didn't talk much on their Sunday drive to the country. From the car radio "Free Bird" by Lynyrd Skynyrd filled the air that Erin breathed. She admired the countryside and thanked Jack for showing it to her. They drove for well over and hour on a two-lane County Highway, and then Jack slowed his Camaro to navigate a sharp turn onto a one-lane dirt road. They passed a small lake and then started to climb as the road rose with the contours of the hill behind the lake.

"My, this is beautiful, kind sir," Erin said in her best southern accent.

Jack didn't look at her and said, "I knew you would like it."

Near the top of the hill Jack turned onto a rutted dirt driveway that led the way to a small clearing. There was an abandoned silver Airstream trailer at the far end of the property. Jack drove up to the trailer and parked his Camaro next to it.

"This was my Daddy's place. He gave it to me when he passed. We can take our picnic lunch down to the lookoff, you can see the lake from there."

Erin was so smitten by Jack's newfound thoughtfulness that she leaned over and gave him a kiss on the cheek.

Jack opened the trunk to the Camaro and took out two plastic grocery bags and a cooler.

"Let me help you with that," Erin said politely.

"That's okay, I got it." Jack replied as he slammed the trunk and headed off toward the clearing overlooking the lake.

The green grass was tall, very tall, and Jack took a seat under a cottonwood shade tree. Erin joined him. She sat next to Jack but turned slightly to admire the view of the lake and the rolling hills beyond.

"Wow, it's beautiful here."

"Uh-huh" Jack replied in his usual, brief, monosyllabic response. As he rose, he said, "I need to take a leak. I'll be right back." He headed off behind the tree, in the opposite direction from the lake, where the brush was thicker.

Erin didn't think anything of it, as she remained seated on the grass admiring the view and glad that Jack was being so charming, so chivalrous.

A shot from a high-powered rifle was heard. It echoed through the hills. The sound of gunfire was a common occurrence in the rural southern wilderness, something that wouldn't draw anyone's particular attention.

Erin slumped over onto the long stems of the green grass. The hollow core projectile from the thirty-aught-six had passed through the back of her head.

As soon as the projectile hit the back of Erin's head (just above the hair-tie she used to pull her beautiful hair back) it expanded to maximize soft tissue damage as it passed into her brain. The hollow core ammo performed exactly as it was designed. To expand upon contact thus transferring its kinetic energy to its victim, as a way to maximize damage. Erin never knew what hit her. She died instantly.

Jack emerged from the thicket and walked toward where Erin lay dead. He reached down and grabbed her arms just above her wrists and pulled her arms back. He dragged her about thirty feet to the far side of the majestic cottonwood.

He stopped beside a freshly dug grave, almost five feet deep, cut into the deep grass and topsoil of the Carolina rolling hills. Jack let go of her and Erin's limp arms fell to the ground. Jack got on the opposite side of Erin and placed his boot just under Erin's midsection. Then he stopped and removed his boot. He turned and moved to Erin's feet. He lifted her legs and pushed up her spring dress with the tropical fruit pattern on it.

Jack pulled her panties off and pressed them to his face and breathed in Erin's essence. He stuffed her panties into the left pocket of his jean shirt and snapped it closed. Then he returned to her side and put his cowboy boot under her, just above her hip. He pushed her into the grave with the thrust from his leg. She landed in the bottom of the grave with a thud and her dress flew up, exposing her pubic region. Jack immediately moved to the pile of dirt, adjacent to the hole and picked up the shovel, just where he left it the day before. He pitched the shovel into the loam and tossed it into the hole where it landed on Erin's dead body.

*   *   *

It was the first week of the month, and Erin had just paid the rent. The landlady didn't think much of Erin not being around. She figured she got the rent and that Erin just went on a vacation without telling her. Erin had no steady friends in Charlotte, so no one noticed she was gone, until the following month, when the rent was due.

By that time, Jack had already fabricated an ironclad alibi with witnesses to his whereabouts the whole weekend that Erin was killed.

Part III

"Being deeply loved by someone gives you strength; loving someone deeply gives you courage."

~ Lao Tzu

Chapter 30

Brad's Apartment, St. Andrews
Saturday March 3, 2018

Tina didn't want to seem presumptuous, but she felt like Brad wouldn't mind if she made herself some coffee. As she downloaded her route from Minneapolis to Los Angeles into her GPS the kettle began to boil. *Brad lived a pretty meager existence*, she thought. "What do you expect from a college kid," Tina said out loud and a little embarrassed.

Tina had broken a promise she had made herself when she first became a professor at Bards College. "Don't sleep with the students." She repeated it to herself and then said, "Jesus, what were you thinking. You weren't thinking - that's your problem. Fuck - how am I going to explain this to Patsy?"

Tina brewed as she put a heaping teaspoon of Folgers instant coffee into a mug. The steam rose and filled her nose with the calming smell of coffee. It was instant coffee, but it would have to do. Tina reached back into the cupboard and took down the Carnation coffee creamer. It was mint flavored, and Tina felt content for the little things in life.

She sat at a small kitchen table and studied her route to L.A. as she took small sips of the hot coffee. Tina's neuron-sensors welcomed the caffeine and she began to feel better. Just then her cell phone rang. She didn't recognize the number and wasn't going to pick up. But with all the shit that was going on lately she decided to answer it.

"Hello."

"Hi, I'm so glad I reached you!"

"Chanal? Is that you?"

"Yes. On a whim, I decided to come to the States on a surprise visit. Surprise!"

"Wow! This is a surprise. Where are you?"

"I'm in New Jersey at my cousin's place. Saeed is away on business, so it was a good time to get away." Chanal lied. Saeed had been missing for over two and a half years.

"Oh, shoot. I wish I knew you were coming. We could have made plans to get together. I'm on my way to L.A. for spring break."

"Oh no problem. I can meet you in L.A."

"Hmm. I'll be there in about three or four days based on the route Google Maps is telling me. I'm taking a road trip."

"A road trip! My, you've always been the adventurous kind," Chanal said with much admiration for her old roommate and dear friend.

"Okay it's a deal. I'll look you up when I get there. Just text me the address. It will be fun to catch up."

"Yes, I'll text you the address. I'll be at my uncle's place in Echo Park. He has a big house and you're welcome to stay with us."

"That sounds like a plan. Listen sorry to cut the conversation short but I've got to get on the road if I'm going to make it all the way to L.A."

"No problem. I'll see you in L.A." And with that Chanal was now back in Tina's thoughts.

As Tina finished her coffee and rinsed out her mug, she was beginning to have second thoughts. She also felt a little guilty just leaving Brad a brief note that she'd gone on a road trip (not mentioning L.A.) and that they'd talk when she got back (and not calling him and leaving him a message, and her new phone number, because she had no intention of talking to him while she was on the road).

Brad was a nice guy, but he's just a kid, Tina thought, and she had no intention of starting a serious relationship with him. Yeah, the sex was good, but she was drunk and vulnerable (not that she was making excuses) but a one-night stand was as far as it was going to go. She hoped that Brad was going to be discreet and not blabber to his hockey buddies that he had just banged the coach's girlfriend.

Tina had a long road trip ahead of her and there would be plenty of time for introspection with nothing but open road ahead of her. As she turned on her Ram Hemi pick up the GPS screen lit up on the dashboard and the Google voice said, "Turn left and head south." And with that Tina was off.

*   *   *

In a black Mercedes on the other side of town a red dot appeared on the computer screen indicating that Tina was on the move.

Interstate 35 between Minnesota and Iowa

Tina certainly had mixed emotions as she headed out for her spring break road trip. She was excited to be going away. – albeit not fully planned out, but that just added to her excitement, and more importantly, her anxiety. She also felt melancholy about breaking up with Jeff. She knew that breaking up was inevitable because they had been fighting more recently. As Tina's pickup turned onto the interstate on-ramp, Kathleen Edwards' country song "Asking for Flowers" started to play. Tina had set her iPod on random play and she then realized it was no accident that that song was playing now that she was making her escape from Jeff.

Country music has a way to cut through the bullshit in life. To Tina, the lyrics to the song laid out the unvarnished truth. She listened closely and thought the song was written about her life. So, by the time she merged onto I-35, she was crying.

She banged the steering wheel hard with her hand and shouted, "Fuck! Why does this always happen to me? That fucking asshole is so self-centered. It's always me, me, me! If I hear about how he played on the New York Rangers and scored the goal that put them in the fucking playoffs, one more time, I'm going to scream!"

255

Tina wiped her eyes with the sleeve of her blouse. She was heading due south. The sun had yet to rise but its presence was felt. Mercury and Venus were peeking out in the eastern sky. Tina usually noticed these things but today she was too upset to pay attention. She had to put many miles of interstate asphalt behind her if she was going to make it to L.A. in three days.

The road was so straight that Tina just put the cruise control on to allow her time to think. Yeah, she had plenty of thinking time on this trip. It would be a welcome break from all of Jeff's B.S. So, Tina began a trip of introspection. She promised herself that she would lie out the absolute truth, just like country music, no matter how difficult it would be to deal with. She knew that just understanding the problem was the key to dealing with it. And if she didn't come to grips with the root of the problem, then she would repeat the same relationship cycle with the next guy she dated.

Tina didn't know how all this introspection stuff was going to work out. The first thing she thought was, *I'm part of the problem.* As difficult as it was to admit, Tina blamed herself, *my personality deficiencies allowed these things to happen. The problem started not when the fight began. The problems began way before that when I decided to go steady, and I allowed these jerks to complete me.*

She was not a victim. Previously unbeknownst to her, she now realized that she was in control of what happened (although it never felt that way). And the reason she felt she wasn't in control was that she tended to merge with what the guy thought, and she failed to maintain her own identity. The boundaries that defined her as a complete whole were blurred. Most importantly, she failed to take measures necessary to protect herself when something undesirable came up.

"I don't know what I saw in that guy. He gets mad all the time, especially when I'm talking to other guys," Tina said out loud as if she was talking to a shrink. "That jerk even wanted me to delete photos of the guys I had on my phone. What a creep. He would sneak my phone and go through the text messages. And shit, he got obsessive about texting him back right away. And the thing that really pisses me off is when he's critical of what I wear. He thinks that I sometimes dress like a slut. I should've smacked him when he said that to me. Fuck, this makes me so angry!" Tina yelled as she hit the steering wheel again, this time with both hands.

The pickup swerved by the jolt to the wheel, which Tina had to correct as she yelled, "Fuck!" again, and started to cry.

Brad's Apartment, St. Andrews

The door to Brad's apartment swung open and banged against the wall. There was an impression of the doorknob in the plaster from the many times this had happened before.

"Honey, I'm home!" Brad cracked, jokingly expecting to find Tina there. His arms were full of grocery bags, which he negotiated through the door jamb and muscled into the kitchen. He kicked the door with his foot to close it.

"Boy, we had a great practice. The coach didn't show. So, we had a scrimmage." Brad stated in a voice loud enough so anyone in the small apartment could hear. He put the items that required refrigeration in the fridge and walked into the bedroom expecting to find Tina lying there, waiting for him, but the window blinds were still closed, and the bed was made.

Hmm… Brad thought to himself. *I wonder where she went.*

Brad went into the bathroom and saw the post-it note Tina left him on the mirror. Brad read the note and was a little taken back by its brevity and lack of affection. Feeling a little hurt, and mostly disappointed because that meant no more sex, which he was counting on.

"Shit," he said out loud, realizing that he didn't have Tina's new cell phone number. She always used burner phones and changed them constantly. He once asked her about this. She said that she needed to because she kept receiving anonymous text messages and phone calls. Then she joked that due to her subversive activities, she was probably being followed by someone from the FBI.

"Yeah, maybe I should call the coach and ask him for his girlfriend's phone number." Brad laughed as he went back to the kitchen to finish putting away the groceries, satisfied with himself that he had fucked the coach's girlfriend. He had a smirk on his face as he thought, *I banged her really hard, and she really loved it.* He then wondered, *does anyone else know?*

Tina's Apartment, St. Andrews

The hockey team was streaming out of the locker room after the scrimmage that was supposed to be a practice, except the coach hadn't showed up. Peter Trammell, the captain of the team was a senior and in his fourth year of playing. In his four years, he had never known the coach to not show up.

At least he would've called, he told himself.

The rest of the team felt Jeff was an asshole, which he was. However, Peter expected that the coach would follow through with his promise to get him a tryout with an NHL team. He didn't want to leave it to the end of the season, the coach hadn't said anything more about it, and Peter didn't want to miss his chance. He was working hard, and was in his best shape ever, and he wanted his shot at playing professionally. So, Peter looked up the coach's phone number on the club roster and called him.

"I'm sorry, but the number you have called is not accepting messages at this time because the mailbox is full. Goodbye," said the automatic recording.

"Shit!" Peter said, turning off his android phone. Peter looked through the photo gallery of his phone. He seemed to recall that he had a photo of the coach's address from the end of the season barbecue the coach had a year ago. He searched through the photo documents but couldn't find it. "Shit! I guess I'll just have to go over there and hunt around to find his place."

                    *   *   *

The town of St. Andrews wasn't very big, and he remembered that the coach's place was just on the outskirts of town, in a new condo development. Peter found the complex without any problem. He looked on the directory and found the coach's name. Building "C" condo 230. Peter pulled his car around to the far side of the complex and spotted the coach's Yukon SUV and pulled in alongside of it. Peter ran up the stairs and knocked on the door. No answer. He knocked again and waited. No answer. He called the coaches cell phone again and heard the phone ring with a distinct ring tone that played "Don't Stop Believing" by the band Journey.

Peter remembered that ring tone because the whole team would roll their eyes when they heard that sappy song and tease the coach about it. The sound was muffled coming through the door, but it was definitely the coach's phone ringing. The phone went to the recorded message again, so Peter hung up the phone. He knocked again and waited. Still nothing. Peter went back to his car to wait.

He waited about five minutes and then got out of his car and was walking towards Jeff's condo again when the old guy that lived next door opened the door and came outside.

"Can I help you?" asked the old guy with teeth stained from smoking and the smell of alcohol on his breath.

"Yeah. I'm looking for my coach," Peter said hopefully.

"Haven't seen him this morning. He had a hell of a fight last night with his girlfriend. We heard the whole thing. The walls in this condominium complex are paper-thin. His girlfriend said she was going to kill him and then she stormed off. My guess is that Jeff is sleeping off a hangover."

"Wow. That's probably why the coach didn't show for practice this morning. Listen, when you see him please tell him to call Peter Trammell. I'm the captain of the team."

"No problem," said the old guy as he turned to go back into his condo.

Peter waited a second before he turned to go back to his car. *Fuck*, he said to himself, *I need to talk to the coach to arrange a tryout.* But he realized that he didn't want to be around the coach when he had a hangover. The coach was a big enough asshole when he was in a "good" mood. Peter didn't want to take his chances when he was in a bad one. So, he drove back into town and would wait for the coach's call.

Chapter 31

FBI Headquarters, Manhattan
Saturday March 3, 2018

Special Agent Foley was in his office on the twelfth floor of the Manhattan Bureau of the Federal Bureau of Investigation. He had been working a ton of overtime on a complex case that kept him up at night. It was just after lunch and he was starting to nod off from the impending lunch coma, when his office phone rang, and he snapped out of his stupor.

"Foley here," he answered.

"Foley, this is Matheson. I need you to come to my office immediately, there is an important matter that I have to discuss with you in person."

"Sure, thing Chief. I'll be right up."

Oh God. What does he want now? I'm already busting my hump. And why is he even in here on a Saturday, Foley sighed to himself as he got up and straightened his necktie.

Foley rode the elevator up to the fifteenth floor. It wasn't often that he would get summoned to the big boss's office. The Chief's office was at the end of the corridor. A glass box in the corner of the building. The Chief saw him approach and waved him to come in. From the office you could see the Hudson below and New Jersey on the far side. Foley was trying to admire the view when the Chief motioned him to take a seat.

"Listen," the Chief said, "do you remember when I told you to keep an eye on Agent Mark Dunphy?"

"Yes," Foley replied not knowing where this conversation was headed. "I tailed him for a few weeks a few years ago and filed my report with Internal Affairs. As I recall, there was nothing of real interest to report other than him breaking a few filing protocols."

"Well Foley, it appears that Mark knew you were following him and was on his best behavior, or at least that's what he wanted you to believe," the Chief said rather annoyed.

"It appears that Agent Dunphy has been off the reservation for a very long time. How long? I don't know. Here is a thumb drive with all of the shit that Mark has been involved with. At least the stuff we're aware of. I want you to dive into this and find out what we don't know. Powerful men, well above my pay grade, are interested in this. So, you'll need to drop everything you're doing and get on this."

"But Chief, I've been working-"

"I know what you been working on," the Chief cut him off. "As of right now, I've taken you off your current assignment and I'll assign your case to another Agent."

"… but Chief, I'm near a big break in the case summation …" Foley exclaimed pleading his case. "Plus, I don't want this babysitting assignment. Mark is an asshole. No one likes him. Hell, he was an asshole when he first entered the Academy. No one liked him even then. He's always had unorthodox methods. Hell, he has that stupid man bun, but he got results. You said so yourself."

The Chief took off his reading glasses and came around to the other side of his desk. He propped himself on the edge of the desk and folded his arms.

"Listen," the Chief began in a lower tone, "this is not a babysitting assignment. There is some deep, deep shit that is going on and I think Mark is under cover way over his head. I should have seen this coming. So, this is my fault. And if it blows up, I'm going to take the hit. That's why I'm assigning my best guy to this.", he said looking straight at Foley. "You'll have access to all the resources you need. But unfortunately, you'll need to use them sparingly. Who knows who else is involved in this thing?" The Chief said, using the word "we." Seeming to infer that Foley would also be implicated if the shit hit the fan because he did the original investigation on Mark. Even though that investigation ended a few years ago. "I've given this a Code 5 and everything you report goes straight to the top," The Chief continued.

Oh Christ, a Code 5. That meant that this thing was a matter of national security, Foley thought to himself.

"I want you on this starting right now. I'll assign an Agent to your current assignment. You'll have to brief them this afternoon. I am counting on you on this one. If there was ever a time when I needed your absolute best work, this is that time. Can I count on you?" The Chief said extending his arm and placing his hand squarely on Foley shoulders.

Foley looked up, straight into the Chief's eyes. He knew the Chief wouldn't dump this on him if he didn't think it was really important.

"Yes Chief, you can count on me."

"Thanks," the Chief said holding out his other hand.

Foley rose from his chair and shook the Chief's hand. Nothing else needed to be said. Foley was the best agent for the assignment. He could think on his feet and wasn't afraid to make a decision, the right decision. The decision that the Chief would agree needed to be made with the information known at the time.

On the elevator ride down to his office, Foley was already planning his strategy on how he was going to tackle this new assignment. The first thing he needed to do was wade through the steaming pile of shit that was on the thumb drive the Chief just gave him. The second was to realize that he couldn't trust anyone on this, and he'd need the help of outside resources. Mark fooled him once before. It was not going to happen again. Foley would make sure of that.

Sespe Wilderness, Ventura County, California

Bryce was happy to be back in California. He was certainly a changed man from the wide-eyed college grad that had left fourteen years ago. It seemed longer than that, seeing that he accomplished the goals he had set out for himself. Plus, he had made a boatload of money in international finance. His confidence level was sky-high because he knew he had the intellect to compete with the world's best and brightest. The years he was away, he was always on call. Working crazy hours to get ahead and compete in the dog eat dog world of capital finance. He felt proud of what he accomplished in spite of the un-pleasantries he ran into. He hoped there were no hard feelings at the Bank of Uppsala. He was very appreciative of the opportunity they had given him, but it was clearly time to move on. At least it was clear to him.

Bryce was surprised that the executive management took it so hard that he was leaving. They thought he was just burned out, and after an extended rest he would be back. They really admired Bryce's skill and that he was such a cool cucumber in the thick of the negotiation battles that always raged at all hours of the day or night. The executives were happy that Bryce was on their team, and that they didn't have to compete against him.

Bryce felt like he had been in a hyperbaric chamber when he was away from Ventura County, and now it was time to decompress. He took a deep breath of the clean Ventura County air as he stretched out his arms in preparation for his morning ride. Lifting each arm around the back of his head and pushing on the elbow while counting to ten. It was part of the stretch and flex routine he went through each time he was going to exercise.

He could feel the burn in his muscles from the four hours of surfing the day before. It was a good feeling, in spite of the pain, because he knew he was getting back into shape. He had lost some of his surfing form, but with all of the downtime he had ahead of him, his immediate goal was to regain what he had lost in the years he hadn't surfed regularly. He knew it sounded crazy, but he would not take on another job unless he was less than an hour from a beach with a decent surf break. But he didn't want to think about that right now. This was his free time and he was planning to maximize his enjoyment of every moment.

Bryce thought about Erin briefly and wondered what she was doing. But they hadn't spoken since he left North Carolina. He figured that such an attractive woman was now hooked up with some good-looking guy. He was glad to be away from the women in Manhattan. At least the ones he had dated. They were more into social climbing and Bryce never felt a real genuine connection with any of them. Those women were more into the conquest than in making a deep connection. And when Bryce was being brutally honest with himself, he realized he behaved that exact same way in that he didn't want a long-term relationship either.

Bryce had pushed away the one person he really wanted to truly be with. He made a mental note to call Tina when he got back from his ride. They stayed in contact over the years, but it had been too long since he had talked to her for any length of time and he wanted to invite her to his ranch with the white picket fence and the stable of beautiful horses.

Jorge, the very able stable hand, had readied Bryce's favorite horse. The gray steed was waiting patiently for Bryce in the paddock, having just finished his breakfast of California grown oats. Bryce lifted his foot into the stirrup. When he felt the heel of his cowboy boot engage the stirrup, he lifted his large frame and swung his leg over the back of the beautiful animal and readied himself for a ride up the Topatopa mountains and into the Sespe Wilderness.

Sunlight was peeking over the hills to the east. It was early enough, and Bryce hoped to catch a glimpse of the California condors as they soared overhead in search of their breakfast. He double-checked the saddlebag that Jorge prepared to make sure there was plenty of water and a snack for him. Bryce was planning on visiting one of the many hot springs that dotted the Sespe Wilderness. Other than that, Bryce's mind was clear, ready to enjoy his ride and enjoy nature.

Bryce grew up hiking these mountains and knew every hill and stream. Today he decided to take a route he hadn't taken in a very long time. It would take a little longer to get to the hot springs, but it would bring him within arm's reach of the Condor Sanctuary. He just knew inside that today he was going to see these magnificent creatures. He put his gray steed through his paces and at one point was up to a full gallop. But today he wanted to take it easy, so he kept his eye to the sky.

*   *   *

265

It was almost 10 AM and Bryce hadn't seen any condors. So, he decided to take a shortcut down into the valley that separated the Sanctuary from the Sespe. The spring water was flowing. He stopped, got off and let his steed have a drink from the cool mountain spring. Bryce sat on a rock and watched the steed drink, pleased that the day was so tranquil. From a distance a gunshot was fired, and the horse jumped. Being in the valley, it was hard to tell where the shot had come from because the sound echoed back and forth. It wasn't hunting season. And even so, no hunting was allowed in the Wilderness.

"Hey, I'm down here!" Bryce shouted - thinking that whoever fired the shot mistook him for some wild game. And then another shot was fired. This time Bryce could hear the bullet quite clearly as it whizzed by with its distinct Doppler sound. Bryce held the reins as he quickly mounted the steed and galloped downslope further into the valley, away from where he thought the shots were coming from.

The steed performed magnificently galloping through the water, avoiding the large boulders that lined the stream. Bryce paid attention to every move he made to avoid being clotheslined by the low hanging tree branches. Galloping in a rock stream was extremely dangerous and he didn't want to be thrown. One more shot whizzed by Bryce's head as he made his escape.

Initially, Bryce thought he was being shot at by mistake, but now he knew it was intentional, so he didn't want to stick around and let them have another shot at him. He was out of cell phone range; otherwise, he would've called the park ranger.

Bryce kept the steed in full gallop until the stream valley opened into a wider clearing and he felt like he was out of danger. He slowed his pace to a brisk trot and for a brief moment thought about cutting his trip short and heading back home. But he wasn't going to let being shot at ruin his otherwise fine day. So, he turned the steed to the east in the hopes of making it to the hot springs by lunch.

*   *   *

The sun was almost overhead. Bryce shaded his eyes as he looked up at the Topatopa Mountains wondering if the condors decided to grace him with their presence. He squinted and thought he saw one, but it was just a crow. He dismounted and tied the reins to the branch of an alder-wood that grew in abundance in the streambed.

Bryce stripped down out of his clothes and underwear as he always did since he was a little kid visiting the hot springs. He was literally in the middle of nowhere, far from civilization. The hot springs were at first too hot to touch, but it felt liberating to have the mineral water warm his naked body. Bryce soon acclimated, and he dipped into the hot pool of mineral water. He floated on his back and looked up at the clear blue sky.

Bryce remembered Billy telling him of pot growers cultivating their plants in the wilderness to avoid government regulation. He questioned Billy about why anyone would still be growing pot in the wilderness, now that pot was legal in California. Billy said that yes, it was theoretically legal but there were so many regulations, and the cost of a license was so expensive that it drove many not to abandon their already thriving underground pot farms and existing buyers.

"Legalizing pot was just another government grab to shake down everyone for more money to fund their wasteful bloated bureaucracy. Those smug progressive ass clowns make me want to puke," Bryce could just hear Billy complaining. As a Libertarian, Billy was always bagging on the government - and for good reason.

Bryce would now have to reconsider his position that the days of farming pot in the wild and shooting at people were coming to an abrupt end. He thought that it was probably illegal pot growers that shot at him but made a note to call the Bureau of Alcohol, Tobacco, and Firearms when he got home. Right after he called Tina; who he was starting to miss. Bryce started to have feelings of anxiety that he had blown his opportunity to be with her.

Chapter 32

Interstate 35 between Minnesota and Iowa
Saturday March 3, 2018

The sun cleared the horizon and Tina had settled down. "No more crying," she said to herself. Saying it out loud reassured her. Her pickup truck was on cruise control. The highway was so straight that she rarely needed to turn the steering wheel.

Tina reflected back on the self-contemplation she had been doing for the past few months, trying to better understand herself. In her research she came to the regretful conclusion that she had codependent tendencies. She came to that conclusion because she felt she gave too much in a relationship and fell prey to exploitive and narcissistic men.

It was hard for her to believe what she read in Psychology Today and other online self-help columns. But the more she read, the more she came to realize that, *yes, she was in control of what happened to her in a relationship. And if she was being treated like shit it meant that she was doing it to herself first.*

In her opinion, the one thing each of these articles agreed on was that getting over codependency behavior was hard because it required her to examine many painful things, and throw out many core beliefs, to heal the scars caused by abusive behavior inflicted by others. This painful path was the only way to gain her self-respect Tina realized. She was willing to put in the hard work to correct this and release her true, authentic self from the shackles that had bound her to a deadbeat like Jeff.

"Well, the first thing you need to do Miss Wood," Tina said, again out loud, so as not to hide from the hard work ahead of her, "is that you are not to overvalue the relationship with the guy at the expense of your dignity. You don't want to be alone, so you value the physical connection to a guy more than you do protecting yourself. You love too much and don't get enough love and respect in return. Wolves will eat those who behave like sheep. Well, girl that shit stops right fucking now! No longer will I allow myself to be used," she said switching from speaking to herself in third person to first person. "I have been blind to the bloodsucking grooming phase of these narcissistic guys."

She was trying to remember that famous saying that went something like, "Your happiness begins when you don't allow some guy to control your emotions."

"Now, all I need to do is to find the right guy," Tina laughed despite herself.

"Incoming message from Bryce St. James," Tina's Bluetooth control console said as if on cue. The planets in the cosmos were certainly in alignment. Tina smiled as she pressed the button to hear the message. A mechanical voice read the message: "Hi kiddo. I just got a call from Chanal and she said you are going to be in L.A. I moved back to Ojai, so let's get together when you are here. Hugs, Bryce."

Tina couldn't believe her luck. In the space of a moment she went from feeling sorry for herself to the elation of looking forward to the one guy she felt she had a true connection with. Hopefully this time it would be different, and Bryce would be more receptive to a deeper, long lasting relationship. Nevertheless, she was glad that they agreed to be best-friends-forever since they first met in Turkey, and that he was the first person she called when she got a new cell phone. He never asked her why she changed her phones so often. He was just glad that she called to catch up. They would talk for hours, and Tina would feel safe knowing that Bryce was out there and that they could talk to each other at any time.

FBI Headquarters, Manhattan

Agent Steve Foley didn't realize that everyone had already left the office. He was deep in thought, studying the documents on the thumb drive that the Chief gave him and doing his own search on what Mark was up to. It was worse than he was led to believe in his brief conversation with the Chief. Perhaps this was on purpose, although he doubted it. The Chief probably didn't realize how bad it was, because if he had known he would have confided all of the facts with him.

From what Steve gathered, Mark had been in constant contact with field operatives in Turkey. The NIOT Bureau Chief in Ankara was pissed that Mark had broken all protocol and most likely jeopardized their investigation of illegal arms sales. In the files he received, there were a number of documents in Turkish that he couldn't read. He recalled a college professor from Columbia that did translation work for the Bureau a few years ago. He thought she would be perfect for this assignment.

A Google collection of data is child's play compared to the shit the U.S. government has on everybody. The only thing that keeps an American citizen safe from search and seizure is that there is way too much stuff to wade through and too few resources to do the wading. This was the only thing that limited what was searched and who can do the searching. The Patriot Act allowed this collection of information to go on pretty much unchecked. Now that the Chief gave this assignment a Code 5, that meant that Steve had unfettered access to all that information. (Although in reality, anyone with a government security clearance can search to his or her heart's content. Luckily most of those that worked for the government aren't that ambitious).

Steve knew that time was of the essence and so he needed to find the professor right away. A few quick searches in the Bureau's databank led him to St. Andrews Minnesota and a cell phone number. He was going to call her right away but figured that she may have left the service of the FBI. So, Steve decided to use the security contact protocol developed for all contract civilians with top-secret security clearances. In his research he did note that the professor's clearance was current, and at level 5.

Interstate 35, Somewhere in Iowa

Tina was in a much better mood, now that she gave herself permission to regain her ego strength. She wasn't going to let the next guy she dated walk all over her. She was especially excited that Bryce had contacted her, although she was somewhat guarded in her elation. She didn't want to get her hopes up and then have Bryce again decide that the life of international finance was more important than being with her.

Tina had been cruising for a few hours now. She lost track of time, although her bladder hadn't, and she needed to pee badly from all the coffee she drank before getting on the road. She checked Google maps and there wasn't anything close. So, she decided to pull off the highway and take a pit stop in the woods.

The French pop group Marie et les Garcons shuffled from her iPod and their hit "Re-Bop" started to play on the stereo. Tina turned up her music and started to groove to the beat, since she was starting to feel better about herself. She pulled her pickup off the interstate into a clearing by the side of the highway. She left her pickup on and opened the doors, so she could hear the music as she dashed into the woods to pee in a thicket of pine trees. As she pulled her pants down and starting to squat, she heard the music stop and her phone announce on the Bluetooth, "Incoming call from an unknown source."

With her pants down around her ankles Tina was not going to run back to her truck to answer the phone. She would just let it go to voicemail. Then the music started playing again as she started to pee. Tina breathed deeply as she relaxed, and the steaming pee formed a puddle on the pine needle covered ground. Then the Bluetooth came on again, "Incoming call from an unknown source."

Wow, Tina thought, *someone really wants to get a hold of me. If it was Jeff begging for forgiveness, then he can just go and fuck himself.*

Tina wiped herself dry and pulled up her panties and pants and tucked in her blouse. *Boy that was a relief. I guess I was too upset to notice that I needed to go,* she thought as she approached the truck. Again, the music cut out and the same Bluetooth announcement came on. She got in the truck and pulled the door closed. She checked the Bluetooth console to see who had called. It was from the 209-area code. She recognized it as being from New York City.

It was probably a robocall from a telemarketer, she thought as she put the truck in gear and continued on her way down the interstate.

Ten minutes later, the phone rang again. And Tina answered it, "Hello."

"Oh hello, I think I've reached the wrong number. Amber," and the man hung up.

That was strange, Tina thought as she kept driving. "Convento de Sant Anna" from the "English Patient" soundtrack was playing on her iPod and Tina kept going over what had just happened on the phone.

"Think Tina, this means something," she said out loud and then it hit her. Amber was her codename. When she was going through her training to get top-secret security clearance, she recalled the instructor telling her to pick a name that she would remember but wasn't associated with her in anyway. She always liked the name and picked it for her codename.

Miss Donaldson used it infrequently, so it just slipped her mind. Tina thought the reason she didn't use it was that Miss Donaldson wanted to make a real connection to another woman in the male dominated world of the FBI, and using a codename for her would have seemed way too impersonal.

Now her initial training was all coming back to her. Yes, of course someone was trying to get ahold of her but wanted her to use a secure line, a line that couldn't be traced or tapped. The protocol was three successive phone calls followed by a message that they had the wrong number, and then state your codename. In all the years Tina had been doing contract work for the Bureau this contact protocol had never been used with her.

Wow, something important must be going on, Tina thought to herself as she checked Google maps for a place to stop and make a call from a landline. Luckily this was the prairie and payphones still existed, due to cell phone coverage being spotty in lots of rural towns. Besides it was past lunchtime and Tina was getting hungry. She had been too involved in her introspection that she didn't notice passing the state line and was now in Iowa. There was a truck stop at the intersection of I-35 and SR-30 near Ames – the perfect place to get something to eat and make a phone call.

The parking lot of the truck stop was full of eighteen-wheelers and double long trailer haul rigs. Tina parked her pickup upfront next to the restaurant. She was stiff from sitting for so long and she stretched before going inside. The restaurant was busier than Tina anticipated, and she noticed payphones on the wall of the hall that led to the bathrooms. Tina picked up the payphone, deposited a quarter and heard the dial tone. She dialed zero for the operator, and heard "AT&T, this is the operator, how may I direct your call?"

"I want to place a collect call to 209…" Tina said as she read out the number on her cell phone from the man that had just contacted her using her codename.

"Who may I say is calling?" The operator asked.

"Amber."

Tina could hear the number being dialed and going through the different phone exchanges as the electrons went from Ames Iowa to New York City; a chasm of not just distance but culture, and a whole bunch else.

"Foley," said the man who picked up the phone. Tina thought she recognized his voice, but she wasn't sure. She was trying to remain calm and collected because she didn't know what was going on, but it must be something important.

"Collect call from Amber, do you accept the charges?" The operator said to the man who answered the phone.

"Yes," the man replied.

"Go ahead" the operator said as she patched Tina through to New York.

"Hello this is Amber," Tina said.

"Are you on a secure line?" Foley asked.

"Yes, I think so. I'm on a payphone in Iowa."

"Good. This is Special Agent Steve Foley. I met you a few years back when you were still at Columbia."

Tina's brain was working faster now, and she replied, "Ah yes, I remember. How can I help you?"

"As you know I cannot go into any details of my investigation, but I need you to translate some documents for me."

"Well, I'm on the road right now. It is spring break, so I couldn't possibly get to it until I return in a week or so," Tina said trying to sound as pleasant as she could.

"Hmm," said Foley, "I need it done right away. It is a rather important matter and I wouldn't press you if I didn't think so."

"Isn't there someone else you can ask?" Tina asked, knowing the answer to her question.

"No, I'm afraid not. The documents are in Turkish and you're the only one connected to the New York Bureau that can translate these. It is my firm belief that it is a matter of national security. I wouldn't impose it on you if it wasn't important," Foley said pressing his case.

"Yes, I know," Tina said, knowing that her plans were going to have to change to accommodate this urgent request. "All right, I'll do it, but you have to know that I'm on the road right now at a truck stop in BFE Iowa."

"No problem. I'll send you an email with instructions to a VPN, and how to access the secure folder that's all set up for you."

"A VP what?"

"A VPN - A virtual private network. It's a fancy way of saying a secure line. Don't worry no one can hack into it."

"Okay, thanks. It will probably take me a few days to translate the documents. Although I'll only know once I see the documents. Once I've had a chance to evaluate them I'll give you an estimate of how long it will take. I know this is urgent, but you have to understand that Turkish is one of the most complicated written languages."

"Yes, I understand. Listen, I really appreciate your help on this," Foley said, "This stuff is being directed all the way from the top."

"Oh, okay," Tina said not knowing what "The top" actually meant, although she understood it was super important.

"The email is on its way to you right now."

"Okay, thanks."

"Only use secure communications and the VPN to contact me."

"Yes, yes of course."

"Thanks. I'll be in touch," and the man hung up without saying goodbye.

As Tina hung up the phone her heart was racing, and her mouth was dry from the anxiety of the excitement. Her knees were shaking, and she had a little difficulty walking back to her truck to get her laptop.

Girl get a hold of yourself. Yeah this is going all the way to the top, but you've done this before, Tina said to herself trying to make sense of her new assignment.

*   *   *

Tina settled into a booth in the back of the diner and was grateful that the truck stop had Wi-Fi. She was logging onto her laptop when the waitress came by to take her order.

"What can I get you to drink, sweetheart?" said the waitress in a raspy smoker's voice.

"Hi, I'll have a cherry coke, a cheeseburger, well done, and fries." Tina replied realizing she was really hungry.

"Everything on it? Pickles?"

"Yes, the works…and extra pickles. The sweet ones."

"You got it. Oh, the password for the Wi-Fi is 'route66,' all lowercase and no spaces."

"Thanks," Tina said, appreciating the small act of kindness and service with a smile. Tina had already logged onto the Wi-Fi when her cherry coke arrived.

"Thanks" Tina said looking up from the screen.

"You're not from these parts," the waitress said.

"No. I'm from all over. My parents are in the Navy and I moved around a lot."

"Well, welcome to Iowa, sweetheart"

"Thanks."

The waitress turned and walked back towards the kitchen. Tina didn't want any prying eyes on her screen as she read the email from Agent Foley. She logged on to the VPN following Foley's instructions and was able to open the folder he set up for her and view the documents placed there. She flipped through the PDF files and a feeling of déjà vu passed over her. *I've read these documents before, but when?*

Think, Tina think, she thought to herself as she put her head in her hands.

Tina didn't notice that the waitress had returned with her burger and fries.

"Lunch is ready," said the waitress.

Tina looked up and then she pushed the laptop to one side and closed the lid as the waitress placed her plate in front of her.

"Oh, looks yummy, thanks."

"There's ketchup and mustard there," the waitress said pointing to the bottles at the side of the booth. Is there anything else I can get for you?"

"No, I'm good, thanks."

"Enjoy."

Tina was indeed hungry. She wolfed her cheeseburger and fries and washed them down with a large gulp of cherry coke. She concealed a burp, thinking it was unladylike to belch; even at a truck stop. She slid her clean plate (except for two butter pickle slices) aside and pulled her laptop closer. She was deep in thought searching frantically through her filing system trying to locate the translation work she remembers doing.

"Wow, sweetheart you polished that off, didn't you?" The waitress said rhetorically, startling Tina. "I guess you saved some room for dessert?"

"Uh, sure, what the hell, I'm on vacation," Tina said in a carefree manner, now confident that she had indeed translated the documents before; now all she had to do was find them.

"Uh... do you have any fresh apple pie?" Tina asked.

"You betcha. Want ice cream with that?"

"Yes, please. And coffee."

"Coming right up," the waitress said smiling. She liked women that ate a proper dinner and didn't just pick at their food.

Tina took her hands from the keyboard and leaned back in the booth. "Think, Tina. Think," she said softly to herself. "Try to remember the circumstances under which you reviewed those documents. When was the last time you did any translation work in Turkish?" She closed her eyes to help her visualize the setting.

"Well, my oh my, what's a pretty young thing like you doing in a place like this all by your lonesome?" Came the drawl of a young trucker.

Tina leaned forward and opened her eyes. "Well, that has to be the most overused, tried and failed pickup line east of the Pecos. Surely, a sophisticated truck driver such as yourself could come up with something more intelligent and wittier. Aren't I right?" Tina shot back at the young man standing next to her table with his Wrangler jeans and big belt buckle (with his beer belly flopped over). Having been around many Navy bases with young horny sailors, Tina certainly knew how to handle herself in these situations. And with her two years teaching at the college level, she was always in command of herself.

"Yes ma'am."

"Well, as a smart young man you'll be able to recognize that I'm busy and trying to get some work done. So, I would be most obliged if I could be left alone."

"Yes ma'am, sorry ma'am," The young truck driver said as he turned and bumped into the waitress returning with Tina's dessert and coffee. The coffee mug was hit by the trucker's elbow and some of its spilled on the floor. The waitress jerked back trying to avoid being scalded by the hot coffee and then the scoop of vanilla ice cream rolled off the hot apple pie and made a splat as it hit the tile floor.

"Now look what you've done, you clumsy fool," the waitress scolded the trucker.

"Sorry ma'am," the trucker said as he quickly took his leave and made his exit back to the safety of his rig and those lonesome country songs he played on the road.

Tina smiled at all of the commotion. "Let me help you," she said to the waitress as she started to get out of the booth.

"Oh, that's alright dear. I've got it. I'll be right back with a fresh piece of pie."

"Nah, don't worry. The pie is fine, and I didn't need the ice cream anyway."

"Are you sure?"

"Yes, yes of course."

The waitress set the warm apple pie in front of Tina, "Let me top off that coffee, dear."

"That's okay. If I have any more to drink, I'll be stopping every 10 miles to pee."

The waitress left Tina to her thoughts of international intrigue and walked back into the kitchen with a scoop of vanilla ice cream, folded in several napkins, neatly tucked into the front pocket of her apron.

"Eureka," Tina said out loud, as if someone was paying attention (which they weren't, now that she had shooed away the young trucker; with his tail between his legs). Tina remembered when she translated the documents Agent Foley just sent.

She searched through the directories on her hard disk. She kept all her work extremely well organized. And boom! She found them. As she was copying the files to the secure FTP website Foley gave her, she wondered why he couldn't have found these documents himself. She translated them when she was still a postdoc at Columbia and gave them to Miss Donaldson from the FBI document control department.

All translated documents were to go through Miss Donaldson. That was the protocol. It was necessary to do it that way, so each document could be catalogued and filed for ease of search and document retrieval. Tina just figured Foley didn't bother to look for himself or have one his staff look for him; not realizing that this was a somewhat dated document and Foley didn't even know it had been in the FBI's possession all this time.

Tina wrote the following note to Agent Foley: "Hi, this is a link to download the files you sent for translation. I translated them over two years ago when I was still in New York. I gave them to Miss Donaldson in document control."

Satisfied that she had earned her keep, Tina packed up her stuff and left the waitress a tip. In the parking lot she could see a big rig pull out of the lot. She caught a glimpse of the driver and recognized him as the guy she had just shooed away. She could tell that he was watching her but turned away when she looked up. Tina shrugged it off and walked to her pickup.

The song "Drive" by the band Incubus started to play on her iPod as she headed out of the parking lot. She obeyed the speed limit when she merged onto the highway. She remembered that the cops hung out near truck stops with the intention of giving speeding tickets to unsuspecting truckers.

She was feeling better now that she was making real time on her road trip to the coast. It would be good to see the ocean again. *Maybe she could go surfing with Bryce!* She thought. And with that thought in mind she pushed the accelerator pedal down just a little bit more, with a smile on her face.

Chapter 33

FBI Headquarters, Manhattan
Saturday March 3, 2018

Tina's email message flashed at the bottom left corner of Foley's computer screen. He clicked on it right away. "Shit!" he said, reading that he was two years behind in the chase.

Miss Donaldson had retired over a year ago. So, he forwarded the message to her replacement. Foley remembered him as a nice young gay man that was a spiffy dresser. Too spiffy in Foley's opinion, but to each his own, he would say. As long as they did their job, what they wore and did on their own time wasn't his concern.

Foley's message read, "This is top priority Category 5 request. Please find the documents that are linked on this email in the FBI's records. I need this right away!"

Foley click the links in Tina's email and downloaded the documents. He got up and went to the kitchen for another cup of coffee, his third that day and it wasn't even dinnertime. The first document was downloaded by the time he returned to his desk. The others were still downloading. "Shit, these are big files," he grumbled.

He opened the first document and started to read. There was an introduction to the document by Tina that she wrote two years ago, "This document was translated from Turkish. The original document was very technical. Turkish doesn't translate well into vernacular English; this combined with the technical subject matter makes the translation into English very awkward. Every attempt has been made to make the document as readable as possible to an American reader. Few literary liberties have been taken; therefore, the sentence structure will be somewhat 'choppy.' Just think of it like the first time you read "Huckleberry Finn." You have to get into a certain rhythm to understand the colloquialisms."

Foley remember the first time he met Tina. He was struck by how attractive she was and that her hair was always unkempt. He formed a crush on her almost immediately and figured he still hadn't gotten over it completely.

Foley read further, and then started to skim through the document. He stopped cold when he saw the name TRX. *Holy shit! This is worse than I thought. That dumb fuck has gotten himself chasing down international gunrunners. Only heaven knows how deeply he's gotten involved in that shit.*

Foley leaned back in his chair and wiped his hands across his mouth and chin. He picked up the phone and called the Chief.

"Yes," the chief answered abruptly.

"It's worse than I originally thought. I'm going to need support," Foley said calmly but with a sense of urgency.

"Sorry, can't do it buddy. Everyone is up to their eyeballs in shit. You know how much corruption there is in New York City. Plus, I had to assign two Agents to take over your last assignment."

"Two?" Foley asked a little pissed off. "I was doing that assignment by myself."

"Like I said, you're my best guy."

"Gee, thanks," Foley replied sarcastically. "God only knows what shit Agent Mark Dunphy has gotten himself into."

"What can I tell you? Once you have something solid, I'll bring in reinforcements. But until that time, you're on your own."

"Gee. Great. Thanks," Foley said dripping in sarcasm as he hung up the phone. He again leaned back in his chair and wiped his hands across his mouth. "Fuck," he muffled to himself. He knew that he needed to figure something out, and fast.

He sent another email to the guy in document control. *He has an earring for Christ sake, where does the Bureau find these guys?* Foley thought to himself as he wrote, "One more thing, I need to know the names and dates of everyone that has viewed these documents."

A reply email was sent almost immediately. "Hi, this is Joseph from document control. I'll be on vacation for two weeks."

"Shit" Foley said, "it looks like I have to do everything myself around here." This probably wasn't too far from the truth.

Interstate 80 between Iowa and Nebraska

Tina had been on the road for three and a half hours when she pulled off to have lunch at the truck stop just outside of Ames. Her goal was to make it all the way across Iowa and most of Nebraska before she would stop for the night. It was another three hours to Lincoln, Nebraska. When she got to Lincoln, she would evaluate how she felt, and whether she would stop or push on.

Unlike her usual self, Tina didn't do any preplanning for this trip. All she knew, when she started, was that she wanted to get as far away from Jeff as possible, to clear her head, and figure out her long-term plans. Making it all the way to California would be great, especially if she was able to see Chanal and rekindle her relationship with Bryce. She didn't want to get her hopes up too much, about getting back together with him. He was a free spirit and marched to his own drummer. Not that they didn't have a special bond, she just wasn't sure if Bryce was ready for a committed relationship with her. Tina decided to not make any plans and just see what happened.

Also, as a lark, Tina decided at the start of the trip that she was going to pop in and see Dean Reed at his ranch in Utah. He had invited her on numerous occasions, but now she figured this was her chance to see him again. Although they remained in contact, by text and emails, she hadn't seen him in person since she left New York almost two and a half years ago.

It was 3 PM. Tina was approaching Lincoln on I-80 and she wasn't tired at all. She decided to press on to Lexington - another two and a half hours away. She figured she would stop there, get something to eat, and have a good night sleep. She knew that tomorrow would be an even longer day if she wanted to make it to the Dean's ranch in Utah.

*   *   *

Tina jumped up in bed when the alarm went off. It was four in the morning, but she was well rested, having gone to bed early. She took a quick shower to freshen up. Before she went to bed, she had planned out her trip for the day. She tried to remember where the Dean lived. She hadn't been to Utah other than Salt Lake City and Zion National Park (and that was many years ago). She wasn't familiar with the rest of the state. She was going to call the Dean, but she wanted her arrival to be a surprise. She remembered that his ranch was just outside a small town, adjacent to a National Park. When she looked at the Google map, she realized that was just about every place in Utah.

What did the Dean mention about his place? She asked herself, pacing in her motel room just in front of her queen-size bed with the bedspread that had a tropical motif. The town was the gateway to Arch National Park. Tina did a Google search and was corrected, "Showing results for Arches National Park."

"Okay the town had a funny sounding name." That was a lot to say, coming from a linguist. "Moab. Yes, I'm pretty sure that's it. It was four hours and thirty-eight minutes to Denver. She would transition from I-80 to I-76 in a place called Julesburg. From Denver she would take I-70 for four hours and forty-five minutes to Crescent Junction, Utah. Then it was a short thirty-two-minute hop south on SR-191 to Moab.

Tina was so excited to be on a road trip. She was looking forward to catching up with the Dean. He had been so nice to her over the years. She thought of him as a surrogate grandfather.

Chapter 34

**The Dean's Ranch, Moab, Utah
Sunday March 4, 2018**

It was about noon, and the bedroom was lit by the sunlight. The Dean was fixated on Joseph's earring as he watched him bob up and down on his stiff member.

"God, you get me excited," the Dean said.

Joseph stopped, looked up, and smiled.

"Oh, don't stop. It feels so good," the Dean said emphasizing the word 'good.'

Joseph obeyed, as he always did.

They had met a year ago at the small private retirement party for Miss Donaldson held at the Dean's apartment in Manhattan. The group was small because the Bureau discourages socializing between staff and hired contractors. The Dean hadn't invited Tina, thinking she would frown on the get together. Plus, the Dean was still somewhat ashamed of being gay and that a good part of his free time consisted of partying with boy-toys like Joseph. So, with the non-socializing policy both the Dean and Joseph kept their tryst secret. In the short time he had worked for the FBI, Joseph had learned how to cover his tracks, especially his digital footprint. Nobody knew that Joseph was staying with the Dean for spring break.

The Dean and Joseph had just hosted a rave party for the underground gay community that called Utah home. They were a small but active group that knew the Dean well. The Dean, for his part, knew what it was like growing up gay in such an unwelcoming place and he strived to provide a safe haven for the young gay men at his sprawling ranch. Plus, he loved having all that hot, young, vibrant male flesh hanging around to look at and fondle.

It was about 2 PM and the Dean and Joseph were still in bed. All of the partygoers had left the premises and left behind a mess of empty liquor bottles, drug paraphernalia, and used condoms.

After the Dean climaxed in his mouth, Joseph got out of bed to go downstairs to the kitchen and make coffee. He was a little hung over and didn't notice the man sitting at the head of the dining room table. Joseph yawned as he opened the fridge to get the coffee jar. He never quite understood why the Dean kept the coffee in the freezer, but like a lot of things in life, Joseph didn't ask too many questions and just went with the flow. The Dean was really nice to him and constantly bought him gifts. In New York, his friends would tease him that the Dean was his sugar daddy. And Joseph would deny it, although it was true. It was also true that those that teased him were jealous and secretly wished they had a sugar daddy as generous as the Dean.

Joseph filled the coffee carafe with tap water. He knew the Dean liked to use Arrowhead bottled water to make his coffee but figured since the Dean wasn't around, he wouldn't know the difference. As he turned from the sink, with a full carafe of water, he froze. The man at the dining room table had risen and was now standing at the entryway to the kitchen.

"I take mine black," the man said in a thick Middle Eastern accent.

Joseph was so scared that he let go of the carafe and it smashed on the tile floor, splashing water all over himself. A few drops and shards of glass came to rest just at the feet of the Middle Eastern man, but nothing landed on him.

"Oh, that's okay. I've already had two cups today, and I'm trying to cut back," the man said with a wry smile. He reached inside his long black jacket and pulled out an Italian made pistol. With a flick of the gun, he motioned to Joseph, "Let's go see if your sugar daddy is up."

As the door to the bedroom opened the Dean said, "Oh you're so good to me. Thanks for…" And then he stopped when he saw the man behind Joseph.

The man pushed Joseph into the room. Joseph stumbled forward, lost his balance and fell to the floor, where he remained, too afraid to get up.

"Leave him out of this," the Dean commanded.

The man didn't pay attention to the Dean as he entered the bedroom. He moved like a cat to case the place and check out the master bathroom, to make sure no one was in there. All the while keeping the gun fixed on the Dean.

"Get dressed," the man said to the Dean. "It seems like you were expecting me."

"I figured eventually someone would come looking for me. But the boy is innocent so leave him out of this."

In one swift motion, while keeping his eyes on the Dean the whole time, the man moved his arm and shot Joseph in the middle of the forehead. Joseph's head hit the floor with a sickening thud, and a pool of blood formed on the carpet.

The Dean shrieked, "Oh my God, you fucker, you killed him!"

"I give the orders see. Now get out of bed and get dressed like I asked. I'm not going to ask again." The man said with a certain measure of authority, seeing that he had just killed a twenty-something man in cold blood.

The Dean was shaking as he rose, completely naked. He had to step around Joseph's body to get to the chair where he had hung his clothes the night before. He couldn't find his underwear, so he put on his pants without them.

Just as the Dean put his arm through his shirtsleeve, the man said, "Okay let's get going" as he motioned to the door.

The Dean walked barefoot toward the door and finished putting on his shirt as they walked downstairs into the dining room. The Dean could see the battery and electrical wires laid out on the table and started to turn away. The man jabbed him in the back with his pistol and said, "Forward. Sit in the chair and put your hands behind your back."

The Dean hesitated, and the man hit him in the back of the head with the butt of the pistol. "Sit," he commanded.

And the Dean obeyed.

The man put his pistol back in his holster and moved behind the Dean. He yanked the Dean's hands back behind the chair and with a nylon zip tie secured his hands behind him.

With his precision motion it was obvious the man was skilled at this. The Dean sunk into the chair with drooped shoulders and his head down, looking at the floor.

"What is amazing to me is that it's always the smart ones - the intellectual ones that are caught. Almost like they wanted to be caught. Am I right professor?"

The Dean didn't answer.

"I've been following you for some time now. With a thief like you, we always play out enough rope knowing that you'll eventually hang yourself and the others in your den of thieves. Yes, yes you came to our attention quite some time ago in Pakistan. It's not every day that a big shot college professor from New York visits Islamabad. And one that likes young boys. Yes. You thought you were so clever, and you were able to hide, but you 'stuck out like a sore thumb' as they say here in America. We were just having a little fun with you when we demanded money in exchange for silence from letting the American authorities know about your sexual proclivities. If they found out that you liked young Pakistani boys that would probably make the New York Times, don't you think?"

The Dean didn't move or look up.

"Yes, yes I think it would. Maybe not the front-page but at least the Metro section. Yes, I can picture the article now 'great professor travels to Pakistan to have sex with boys' or maybe they would say 'boy-toys.' Yes, yes that would be more accurate. Wouldn't you agree professor?"

The Dean didn't move.

"Yes, we found it all so amusing that you would publish your little papers about the Urdu language to cover your tracks and not raise any suspicions. So, you were having fun, and we thought it only fair that we have our fun too. We didn't mean to hurt your feelings. We just wanted to 'balance the equation' so to speak. Yes, we were all having fun. Your fun was buggering young boys and ours was watching you squirm, too afraid that we would tell the American authorities. That is quite ironic don't you think professor? That the American authorities would believe anything those Islamic extremists would say, over the word of a distinguished professor. A Dean from Columbia, no less. Yes, we got a good chuckle out of that. All extremists have a fatalistic sense of humor. Like a work of Shakespeare, no? And we were going to let it go at that. 'No harm, no foul' as they say here in America. Yes, we were growing tired of the little charade. Some of the guys 'back at the office' actually wanted to let you off Scott-free. For a brief moment - and I mean very brief - I was considering it myself. It never would've happened, but I just wanted to show you how charitable we are, that we even thought about it."

The Dean was trembling as he slouched down even more.

"Sit up straight, professor," the man barked.

The Dean fidgeted in his chair but didn't sit up straight.

"I said sit up straight," the man repeated, emphatically stressing every word.

"Don't hurt me. I beg you," the Dean said looking up with tears streaming down his face.

"Don't hurt you? Don't hurt you!" The man screamed, getting very angry. The man took a deep breath, rolled his shoulders back and moved his neck to one side, cracking it with a small twist of his head. As a skilled revolutionary and Executioner, he knew how to remain calm and that losing your temper caused you to think irrationally.

"How can you say such a thing professor?" The man continued calmly. "For it is you that has hurt me. You've stolen from me. And by all accounts you've been doing it for many years. Of course, you might be the mastermind of the whole operation. No offense mind-you, given your esteemed position as Dean of Linguistics at Columbia University in New York City. No, no, I don't mean any offense, even though it is you that has offended me. But I need something from you. And it is something only you can give me. And that is information. I need to know everything you know about the operation. I need names, dates, places, and amounts. Everything. You see I came from a country that is very different from America. Americans are always in a rush. Where I come from, we have all the time in the world. I have learned to be a very patient man. So, let's start from the beginning, shall we?"

It was midafternoon. The Dean asked, "Can I please have a cup of coffee?"

The man looked at the Dean and said, "I will let you have your coffee, but you have to give me something in return. I need the names of everyone involved in the scheme to steal the profits from me. International gunrunning is very risky. Therefore, profits have to be high to make it worth my while. I don't want to rot away at Guantánamo Bay. So, professor, a name for a cup of coffee."

After hearing the lecture from this Middle Eastern asshole, the Dean had gathered his composure. Yeah, the guy had just killed Joseph, but Joseph was just one young boy who liked having the Dean as a sugar daddy. Beside the Dean was growing weary of the illegal arms business. And sick to death of being blackmailed by Ahmed.

The Dean knew that he would eventually be caught, if not by the FBI then by the backstabbing Islamic extremists. They had so many different groups forming and reforming it was hard to keep track. They kept splintering off, forming a new group, and giving themselves a new name for their group. Of course, all in the name of Allah and in the strict accordance with the Koran, or so they said.

The Dean was an international scholar. And according to him these fucks didn't know shit about Allah or the Koran. It still made the Dean angry to remember how he cowered the first time Ahmed came to him with the video of the Dean having sex with boys in Pakistan. He was so afraid of being found out he would have done anything to prevent the video from being released. So, he agreed to launder money for the group Ahmed was involved with at that time. But Ahmed's loyalties changed all the time.

The Dean was smart enough not to ask too many questions about Ahmed's operation. The less he knew the better off he was. No one suspected that a college professor (a Dean no less) would be involved in international gunrunning and money laundering. It was the perfect cover. He traveled the world over, all under the guise of his scholarly research. The guy had balls. He would even apply for government grants to cover the expenses of his trips, writing papers, and giving lectures. Of course, the Dean didn't need the grant money. It was all part of his elaborate ruse.

The Dean would launder money through the Bank of Uppsala. He was a quick study and soon realized that some bankers were as crooked as the Islamic extremists. The Dean had sized up Ahmed. Yeah, he talked tough. And he was tough. But he was as dumb as a bag of rocks. At least compared to the brilliant professor. So, the Dean started to skim a little off the top from each transaction he made. Actually, it was quite easy to do. With the corrupt banker's help he was able to obfuscate his transactions and in the convoluted process take a little for himself and convert it into crypto currency – certainly, the currency of choice for gunrunners, sexual deviants, and thieves. The gunrunning business was booming, and the money kept pouring in. And the Dean's illicit fortune kept increasing, both from the amount he was stealing as well as the insane increase in the value of crypto currency.

The Dean figured that the jig was up, and he better start to plan his exit strategy. He had one close call. Some hotshot from the FBI started to snoop around the Bank of Uppsala, asking questions about irregularities in the paperwork. The Dean's broker at the bank called him one morning to tell him he would take care of it, and not to worry. Obviously, that was the broker's way of fishing for a bonus. The Dean took the hint and threw the banker some crypto currency for his troubles. The Dean never thought about it again, and figured it was all taken care of.

The Dean planned to make his escape to Bangkok – a place where everything was for sale, for a price. And more importantly, they didn't have an extradition agreement with the United States. Besides the Dean rather liked the southeastern boys there.

"So, you want a name. Well I'll give you a name but first you must untie me. Look I'm no threat to you. And I certainly can't outrun or outwit you. So, I ask that you untie me, let me have a cup of coffee and I'll tell you all I know."

The man looked straight into the Dean's eyes and realized he was no threat, a middle-aged, balding man, with a bit of a paunch. So, the man came over to the Dean's side of the table, clicked open a 6-inch switchblade and cut the zip tie that bound the Dean's hands.

"Go make your coffee, before I change my mind."

It was almost 3:00 in the afternoon, as the Dean started to make morning coffee.

Chapter 35

Mark's Undercover Van, Moab, Utah
Sunday March 4, 2018

On the dirt road just off SR-191 on the way to the Dean's ranch, Mark's van pulled off into a clearing. When the Dean was away, on one of his many trips abroad, Mark had bugged his ranch home. Usually a Field Agent, such as Mark, had specialized technicians who did the actual installation of the latest high-tech gadgets. But Mark did not want to compromise his operation. This was all his, and he didn't want any geek numbskull fucking it up for him. Mark paid attention during all his classes at the Academy, and he had developed a knack for integrating technology into his field operations. So, he would collect not only audio, but video as well, of every sordid sex act the professor had with the young gay community of Utah and parts surrounding.

Mark was able to record everything that happened in the house. He left nothing to chance. He could even tell when the professor, or one of his many boy-toys, was taking a dump. But now he was trying to videotape the conversation between the Dean and the Middle Eastern man. Mark was searching through the voluminous amounts of data he had gathered on these gunrunners. His best guess based on the Turkish accent was the guy affectionately known as 'The Executioner.'

Mark figured it would be a miracle if the Dean made it out of that house alive. That wasn't Mark's immediate concern however. No, he wanted to keep track of the big fish. The fish that would tie this whole sordid mess back together (at least that's what he was going to put in his official report). If there was collateral damage, well too bad. This was a messy business, Mark always figured. He had no problem stepping over corpses to get to his ultimate prize.

Mark could see the Dean shuffle off into the kitchen to make his coffee. For Mark, this was his entertainment. He lived

for this shit. He was a master manipulator and loved being a
voyeur.

Dean's Ranch, Moab

The Dean had just finished making his coffee. For a
dead man the Dean was behaving rather calmly. "Would you like
some coffee?" The Dean shouted to the man who had stayed in
the dining room.
"No."
"Okay, suit yourself."
The Dean walked back into the dining room with his cup
of coffee like a changed man. Gone was the cowardly sniffling
of just five minutes ago "shall we get started?" He asked the
man.
"Yes, please begin."
"Oh yes. You wanted a name." The Dean replied with
the air of the international scholar he was.

Mark's Undercover Van

Secure in his van, Mark put his headphones on, because
he didn't want to miss anything the Dean said. He adjusted a
couple of knobs on the high-tech recording equipment. The
micro cameras he installed had tilt, zoom, and pan capabilities.
Mark tilted, zoomed and panned the camera to get the best
possible view of the Dean ready to make his last confession.
In the video monitor in Mark's van, you could see the
dining room of the Dean's ranch home.
"I'll do you better than a name. I'll tell you the whole
story, as far as I know it," the Dean said.
"Yes, go on," motioned The Executioner.
Then without missing a beat, the Dean started to speak
in Turkish, that only had the slightest hint of a Western accent.

*   *   *

Inside Mark's van you could hear him yell, "Shit!" He growled, fidgeting with the knobs of the instruments as if they were capable of translating what the Dean was saying.

"Fuck!" Mark yelled, slamming his fist down on the top of the recording cabinet. "Fuck!" Mark watched the captured video of the Dean talking to The Executioner. But he was helpless to understand what they were talking about. The Turkish language was just gibberish to him.

About five minutes into the conversation Mark clearly heard the Dean say, "Dick Danger." So, he sat up and took notice, because that was the nom de guerre he'd given himself.

Mark's devious mind was racing again.

Then he heard The Executioner reply back saying "Dick Head."

Mark watched as both men laughed, and his anger grew from being the butt of their joke that he couldn't understand. He was not going to be an FBI manqué and both men would pay dearly for their transgressions.

The conversation between the two men continued for well over an hour. Punctuated at times by laughter. Mark found this all very strange, given that The Executioner had killed the Dean's boy-toy lover a few hours before and the body was lying in the Dean's bedroom in a pool of blood already developing rigor mortis.

Outside the Dean's Ranch, Moab Utah

It was late afternoon and Mark had nodded off; no longer interested in that which he could not understand. He didn't notice the pickup truck drive past his parked van, even though it kicked up gravel from the dirt road and left a cloud of dust behind it. A couple of small pebbles hit Mark's windshield, but he was oblivious to it.

294

Tina traveled at a good clip on the dirt road, not knowing exactly where the Dean's house was. She veered around a blind curve and slammed on the brakes, when she saw a small roadside sign hung under the mailbox. The sign in Latin read "Per Multas Lingus Lingua Est." Tina immediately translated this "Through Many Tongues, One Language." She figured this had to be the Dean's place. She remembered him describing it to her when he first bought it, many years ago.

She tugged on the steering wheel to navigate the tight turn at her present clip. The sun had gone down behind the hills to the west, as she raced up the incline hoping that she would be able to meet the Dean. The Dean's house was set back from the road. Far enough back that Tina began to think that she may have gone too far. The sun's glow still lit the sky, but it was starting to get dark. Finally, Tina saw the house. There was a Land Rover with Utah plates parked just in front. Tina was tired from her long day's journey and she didn't notice the black Mercedes with New York plates off to the side of the house.

The house was much larger than she would have imagined. She thought, *how could the Dean afford such a mansion on a professor's salary? Yeah, he was the Dean but so what; this place is huge.* She wasn't exactly certain that she was at the right place. *What the hell. She had come all that way*, she thought as she rang the doorbell. There was a long pause and no response. She rung the bell a second time. The porch light came on, even though there were no lights on within the house. Tina saw a figure approaching the door. She recognized the Dean and started to smile. The Dean was not smiling, and Tina's initial feeling was that it was a mistake to surprise him by just barging in. The door opened swiftly; too swiftly. The Dean emerged and hugged Tina. He then whispered in her ear speaking in Latin, "In magno periculo sumus. Opus est ut de hic statim." *We are in great danger. I need to get out of here, immediately.*

Tina was dumbfounded. She didn't respond but allowed the Dean to take her arm by the elbow and lead her quickly toward her pickup. They both rushed toward the waiting vehicle that Tina left unlocked.

Behind them, The Executioner emerged from the house shouting, "Stop!" as he fired a warning shot into the air.

"Drive, Tina, drive!" The Dean shouted.

Not needing an explanation, Tina floored it, accelerating toward The Executioner. She started to turn the steering wheel to avoid hitting him, but the Dean grabbed the wheel from the passenger's seat, steering the truck toward the man. The Executioner jumped out of the way, just in time to avoid being hit by Tina's pickup.

"Hey, what's going on?" she shouted, regaining control of her vehicle, and noticing that the Dean was not wearing any shoes.

"No time to explain, my dear, just drive like the wind," The Dean replied as the passenger side rearview mirror was shot out. "Fuck!" the Dean shrieked.

"Well Dean, I wanted to surprise you. You always said to drop in if I'm in the neighborhood…"

"So good to see you too Tina my love, but right now I'm in a bit of a pickle. I got mixed in with the wrong crowd."

Headlights flashed in the rearview mirror. The Executioner was chasing them in his black Mercedes. Gunshots were heard but nothing hit the truck. Tina was on autopilot, remembering the stories her Dad and his SEAL buddies used to tell her about what to do when you're being chased.

Never drive in a straight line, she could hear them say.

Not knowing the terrain, Tina was doing the best she could to keep from being shot. The Dean was holding on for dear life, as Tina drove her 4x4 Ram Pickup like it was a military Humvee. Unfortunately, it didn't have all of the same armament, or even better a 50 mm cannon.

She remembered the sharp curve from the driveway onto the main dirt road.

"Hold on!" she yelled to the Dean, knowing that she was not going to slow down to navigate the turn. When she was partway through the turn, holding the steering wheel to counteract the G forces of the turn, a white van emerged on the main road. To avoid a T-bone collision with the van, Tina had to drive off the road. She tried to hold the truck to the edge of the road but the forward momentum, from taking the curve too fast, forced them off the road and into a dry creek ravine. The truck bounced down the steep hill and lurched forward when it got hung up on a large boulder. The truck came to an abrupt stop and the Dean was launched forward and smashed his forehead on the dashboard.

"Dean, are you okay?" Tina shouted as she frantically tried to get traction from the wheels. She put the transmission in four-wheel-drive and tried again, still no luck. "Shit, we're stuck!" she shouted, slamming the steering wheel.

The Dean panicked and opened the door. As he emerged from the vehicle he was immediately shot in the back of the head. Tina dove down, trying to stay low and out of sight. The truck was now illuminated by the high beams of the Mercedes up on the dirt road above them.

"Dean, can you hear me?" Tina called out to the Dean but there was no reply. Tina was trying to stay as calm as she could.

Panic is your worst enemy, she could hear her father say.

Tina always carried a .45 MEU pistol under the driver's seat. She didn't have a permit for a concealed weapon, so she kept the gun unassembled in a leather pouch. That way if she was ever pulled over and they searched her truck she could always claim that she was just transporting it and had no intention of actually using it. Well, now she had to use it. And fast. She reached under the seat but couldn't find the case. It was shoved to one side when the truck came to an abrupt stop. She got down on the floorboard and extended her arm; groping in the dark. Trying desperately to find the case. Her fingers reached out and touched the edge of the case, but she couldn't grab a hold of it.

A shot was fired, and the back window was shot out. Tina pushed under the seat and was able to move the gun case slightly closer to her. She pushed her feet again against the dashboard and moved her head under the seat. She stretched her arm as far as she could and was finally able to grab the case. She swiftly pulled it from under the seat and stayed down as she pulled open the zippered case. She started to feel for the different pieces needed to assemble the pistol. She kept her focus as she snapped the pieces together and then finally slammed in the magazine.

Tina stayed perfectly still with her pistol at the ready. She dared not exit the vehicle, thinking she would suffer the same fate as the Dean. She could hear someone approaching and then saw his shadow cast in his own headlights. Tina was trying to determine if he was going to approach the vehicle from the driver's or the passenger's side. She needed to know this, so she could get ready to get off the first shot.

She felt the truck move, as the man steadied himself against the tailgate on the steep terrain. She saw his shadow move toward the driver's side. *Good, at least she would able to get off a clean shot from where she was currently positioned*; crouched on the floor on the passenger's side of her pickup.

The man crept forward slowly. Tina felt like it was taking him an eternity to move the length of her pickup. His shadow was looming larger and larger. She waited patiently like a sniper, not wanting to fire too soon and lose the element of surprise. She could hear the man's heavy breathing as his hand came to rest on the driver's door window. The door was locked so Tina would need to shoot through the glass. As the man's frame started to appear in the window a distant shot rang out and the man was hit from behind. The bullet went through the man and smashed out the driver side window. Tina was sprayed with glass but didn't move. She tried to control her breathing, so she wouldn't panic.

She figured her best position was to remain as still as possible and keep the element of surprise because she heard another person coming down the embankment toward the truck. There were now two dead men on each side of Tina's immobile truck. Tina dared not exit.

"Tina. Tina Wood!" She heard her name being called out, "This is FBI Special Agent Mark Dunphy. Please identify yourself."

Tina didn't know what to think, how could she have been caught up in all this shit? Hell, her relaxing spring break wasn't turning out as she had planned.

Again, she heard her name being called out. "Tina Wood. This is FBI Special Agent Mark Dunphy. Please acknowledge yourself. You are wanted for questioning in the murder of Jeff Webster."

"Yes, this is Tina Wood. Do not shoot!" Tina shouted. "How do I know that it's really Mark Dunphy? What happened to Jeff?"

"You'll just have to trust me!" Came the shouted reply.

"Yeah, I was afraid of that! On the whole planet you are the one guy I am least likely to trust!"

"Well, I'm sorry about that Tina. That was a long time ago. I was an immature college kid. I'm a changed man! Now I need you to exit the vehicle and raise your hands above your head. Put your 45 on the dashboard and exit the vehicle keeping your hands where I can see them!"

Initially, Tina didn't think that she had a choice. She was shocked that Jeff had been killed. She didn't know what shit the Dean had gotten himself into and could only guess that it had something to do with the translation work he did for the FBI. She didn't want to get wrapped up in any of this stuff although she had no choice since Jeff was dead. *Oh my God, Jeff was dead*, she thought to herself, trying not to panic. She was on spring break for Christ sake, and now all of these things had come crashing down on her.

Trusting that fucking worm Mark Dunphy was something else. Something she was not prepared to do, even if he did work for the FBI. *Well, fuck him,* she said to herself as she took a deep breath. Staying low she moved across the truck to exit the opened passenger side door. Tina pushed herself out backwards, being careful not to step on the Dean's dead body lying on the ground, slumped where he came to rest from the fatal shot of The Executioner's gun. Tina thought *how did that fuck know I had a 45?"* There was no fucking way she was

putting her weapon down without a fight. She grabbed her purse
and readied herself to make a dash for safety.

When she hit the ground, Tina moved like a cat and with
fluid and agile motion moved around the opened passenger door
and ducked down next to the front wheel well. She slung her
purse strap around her head and tucked it up under her arm, in
preparation for the run of her life. She didn't trust Mark and only
God knew what kind of shit he was trying to pull. He had already
killed one guy in cold blood, and Tina didn't want to be his next
victim. She didn't give a shit if he was an FBI Agent; to her he
was a worthless motherfucking scoundrel.

Tina turned away from the truck and surveyed where she
was going to make her dash. The ravine had several large
boulders that would provide some immediate cover. She dared
not make a run upslope, back to the road, figuring she would be
a sitting duck for a shot from Mark. So, having figured her best
plan, Tina bolted, staying low.

She was almost to the first boulder when she heard,
"Stop! This is the FBI!"

As she ducked behind the first boulder a shot was fired
and it ricocheted off the boulder she was hiding behind. Tina
ducked lower but knew she had to keep moving away from Mark
and all of his poison. She got up in a crouched position and
moved as quickly as she could until she was beyond the range
illuminated by the headlights of the vehicle. Then she raised
herself up and was in a full out sprint, running as fast as she
could. It was almost near dark, and Tina's eyes were still
adjusting to the dim light. She tripped on a large rock and lost
her footing. She lunged forward, and her hands broke her fall.
She tore her pant leg and skinned her shin.

"Fuck," she said in a muffled tone, not wanting to yell,
so as not to give away her position. She took a breath and rose to
her feet. She knew she could outrun Mark. The last time she saw
him was in New York City. She was across the street from the
FBI building and saw him exit. She ducked behind a parked car,
not wanting him to see her, but she got a good look at him. There
he was in his full FBI G-man splendor with his male pattern

baldness, that stupid man bun, full-on gut, and that cheap polyester suit.

What a fucking creep, she thought at the time, *what could I have possibly seen in such a creep. Yuck!*

Tina heard a car door slam closed. She figured Mark was not going to try and chase her on foot and had headed back to his van to try and pursue her from the road.

What a lazy good for nothing fuck, Tina thought, as she knew she had him beat and there was no way he was going to catch her. But now she had to make some important decisions.

The ravine paralleled the road, which lay above it by about 50 feet. Tina ducked down just in time as a bright flashlight beam scanned the ravine. It was Mark, looking for his prey. Tina stayed perfectly still as the beam moved down through the ravine. For the time being, she thought it was best just to stay put and figure out her next move. When the flashlight beam had moved a few hundred feet further away, Tina decided to move up the far slope, opposite the road.

The ravine was steeper than she originally thought. She was breathing heavily when she reached the crest, and she felt safe enough to stop and clear the sand from her Nike running shoes.

Jesus, what did the Dean get himself into? She thought, sitting on a large rock as she empty sand from her shoe. *My truck is inoperable. Now how am I going to get to L.A.? Better not go back there. It was a crime scene for sure and I need to get the hell out of here, but how?*

Tina hadn't eaten anything since lunch. It was almost 6:30 PM and she was hungry. *Need to stay strong Tina Wood. Focus girl. What would Dad do*? She thought for a few moments trying not to panic, then decided that she would walk back to the town of Moab, get something to eat, call Bryce, and stay clear of Mark.

It was almost 9 PM when Tina made her way back into town. At one point in her trek, she thought about walking back on the road but decided not to risk it. So, she didn't make great time, bushwhacking it through the Utah desert with a cut shin, and sand continually getting in her shoes.

From a distance she could see a row of streetlights and figured it was the main drag. As she got closer, she could make out the golden arches of McDonald's. It certainly wasn't her first choice but would have to do for now. She didn't want to spend much time getting something to eat.

Chapter 36

McDonalds, Moab, Utah
Sunday March 4, 2018

Tina squinted her eyes when she first entered McDonalds. She was grateful that there were no customers in line which meant that she could order right away. When she was ordering her Big Mac, fries and orange juice she thought she saw Mark's van pass by on the street. Her reflexes kicked in and she ducked down.

The clerk that was taking her order saw her duck down and said, "You alright ma'am?" Thinking it was odd to duck when you're placing your food order.

"Yes, thanks," Tina said trying to pretend she was fixing her pant leg that had ripped during her trek through the desert.

"Ma'am, do you know your leg is bleeding?"

"Yes"

"I can get the first aid kit."

"No, that won't be necessary. Thanks. I just need a septic wipe."

"You got it," said the McDonald's clerk has he turned to go into the back area and fetch the first aid kit. He returned about thirty seconds later with a septic wipe and a large size Band-Aid. "Here you go. Your order will be right up."

The night was a little chilly as Tina walked on the sidewalk immediately adjacent to McDonald's towards the back-parking lot. She figured she would eat her Big Mac in peace and then call Bryce. As she passed the back corner of the building something didn't feel right, but it was too late. She was hit on the side of the head by a punch thrown by Mark. He saw her inside McDonald's and had circled back. He was lying in wait for her to exit the building.

Tina was knocked to the ground and she dropped the bag with her food and orange juice. "You're going to buy me another Big Mac asshole," Tina said holding the side of her head.

But Mark didn't wait for her to get up and lunged at her again trying to kick her when she was on the asphalt pavement. Tina tried to move but was too slow and Mark's foot hit her already bloodied shin.

"Ah!" Tina screamed in pain.

"You ruined my investigation! Why did you have to show up?" Mark yelled as he tried to kick Tina again. But this time Tina moved out of the way and Mark's foot only grazed her.

"Now, you're a dead man," Tina snarled as she pressed her hands to the pavement and slowly pushed herself up.

Mark was 5'10" and outweighed Tina by at least 50 pounds. However, Tina knew how to use imbalances to her advantage, if she could get the leverage she needed. There was no way she could take him head-on. Tina was on her feet and she took a step back and raised herself up on the balls of her feet. Then she sprung forward like a cat and with a sweeping motion (like kicking a soccer ball in the opposite direction) kicked Mark's right knee forward. Mark's leg buckled, and he stumbled but quickly regained his footing.

While Tina was off balance, he gave her a straight arm right to the chest. This blow forced Tina back and she again fell to the pavement. By reflex her arms came out to break her fall but she skinned her hands on the hard asphalt pavement. Mark wasn't going to allow her to get up again and moved toward her in a brutish fashion, with his weapon drawn and aimed at Tina's head. Tina quickly reached behind her and with her bloodied hand pulled out her pistol that she had placed in the back of her pants. In one fluid motion, she discharged the weapon and shot Mark in the fleshy part of his thigh; a non-lethal shot that just grazed him.

"You bitch! You fucking bitch! You shot me!" Mark screamed in pain covering the entry wound that was now streaming blood. The shot only momentarily stopped him, and Mark kept moving forward - with a limp leg, rage in his eyes, and his gun in his hand. Mark shot at Tina's head when she was still on the ground. He missed and the bullet grazed her shoulder and ricocheted off the pavement.

In a split second, Tina figured she would just wound Mark, with the hope that this would stop his forward advance. Since he kept coming and shot at her head, Tina aimed her pistol again. She was leaning back on the pavement at the McDonald's back parking lot in Moab Utah.

Mark was looming large above her screaming like a mad man. The bullet entered Mark's lower jaw with a trajectory that traversed through the roof of his mouth and cerebellum and exited the backside of his head. Mark dropped like a rock, face first, toward Tina. Due to the brain damage, caused by the bullet, Mark's reflexes failed to respond to his fall and his hands did not project out to brace the fall. Mark's face smashed against the pavement with a loud cringing 'splat', and he partially landed on top of Tina as his face hit the cold black surface of the parking lot.

A moment before Tina fired the fatal shot into Mark's head, a car squealed into the McDonald's driveway from the main drag. The car's headlights illuminated the last parts of the deadly struggle between Mark and Tina. The car wheels screeched to a stop and smoke from the burning rubber escaped into the cool clean Utah air. The car's door flung open and a man got out and crouched behind the open door.

"Tina, please put down the gun. This is Special Agent Steve Foley of the FBI."

Tina turned to look in the direction of the voice. She couldn't identify who was talking due to the headlight blinding her and she thought it was another trick.

"How do I know it's you?" Tina said pushing Mark off her and rising from the pavement, still holding her weapon.

"Tina, I got your email. I was able to locate Mark's data bank and uncover the shit he was into. I figured out he would be back here because he had been tracking the Dean for years. Something terrible has happened to your boyfriend. And I don't want you to get involved in the shit that Mark has wrought. So, I ask you to please put the gun down."

Tina was stunned. Tears welled up in her eyes as she bent over to place her shiny Marine Expeditionary Unit, Special Operations Capable pistol on the cold pavement.

Agent Foley came out from behind the car door and approached Tina. "I'm afraid I have some terrible news," he said in a low stern voice.

"Yes, I know. Jeff's been killed."

"I'm so sorry, my dear," Foley said, looking at Tina and knowing the hurt she was now going through.

Tina couldn't hold back her tough woman persona any longer and began to sob. Foley put his arms around her and hugged her as she cried on his chest.

"I'm so sorry you got mixed up in all of this. The Bureau appreciates all of your hard work and dedication beyond the call of duty," Foley said, trying to console Tina.

"Thanks," Tina said through the labored breathing of her sobs and wiping the tears from her face, "I was just trying to get away for spring break."

"I'm sorry your vacation was ruined. I'll try and make it up to you. Your email was the big break that cracked this case wide open. Thanks for taking the time to respond," Foley said giving her another hug.

"My truck is in a ditch by the side of the dirt road back there," she said motioning in the direction from where she had trekked. "The Dean is dead. And there's another dead man by the side of my truck. Mark shot him from behind," Tina said looking down now feeling cold as she rubbed each of her arms trying to get warm.

"Please sit in my car. I'm going to have to call this in to the local sheriff. I'll need you to take me to your truck." Agent Foley said in the manner of an experienced G-man having done this type of grisly work before.

"Yes, okay," Tina said as she walked towards Foley's car. She now noticed the small crowd of people, mostly the night crew from McDonald's, gathering on the sidewalk. The car was still running as she opened the front passenger door. She sat down and reclined her seat. She reached forward to turn on the car heater. Foley came around to the far side and reached inside to get his radio. He stood beside the car and called the Moab County Sheriff.

"This is Special Agent Foley of the FBI. I need local assistance at the McDonald's off of Highway SR-191."

"Agent Foley, this is the Moab County Sheriff Dispatch" came the squawk of the radio. Your call is acknowledged. We'll have mobile units there shortly."

"I'll also need the County Coroner."

"10-4, the coroner will be called."

*   *   *

Within minutes, the sirens of the Moab County Sheriff cars were heard as they raced toward the McDonald's. It wasn't every day they got a call from the FBI, so the whole force came out. There were five squad cars all parked haphazardly behind Foley's sedan with the federal license plates.

"Agent Foley? I'm Sergeant Brent Scowcroft of the Grant County Sheriff's Department. What have we got here?" the sergeant said, reaching out his hand.

Foley shook the sergeant's hand as he said "sergeant we have a homicide of FBI Agent Mark Dunphy. The lady in my car is Dr. Tina Wood. She is a security contractor for the FBI and has top-secret security clearance. She shot Agent Dunphy in self-defense. I witnessed the fatal shot and want to be present when you take her statement. It is my belief that this is a matter of national security and all information gathered by the Sheriff's Department needs to be kept in strict confidence. We'll need the coroner's office here immediately."

"Oh okay. Getting the coroner here is going to be a bit of a snag. We don't have much call for one in these parts, so we contract with Salt Lake. They said they'd have someone here in a jiffy."

"Okay, that should work. I want you to take command of the cri…" Foley's voice tapered off from saying 'crime scene'

307

and then said. "You can get Dr. Wood's statement afterward. Right now, she has to show me another location not far from here. I'll need you to assign two of your men to me until I get federal Agents here. Once I visit Dr. Kim Reed's house, I'll set up a command post. Remember everything is to be secured in strict confidence and everything has to go through me. Got it?"

"Yes sir," said the Sheriff not used to being ordered around by an Agent of the federal government, but he was impressed with Foley's command of the situation.

"The sergeant called on his radio, "Rich and Pete I need you to follow Special Agent Foley and to take direction from him. He is heading out now to another crime scene and he'll need you to secure the place. I've called for backup."

"10-4 Sarge," came the reply over the radio from the two units now assigned to Foley.

Agent Foley got back in his car. "Tina, I need you to stay strong. This is going to be a long night. Now you'll have to direct me to your truck."

"Yes, of course. It's not far. I walked here from there." Tina said sitting up and adjusting the back of her seat. "Go back to the highway, head south and take the first dirt road east."

Chapter 37

Outside the Dean's Ranch, Moab
Sunday March 4, 2018

It was a moonless night and completely dark. The headlights of the three vehicles cast an eerie glow on the bushes and dust kicked up on the unpaved road.

"Slow down. Getting close" Tina said peering over Foley trying to look out the driver's side window for something she recognized. "That's it, just down there."

Foley pulled the car to the far side of the road, adjacent to the downslope. One of the cruisers pulled ahead of them with its rotating red lights lighting the gloomy night air. Both cruisers turned on their spotlights and immediately lit the area where Tina's truck had come to rest.

"I need you to wait here while I check this out," Foley said putting the car in park, but leaving the engine running. He opened the driver side door and got out, closing it behind him. Tina could see Agent Foley talking to the two Sheriff's deputies; directing them what to do. She saw them get flashlights from the cruisers and then head down the embankment. She thought about going down there to fetch her fleece jacket from her truck but figured Agent Foley wouldn't allow it. Now that her Dodge Ram pickup was now a federal crime scene, with two dead bodies on either side of it.

Before she had time to start feeling sorry for herself, Agent Foley was back. Getting quickly into the car and putting it in gear he said, "I need you to direct me to the Dean's house."

"Yes, it's just down here a bit," Tina said motioning forward.

Foley pulled out around the forward cruiser and started heading down the dirt road. The cruiser in the back followed them. They hadn't gone 50 yards when they stopped again. Parked on the side of the road was the black Mercedes driven by

The Executioner that had chased Tina and the Dean, and who now laid dead at the side of her truck.

Agent Foley pulled over and stopped by the car. "I'll just be a moment," he said opening the car door.

Tina just looked straight ahead and didn't say anything. Agent Foley approached the car putting on his gloves. He opened the door and pressed the button to lock all the doors.

Tina could hear him say to the Sheriff's deputy that was behind them "we'll come back to this car. Right now, I want you to go up to the house with me."

The ride was bumpy up the dirt driveway to the Dean's house. Finally, through a clearing Tina could see an outline of the house. It was huge - something that didn't register completely when she first drove up to it. Foley parked almost exactly in the same spot she had only a few hours previous. Tina thought about the things that had changed since then. *She found out her boyfriend had been killed, the Middle Eastern guy driving the black Mercedes tried to kill her, her mentor and confidential advisor for many years was killed in cold blood right before her eyes, and to top it off - she killed the guy she had once dated. Shit, my day didn't turn out like I thought it would when I first hatched the idea of dropping in on the Dean and surprising him.*

Tina was a little dazed and probably in shock when Agent Foley said "Tina, this house is a crime scene, otherwise I would invite you in. Please stay here. I know you're upset but you'll just have to bear with me for the moment."

Tina nodded slightly in acknowledgment, knowing that as soon as she was alone in the car, she was going to call Bryce. And she hoped like hell that he would answer. Tina clicked on the recently called numbers on her Samsung Galaxy smartphone and hit Bryce's number. Unlike so many times before he picked up after the first ring.

"Hey, kiddo how's it going? I was just thinking about you."

"Bryce, I'm in trouble and I need your help. Please listen carefully. I'm going to tell you things that will cause you to have many questions. But I ask you to hold your questions and I'll answer them when I see you in person. Right now, I just want you to help me as best you can." Tina paused to give Bryce time to respond.

"Anything for you, kid. You know that."

"Thanks, I always knew I could count on you. I never told anyone this before and I cannot completely divulge my role. The most I can say is that I have top-secret security clearance."

"Go on, I'm listening," Bryce said knowing that Tina was serious, and he knew better than to crack jokes when she was being very direct with him.

"Right now, I'm in Moab Utah at Dean Reed's ranch house. There have been multiple shootings and I think I need a criminal lawyer."

"Ah…ah let me think for a moment," Bryce said with his mind racing. He paused and then said, "I know just the guy. But he lives here in L.A. Do you want me to contact him?"

"Yes, please do so. The sheriff is going to take my statement and I know enough about these things that I want my own representation. There is some really deep shit that has gone down."

She was going to add 'matters of national security' but decided that would only complicate the already complicated and confusing circumstances.

"I am not involved with what is going on and do not want to be collateral damage when everything comes out. I trust that my government handler will be fair with me, but this is a real shit show and God only knows what will happen when this goes above his level."

"Got it. Let me call my guy and I'll call you right back."

"Okay thanks," and with that, Bryce hung up.

It used to really bug Tina that Bryce never said "goodbye" on the phone, but over the years, she just got used to his little quirk. She once asked him about it, and he said the reason that he never said "goodbye" to her was that she was always on his mind so there was never a goodbye really.

She found his explanation endearing but it took her awhile to overcome the abruptness of not saying goodbye. Tina put her smartphone back in her purse and reclined her car seat. She laid back and tried not to think about the rotating red lights from the sheriff's cruiser sitting not ten feet away from her.

She could hear the crackling on the police radio but tried to put it out of her mind. She needed to pee but didn't dare go in the Dean's house. She briefly thought about peeing in the bushes but thought the sheriff would catch her. The best thing was to try not to think about it. And just then her phone rang.

Boy that was quick, she thought, thinking that Bryce was an amazing guy.

"Hello," she said hopefully.

"Listen, kiddo I was able to get ahold of the L.A. attorney, but they don't do any work in Utah, so he recommended a guy in Salt Lake. Apparently, there aren't that many lawyers outside of Salt Lake. Not much call for it, I guess."

"Yeah, that's what I've heard."

"Well listen, I called the guy in Salt Lake. He's going to send one of his associates out to you right away. He's taking a helicopter to the town of Moab. His name is Jon Hawk and his cell phone number is..." Bryce recited the number he had been given. "He's going to call you right away. I am going to hang up, so he can get a hold of you."

"Thanks Bryce. You're the best," Tina said with tears in her eyes.

"Don't worry kiddo, everything is going to be okay. Bryce St. James is on the case. I'll cover the cost. I just want you to be safe. Talk to you soon." And with that he hung up. And almost immediately after that the phone rang again. Tina could see it was the number of the lawyer Bryce had just given her.

"Hello, this is Tina Wood."

"Hello, Dr. Wood. This is Jon Hawk. I just spoke with Bryce St. James from Los Angeles and want you to know that I am en route to the Salt Lake airport. I'll be chartering a plane and should be in Moab within an hour. I'll call you when I land.

As you may know, do not give a statement to the authorities until I've had a chance to talk to you. I will also need to be present when you're being questioned and giving your statement. These are your constitutional rights. The sheriff should respect that."

"Understood. Thank you for helping me."

"My pleasure Dr. Wood. Just sit tight and I'll be there as quickly as possible."

"Thanks, I'll see you when you get here."

"Goodbye," and with that, the phone went silent. Tina wished he would've stayed on the line a little longer, so she could explain what was going on. She figured that she'd just have to wait a little longer. She felt bad that she wasn't able to tell Bryce more on the phone. As she began to recline her seat, she saw Agent Foley talking to the sheriff's deputy on the porch of the Dean's house. Most likely giving him instructions, because the deputy went back into the house and Agent Foley started walking towards the car.

"We have to go back to McDonald's, then I'll take you to a motel. I've asked the sheriff to make a reservation for you. I know this has been a long day for you, as it has for me as well. I certainly appreciate your patience and all that you've done for the Bureau."

Tina puffed her breath, trying to stay calm and not lose it. "Agent Foley, I've been more than patient. I want to go to the motel now. Please take me there."

"Well my dear, things have indeed been hectic and traumatic. I completely understand. I'll take you to the motel and will arrange for you to give your statement after a good night's rest." And with that, Agent Foley put the car in reverse. The red lights of the cruiser illuminated a strobe across the cool Utah night sky blocking out the tranquil flicker of the stars above.

Chapter 38

Grand County Sheriff's Station, Moab, Utah
Monday March 5, 2018

They arrived in droves – some by themselves, others with their partners. But they all came. Word spread quickly that an FBI Agent had been killed in the line of duty. His fellow agents were out for blood. Rumors abound. Some said his scorned lover killed the agent. Some said that he was a rogue Agent involved in a prostitution ring.

Others countered, defending the slain Agent, by saying that he needed to give the appearance of being rogue, if he was going to be deep undercover and believable to those criminals he had infiltrated. There was an element of specious facts that surrounded these rumors. But the one thing they had in common was that conclusions had been reached without knowing all the facts.

Utah Bureau Chief Tad Edwards had been awakened by a phone call from the governor, no less, who demanded that this sordid mess did not damage the clean image of the great State of Utah. The governor didn't want some underling to be assigned to the investigation. He demanded that the Bureau Chief devote himself to the case and take charge of the situation. And that is what Chief Edwards intended to do.

Overnight the Grand County Sheriff's Department had been essentially taken over by the FBI. The sleepy town of Moab, Utah was abuzz with police activity and word spread quickly that their famous native son, the international scholar, Dean Kim Reed had been killed. In the live and let live County, with the mighty Colorado River flowing through it, some were shocked to learn that the Dean was gay, and that his gay lover had also been slain in the Dean's bedroom by a bullet to the middle of the forehead.

"How could such a thing take place here in Grand County?" the residents asked each other. And now the news media wanted to know too. It was the job of the FBI to get the answer to that question… and never tell anybody, unless they had a top-secret security clearance.

*   *   *

The conference room at the Sheriff's Department was small and had never seen this level of activity. Not even the Christmas Toy Drive generated the buzz that now swarmed over the place. A sheriff's deputy, who also doubled as the IT guy, was down on his hands and knees trying to figure out which cables to use to patch the video feed in from Salt Lake. The Salt Lake FBI Bureau Chief had scheduled a conference call for 8 AM with the Agents that were on the ground in Moab. The office phone was in the middle of the conference room table; its cord stretched across the room to the wall outlet, creating a tripping hazard for the standing room only crowd.

It was already 8:05 and the Bureau Chief was impatient to get going. He didn't want to wait for the video screen to be set up.

"Alright, let's get started. This is FBI Bureau Chief Tad Edwards here in Salt Lake. I just want you to know that I received calls from the governor, and both of our federal senators. They have given me complete charge of this investigation and have expressed to me that they want the sordid characters involved in these hideous crimes, to be dealt with to the fullest extent of the law. All officers involved - local, state, and federal - are to conduct themselves in the most professional manner, especially when gathering evidence. They do not want some critical piece of evidence being thrown out of court on some technicality. I've also been in contact with the New York Bureau Chief and he informed me that Special Agent Steve Foley is the most knowledgeable of the facts surrounding these events and that we should keep him informed of all information that is gathered. I have assigned Special Agent Roger Helmbuck to be my right-hand man, and to lead all that are involved at the site. Roger please fill us in on what's going on there in Grand County."

Just as Agent Helmbuck started to speak, the IT deputy cheered, "That's it!" As the video screen flickered to life illuminating Bureau Chief Edwards, drinking coffee and eating his Dunkin' Donuts.

"Thanks Chief. Before I begin, I would like Agent Foley to fill us in on the background of this case. I think it would be helpful for all of us to understand what we are dealing with."

Special Agent Roger Helmbuck was a by-the-book G-man. A no-nonsense former Marine who most people described as a humorless hard ass.

Agent Foley hadn't gotten much sleep and wasn't prepared for a long stay out of New York, so he looked like he slept in his clothes and hadn't had time to shave. He was also in no mood to deal with hard-asses like Helmbuck. He was assigned this investigation and planned to see it through to the end regardless of what the Utah FBI thought. That little shit Mark Dunphy had escaped his grasp once before. Foley didn't want that to reflect poorly on his handling of the initial internal investigation of Mark's eccentric behavior.

By the time Foley arrived at the Grand County Sheriff's station the place was already packed. It was certainly going to be a good day for the local Dunkin' Donuts shop, and from all early indications, a good week as well. Foley was standing in the back, the lone black man in a sea of white faces. As he began to speak those assembled in front of him moved to the side, so that he could advance toward the conference room table.

"It is my firm belief that this is a matter of national security. And as such, only federal Agents, with top secret security clearance, will be able to view privileged information," Foley began.

"Oh, cut the crap, Foley!" Helmbuck retorted, "I don't want to hear any sorry excuses defending how the New York bureau screwed up this case and now want to stay in charge. In case you didn't notice, you're in Utah now. And the sworn officers have a right to know what they are up against."

"In due time the Sheriff's Department will be brought up to speed about the background of this case. But it will only be on a need to know basis. It is my belief that events are still unfolding, and I do not want to jeopardize the overall investigation with information being released prematurely. Thus, I must ask that the room be cleared of all personnel accept FBI Agents.

"Hey, just wait a cotton-picking moment!" the Grand County Sheriff said seated at the head of the table. Unlike Foley, he had arrived early to the meeting to secure his place at the head of the table. He was up for reelection this year and didn't want to let the biggest crime event in Utah's history to pass him by. "I am sheriff of the county and me and my deputies need to know what the hell is going on."

"I truly appreciate that Sheriff, and I indeed intend to brief you personally this morning. But right now, I need time to discuss the case with the Utah FBI."

"You're not going to waltz in here to my Sheriff station, from New York of all places, and start telling us what to do."

"Alright, alright! Enough!" boomed the distorted voice of Tad Edwards over the speakerphone. On the video screen you could see that he had just finished his donut, there was white confectioners' sugar on his chin and was talking with his mouth full. "Sheriff, I fully appreciate your position, but right now I'm going to have to agree with Special Agent Foley, and kindly asked that the FBI be allowed to caucus. I'll plan on calling in when you talk separately with Agents Helmbuck and Foley. But right now, the conference room needs to be cleared of everyone except the FBI."

'Smack!' Came the noise of the Sheriff's hand as it slapped down on the conference room table signifying his displeasure at being dismissed. "I'll be in my office waiting for the meeting," he said in an angry voice as he rose from his chair at the head of the conference room table.

The Sheriff deputies now started to file out of the room. Foley waited for all to leave before he closed the conference room door and took a seat at the head of the table - the one previously occupied by the Grand County Sheriff.

After a brief round of introductions of the FBI Agents that remained in the conference room, Foley began. "Special Agent Mark Dunphy assigned to the New York Bureau of the FBI was shot and killed last night in the McDonald's parking lot in the town of Moab, Utah. The alleged assailant is Dr. Tina Wood, an FBI consultant contracted by the New York Bureau to provide translation services. Also killed last night was Dean Kim Reed, who also was a translation consultant to the New York Bureau. Also killed in the Dean's house was Joseph Sweat who is a document control clerk at the New York Bureau." Foley paused realizing that this was indeed a total shit-show brought to the peaceful town of Moab.

He continued as he looked around the table at the assembled local FBI Agents. "Also killed was an Iraqi national who goes by numerous aliases. He is affectionately known in the Islamic underground as The Executioner. At this point in time, we do not know his true identity. Sometime within the last week Dr. Wood's partner Jeff Webster was killed in St. Andrews, Minnesota. I believe that this is also linked to the events that unfolded here in Utah. Dr. Wood is a person of interest in Jeff Webster's murder. At this time, she is not a suspect."

"Jesus, what a cluster fuck, Foley. The New York Bureau has spread its Gomorrah to the peaceful state of Utah. Please tell us more. I'm waiting for the part about national security interest. And it better be good, otherwise you just pissed off the sheriff and all his deputies for no good reason," Helmbuck interrupted.

"All right Roger, that's enough. We're all supposed to be on the same side," the Utah Bureau Chief interjected, trying to keep peace in the family. "Yes, Foley were all waiting for the national security part."

The people in Utah were so polite, compared to what Foley had to put up with in New York. Even when they were trying to act all high and mighty and pissed off, they couldn't hold a candle to the certified jerks and assholes Foley dealt with every single day in New York.

Foley continued unfazed by the interruption. "The Iraqi national that was killed last night has been on the FBI's watch list for years. He has to be in the U.S. illegally, possibly coming through Mexico or Canada. Or he could have used one of his many aliases to fool the TSA. Approximately three years ago Agent Mark Dunphy was under an internal investigation. It was believed at that time he was in over his head in an undercover investigation of international gun sales through the Turkish distributor of an American company. It now appears that our internal investigation was prematurely called off. At that time Agent Dunphy was reprimanded for not following investigation protocol and put on a short probation. The Agent cleared probation and return to active duty, to what appears now to be certainly unsanctioned activities. It is my belief that he was investigating the blackmailing of the Dean. It appears that the Dean was exchanging money-laundering services for keeping his pedophilia concealed. We think the Dean was being blackmailed by Ahmed Ali Raheem who runs a nightclub in Manhattan, and I believe to be the U.S. contact, and clearinghouse for all the illegal arms sales and money laundering."

"Make sure his picture and info are posted at the Utah bureau," Helmbuck interrupted again, trying to appear to be in charge.

Foley continued, ignoring Helmbuck, "I have a hunch that Ahmed and the Dean were skimming off the top from the money laundering operation they ran, and that is why The Executioner was sent here to deal with them."

"Well how does this figure when the girl is the one that popped Agent Dunphy? And now her boyfriend has been killed as well. Seems pretty suspicious to me," Helmbuck interjected.

"I caution all of you that we must not jump to any conclusions. Right now, we have to gather all the evidence we can. The tapes that Agent Mark Dunphy recorded in his surveillance van need to be reviewed and cross-referenced to information we already have. We cannot rush to judgment because it may cause us to overlook something that may appear to be insignificant or irrelevant but could turn out to be the clue we need to break the case wide open. International gun runners are well financed and will hire the best criminal attorneys available that will pick apart our evidence and claim that we didn't follow proper protocol in an effort to get key pieces of evidence dismissed. We cannot let this happen, so we all have to shadow the local sheriff's deputies to make absolutely certain proper protocols are followed."

The Utah Bureau Chief came back on the line, "Well, speaking of the best criminal attorneys. Your doctor friend certainly knew the best in the state of Utah. I was just handed a note that she has retained Smit, Weiss, Jenner, and Buchanan and that all communications with their client needs to go through them. They sent one of their associates to Moab to meet with Dr. Wood."

"See, what did I tell you? All seems too suspicious to me," Helmbuck piped up.

"Listen, if I hear any more of your innuendo or half-baked suppositions, I'll personally petition the head of the Bureau in Washington to have you removed from the case," Foley said to Helmbuck. The statement was also meant as a challenge to Edwards.

"Well fuck..." Helmbuck started to say until the Utah Bureau Chief cut him off.

"Gentlemen, gentlemen we need the two of you to get along, or I'll remove you both from the case. Do I make myself clear?"

Foley, who was used to high-pressure situations, and grandstanding Agents said, "Yes, of course. I'm here to see that justice is served." And he made a mental note that he was going to need help from the brass in New York to deal with these two clowns that were going to fat-finger the investigation and fuck it all up.

There was a pause as the Chief waited for Helmbuck's reply, "Well, Roger what will it be?"

"Yes, Chief, you have my word."

Foley was surprised that Tina had already hired outside counsel. *When did she have time to do that?* He wondered. *Was there something going on that he didn't know about?* He thought to himself, not letting on that he was surprised. Foley was not someone you wanted to play poker with.

"So, Agent Foley we've now heard all of *your* half-baked ideas and suppositions where are the facts that point to this being a matter of national security?" The Utah Bureau Chief now shot back, not one to back down to a challenge, especially from a New Yorker.

"That's it. That's all I have for you. You now know what I know," Foley answered the Chief's one-uppance. Not willing to reveal any more of his theories, especially since he didn't have the facts and evidence to back them up. And he was now worried that he may have actually said too much to these bumpkins from the backwoods of the country. No, that was enough. He would suffer their ridicule because TRX was his. If he let it get out he was going after them, he knew that they would have very powerful allies in the U.S. government that would side with them to marginalize him and shut down his investigation. No, this was something he needed to do by himself, but he knew he would need the help of a special person. And that special person had just hired the best attorney in the State of Utah.

"Yeah, what about your girlfriend," Helmbuck continued, ignoring his pledge of not ten seconds ago of vowing to get along. "I heard she went for a ride along with you all last night, and now you let her get away without us interrogating her. God you must have a crush on the good Dr. Wood."

Agent Foley just smiled. He had certainly dealt with plenty of dickheads that thought they were smarter than they were. The morons thought that if they acted tough, others would bend to their will.

"I think I've heard quite enough from the fine Agents here in the great State of Utah," Foley said, dripping with sarcasm, as he rose from his seat. Foley was not one to be baited by the likes of Helmbuck. *Let that amateur have his 'interrogation'* he thought. He knew Tina could handle herself.

And he was glad that she hired legal counsel. With the shit that had just gone down, the brass would be out for blood. They had been in denial about Mark's undercover operation. Foley would have to get more evidence to figure out this whole mess.

Chapter 39

Tina's Motel, Moab, Utah
Tuesday March 6, 2018

The small hotel where Tina had spent the night was right out of a Route 66 movie from the 1960's. A well-built brick structure with a space age architectural motif and a few Art Deco touches thrown in for good measure. All these fine details were lost on an exhausted Tina Wood as she made her way to her room, after being dropped off by Agent Foley.

Despite being exhausted, Tina had a restless sleep. The events of the previous day kept playing over and over in her mind. Her mind kept trying to figure out who could possibly want to kill Jeff. She realized that she didn't love him and hadn't for many months, but she still felt remorse that he was dead. And most likely because of the shit Mark had caused. *That fuck deserved to die* she thought vindictively. She was trying to find something less harsh to think, but she hated his guts and all the pent-up emotions came out that she had buried deep in her from when they were briefly together in San Diego.

Tina received a text message from the lawyer Bryce hired for her. He said that since she was too tired to meet in the evening, they should meet at Denny's for breakfast. In his text he also mentioned that he had been in contact with the Utah Bureau Chief of the FBI.

Tina was a bit dazed from everything that had happened since spring break started. So, she didn't notice the crew working on the neon hotel sign at the edge of the driveway. The motel owner had made enough money from the increased number of guests over the past few years that he decided to spruce the place up a little. He was even toying with the idea of listing the place on the State's Registry of Historic Places. Had Tina known, or even cared, she would have advised him to fix the plumbing, first. She was not too pleased with the lukewarm shower that she took that morning. The water pressure was so low that the slightly brownish water hardly flowed from the showerhead.

Tina received a call from Agent Foley at 6 AM. He left her a message that he had a tow truck pull her truck from the ravine. It was not in an operable state, but that he had retrieved her personal items from the truck and that they would be dropped off at the motel, along with a rental pickup truck - courtesy of the New York FBI. Tina thought they would impound her truck but was pleased that Foley was able to get her stuff for her and get her a replacement vehicle. She was trying hard not to lose it and meltdown from the stress of the last few days, and it was comforting to know that Foley had her back.

With her hair still a little damp, Tina pressed the ignition to her rental truck. She sat in the driver's seat looking straight out the window, but not seeing anything in particular. No, she was looking inward. Trying to picture how the events of the coming day were going to play out. She could not recall ever talking to a lawyer before - especially a criminal defense attorney. Tina was trying to think what her father would do in the situation. She could hear him say to her, "Just be you. The truth will set you free."

She had killed an FBI Agent, so she knew they were going to come after her hard. And the circumstances surrounding Jeff's death didn't look good either. Tina could just picture the nosy neighbors telling the police about the big fight she had with Jeff and that she had stormed off. Now that Jeff was dead, they would certainly embellish their stories. Tina took a deep breath as she put the truck in gear and pulled out of the parking lot. She had her game face on, and she wasn't going to take shit from anyone. "Take no prisoners," she said aloud as she pulled out onto the two-lane highway that led to Denny's.

Denny's, Moab, Utah

Tina listened to what she called ambient music whenever she needed to calm down. Others would call it new age electronica, but to Tina's discerning taste there was a big difference between the two genres. A random selection on her iPod pulled up the album "Calling Down the Sky" by Robert Rich, and the song "Vertigo" began to play. Almost immediately she was transported to a different place as she drove down the quiet country road. Tina visualized what was going to happen to her after the events of the previous day. Space-time was a continuum and she could sense that she had lived these events before. So, she was not afraid.

*   *   *

Denny's was busy at 7 AM. Filled with tourists that wanted to get a jump on the day, and not miss out on anything during their short spring break. The hostess barely had time to say "good morning" when Tina spotted her lawyer. She had never seen him before, but he dressed like a lawyer, even in casual clothes.

Tina said, "Good morning" to the hostess and walked straight to the lawyer's table. He slid out of the booth and rose to his feet to greet her.

"Jon Hawk. It's a pleasure to meet you Dr. Wood."

Jon was a handsome man of forty-six with an athletic build. He had the kind of look women would swoon to. He enjoyed rock climbing and canyoneering in Zion National Park. He married his high school sweetheart and they had one daughter. But before they got married, Jon had done a stint in the Navy as a JAG.

"Thanks. Please call me Tina" all my friends do. Tina said trying to break down formal barriers between her and the guy she was now going to have to bare her soul too.

"Tina it is. Please have a seat."

Tina slid into the booth opposite Jon and put her hands out on the table in front of her. She was about to speak when the waitress interrupted, "Coffee?"

325

"No, thank you. A tall orange juice on ice please" Tina said taking a deep breath and trying to relax.

"You got it," the waitress replied handing them both the large Denny's menus with the wonderful pictures of breakfast meals they could order. "I'll be back to take your order."

"Listen," Tina began to speak at the exact same time Jon did, and stopped.

"No, you first" he said gesturing to her.

"Well this is the first time I've talked to a lawyer and I'm a little nervous."

"Please try not to be. I am your absolute advocate and will be with you every step of the way to get you through this most difficult time. The one thing that I do ask however, and this is for your own benefit, is to tell me the unvarnished truth, no matter how embarrassing, or damaging it may be. I need to prepare the best representation possible, and I can only do that with your help. Agreed?"

"Yes, agreed."

"I am going to appear very blunt at times and what I say and do may appear harsh and you may think that I need to 'tone it down' so to speak. But the first class you take in college to be a criminal defense attorney is called Asshole 101. Trust me I'm not an asshole, but sometimes in the heat of battle I need to be. Do you understand?"

"Yes," Tina said nodding her head in agreement, a little surprised at the strong words coming from such a polite Mormon.

"Good. Well let's get to it. There is little time to waste. Your hearing is at 10 AM with the federal judge. I've already talked to the Salt Lake Bureau Chief about the events involving you and they're going to come at you hard. Very hard. They're going to invoke the Patriot Act and essentially throw the book at you. So, I need you to stay strong and be direct in your response to my questions and the questions from the U.S. Attorney General's representative. He's going to be a bigger asshole than I am because a federal agent is dead. And they don't take too kindly to that. They are out for blood and that can blind justice.

Compounding all of this is the fact that your live-in partner is dead as well."

"Jeff was my boyfriend" Tina said correcting Jon. "We had a big fight and I stormed out. I didn't kill him. I did kill Mark, but clearly in self-defense. Do you know what? Both of those guys sucker punched me" Tina said her voice rising. "They fucking sucker punched me!" Tina repeated, not caring that she was swearing or showing emotion.

"I'm so sorry, but I need you to stay calm. We need to appeal to the judge, who is a no nonsense kinda guy, and who will see through the embellishment of the U.S. Attorney General's rep. However, in order for him to do that you need to just be yourself and the truth will set you free."

Tina regained her composure quickly and smiled slightly. Jon caught it.

"What?" Jon said sensing a connection with her.

"Oh, that's just something that my Dad would've said."

"Well your father is a wise man."

"Yes, he is. He is indeed," and with that, Tina felt comfortable and dropped her defensive position and opened up to Jon. Helping him prepare for the hearing. She was now fearless.

Chapter 40

Grand County Courthouse, Moab, Utah
Tuesday March 6, 2018

Tina's hearing was held at the Grand County Courthouse. A stately building of white marble and two-story tall Ionic columns at the entrance to the building that served as a warning to all 'if you do bad things you'll end up in here and we'll put you down.'

The courtroom was sparse. It was Tina's first time being in one and it seemed like a place out of some old movie. Dark walnut wainscoting lined the walls. The judge's dais rose over the two tables in front of it. All made from the same dark walnut. Tina sat next to Jon. They were the first to arrive. The bailiff showed them to their table. At about 9:55 AM the U.S. Attorney's representative arrived, and Agent Roger Helmbuck followed behind him. They didn't make eye contact or even acknowledge Tina and Jon. Just before 10 AM, the bailiff re-entered the courtroom and asked the U.S. Attorney's rep if he was expecting anyone else. The U.S. Attorney's rep said no.

Tina thought it strange that Agent Foley wasn't present. She was going to say something to Jon about it when the bailiff announced, "All rise, the Honorable Judge Hubert E. Lawson presiding."

At the same time all four in attendance rose as the judge entered the courtroom from a door partially obscured by the high dais. A stenographer followed behind him and set up her stenograph in front of the dais.

"Be seated," the judge commanded. The judge was a sixty-year-old slight man with stooped shoulders. His black robe enveloped him, almost looking comical with his small bald head sticking out. His bald head had a small band of gray hair that wrapped around the backside. The judge hit the gavel on the wooden block and called the hearing to order. "This is the federal hearing into the death of Agent Mark Dunphy of the FBI.

The hearing is informal by nature, but the U.S. Attorney's office has requested that we must follow the rules of the Patriot Act. Thus, I asked that the bailiff seal the courtroom."

"Your Honor," Jon said rising to his feet, "I asked that the judge reconsider invoking the Patriot Act. The rules are not applicable in this instance. Especially when it concerns my client, Dr. Wood."

"Your Honor!" the U.S. Attorney's rep shouted out, "based on the matters surrounding this case it is absolutely necessary that the rules of the Patriot Act be employed. This is a matter of national security!"

"Be seated gentlemen. I'll decide if the Patriot Act needs to be invoked. But first I asked the U.S. Attorney to present, then Mr. Hawk can present his side of the story."

Jon's brain was in overdrive. Trying to remember the Patriot Act hearing he attended as a Navy JAG. There certainly wasn't much call for this knowledge in sleepy Salt Lake. He started taking notes as soon as the DA started to speak.

"Thank you, your Honor. The federal government is going to charge Dr. Christina Clare Wood with the first-degree murder of FBI Special Agent Mark Dunphy. We also ask that she be held without bail because we deem her to be a flight risk with connections to Muslim terrorist operatives working out of Pakistan. Dr. Wood is also wanted for questioning and is a person of interest in the killing of her boyfriend Jeff Webster in St. Andrews, Minnesota. According to local police records Dr. Wood had a fight with Mr. Webster. It is believed that she was having an affair with Bradford Hayworth the backup goalie of the college hockey team that Mr. Webster coached. She flaunted her affair with the goalie the day Mr. Webster was killed. A fight ensued between Dr. Wood and Mr. Webster. She killed him and spent the night with her lover. She made her getaway to meet with her Pakistani handlers operating out of the safe house in New Jersey. Our records indicate the phone call came from Chanal Aslumani, a Pakistani national. Chanal Aslumani's husband Saeed Balmsa is wanted by the NIOT due to his connections with illegal arms dealing to known Islamic terrorist groups."

The U.S. Attorney's rep stopped for a moment and returned to the table to check his notes. He picked up a yellow legal pad and flipped through the first few pages. He held the flipped pages on the back of the pad as he turned towards the judge and continued his prosecution. "It is believed by the Bureau that Chanal Aslumani is Dr. Wood's handler and that they plan to rendezvous in Los Angeles. On her trip to Los Angeles, Dr. Wood stopped in Moab to get instructions about illegal arms sales from her colleague at Columbia University, Dean Kim Reed, The Head of Linguistics. Agent Dunphy was investigating the Dean, and Dr. Wood fouled up his investigation. The details of the ensuing gunfight at the Dean's ranch are still being investigated. But suffice it to say that Dr. Wood is a flight risk because she has traveled the entire globe, speaks twenty-seven languages, and her defense is being financed by one Bryce St. James. Mr. St. James is a wealthy international banker at the Bank of Uppsala in New York City. The bank is under investigation for conspiring to participate in international money laundering. Dr. Wood and Agent Dunphy were lovers in college at the University of California in San Diego. It is alleged that Dr. Wood still carried a flame for Agent Dunphy and that she never got over being dumped by him. Thus, it is the desire of the federal government that Dr. Wood be remanded into custody of the FBI and held without bail at the federal corrections maximum-security prison in Columbine, Colorado."

The U.S. Attorney turned to head back to his seat. Satisfied with himself that he just nailed a domestic terrorist with connections to Islamic extremists. This would certainly play well in his career advancement.

As the U.S. Attorney rep begins to sit the judge asked, "Is that all?"

"Oh yes your honor. I think that's enough." The U.S. Attorney says with a smirk. Agent Helmbuck almost high-fived him when he sat down.

"Mr. Hawk, the floor is yours," the judge said as he peered out over the top of his reading glasses.

Jon had his head down and had been writing feverishly the whole time that the U.S. Attorney's rep had been speaking. Ten seconds passed, and the judge sternly said, "Mr. Hawk?"

Jon put his pen down, picked up his pad, and pushed his chair back away from the table. He started to speak while still sitting. Unbeknownst to Tina, this was a sign of great disrespect in a court of law. Jon knew what he was doing. He wanted to establish that he was in control.

"Your honor, when this hearing began you said that it was an informal hearing. You did not say that the hearing was to be a slanderous affair of conjecture, half-truths, salacious details stated only to inflame, gross inaccuracies, and specious arguments all cobbled together by the Utah Barney Fife Corps of the Federal Bureau of Investigation."

Agent Roger Helmbuck took the bait and slammed his fist on the table. "I object. What does this country lawyer know?"

Immediately the U.S. Attorney's rep moved his hand over to calm Helmbuck as the judge scolded him, "One more outburst from you sir and I'll have you fined for contempt of court. You had your turn." The judge turned to Jon and said, "Counselor, please continue."

Jon's opening statement had the desired effect of getting Helmbuck all steamed up. He had been given an anonymous tip the previous evening about Helmbuck's demeanor and used the information masterfully. In the dynamics of the hearing, he wanted to contrast this hot-headed buffoon with the eminent college professor Dr. Wood. Jon reached over and squeezed Tina's forearm to reassure her that everything was going to be fine. He rose from his chair and started to speak from behind the table, showing his command of the court learned from his stint in the Navy. "Your honor, I'm going to call Dr. Tina Wood to the stand. She will waive her fifth amendment rights."

The U.S. Attorney's rep sat up straight with raised eyebrows at Jon Hawk's announcement that he'd get to question the defendant. That never happens and he was now planning to shred her testimony.

The bailiff approached from the back of the courtroom. Jon motioned to Tina to rise. She walked confidently towards the bailiff and raised her right hand.

The bailiff began "Do you swear to tell the truth, the whole truth, and nothing but the truth, so help you God?"

"I do," Tina replied.

The bailiff directed her to the witness stand adjacent to the judge. Tina sat on the hardwood chair and looked straight at the U.S. Attorney's rep. He averted her glare by looking down.

The judge turned to her and said, "Please, state your name for the record."

"Christina Clare Wood, your Honor, my friends call me Tina."

"Thank you my dear", the judge said in his folksy way. "Please begin counselor."

"Thank you, your Honor" Jon said as he came out from behind the table and approached Tina.

"Dr. Wood, please tell us what you do for living."

"I teach French and Latin at Bards College in St. Andrews, Minnesota."

"And what else?"

"I am an independent contractor for the FBI in New York. I translate documents from foreign languages into English."

"Are these special documents?"

"It varies, depending on the assignment. To do this work requires a top-secret security clearance, level V."

"How many languages do you speak?"

"I speak eleven languages fluently and have a working knowledge of approximately twenty others. Lately the assignments have been to translate documents from languages spoken in the Middle East. Geographically the area covered by the late Ottoman Empire."

"Where did you graduate from high school?"

"At the Anderson International School in Ankara Turkey. My parents were in the Navy and we traveled all over the world."

"What did your parents do in the Navy?"

"My parents spent their entire career in the Navy. They are both retired now and live on the Big Island of Hawaii. My mother was a flight surgeon and my father was a Navy SEAL."

Who was your roommate at the Anderson School?"

"Chanal Aslumani. When you travelled as much as we did it was difficult maintaining friendships. But Chanal and I have remained close over the years. Her boyfriend from high school was Saeed Balmsa. They eventually got married. I also met my first boyfriend in Turkey. Bryce St. James. He was the son of the U.S. Ambassador to Turkey. And we remained close friends over the years as well. It is my spring break and I am traveling to Los Angeles to visit both of them. Bryce no longer works for the Bank of Uppsala. He left the bank a few months ago and moved back to his hometown of Ojai California."

"So, what do you make of these accusations that Chanal is your 'handler'?" Jon said lifting his hands and giving the quotation sign as he said the word 'handler'.

"It's preposterous. Both Chanal and Saeed are Jantis Muslims and they wouldn't hurt anyone. I was planning to stay with Chanal at her uncle's house in Echo Park. Her uncle is the Head of Thoracic Surgery at the USC University Hospital in Los Angeles. Hardly Muslim terrorists."

Jon waited a moment to let this sink in with the judge. He knew he needed to counter each specious argument by the U.S. Attorney and to do it in such a way that the judge could digest it and rule in Tina's favor.

"What happened the day before you left St. Andrews, Minnesota?" Jon said as he referenced his notes.

"I went to the rink to bring Jeff his favorite Starbucks coffee. Bradford, the backup goalie, is my best friend's kid brother. I was sitting alone, and he wasn't playing, so he came over and sat next to me and we chatted. I went to the rink to see Jeff and see if I could patch things up. Our relationship was getting very strained. Jeff gets very jealous when I talk to other guys. So, when I got home that evening, he had been drinking heavily. He sucker punched me and called me a whore. So, I packed my bags and decided I was going to move out. I didn't have any place to stay so Brad offered that I could crash at his place."

For a second, Tina thought about adding, *and had the best sex she had had in a long time with the backup goalie*, but wisely left that part out. Knowing some things were better left unsaid.

"When I left Jeff, he was very much alive. Drunk, but alive. I don't know what happened to Jeff or why anyone would want to kill him."

"Why are you in Utah?" Jon continued.

"On my way here, I figured I would stop in and surprise Dean Kim Reed. The Dean was my Ph.D. advisor at Columbia University. He was the one that recommended me for translation work at the New York Bureau of the FBI. This hearing really needs to have Special Agent Steve Foley present. He was my first contact at the FBI and was here in Moab yesterday. I don't know why he's not at this hearing. He would certainly corroborate my statements."

Upon hearing this the judge raised his eyebrows with astonishment. "You mean to say that an FBI Agent from New York is in Utah and you spoke with him yesterday?" The judge said, interrupting Jon's line of questioning.

"Yes, your Honor. He pulled into the driveway at McDonald's when Mark…Agent Dunphy was attacking me."

The judge made a puffing sound with his mouth and shook his head in disbelief that the U.S. Attorney didn't mention this important fact.

"Go on Dr. Wood," the judge said.

Jon sensed a big opening that he was going to exploit with his line of questioning.

"Well, I was walking out of McDonald's when I was punched in the side of the head – a sucker punch thrown by

Agent Dunphy, and I fell to the ground." Tina turned her head, so the judge could see the left side of her swollen face.

"Why don't you explain what took place before that!" The U.S. Attorney's rep burst out.

The judge banged his gavel and shouted "No more outbursts from that table or I will find you in contempt of court. You had your turn, now let her speak."

Just then there was a pounding on the locked courtroom door.

"Sheesh, what now?" The judge said in frustration. "Bailiff, go see who that is!"

The bailiff hustled to the door and unlocked it. Special Agent Steve Foley barged in, holding his badge aloft, as the bailiff tried to restrain him.

The judge shouted, "This is a sealed courtroom!"

"Your Honor, I'm Special Agent Steve Foley of the New York Bureau of the FBI. I am in charge of this investigation and must speak to you about important matters related to this hearing."

The judge shrugged, "Well, it can't be any stranger than what I've heard so far. Bailiff allow him in. But lock the door!"

Agent Foley strutted to the front of the courtroom not looking at anyone and stood in front of the judge, with the judge looming over the proceedings on the dais.

"Your honor I'm in charge of this investigation, and the investigation of all the events that happened in Moab yesterday."

"You are not!" Helmbuck shouted.

The judge whacked his gavel. "Five thousand dollar fine to you sir. I do not want to hear another word from you, or I'll have you removed from my courtroom. Am I perfectly clear?"

The U.S. Attorney glowered at Helmbuck and put his hand on his shoulder in a gesture of 'shut the fuck up you moron'.

"Yes, your honor," Helmbuck said begrudgingly.

"Well, as I was saying your honor, I followed Agent Dunphy from New York. This is the second time he has been under internal investigation by the New York Bureau. Agent

Dunphy was deep undercover and we believe got in way over his head. I have jurisdiction over all the events related to this investigation. This is a letter from the Deputy Secretary of the Justice Department." Foley said, reaching into his crumpled suit coat breast pocket producing a letter that he hands to the judge.

"I had this letter prepared before I left New York in anticipation of encountering uncooperative law enforcement in my investigation."

The judge raised his hand, signaling that he wanted Foley to stop talking as he began to read the letter on Department of Justice letterhead.

The letter read:

"To whom it may concern,

This letter has been written to inform you that Special Agent Stephen Foley is on a case of national security importance. He is in charge of all matters involving the investigation of Agent Mark Dunphy of the F.B.I. Your utmost cooperation with Agent Foley is expected and considered your duty. Failure to cooperate with Special Agent Foley will be dealt with swiftly by the Department of Justice.

Sincerely, James Tucker,

Deputy Secretary, U.S. Department of Justice"

The judge looked up from the letter and said, "Impressive letter. It was short, but effective. So, Agent Foley, what do you have to say pertinent to this hearing?"

"First, I need that letter back, Your Honor. Heaven knows if I'll need to use it again before my investigation is complete."

"Yes, of course," the judge says handing back the letter.

"This hearing should never have taken place. Local authorities have taken it upon themselves to try and take over this investigation and in a rush to judgment, are trying to railroad this fine lady, who is a critical asset needed to further this investigation. Dr. Wood is an FBI contractor, with a level V security clearance. She has been on special assignment for me and has been caught up in these most unfortunate events. Hell, she translated a critical document for me just a couple of days ago that gave me a significant break in my investigation. There are details that I cannot go into because my direction is coming straight from the Justice Department. This is the protocol when there is cause to believe that we have a matter of national security and there may be co-conspirators within the government."

"That's all well and good, and certainly very impressive and compelling. So, what do you have to say to your esteemed colleague?" the judge asked as he motioned toward Helmbuck and the Utah representative of the U.S. Attorney's office, "that Dr. Wood should be charged with first-degree murder of Agent Dunphy and held without bail at a maximum-security prison because she is a flight risk."

"With all due respect, Your Honor, that sounds like the bumbling investigation style of Barney Fife. Dr. Wood is certainly not a flight risk. Yes, she lived abroad because her parents were in the Navy, but she is a patriot. Why else would she be doing the translation assignments for the pittance the Bureau pays her? This is her service to our country. Much like that of her parents. She has a special God-given talent that she has offered to share. I intend to continue using her services. I have a copy of the security video from the McDonald's where Agent Dunphy attacked Dr. Wood. I want to show you this video," Foley said as he turned and placed his briefcase on the table right in front of the U.S. Attorney rep in a show of "who's your daddy now, you dumb fuck."

He unzipped the case and pulled out his laptop. The computer was in sleep mode because he grabbed it when he learned that this hearing was taking place. The computer came to life after a brief boot up with the FBI symbol flashing to life on the screen. While this was happening, the judge left the dais and came to stand next to Agent Foley to view the screen. And soon everyone in the courtroom had gathered round to get a peek of the computer screen.

Agent Foley used his large fingers on the small pad to click on a file on his desktop. The video file opened up showing McDonalds from the drive-through point of view. Foley took the cursor and advanced the video to the point when Tina exited the side entrance of the McDonald's.

They all watched Tina walk out of the side exit heading to the back-parking lot. Then a man from behind the corner of the building punched Tina. She fell to the pavement.

Agent Foley paused the video and pointed to the screen, "The man that jumped out and punched Dr. Wood is Agent Mark Dunphy of the FBI."

Foley restarts the video, and they see Tina trying to scramble away on the pavement, but Mark was looming over her. Mark had his revolver drawn and pointed at Tina. Then the scene is illuminated by a car's headlights.

Again, Foley pauses the video and said, "You can see the scene being lit from my car's headlights. I witnessed the whole firefight."

There was no audio, so they couldn't hear any words exchanged. Foley restarted the video and there was a brief flash from Tina's pistol as she shot Mark in the thigh. Mark reached down to touch his leg but kept moving toward Tina with his gun drawn and pointed at her head. There was a flash as Mark shot at Tina's head and missed. Within an instant there was another flash from Tina's gun as she shot Mark through the jaw and he fell on top of her. Then Tina pushed Mark off her and got up placing her pistol on the pavement and raising her hands. Agent Foley then enters the frame and takes Tina's arm to lead her away from Mark's fallen body.

Foley clicked the video off.

"I am the eyewitness to the shooting of Agent Mark Dunphy. And if what you just saw wasn't self-defense then I don't know what is."

"But judge…" Helmbuck started to say.

"The next time you speak without me asking you to talk you will spend thirty days in the federal lock-up" the judge scolded Helmbuck as he shook his head and returned to the dais.

"Please take your seats everyone. Agent Foley what is your explanation for the events that took place in Minnesota, and the killing of Jeff Webster?" the judge said as he sat down.

"Well your honor, not all the facts are in. However, it is my belief that he was the unfortunate victim of a turf war between the Islamic money laundering syndicate in the United States, headed by Ahmed Ali Raheem. Agent Dunphy was investigating this syndicate. From what I gathered so far Agent Dunphy compromised Dr. Wood's cover as a translator for the FBI. She is the only one we have that speaks fluent Turkish. Ahmed is a Turkish national and is on the FBI's most wanted list. He is a man of many identities, and it appears that Agent Dunphy got in over his head and gave them Dr. Wood's name. So, Ahmed was coming for her and Jeff Webster was in the wrong place at the wrong time. Most unfortunate."

"Agent Foley, you say that not all of the facts are in… and your belief is… and it appears. I run a court of law and we deal with facts, not hearsay," the judge said, wanting to give the benefit of the doubt but not totally convinced.

"I'm sorry judge but that is what it's like in the shadowy underworld of international crime syndicates. We may never know all the facts or have videotape of all of the illegal activity. We are dealing with trained killers who would shoot you in cold blood while they ate their turkey sandwich and wouldn't think twice about it. Trust me when I say, at the conclusion of my investigation all responsible will be brought to justice. Agent Dunphy was under internal investigation by the New York Bureau. I am in charge of that investigation and think this hearing should never have been held. I respectfully ask that this hearing be concluded, and you release Dr. Wood. I will be personally responsible for her oversight."

The judge again made a puffing sound with his breath and leaned back in his chair. He stopped and thought for a moment before speaking, "Agent Foley I will grant your request and asked that a written report be sent to me and the U.S. Attorney from Utah in thirty days documenting the findings of your investigation. At that time, I'll evaluate what direction (if any) this hearing should take. This hearing is adjourned." Judge Herbert E Lawson whacked the gavel, rose and left by the same door that he entered.

*   *   *

Agent Steve Foley had certainly been very busy since he arrived in Utah. The shit hit the fan when Agent Mark Dunphy was shot and killed, especially by an FBI contractor. The New York Bureau Chief called him to demand answers. Answers that Foley wasn't able to provide, or worse, answers that the Chief didn't want to hear. On the positive side Foley was now able to get the backup New York Agents he needed. And word of what happened at Tina's hearing quickly spread amongst the Utah FBI Agents.

The Utah Bureau Chief put Helmbuck on desk duty, temporarily, while the shit storm blew over. Needless to say, his behavior was an embarrassment to the department. The U.S. Attorney was even more pissed. He let his false pride take over his better judgment. He thought he would be a big shot and arrest a domestic terrorist. Instead he was now the laughingstock of Utah law enforcement, by getting his hat handed to him by Foley.

The Utah Bureau Chief called Foley to clear the air. He had heard of the letter from the Deputy Secretary and didn't want to get on the bad side of the Justice Department. Although he didn't actually apologize, he did eat plenty of crow telling Foley that his department was at his disposal to assist in his investigation. Foley was magnanimous in victory, but it wasn't the victory he needed. Yes, it was good that the FBI had stopped the infighting, but he needed to break up the gunrunning and the money laundering. And truth be told, he saw the Utah Agents as a bunch of redneck hillbillies that he was going to assign to the FBI equivalent of meter maid while he had the New York crew fly in for the serious investigative stuff.

340

Chapter 41

FBI Impound Yard, Moab, Utah
Tuesday March 6, 2018

The Utah Agents impounded Mark's van but had no idea what to do with the electronic surveillance equipment in the back. Foley still had his suspicions that Mark wasn't acting alone. He had to be careful about who knew what. Mark tripping him up on his first investigation still ate away at Foley. He didn't think of his current investigation as revenge or setting the record straight. No, it was way more personal than that. Foley was upset with himself that he allowed it to happen. So now he had a chance to do the right thing and see that justice was done.

Foley made sure he was the Agent that inspected the van. He had his own solid-state external drive with him and surreptitiously downloaded all the files Mark had stored. When he left the impound yard, he told the Utah Agent "I want that van sealed and no one, absolutely no one goes inside without my prior consent. If the seal on that van is broken it will go into my report to the Utah Bureau Chief, and that would not be good on your record. Am I making myself perfectly clear?"

"Yes sir. I'll seal the van personally and make sure no one gets inside."

Foley smiled as he turned away to leave the impound yard. *These guys are a bunch of bumpkins,* he thought to himself. Foley was jaded by the attitudes displayed by the Agents in New York. The New York Agents would have told him to seal the van himself and get stuffed.

*   *   *

Foley loaded the videos on his laptop and started to watch them when he got back to his car. Starting at the ending, where he rightfully thought the important stuff was. He watched

Dean Reed and The Executioner talking to each other. They were speaking in a foreign language that he didn't recognize. The only words that he could make out were "Dick Danger" and "Dick Head." A flash thought raced over him. *He was going to need Tina's services after all.* He was just bullshitting the judge previously about getting her continued assistance to make sure that he got his way, and that Tina was released. But now he realized that he needed her more than ever. He needed her immediately, otherwise the investigation would come to a standstill without knowledge of what was being said on the tapes that Mark made.

Tina's Motel, Moab, Utah

The Chevy Malibu's front wheels wailed as it navigated the tight turn into the motel where Tina was staying. The crew working on the neon sign looked up as Foley's car came to a screeching halt right next to Tina's rental truck. Tina heard the commotion and came out of the motel room to meet Foley.

"You know my lawyer said I should not talk to you," Tina said squinting from the glare of the sun.

"Yeah I figured he would tell you that. I would too if I was your lawyer. But I'm not, and I need your help." Foley said, almost pleading with her.

"He also said I should get out of the translation business for the FBI."

"Yeah, he's right again. So, what can I say? I need you to look at these videotapes and let me know what they are saying. Then I'll owe you one."

"No, this one's on me. I'm so grateful that you came to my rescue. That clown, Helmbuck and the U.S. Attorney were going to railroad me and put me away for a very long time. But can this wait? I need to get on the road if I'm going to make it to Los Angeles."

"I'm afraid this can't wait but it won't take long. I'll sit with you as you watch the video and transcribe what you say they are saying. We'll record your translation, so we'll have a permanent record. Listen, if you do this for me then I'll have you flown to L.A. and your truck shipped there courtesy of the federal government."

"Well okay. You have yourself a deal Agent Foley," Tina said holding out her hand. They shook hands on the agreement.

"Listen" Tina said, "is it true that Ahmed Ali Raheem is out to kill me?"

"Yes, I think so. I believe that the key to his arrest lies in the videotape you're going to translate. If I didn't believe in this so strongly, I wouldn't get you to do it. I know you been through so much in the last few days."

"Okay let's get to it" Tina said getting her game face on.

Naval Air Station, Point Mugu, CA

The Grumman C-2A Navy cargo plane thundered over the beach at Naval Air Station Point Mugu, in Ventura County California, on its landing approach. The naval base was a sealed facility, but Agent Foley received clearance for Bryce to be there to greet Tina when she arrived. The massive plane landed in the distance away from the hanger Bryce was waiting in. He could see the plane taxi in toward the hanger. Agent Foley had made good on his promise to have Tina flown to Los Angeles. He just didn't say how. The plane came to a stop just outside the hangar and the revolutions on the propellers slowed down. The tail hatch was lowered, and Tina slowly walked down the ramp onto the tarmac. The Navy ground crew directed her towards the hanger. When she saw Bryce in the doorway of the open hangar, she began to run toward him. The ground crew were following her, carrying her bags.

Bryce started to run to Tina, and they met on the Navy tarmac under the wing of the massive cargo plane. They hugged each other with the passion of a thousand sleepless nights. Bryce

343

kissed Tina on the mouth, and the embrace lasted until the Navy ground crew walked past them.

"Listen kiddo" Bryce said still holding Tina. "Let's get out of here and have some fun."

"That's the best thing I've heard all spring break" Tina said smiling as they turned and started walking toward the Navy hanger, hand in hand. Bryce reached over and gave Tina a kiss on her forehead.

Motel 6, Blythe, CA
Thursday March 8, 2018

The sun was just about to set, but the sky was illuminated with the glow of orange and red. The Motel 6 just outside of Blythe, California could be seen in the distance. The two-story concrete block building was surrounded by an asphalt parking lot. It wasn't the Ritz, but it sufficed for anyone bothering to visit Blythe. The place appeared to be about twenty-five percent full. There was no vegetation, as far as the eye could see. A white Chevy Malibu pulled into an empty parking stall about midway down the right wing of the building.

Off to the east side, an armored vehicle pulled up quietly and stopped behind the back of the building. A squad of six heavily armed men exited the vehicle and made their way rapidly to the front of the building; moving in a low crouched position, with their automatic weapons out in front of them. A tall black man exited the Chevy Malibu and walked toward the motel building. He stopped at a room two doors down from his car. He stood two feet away from the door and lifted his left leg. He rammed his leg into the door. The door latch broke, but the door didn't open.

At the exact same time, the armored squad arrived with a round ram tube approximately 8 inches in diameter and 5 feet long. Two men grabbed the handles on each side of the tube and smashed the ram into the door. The door flew open and the squad was met with a hail of automatic gunfire from inside the hotel room. The men ducked down but the man on the right side of the ram was hit in the arm. The armed squad quickly returned fire, and a firefight ensued in a hail of bullets.

Bryce's Ranch, Ojai, CA

Tina had been in California for two days but didn't want to leave Bryce's house in Ojai. Not even to get dinner.

"Listen, do you want to talk about it?" Bryce said, worried about what was happening, and that Tina wasn't her usual cheerful self.

"I can't right now. I'm waiting for a message that the coast is clear. As soon as that happens, I'll explain everything to you," Tina replied as she gave him a kiss. "I hope you understand."

Bryce teased, "You're not going to tell me that you work for the CIA, are you?"

Tina snickered but couldn't be cajoled into going out and having fun. Bryce tried to get Tina out of her funk, but Tina was just not herself.

Tina and Bryce were on the couch watching Netflix and sharing a bottle of California Butter Chardonnay. It was about 9 PM and the sun had set. The landscape lighting to Bryce's ranch house automatically flickered on. Tina's smartphone was on the coffee table in front of her. Her phone pinged, indicating she had just received a text, "Ahmed taken care of. The coast is clear. S. F."

Tina let out a sigh and reached over and gave Bryce a hug and kissed him on the mouth. "Sorry I've been a party pooper since I arrived. That was the text I was waiting for. Now we can have some fun. Let's have Chanal and Billy come over tomorrow for a pool party and barbeque. We can swap stories about what happened to the both of us. Why you quit the bank and what happened to me in Utah."

"That sounds great. I was dreading that our time together was coming to an end and that you had to get back to Minnesota." Bryce said somewhat guarded.

"No, I resigned my position at the college. I'll never again set foot in Minnesota or Utah."

Bryce pulled Tina closer and slid his hand behind her back into the back of her jeans under her panties. "For You" by Singer-songwriter Mahrs was playing softly from the Bose Bluetooth speakers Bryce had placed throughout his ranch house. Tina put her hands up Bryce's pant leg as they exchanged a wet kiss. Do you want to go into the bedroom?" Tina asked, her face getting flushed.

"No. I don't want to spoil this. I let you get away once; I'm now not letting you out of my sight. Let's stay right here." Bryce said reaching behind him to turn off the light.

Tina unzipped Bryce's zipper and freed his now rigid member. She caressed it as she put it in her mouth. Bryce watched Tina's beautiful face bob up and down as he gently held the side of her head. He was too excited to wonder how he could have let Tina get away. Now that she was back in his life, he would not make the same mistake again.

He was so excited and wanted the moment to last so he pulled out. Through gasps of air Bryce said, "On second thought, let's go to the bedroom. We'll be more comfortable there."

Epilogue

"Courage is like love; it must have hope for nourishment."
~ Napoleon

Chapter 42

FBI Headquarters, Manhattan
Monday March 26, 2018

Two weeks have gone by since the death of Agent Mark Dunphy's arch nemesis, Ahmed Ali Raheem. Special Agent Foley was at his desk in New York. It was 7 AM and the office was nearly empty. Foley had been full-time on the case, even when he was at home, and still some things just didn't add up. Foley had commandeered the main conference room where he had plastered the walls with images of all the characters and events related to the case.

Foley got up from his desk and walked with his coffee mug into the conference room and turned on the lights. He sat at the head of the table and surveyed the items taped to the wall. Taking a sip of coffee, he suddenly slammed his hand on the table, "That's it! God dammit she's right. You sneaky little shit, Dunphy."

El Segundo, CA and Ankara, Turkey
Wednesday March 28, 2018

Agents from the FBI and the ATF arrived at TRX's headquarters in El Segundo California. Simultaneously the NIOT arrived at Roketsen in Ankara Turkey. At the El Segundo offices, two men were arrested, and the FBI hauled off a shit load of computer equipment. In Ankara a dozen men of various nationalities were arrested and brought to a CIA dark site for questioning.

JFK International Airport, New York

9:45 AM, a British Airways flight from London arrived at JFK. The passengers were anxious to deplane and stretch their legs. However, the captain came on the P.A. and announced that there would be a slight delay at the gate. A collective groan could be heard from the crowd.

Agents from the Manhattan Branch of the FBI boarded the plane and took Ulf Samuellson into custody. There was a slight scuffle, but Ulf was easily overpowered by the two agents and put into handcuffs.

Miami Florida

Agent Foley was monitoring all events from the FBI command center in Miami Florida.

When he was confident that all of Mark's accomplices were safely under arrest, he called the New York Bureau Chief.

"Well this sad saga is finally over Chief. I don't think there is much you can do when an Agent goes rogue. Especially someone as intelligent and devious as Dunphy. Did you know the coroner's report stated that Mark was addicted to anabolic steroids? And from what I can tell he did not have a prescription for them. The coroner also mentioned that this addiction could be a cause for Mark's erratic behavior."

"Yeah, I'm just glad to put this shit show behind us. Tell me how you finally broke the case" the New York Bureau chief asked, now relieved that all responsible were either dead or had been arrested.

"I didn't." There was a slight pause, and then Foley continued, "do you remember that cute college professor that translates documents for us?"

"Yes, I've heard of her work, but I've never met her."

"Well, she's the one that broke the case. After everything that went down in Utah, I uncovered some documents that I needed to be translated. She was a real trooper and took on those assignments without complaint. Then late one night she calls me from Ojai, California and says she has something important to tell me. She says that all the documents she was sent to translate were just a ruse. At first, I thought she just wanted to get out of the assignment. And then she explained to me her take on all the shit that had gone down."

Foley waited for the chief to respond, and when he didn't, he continued. "Tina said The Executioner and Ahmed actually worked for Mark. That Mark was the mastermind behind the gun running out of Turkey. He controlled everything including the two guys we just arrested at TRX in California. They had links to weapon orders that went to Turkey. The documents that accompanied the arms and munition shipments from the U.S. always undercounted what was included in the shipments. So, it was so easy to skim off the top when the crates arrived in Turkey. They just took the extra weapons that were not accounted for on the shipment manifest. However, the guys in Turkey were much greedier than the two clowns we just arrested at TRX. So, to keep order, Mark brought in The Executioner; a guy he had never met in person but had come highly 'recommended' in his line of work. It was a little like hiring the Hells Angels to do security detail. Yeah, things were secure, as far as Mark was concerned, but The Executioner used a very heavy hand in carrying out his duties. As a sadist, let's just say he enjoyed his work.

Mark was making a boatload of money and needed to launder it here in the states. It was also a ruse that he lived in a shitty little apartment in the Bronx. He had properties all over the states, and in other countries. So, he set up a club in Manhattan that catered to all types of deviant sexual preferences. The perfect camouflage to launder his money right under our noses. The Club 69 is a block from FBI Headquarters. He brought in Ahmed to run the place, which was ultimately his downfall because Ahmed was not only greedy, but a sexual deviant. However, his worst offense was that he was careless and used the Columbia Dean to make the money laundering transactions. The Dean did it because he also was a pedophile and went overseas to have sex with teenage boys and was being blackmailed by Ahmed for his indiscretions. Needless to say, things got out of hand.

The Executioner came stateside to team with Ahmed to try and take back control from Mark. That's when the turf war started, and Tina got caught in the middle. This is all pretty ingenious detective work on Tina's part, which I think we would have eventually figured out. No, she figured out the key to this whole house of cards was Mark's undercover act. Mark actually prepared bona fide reports on this whole fucking operation, even the shit going on in Turkey. True to form, Mark never filed his paperwork properly, so it took a while to find all his documents on the F.B.I. server in New York. But they are all there. That was also a big part of his ruse. He was able to use the full power and resources of the federal government to run the whole shebang for him. But he needed to still launder all that money. So, he chose an indiscreet Swedish bank called the Bank of Uppsala.

He did his homework and didn't select them randomly. No, they had a somewhat checkered past of not asking their customers too many questions on obviously shady deals, as long as they made a handsome profit. And they always filed shoddy paperwork. Mark would write them up on shoddy paperwork charges and launder just gobs of money through their New York office.

There were a couple of people at the bank that were handling the citations on incorrect paperwork that almost caught on to Mark's scheming. But Mark was always one step ahead of them thanks to the full force of the Justice Department that he used to threaten the bank's vice president from Sweden, Ulf Samuellson. So, after Dr. Wood told me her theory, I just put all the characters and events in order and was able to corroborate her theory exactly. Initially I wondered how Tina knew so much about Ulf and the shit that went down at the B of U. Then it dawned on me, *duh, of course.* Tina was with Bryce and he filled her in on the stuff he knew. However, she was the one that made the connection between Mark, the B of U, Ahmed, the

Dean, and the Executioner. And it was more than a wild ass guess."

"Okay, so how did a college professor, that did contract translation assignments for us, figure all of this shit out?" The Bureau Chief asked incredulously.

"Funny you should ask that, because that's exactly what I asked her when she called me that night from Ojai. And do you know what she said?"

"No, what?"

"Elocution lessons. And then she hung up the phone without even saying goodbye."